TO BE INTERESTING

I'm going to pinpoint EXACTLY what it is
that makes a person worth caring about
and then do it.

I'll let you know how I get on.

It's not going to be easy.

But then interesting things never are,
are they?

the MANIFESTO ON HOW TO BE INTERESTING

HOLLY BOURNE

USBORNE

To Owen – I officially forgive you for being popular at school...

First published in the UK in 2014 by Usborne Publishing Ltd., Usborne House, 83-85 Saffron Hill, London EC1N 8RT, England. www.usborne.com

chapter one

Bree supposed it was quite an achievement really – to be a failed novelist aged only seventeen.

Most people her age didn't have a clue what they wanted to do with their lives yet. Let alone know, work really hard for it and then fail miserably. She was miles ahead in the life-ultimately-sucks realization that takes most people their twenties and thirties to figure out.

But Bree wasn't most people. Well, she didn't think so anyway.

She looked at the rejection letter in her hand, hoping, somehow, if she stared at it hard enough her longing would melt the ink on the page into a "yes".

Dear Bree
Thank you for your submission. We regret to tell you that your novel isn't something we think we can take forward

BLAH BLAH BLAH.

Generic response. They hadn't even bothered personalizing it. That's how much of a failure she was.

Four years ago, when Bree decided to become a novelist, she'd done what she'd always done – obsessively planned, researched and plotted a no-fail manifesto. She'd read everything she could about writing, including a book by Stephen King, aka GOD. He'd apparently been rejected LOADS – so much that he hammered a nail into the wall above his desk to spike all the "no" letters on. Delighted at the self-deprecation of it all, Bree also hammered a massive nail into the perfect plastering of her bedroom wall. And, month by month, year by year, the nail got clogged up with her own swell of rejection letters.

Ha ha, just like Stephen King, she'd thought, spiking the first "no" letter and flipping it the middle finger.

Then more came, and more.

"I can't wait to talk about this emotional part of my journey when I'm being interviewed by the *Guardian* about my number one bestseller," she'd told the clogged nail as she impaled another rejection letter. Yes, she'd got to the point of talking aloud to it. Like it was a person.

Now that *Guardian* interview seemed as likely as J K Rowling asking Bree to be her best forever friend. Her first novel had been rejected by every agent and publisher in the UK.

Then her second.

What the hell was she going to do now?

"Bree?" Her mother called up the stairs. "You're going to be late for school."

She stubbed the new letter onto the nail, pushing hard to make room for it.

"It's alright. I'm almost ready," she called back.

"Well I can't give you a lift. I've got Bikram yoga this morning with the girls."

She always did. Bree thought how ironic the usage of the word "girls" was to describe her mum and her mates.

In a rush now, she rummaged in her drawer and pulled out a pair of pink and black striped tights. She pulled them on quickly, wincing as the fabric brushed against last night's fresh cuts on her thighs. It was the first time Bree had done it for a while. She would pay the price in pain whenever she sat down or stood up for the next two days.

Her phone went. It was a text from Holdo. No doubt double-checking they were still walking in together despite the fact they did so every day.

Sure enough:

Good morning, Bree. Shall we meet at our regular corner at the usual time? Please let me know. From, Holdo.

Holdo didn't "do" text-speak – considered it an aberration of the English language. He wrote everything out in full, with proper punctuation marks. Once, he'd forgotten to use a comma and Bree was subjected to a mammoth apology.

She fired back a response.

Sure. C U there.

She deliberately used the "C" and "U" to piss him off. She wasn't sure why. Bree put on her school blazer and was about to run out of her bedroom door when last night's list caught her eye.

She'd forgotten about it – it lay abandoned on the carpet. She made so many lists, it was hard to remember them all. She'd written this one on an adrenalin comedown. That familiar sensation of calm had reminded her that things weren't that bad and so the list was meant to jog her memory for next time – hoping it may prevent a next time.

Reasons why I shouldn't be so bloody miserable all
the time

1. I live in a massive house, the kind that makes strangers jealous
2. I suppose, in their own sort of way, both of my parents love me
3. I could be pretty if I wanted…
4. I'm much smarter than most people
5. I know what I want to do with my life
6. I have Holdo

That was it. She'd wanted to list ten – because it just feels nicer, doesn't it? But she couldn't think of any more reasons. This, Bree supposed, could be the start of a whole other list.

Reasons to be bloody miserable all the time

1. My life is so crap that I can't even think of ten stupid things that give me reason NOT to be miserable

But she didn't have time for that list. Not now. She was late.

Bree ran down the stairs and into the kitchen. She ignored the bowl of muesli, fresh fruit and organic yogurt her mum had left her and took a Pop-Tart out of the cupboard instead. Strawberry. Just what she felt like. She shoved it into her mouth and held it there as she packed her school bag. Then she set the alarm and half-jogged out of the house.

As she waited for the security gate to open, she thought a bit more about her list. How stupid she could be sometimes – thinking her life wasn't that miserable. Yes, she could list six reasons why things weren't that bad. But those were just starting points for further elaboration. Elaboration that would ultimately collapse each point.

Take number one, for example.

I live in a massive house, the kind that makes strangers jealous

That, on the surface, was true as true could be. Her house *was* gigantic. And on a private road as well. Ashdown Drive was the sort of road poorer people deliberately detoured through so they could stare at the houses. Hers was one of the most impressive. It had a security gate with intercom to get through to the sweeping circular driveway. They didn't have a garden as such – "grounds" was a more appropriate word. It took about five minutes to walk past the property. The outstretched dark-green-light-green-dark-green-light-green stripes of lawn were hidden by carefully manicured privacy hedges. It was the sort of house that everyone peers at, trying to get a glimpse of the lucky ones who live there, and thinks: *Wow. Those people must have the most perfectly wonderful lives. I bet they don't know what a problem looks like. If I lived there, everything would be okay. All the time.*

The truth though? Bree hated the house. Nobody tells you that large houses have this horrible habit of making you feel utterly alone. Constantly. She could scream and nobody would hear her. She knew this, she'd tried once. (On a particularly low day.) And the only response had been her own yells echoing endlessly, bouncing around the marble entrance hall.

The security gate felt like a prison gate. She often wondered what it would be like not to be so rich and figured it would be a lot more fun.

"Shut up, Bree," she told herself.

The gate closed behind her and she walked to meet Holdo. It was October and it was cold. She wished she'd doubled up on the bright tights today. Her mum always despaired of Bree's fashion choices, which led her onto point two…

I suppose, in their own sort of way, both of my parents love me

It depends how you view love, doesn't it? Bree had never wanted for anything. Did that mean she was loved? Her dad worked his arse off pretty much 24/7 so she could live in the aforementioned large prison house. He left home before she woke every morning, even Saturdays, and wasn't usually back until after midnight. She wasn't exactly sure what he did. In return, her dad barely knew how old she was. The extent of their communication went as follows:

Dad: (*In rare moment they bump into each other on the stairs*) You behaving yourself in school?

Bree: Yes.

Dad: Good.

Or, there was that time on Christmas day...

Dad: (*Carving the turkey*) Do you want leg or breast?

Bree: I'm a vegetarian, remember?

Dad: Don't be so ridiculous. (*Carves off a bit of leg and dumps it on her plate*)

Then there was Mum. At least she was around – in physical manifestation anyway. Her mum was a full-time yummy mummy. That's what she liked to call herself. In Bree's unhumble opinion, the word "yummy" shouldn't be associated with anyone over the age of forty.

Her mum spent her time doing a variety of increasingly oddly-named exercise classes, getting facials, fillers and Botox done on her regular day trips to Harley Street, and reading about celebrities in garish magazines she left all over the house. She communicated her love to Bree with a constant stream of gift-wrapped packages left on Bree's bed.

Tiffany necklaces, Hollister jumpers – once Mum even got her some lingerie. Lucky, huh? But to Bree it was as welcome as a cat proudly leaving a beheaded mouse oozing blood on your doorstep. She knew people wouldn't understand. Who wouldn't want a mother who loaded you with gifts? Especially top-notch ones most girls her age could only fantasize about. But Bree didn't want necklaces, overpriced knitwear or fancy knickers. She wanted a mother who helped her with her coursework. Someone who made her a cup of tea after school and asked her about what she'd learned, rather than grilling her about whether she'd made any new friends. All the time. Like being popular was the most important thing ever.

All she got was:

"Why aren't you wearing that jumper I got you?"

Or:

"Is Holdo coming round *again*? Don't you have any girlfriends?"

Or:

"You're so pretty. Why don't you just DO something with yourself? You're putting yourself to waste."

Which led Bree onto…

I could be pretty if I wanted

She could. Now. But she didn't want to be. She'd tried to be pretty once before, on her first day at secondary school, in some deluded burst of naivety that it might change things. Still blubbery with puppy fat, she'd hoicked her skirt up, carefully painted darker stripes through her hair with a home-colouring kit, smothered her face with blue eyeshadow and pink lipstick and shoved two socks down her bra. The result was the worst first day of secondary school the world had ever known. Jassmine Dallington and her cronies had positively dribbled with delight when they saw her, spluttering on their laughter and rushing to lob new and nastier names at her.

She'd been so stupid to try. And now, puppy fat gone and her face fully grown into, she wouldn't bother trying again.

What *pretty* person achieved anything of merit anyway? Who cares what a writer looks like as long as their words are beautiful?

So, much to her mother's despair, Bree made herself as unattractive as possible.

If you control what they laugh at, invite them to dine out on you...well, then, Bree found they usually stop laughing.

She would wash her hair, on occasion. It was a lanky mouse shade at the moment but had been an array of absurd colours in the past – pink most recently, which still hadn't quite washed out. She wore the clothes of a frumpy forty-year-old going through a mid-life crisis – all neon this, and novelty-hair-bobbles that. She ate what she wanted, meaning her skin had a near-constant scattering of spots and her thighs rubbed together when she walked. And none of this mattered because...

I'm much smarter than most people

Being pretty was only important at school. And school wasn't a part of Bree's life she considered essential to her development. It was a time to endure before the beautiful world of adulthood opened its arms to give her a great big hug and a two-book publishing deal. School was a mere drop in the ocean of a human life. And for the pretty girls at school, their moment would soon be over. They were peaking in their happiness-levels much too early. Which is why Bree stayed ugly – to delay the peakage to a more useful age. Another reason why Bree was much smarter than most people.

She needed to hurry up though. Bree was smart but she wasn't very punctual. Like, ever. While Holdo was quite the opposite. She wrapped her blazer tighter around her to keep out the cold, barely allowing herself to think about the penultimate entry on last night's list.

I know what I want to do with my life

But what if it doesn't want you? All she had ever wanted to do was write. Well, for the past four years anyway. To have people read her words. To leave a tiny imprint of herself on whoever read them. What better way to validate your existence – to prove you had one? But maybe it wasn't to be.

She wasn't quite ready to accept that yet.

Though, in the meantime, *she had Holdo.*

There he was, waiting for her, like he always did. His trademark yellow headphones cupped his ears, and he was wearing that Velvet Underground banana T-shirt over his school jumper – an essential wardrobe item for any wannabe-indie boy. Holdo spotted her, pulled down his headphones and tapped on his watch.

"You're late again."

"I'm always late."

"It's disrespectful, you know, to keep other people waiting."

"It's only been five minutes."

They began walking towards school, each too stubborn to break the silence. Holdo, of course, broke it first. After a record holdout of five entire minutes.

"So what did you get up to last night?"

Bree stared at the pavement. "I got another rejection letter. It was waiting for me on the doormat when I got home."

She could see Holdo forgive her lateness as his eyes melted instantly. He never stayed mad at her for long.

"I'm sorry, Bree. I don't understand it. You're so talented."

"I know," she said, giving him a wry smile as an apology. "I don't get it either."

"Do you want to talk about it?"

"Not really." Not with Holdo anyway. When she was this upset, she always found his well-intentioned advice grated rather than helped.

The fallen autumn leaves crunched under her Dr Martens and she stamped to make the crunch louder.

"So what did *you* get up to last night?" she asked, kicking up a pile of yellow and orange ones and watching them float back down to the pavement. They didn't have fallen leaves on her road. The handyman jointly hired by the residents blew them away every morning with a special reverse-vacuum machine.

"I watched *Apocalypse Now Redux*. The three-hour version. It's so enthralling. Have you seen it?"

"Of course."

"But have you seen the extended rough-cut?"

"Yes." She was lying. Bree had only watched the regular cinema version and found the film more puzzling than enthralling. She would never tell Holdo that though. (She'd rather die.)

"Well, we're in the minority. Most people struggle with the regular one just because it's over ninety minutes long. Honestly, the attention span of cinema audiences these days is insane. If there isn't a massive explosion, or a gratuitous sex scene every five seconds, people just don't want to know…"

Bree let Holdo's well-exercised rant wash over her. She'd heard it at least twenty times. It was one of his favourites. Along with the ones about how reality TV was destroying the music industry, how Dan Brown should be hanged, drawn and quartered for his *Da-Vinci-Code*-shaped crimes against literature, and how the film industry had no original screenwriters any more as they spent all their time adapting bestselling novels rather than investing in raw talent.

She sighed. Holdo was her best friend. Her *only* friend, if she was being honest. Bree knew she wasn't a very likeable person, but it didn't bother her mostly. Yes, of course there were moments of crippling loneliness. And, yeah, it would be nice to have a girl to talk to from time to time. But generally she was happy with Holdo.

"...and it just makes me so angry that the Vietnam War was ever allowed to happen, you know? It was just so completely immoral and it's not like America has learned from it, have they? You'd think they would—"

Ahh. The war. She'd wondered when he would start ranting about the war.

Holdo was your stereotypical rich-kid-rejecting-his-upbringing. The indie sort that honestly believed, if he and Morrissey were to meet, they would become the best of friends. His real name wasn't Holdo – it was Jeremy Smythe. He'd renamed himself – yes – after Holden in *The Catcher In The Rye* (although the "o" on the end apparently made it "more original"). But Bree loved Holdo (in a strictly friendship way). He was the only person around who shared her intellect levels and desires to DO something with their privilege instead of resting on the laurels of wealth. Holdo was designing a computer game – he actually knew how to write code for it and everything. It was a cross between *Grand Theft Auto* and *Bugsy Malone*. As Bree understood it, the game involved a bullied geek running amok at school with a splurge gun, squirting bullies with cream. Holdo was eventually going to be a self-made millionaire. Bless him – he just needed to get through school first.

She interrupted his war monologue.

"Holdo?"

He stuttered to a stop. "What?"

"I'm a good writer, aren't I?"

She knew she was. Of course she was. But she could do with some reassurance.

Holdo reached out and squeezed her hand. "Of course you are. I read everything you write and love every word."

She looked at his hand, wondering how quickly she could detach herself. That was the thing with Holdo: strictly-friends-only wasn't an opinion he shared.

"Thanks." She dropped his hand and tucked hers safely back in her pocket.

"Why don't you talk to Mr Fellows about it?"

She'd already planned to. Mr Fellows was her English teacher and the only adult in existence who noticed her.

"I've got English today. I could do."

"He always seems to cheer you up."

Bree smiled to herself.

Holdo had no idea.

chapter two

They got to the school gates and then queued to get through security at the main door. While Holdo somehow slipped through and disappeared with a wave towards his form room, Bree waited impatiently to get her ID card checked. Queen's Hall school cost twelve thousand pounds a year, and half the money seemed to go on ensuring Joe Public couldn't sneak in. Like "being common" was infectious or something.

She stood directly behind Jassmine Dallington and her posse of perfects and could smell the clean strawberry scent of Jassmine's blow-dried hair. As the queue of students shifted and jostled, Bree overstepped slightly and accidently trod on the back of her heel. Jassmine swung her head round, to see who dared touch her. When she saw it was Bree, her nose wrinkled.

"Watch it," she said, her voice full of disgust.

"Sorry," Bree mumbled, looking down at her stripy legs.

Jassmine turned away and must've made a face because the other girls laughed. Not properly – a genuine laugh would make their faces look too ugly – but they sniggered in an attractive way. Gemma Rinestone whispered in Jassmine's ear and there was another wave of giggles.

Bree continued expressing an unnatural interest in her tights and cursed herself for blushing. She didn't care. Of course not. The perfect posse were idiots. But, you know, it was still embarrassing.

She handed her security card to the guy and did her best disappearing-into-the-wall trick while she waited. It wasn't hard. She was nobody here. Bag and card retrieved, she made her way through the maze of corridors to her form room. She would have to sit there for no good reason and listen to her tutor drone on about the importance of success for an hour.

Hugo and his mates were standing in the doorway, blocking it.

"Excuse me," she said, turning her body sideways to try and squeeze past.

They ignored her and Hugo carried on talking.

"Oh my God, guys, the gash hunt on Friday was totally brutal. Those single-sex-school girls are, like, so grateful. I swear, I'm not even lying, this one girl came up to me and offered herself, just like that."

His friends laughed like a pack of hyenas and high-fived him.

"So, did you?" one asked. His face was far too red. Either from unfortunate genetics or overzealous fake guy-laughing. Bree thought his name might be Seth.

Hugo raised an eyebrow. "A gentleman never tells."

"Ha! And when have you ever been a gentleman?"

"Good point, man. Good point." Another high five.

"Actually, nothing happened. I told the girl to get some self-respect and she started crying."

More laughter. Possibly-Seth looked like he was about to combust.

"Great party though, man," the red-faced guy said, tears of laughter in his eyes. "I was so completely wasted. I swear to God I went *literally* blind for a while." He looked round the circle, waiting for the laughter. It didn't come.

Hugo pulled a face. "Christ, Seth. You only had a few shots!"

"No I didn't! I had most of a bottle of vodka. You just didn't see. Probably too busy pushing away all that gash."

Hugo rolled his eyes. "Whatever, man."

Bree used the awkward silence to try and get past. She cleared her throat. "Excuse me."

Now all the boys' eyes were on her.

"What do you want?"

"Can I just get by?"

Hugo lifted his arms and stood back, creating the teensiest bit of space for her. The other boys followed suit, each not quite giving her enough room. She examined the gap, sighed inwardly, and sidestepped her way into the form room. The front of her body brushed against Hugo's.

"Eww, stop rubbing up against me," he said. "I don't like getting touched up this early in the morning."

The boys burst into hysteria. Bree blushed for the second time that day and half-ran to her desk. Her legs twinged as she sat and pulled out her favourite notepad. She could feel her face burning and pulled some lanky strands of hair over her face to cover it.

Stupid school. Stupid school. Stupid school.

The thing was, though she was loathe to admit it, she couldn't help but fancy Hugo. Ridiculous, she knew. Ludicrous. Fantastical. And also so, so wrong, considering he was such an arse arse ARSEhole. He basically stood for everything she hated about:

a) Boys
b) This school
c) Life in general

And yet he was so frustratingly good-looking and lived up to all the clichés that went with that. Captain of the school's trophy-winning rugby team, complete player (though he proudly pronounced it "playa"), the absolute definition of alpha male thanks to his built, toned physique. He was a year older than them, after his parents pulled him from school for a year so he could live in Paris and get fluent in French. Oh – and his parents knew Mark Zuckerberg or someone. He was so wealthy he made everyone else at school look poor.

Of course he and Jassmine had a turbulent on-off-on-off relationship. Even Bree knew every detail of the ongoing saga that was their "love". Every update got broadcast round the classrooms like some really sad version of Chinese Whispers. Bree hoped her own silly crush would ultimately pass and the thought of getting with him wasn't one she indulged. Not only because it would NEVER happen – he was ignorant of her very existence – but also because, well, he was an ARSEhole.

Her form tutor, Mr Phillips, strolled into the room and everyone settled down immediately. That was the thing about private school – people behaved.

"Alright, everybody?" he asked, putting his briefcase on the desk and opening it.

Nobody replied.

"I said, ALRIGHT, EVERYBODY?"

Calm down, Bree thought. *You're not a rock star.*

"Morning," the class chorused.

"Right, UCAS form, UCAS form, UCAS form. I know you're thinking, 'What? But we're only in Year Twelve!' but your parents spend a lot of money ensuring I get you into the university of your choice. And that means applying in good time with a personal statement that's been honed to perfection over a year. Now, does everyone know what subject they're doing and what five universities they want to put down? Oxford and Cambridge applicants, do you know which college you want to try for?"

Bree doodled in her notebook. She'd had her escape to

Cambridge planned since puberty and a word-perfect personal statement and completed practice UCAS form had been sitting on her laptop for months, just waiting for the day she could hit *Send*. So she didn't really need to be listening to Mr Phillips right now. Which was just as well because she was writing another list.

Reasons why it is entirely unreasonable to fancy
Hugo d'Felance

1. I have never heard him refer to the female species without using the words: gash, clunge, flange, pussy, bucket, windsock and the C-word that can definitely not be mentioned. Ever.
2. He is openly racist, homophobic, misogynistic and a massive bigot.
3. I have heard, from anecdotal evidence only, but lots of it, that he's had at least one STI.
4. He once referred to Shakespeare as "that boring dude".
5. If Jassmine ever found out she would gut me with her nail file, burn my intestines and eat my eyeballs with a spoon…
6. I have self-respect. I have self-respect. I have self-respect.

Bree's continuous list-writing had become her coping device. She had a special notebook and everything. The lists weren't useful – just her views on the world at that moment.

Sometimes she fantasized about them being displayed in a museum hundreds of years in the future, secured in glass, in a sell-out exhibition about her "early life". A plaque next to her notebook would read: *Bree's unique insights on her sad teenage years were diarized here, in list form. You can already see her strong narrative voice beginning to emerge, soon to become the voice of her generation that would be treasured until far beyond her death.*

Mr Phillips was still droning on.

"Now, university interviews. We'll be holding training sessions on interview technique closer to summer so you can practise over the holidays. The sign-up sheets will be posted after Christmas. Don't all rush to sign up at once, there are enough slots for everyone. But, in the meantime, I want you to be thinking about your extra-curricular activities. Remember – boring people don't get into Oxbridge! You need to DO stuff. Get doing!"

Bree heard Hugo and his mates laughing and looked over. Hugo had drawn a massive hairy penis on Seth's practice UCAS form and was showing it off.

"Hey!" Seth tried to grab it back. "I need that."

Hugo put it behind his back. "Why do you want a picture of a knob so much, Seth?"

"Ha ha. Gay boy, gay boy," the others sniggered.

"Shut up. You know what I mean. It's my practice form. I need it."

At this point, the teacher noticed the kerfuffle. "Problem, gentlemen?"

Hugo shook his head, the paper still behind his back. "None at all, sir."

"Good." And Mr Phillips went back to harping on about university entry.

Hugo drank in the attention he'd provoked – mainly from two girls Bree knew only from form-time. They giggled at Hugo and flicked their hair. He winked and they giggled harder.

Bree added one last *I have self-respect* to her list.

chapter three

After the bell rang, Bree navigated the corridors – doing her best impression of the invisible girl – towards English. Seeing Mr Fellows always put her on edge so she leaned against some lockers and took a couple of deep breaths before entering the classroom.

He didn't acknowledge her arrival. She took a seat right at the front. More pupils trickled in and sat down, begrudgingly taking their copies of Philip Larkin's poetry anthology out of their designer bags. Bree stared at Mr Fellows. He was marking, presumably, scribbling away on a sheet of headed A4. His conker-brown hair flopped over his eyes. She sucked her stomach in and uncrossed and recrossed her stripy legs.

Finally, Mr Fellows registered his class's existence and straightened up.

"Excellent, wonderful," he said, to no one in particular.

He stood with his back against the interactive whiteboard. "Right. Where were we?"

Bree put her hand up but didn't wait for him to call her. "We'd just read the poem 'As Bad as a Mile'."

She heard a groan. Bree wasn't sure if it was due to the poem or her overeagerness in class.

Mr Fellows picked up his battered copy of poems and skimmed through the pages. "Right you are, Bree."

She shifted back in her chair, bathing in the praise, no matter how small and inconsequential it was.

He found the right page and read it aloud. Beautifully...

"Watching the shied core
Striking the basket, skidding across the floor,
Shows less and less of luck, and more and more

Of failure spreading back up the arm
Earlier and earlier, the unraised hand calm,
The apple unbitten in the palm.

"Right. So in this poem, Larkin tries to throw an apple core in the bin but misses. What did you guys all think about it?"

Some kid called Chuck raised his hand.

"Yes?"

Chuck had jet-black hair, definitely dyed. "I think that Philip Larkin shouldn't try and throw an apple in a bin considering he's such a bloody depressive who can't even breathe without whingeing about it."

The small class twittered with laughter.

Even Mr Fellows smiled. "Is that right?"

Chuck, cocky now, nodded animatedly. "Yeah. I mean, sir, why have you given us something so depressing to read? No other English classes have to read this joker, moaning on and on about his sad life."

This sort of backchat was completely unacceptable in any class other than Mr Fellows's. But Mr Fellows wasn't like the other teachers. He was like an air bubble in a nailed-shut coffin, an interval during a boring play, a palate-cleansing amuse-bouche during a heavy meal, a...er...Bree couldn't think of any other metaphors. Basically he had character. He was actually interested in the students as humans, rather than as high-grade-getters to use as ego-massagers, confirming what a great teacher you were. No one knew quite how he had got or kept the job. Especially as he regularly picked books not on the recommended list, used swear words in class and, rumour had it, once shared a spliff with students on results day.

"Does anyone else feel this way about Philip Larkin?"

Bree's hand shot in the air. "I don't. I love it."

"Surprise surprise," someone whispered and more laughter echoed behind her.

Bree didn't care. Not much.

"Nice to hear at least one of you is enjoying it." Mr Fellows didn't even look at her and she felt worse. "How about the rest of you?"

"It's boring."

"It's so miserable."

"Why didn't he just top himself?"

"Yeah. Why did he have to write so much? Now we have to be miserable too."

Mr Fellows shook his head. "Guys. This is so hard to hear! Philip Larkin is one of England's most treasured poets. Don't tell me you don't like him just because he's miserable."

Bree's hand shot up again.

"Yes, Bree."

"He was sexist as well. Lots of people don't like that he was sexist."

"Good point."

Bree glowed.

"But it sounds like you're all caught up in the depression of it all. Why do you think that is?"

Cocky Chuck put his hand up.

"Yes, Chuck?"

"Because no one wants to read about some miserable loner whingeing on about how crap his life is. I don't care how good his onomatopoeias are. Can't we do someone else, sir?"

"Not at all. Now, come on, let's dissect this poem and I'll get you all to change your minds."

chapter four

When the bell went for lunch, Bree dawdled next to Mr Fellows's desk. He was scribbling again, his hair flopping again. She waited for him to notice her.

"Yes, Bree?" He looked up eventually and she paced from foot to foot.

"I got another rejection letter."

Mr Fellows pushed his chair back and gave her a sorrowful look. "I'm sorry. I know how hard you worked on that second novel."

"I just don't understand why, sir. Like you said, I tried really hard. I put everything into it. And it's still crap."

"It's not crap, it's just…"

She pounced on the pause. "What? What is it?"

He sighed and ran his hands through his hair – agitated. "Look, Bree, you know you're a hard worker…"

"I don't want to be a hard worker, I want to be a good writer. A published author!"

"I know, I know, I know. It's just…well…what you write… Have you thought about how commercial it is?"

Commercial? She shuddered at the word. "You want me to sell out? To write some sappy easy-read?"

"That's not what I'm saying… It has to be commercial enough to be published, remember?"

"I know I can write. I got full marks in my English Language GCSE. The examining board even asked if they could use it as an example piece!"

"I know. I taught you, remember?"

"Well, what's wrong with my writing if it got full marks?"

Mr Fellows rolled back and forth in his wheelie chair some more. He wouldn't look at Bree. Not properly. He hadn't ever since…The Thing happened. But she needed his support. Who else could she ask for advice?

"Your creative writing piece for GCSE was good, Bree – but good for a GCSE creative writing piece. Books are different. They have to sell. And, no offence, but nobody wants to read an 110,000-word novel about a girl throwing herself off the end of a pier…"

She crossed her arms defensively. "Why not?"

Mr Fellows opened the bottom drawer of his desk and took out some sheets of paper. He furrowed his eyebrows and began reading aloud.

"*Rose watched the deep frothing water foam under the cracked weathered wooden planks of the pier. She wondered how long it would take for her body to decompose at sea if she were to throw herself in. Would her body bloat? Would she get eaten by sharks? Or would she just decompose, parts of her body going soft and breaking off, like soggy Weetabix left at the bottom of a white ceramic bowl...*"

Bree stuck her lip out. Okay, so it sounded a bit silly when he read it aloud, but only because he was using THAT voice.

"What's wrong with that?"

He smiled. "Nothing at all, Bree. That's why you got such good marks. It's like a big vomit of metaphors – markers love that. Plus, they were probably so scared that the student who wrote it was suicidal, they gave you full marks in case you were thinking of throwing yourself off a pier for real."

Despite herself, she smiled.

"But to read a whole book dedicated to such misery? Well, it's a little hard-going, don't you think?"

"But that's what life is really like."

"What? All young teenage girls want to throw themselves off piers?"

Bree thought about it for a moment. "Yes!"

Mr Fellows looked at her properly for the first time in ages. His eyes were all wide and watery with sympathy. She felt a bit ashamed and wished he wasn't looking at her after all.

"Look, Bree, you're a very talented writer. You know I already think that. I'm not saying all this to be harsh. I know you're not happy, Bree..." She opened her mouth to object but he ignored her. "…You know you're not. You pretend you don't care but I know you do. Do you not think maybe your writing isn't going anywhere because you're unhappy? Because you're not living the life you could? A life worth writing about? You must know that cliché – write what you know – but what do you know, Bree, when you shut the world out?"

Her eyes started twitching. Couldn't he have just stopped at the "you're a very talented writer" bit? That was all she needed – reassurance. Not to have her life dismantled.

"What about Philip Larkin? He's mega-famous and he was miserable."

"Yeah and look how popular he is with your classmates. They all hate it. It's *too* miserable. You want to write something people *want* to read, right?"

She nodded.

"Well, have you not thought about the possibility that not all your classmates are wretchedly sad? And, even if some are, they may want to escape it for a bit by reading something a bit more…upbeat?"

"No." She scuffed her shoes on the carpet, feeling the heat of friction glow through the soles. She focused on that feeling over the eye-prickling.

"I think you need to make yourself, and your life, more open. Do more interesting things, Bree. Then your writing will follow suit. Be someone you would want to read about."

Her next words came out as barely a whisper.

"What was that?" he asked.

"I said, would you want to read about me?"

He rocked in his chair again and cleared his throat.

"I don't really think that's relevant. I'm just trying to help you. I'm your teacher."

She made herself stare right into his sympathetic eyes. "But you're more than just my teacher, aren't you?"

He wouldn't meet her gaze. "Come on, Bree. Let's not go there again."

"But you kissed me!"

His face went a little whiter, making his chestnut hair look even browner.

"Bree. I didn't kiss you," he hissed. "You've got to stop saying that. *I could lose my job.*"

"I'm not going to tell anyone. I just don't understand why you're pretending it didn't happen."

He stood up. "Because nothing did happen! I didn't kiss you." He ran his hands through his hair again. "Not how you think I kissed you anyway," he admitted, looking back down at his desk.

Her eyes stung harder and she blinked furiously so as not to give herself away. He *had* kissed her. Bree should know. She'd only been kissed by two people in her entire life. Mr Fellows was one of them – in fact, he'd been her first proper kiss. "Proper", in that it was her first kiss where both people partaking in the kiss had actually wanted to kiss each other.

* * *

Her *first* first kiss – as in, the first time another pair of lips had touched hers – had been at a teenage creative-writing weekend. It was one of Bree's most painful and psychologically-damaging memories. On the last night, someone had smuggled in a bottle of wine. Eight of them drank it and pretended to be pissed. They'd played Spin the Bottle, but the bottle kept not landing on Bree. She'd merely watched while everyone kissed each other – some a tentative peck, some of the more attractive people really going for it. There was this one guy, Dylan…he looked like Perfection mixed with Godliness and wrote actual poetry. And just when she thought she'd never get kissed, Dylan spun the bottle and it landed on her. She could've squealed with delight. Trying to appear nonchalant, she'd straightened her back, and tucked a strand of hair away from her face.

Dylan was less subtle.

His face fell when he saw who he'd landed on. He sneered. And said, loud enough for everyone to hear, "Bree? I don't really have to kiss Bree, do I?"

Bree? I don't really have to kiss Bree, do I?

Bree? I don't really have to kiss Bree, do I?

Bree? I don't really have to kiss Bree, do I?

How those words haunted her at 3 a.m. when she couldn't sleep.

Her heart had broken to the soundtrack of gleeful laughter.

Dylan had leaned over and pecked her, just next to her lips. With a wrinkle of his nose and an overdramatic wiping of his mouth (more laughter), he erased fifteen years of Bree's romantic fantasy of her first-kiss moment and replaced it with a painful reality.

But her second kiss had been different.

It had been like she'd always thought it could be.

Last year, she and Mr Fellows had set up a creative-writing group for the younger students. Social suicide, but since when did Bree care? It wasn't like she had much social life to lose. Two lunchtimes a week, they helped Year Sevens write and produce a booklet of their poetry and short stories. After each session, Mr Fellows read her first manuscripts and gave his feedback. In return she listened to tales of his unhappy marriage, his rebellious youth, and how, he too, yearned to be a writer. They always had something to say to one another. He was a dreamer, a creative, someone who understood her urge to put the world into words as a way of understanding why bad things happen. He made her feel warm, like a friend. It wasn't too strange, Bree figured. He was only thirty, after all. (He'd let it slip once while warning her not to marry too young.)

By the end of term, Bree had made a decision. She'd secretly applied to the state school down the road without telling her parents. There were horror stories about there being over thirty students in each class, no help with coursework and disruption in lessons. But she figured she was smart enough to do well anywhere and longed to be somewhere different. Somewhere she could be herself and be accepted. Her label of "weird loner girl" was so entrenched at Queen's Hall, she would be shackled to it for ever there.

She'd accepted her place and told Mr Fellows just before the end of term. He'd looked sad and said, "I'm going to miss you." She'd miss him too. She'd started thinking about him before she went to sleep.

On the supposedly last night of her private-school career, she and Holdo risked an evening of being blatantly ignored and went to the Year Eleven Leaving Ball. Silly name really, as nobody left Queen's. She probably would have been the first. Bree had actually worn a dress – a champagne-coloured clingy number that didn't quite fit properly and her mum had winced at. While Jassmine, Hugo and their minions twirled and bitched and ruled in their tailor-made suits and two-grand dresses, Bree and Holdo spent the night sat alone at a table in the corner…watching them have fun and thinking maybe coming to the ball hadn't been the best idea after all. But then Mr Fellows sat next to them and opened up his suit to reveal a hidden hip flask of whisky.

"You might as well have some," he'd said, passing them the bottle under the table. "It's the only chance you've got of having any fun. Plus…" He leaned over to Bree. "You're not my pupil any more, are you?"

A couple of swigs of whisky later, and the three of them were dancing badly at the edge of the dance floor.

"This is great," Bree called over the music. "I'm leaving

this place and never coming back. I'm free to do whatever I want." At which point she launched into some Irish dancing.

"Freak," she heard Gemma, Jassmine's number one crony, yell across the dance floor. Eight times louder than the music.

Mr Fellows clenched his fists and moved as if to go over but Bree stopped him, shaking her head. She didn't care. She was leaving. For ever. It would all be a bad memory soon.

Holdo went to pee and Mr Fellows leaned in, looking a bit sorry for her. Or maybe she'd imagined it. She hoped she had.

"Do you want to get some air?"

She nodded and they both stumbled out onto the gravel driveway of the posh golf clubhouse.

"I shouldn't really be seen hanging out with just you," he said, smiling. "You're my student."

Bree walked round the side of the clubhouse and Mr Fellows followed until they were out of view.

"I'm not your student any more, remember?" she teased. Was she flirting? Was this flirting? Did she even know how to flirt?

"Don't remind me."

The sun had begun to set in the summer sky and the golf course around them glowed pink. It was a scene in which romance could happen.

"I'll miss you, sir."

She wasn't sure why she said it. Probably the whisky. But it was true. She felt a sudden rush of loss gush through her at the thought of not seeing him every day.

He waved his hand away. "Nah. You'll be too busy having fun with all those poor people."

She laughed. "It's still a good school. It's just free, that's all."

He laughed too. "I know. I think you're making the right decision. Queen's Hall doesn't really fit you, does it?"

She shook her head, sadly. "No."

Then he was clasping her hand.

"It's not your fault, Bree," he said, his heartbeat pulsing through their entwined fingers. "You're different, that's all. And I know it feels like it's you, but it's really not. You're a special person and you deserve happiness. Just because you don't fit in with all the other millionaires' offspring doesn't make you the problem. It's another world out there and it will suit you better. I'm just going to miss you, that's all. Who's going to run the creative-writing group with me now?"

"I'm sure you'll find another social outcast," Bree said.

"You're not a social outcast. You're my favourite student. I'm allowed to say that now you're leaving, aren't I?"

She didn't think he was allowed to say or do anything he had said or done that night. But that was the thing about Mr Fellows. He didn't fit into Queen's Hall either. They were like two sore thumbs, being luminous together on a perfectly manicured pair of hands.

She looked at his hand, still holding hers. "You're my favourite teacher. My favourite person probably…"

They both looked at their interlocking fingers and life paused for a moment. Until they heard a group laughing round the corner and the spell was broken.

"I guess we'd better go back inside," Bree said reluctantly. "Holdo will be out of the loo by now."

They stared at each other for a moment, neither of them making the move to leave. And then something propelled Bree to lean her face towards him. He hesitated but didn't stop her, so she leaned in further and closed her eyes. Her lips touched his, very, very gently. He didn't move. But his lips stayed there a second or two longer. When he pulled back, her lips felt cold.

"You're right," he said. And he coughed, looking embarrassed. "Let's get back inside."

It should have been a beautiful moment Bree could always look back on. But no. Her dad had discovered her plans to move schools and taken a sudden ferocious interest in her future. She was forbidden from leaving Queen's and forced to return that autumn – loaded with fresh teasing-material as the girl who did an Irish jig at the ball.

Mr Fellows's face had gone rigid with shock when she'd entered her first English lesson. Since then, he'd refused to talk about it, wouldn't speak with her the way he used to, and now he was denying their kiss to her face.

Bree was, once again, an embarrassment. And with most people it didn't bother her, but this was Mr Fellows. And he was different. And now he felt about her just like everybody else did.

He put her coursework back into his desk and the tone of his voice changed – all calm and authoritarian.

"Look, I don't think we're getting anywhere. I'm sorry your manuscript was rejected again. I do think you should take on board what I've said. Try and make yourself, your life, a bit more interesting, and the interesting writing will follow. Stop shutting everyone out."

Without another word, Bree ran from the room, humiliated. She streamed along the corridors and bashed through the door to the girls' toilets. She locked herself into a cubicle, pulled down her tights and sat on the loo seat, willing her eyes to stop prickling.

The bathroom door opened. People came in.

"Okay. I completely and utterly have to redo this mascara. It looks like a spider hijacked my face."

It was Jassmine and her posse of perfects. Checking up on their make-up. Of course.

Bree stayed still, fighting the urge to sniff and accidently give away her lurking location.

"You don't look like that. Your lashes look fab." That was Gemma. Sucking up as usual.

"You reckon? You don't think falsies are too much

for school? I thought I'd try it out today."

"Nah. They look amazing."

Bree heard the clattering of a make-up bag being emptied into a sink.

"I'm trying to look my best at the moment. Hugo keeps messing me about and I think it's easier to deal with all that stuff if you look nice, you know?"

"Totally. What's he done now?"

"I dunno." Jassmine sighed. "Just some rumours going round that he was all over some single-sex-slut at that party over the weekend."

Bree leaned forward on the toilet so she could hear better. She'd heard Hugo talking about that girl this morning.

"You believe the rumours?"

"I don't know."

"Why do you do it to yourself? If he makes you feel insecure?"

Jassmine? Insecure? Bree almost snorted and gave herself away.

"I don't know. You're right. We're technically broken up right now...but maybe I should finish it for good."

Bree almost gasped.

"Not before his massive eighteenth though?"

Jassmine laughed. A gorgeous discreet titter. "Of course not. It's going to be the event of the year. I've already got about ten outfits on standby."

"Well then, just make him behave until then."

"Yep." The sound of lips being smacked together echoed

round the tiled walls. "This new lipstick should help. Anyway...maybe I've not been behaving myself either."

A gasp.

"Jassmine? Seriously?"

"Shh. Anyway, we are 'on a break'."

"Who? Who is it?"

Make-up was collected and stuffed back into a bag. Then came the sounds of their heels clicking towards the door.

"Well, you know Seth's party...?"

The door opened and shut and Jassmine's voice faded out until Bree couldn't hear anything else. She was annoyed. She'd been literally on the edge of her (loo) seat, wanting to find out who it was.

That's when she realized.

Jassmine Dallington was interesting.

Bree was interested in Jassmine Dallington's life.

Did she need to be more like *her*? The thought was repulsive. Disgusting. Jassmine was nothing but perfumed vacant air and yet people cared about her. And her horrible friends. They wanted to know what was going on in their lives. What their thoughts were. What they'd done that weekend.

Nobody wanted to know anything about Bree.

She looked down and noticed she'd been scratching last night's scabs. A small droplet of blood dribbled down her leg. She ripped off some loo paper and dabbed it away.

She had a lot to think about.

chapter five

"More wine, please."

Bree held out her plastic beaker and Holdo poured in some red.

"More."

Holdo raised an eyebrow and tipped in another dash until the wine was dangerously close to the rim. "You're going to be troublesome after that."

"Shh. I've had a bad day."

It was later that evening. Friday night. And Bree and Holdo were doing what they did every Friday night: staying in and watching intelligent films – preferably with subtitles – to make them feel even more self-important.

"Why do you only ever have red wine?" Bree asked, taking a generous sip from her beaker. The bottle probably cost at least fifty quid but she never noticed the difference. As long as it had alcohol in it, she didn't mind. Especially after today.

"Why? What else do you want?"

She shrugged. "I dunno. Some vodka?"

Holdo looked disgusted. "Eww. What next? You'll be telling me soon you want to 'strawpeedo' some 'Bacardi Breezers' and follow that with a 'Jägerbomb'."

"It's what everyone else our age drinks."

Holdo opened his mouth into a perfect "O", like he was waiting for someone to pop a grape in there.

"This is an Eastern France burgundy made from grapes grown on a small tributary of the Rhone River." His voice trailed off.

Bree had somehow hurt his feelings and now she felt a little bad. "It's really nice. Thank you."

Both embarrassed, they returned their attention to *Donnie Darko* – one of Holdo's absolute favourites. It was his lifelong dream to lose his virginity while Joy Division played in the background, just like Jake Gyllenhaal does in the film.

Screw that. It was Holdo's dream just to lose his virginity. Period.

Bree snuggled further under Holdo's blanket and took another deep sip of wine. She couldn't concentrate on the film. Mr Fellows's words echoed in her head and she thought once more of the rejection letter spiked on her bedroom wall.

She sighed.

"You alright? We can watch something else." The wine had stained a crimson ring around Holdo's mouth where his lips were chapped. She didn't have the heart to tell him.

"I'm fine. Just distracted, 'tis all."

"You still thinking about the rejection letter?"

Her head was beginning to feel heavy. A giant grey bunny rabbit was bashing its way through a mirror on the television. She didn't reply.

Holdo, sensing her restlessness, muted the film.

"Have you thought about blogging?" he asked, turning his body towards her on the sofa. "That's one way of getting published."

Bree pulled a face. "Blogging?" She said the word like it was poisoned.

"It's cool to blog now, Bree. Bloggers are taking over the world."

"I dunno."

"You should give it a go. Can't hurt, can it? Anyway, if you get a strong following that's a good thing to tell publishers when you write your next submission letter."

Bree put her wine on the floor and lay down heavily on the sofa, putting her head in Holdo's lap. He looked confused and nervously stroked her mousy-pink hair.

"There are no more submission letters. I've tried everyone."

"Well, write another book."

"That's what you said last time. And I did it. That's not worked either."

She looked back at the mute telly. Jake Gyllenhaal was wandering round, dressed as a skeleton.

"Why couldn't I have had the idea to write about a

paranoid schizophrenic who saves the world?" she asked, in a childish whine.

"This film bombed at the box office."

She turned over so she was looking right up into Holdo's nostrils. "Really? But everyone loves it now."

"Yeah, but it didn't open well. Barely sold any tickets. You know what it's like – credible things never do well. But shove a formulaic romantic comedy onto the screen, or yet another superhero special-effects spunk-a-thon, and people trample all over each other to see it."

Bree thought again of Mr Fellows. "Do you not think it might be because people want to escape their humdrum lives for a while? Instead of wallowing in them?"

Holdo scoffed. "Are you kidding? Those populist things aren't *real*. They're not important. They're not going to hang around and make man stop and really think for decades to come. They're disposable trash. In the long run, people want a mirror held up to them. They want to look at themselves and be scared at what they see. They want to be *confronted*, challenged…"

He went on a bit. Holdo was always worse after a few glasses of vino.

"…I dunno, Bree. You're kinda weirding me out. I think you're letting this rejection get to you. You usually HATE all that kind of stuff. Don't change who you are. You're perfect."

He looked down at her blearily, like an adoring puppy. An adoring puppy whose water bowl had been spiked with wine. Bree got off his lap before the alcohol made things happen.

"Come on then." She downed her glass. "Let's get wasted."

An hour later and Holdo was monologuing as the Rolling Stones played on his state-of-the-art stereo.

"I know, I know, I know, they made millions of pounds, but 'I Can't Get No Satisfaction', it's, like, almost prophetic. The way they understood consumerism and just how… empty it is. That line about someone not being a man, you know, because he smokes a different brand of cigarette?"

Bree nodded her head heavily.

"…Well, it just sums us up, doesn't it? How *brainwashed* we are by adverts. And branding. And how segregated we are now. Like, no one knows their neighbours any more, do they? Who lives next door? I dunno. Do you know who lives next door?"

Bree shook her head heavily.

"That's exactly my point. I mean, how are we supposed to be satisfied when we don't even know our neighbours?"

He talked himself out. They sat for a while, listening to the music.

If we were cooler, we would be smoking right now.

Bree wasn't sure where the thought came from but it surprised her. It surprised her more to realize she was right. They should be smoking! An illegal substance preferably. Then this monologue would seem less pathetic, less bitter, less trite and would instead be delivered in a hazy smoky atmosphere of cool, hipster-ness. They *definitely* should be smoking. Wasn't that what young disenchanted people were supposed to do? Not drink two bottles of very expensive French burgundy.

She lay her fuggy head on the armrest and half-closed her eyes. As she stretched out her legs, they brushed against Holdo's. She apologized and drew them back into herself.

"S'okay," he muttered. His own eyes were half-closed and his blondish hair fell into them, hiding the worst of his acne-splattered forehead.

If we were more interesting, we would be having sex right now.

Again the thought came out of nowhere. But again she knew she was right. They should be having sex! That's what people cared about. That's what interesting people did. They shagged each other and then got confused and upset about it and told everyone. And you would listen – interested – dying to know more. If she and Holdo ended up sleeping together tonight that would be a very interesting thing to have happened. She wondered if she should try it. Could she bring herself to? Tentatively, she stretched out her legs again, but this time laid them on Holdo's lap.

If he starts stroking them, what will I do?

She watched his reaction. Holdo looked at his lap and the unexpected human parcel that had landed there. His hand clenched and unclenched and then she was certain she saw him reach towards her, to maybe touch her leg. Her breath quickened with suspense...

But then he dropped his hand like a damp dandelion and scratched a spot on his chin.

Not really disappointed, she closed her eyes and concentrated on the music. Jagger was yelling about not getting what you want but getting what you need.

But what if you needed to get what you want...just once?

She opened her eyes to tell Holdo her clever thought about the song.

"Holdo?"

His head had flopped down and a small snore whistled out his mouth.

He'd passed out.

"Holdo?" she said a little louder, but nothing. He was gone. Bree sighed, bored of this evening, bored of her life. Tired of it always feeling like sludge to wade through. She carefully extricated her apparently unenticing legs from his lap and stood up, wobbling slightly. She took a moment to roll Holdo over so he was lying on his side and put a bin next to his head. She knew Holdo, and he would always vomit when he'd had too much wine. The stain on Bree's bedroom carpet was proof. She examined him for a while – how his face looked when he was sleeping. Maybe he would grow up to be good-looking one day. There was certainly potential. It was just hard to get over the bad skin and, well, Holdo's somewhat difficult personality.

He really needed to learn to stop interrupting people to correct them on their grammar.

She left Holdo sleeping – dreaming about a world where he wasn't him, where he was someone else…

…Someone confident enough to reach out and stroke a girl's legs.

chapter six

The house was quiet when Bree stumbled in. She'd had trouble with the security gate and almost set off the alarm. Now she was having trouble closing the door without making a noise. Every bang seemed to echo around the huge lonely house. She didn't know whether her parents were asleep or out. Her dad was probably still at work. She removed a crystal glass from a display cabinet and pushed the button on the giant fridge to let ice fall. She then filled it with water and downed it as quickly as she could, before opening the cupboard to get out another strawberry Pop-Tart to take up to her room.

She *still* couldn't get Mr Fellows's words out of her head. They merry-go-rounded in her brain over and over. She knew why. It was because he was right. Bree needed to become more interesting.

Closing her bedroom door behind her, she leaned against

it for a moment and stared at her special bookshelf. The shelf drilled into the wall just above her rejection spike. All her favourite books stood lined up on it in pride of place, for her to yank out and reread night after night. She walked over and trailed her fingers along the crusted spines, thinking of the authors who'd created these beautiful collections of words, and why.

She stopped on Stephen King. Alcoholic and drug addict. So intent on self-medicating his demons he still can't remember writing some of his most famous stories...just stuffing tissues up his nose to stop blood dripping onto his typewriter. And yet it was his words that conquered those demons. Writing about them was vanquishing them. His stories mending him, word by word, page by page, until his blood was clean again.

Next was Jane Austen, her favourite. Bree took out her battered copy of *Pride and Prejudice* and leafed through the pages. It was all biting social satire. Jane flicking literary spitwads at the world of romance and marriage, a world she was never invited to join herself.

And finally there was Virginia Woolf. Whose brain composed words of such brilliance, and yet tortured her with such darkness that she filled her pockets with stones and wandered into a river.

Pain, loneliness, darkness.

Bree's three favourite writers; Bree's three most present emotions.

And yet, on her bookcase, all that remained of her heroes'

torments were their stories and their words. If Bree could write, if she could write interesting things that people wanted to read, she too could be immortal. Her pain too could be worthwhile – transformed and transfigured into the redemption of A Good Story.

She just needed something good to write about.

She opened her desk drawer and took out her latest rejected manuscript. She sat down and read the opening few lines.

Rose didn't know why she had come to the pier but the black waters had coaxed her here with their tidal magic. She knew the water would consume her eventually. She couldn't fight its intoxicating force. Misery. It would claim her misery. Wash it away and make her clean again. Jumping was the inevitable conclusion to this visit. She knew that, the pier knew that, the water definitely knew that. But before she jumped she needed to understand her pain and why it had brought her here.

Maybe it was the wine. Maybe it was her teacher's words. Or maybe it was the countless rejection letters. But something finally clicked in Bree.

This. Was. Terrible.

Laughably terrible.

Hysterically laughably terrible.

A snort escaped her nose. A hiccup popped out of her mouth. She reread it again, chuckling to herself. The chuckles turned to hysteria and soon she was laughing so hard she was almost crying. She flopped back on her bed, sinking into the pillows, and let the giggles bubble from her mouth. They sprang through her body until she was hiccupping instead of laughing. High on the hilarity, Bree rolled over and rummaged in her school bag to retrieve her notebook and pen. She turned onto her belly and sucked the end of the biro.

She knew what she had to do.

Her writing was scrawled, messy from the red-wine haze. But the plan was clear. It lay before her, a path waiting to be walked.

How to become interesting…

She wrote several bullet points, the rules she needed to follow – scribbling some out, rewriting them, until the list was complete. Then she turned on her laptop.

Bree signed up to a blogger platform. It was unexpectedly easy to pick a wallpaper, a domain name, and get ready to post. She just had to write and click – then she would be a published writer. Online, anyway. She took a bite of her Pop-Tart and, before she lost her nerve, Bree began to type.

THE MANIFESTO ON HOW TO BE INTERESTING

Hello.

I EXIST. I EXIST. I EXIST. I EXIST. I EXIST. I EXIST. I EXIST.

Isn't this what blogging is all about? Proving our

existence? Leaving a tiny crap mark on the world so when we die it doesn't all seem so horribly pointless?

Good evening, reader. You are reading a loser's blog. That's right. I'm a massive loser. If you go to school with me, you won't know my name. If I walked past you in the street, you wouldn't even notice. If you talked to me, I would have nothing of any interest to say.

Why?

Because I'm not interesting!

I'm boring. I'm a nobody. I don't live life. I don't embrace life. But that's all about to change. Because I am starting a project. Here. Now. For myself. And if you want to come along for the ride then you're very welcome.

What's my purpose? I'm going to become interesting. I'm going to become somebody you want to read about.

How?

I'm going to do all the things you're too scared to do. And then I'm going to tell you about it. If you're really brave, you can do it with me.

This is <u>The Manifesto on How to be Interesting</u>. I'm going to pinpoint EXACTLY what it is that makes a person worth caring about and then do it.

I'll let you know how I get on.

It's not going to be easy.

But then interesting things never are, are they?

She finished typing with a flourish and hit *Publish*. And then, without even brushing her teeth, Bree fell onto her bed and fell fast asleep. Smiling.

chapter seven

Bree woke up with her notepad stuck to her forehead.

Her mouth tasted of dead rats. It was so dry she was quite certain her tongue could sandpaper a piece of wood. Her head was thudding like a giant gong had been erected overnight in her brain and some mischievous kids were constantly bashing it. *Bash. Bash. BASH.*

Despite all this, Bree felt just wonderful. This was the best hangover ever. Because it was a hangover with purpose. She rolled over and picked her laptop off the floor. She logged on and read back what she'd garbled out last night.

Not bad.

It wasn't great literature. But – even though she'd written it herself – Bree got excited reading it back. This was going to happen. She was going to do this.

She grabbed her toothbrush and jumped in the shower of her en-suite. She liked to brush her teeth and wash at the same time, especially when suffering a red-wine hangover of doom. The water was scalding, reviving, and she stayed in until her skin was bright red and she felt light-headed.

"Morning, dear," her mum greeted her as she entered the kitchen. Mum was wearing a crop top. Actual real fifty-year-old midriff was on show. It was only for the gym, but still.

"I've made you a fresh fruit salad."

Bree grunted and opened the freezer to retrieve some veggie bacon for a sandwich. Today was a carb day.

"Your father had to go into work again but he wants us to all have a proper family dinner tonight. That sounds nice, doesn't it? I was going to make a roast."

Bree got out the frying pan.

"I've just come back from spinning. You feel so amazing afterwards. You should come with me sometime..."

Bree emptied the bacon onto the hot oil. It began to splutter and gasp and brown.

"Well, I'm off to Waitrose. What are you up to today? Got any nice plans?"

She flipped the bacon over.

"Bree, I said have you got any nice plans?"

Finally Bree spoke. Two whole words. "Watching TV."

"Is that all?"

She nodded.

"You're not going to go outside or anything? Not even meeting up with Holdo?"

Bree tipped the slightly burned bacon onto some white bread. "I'll go outside when I walk to get the films."

"That's not what I meant."

"I know."

"You could come to Waitrose with me. I'll let you put whatever you want in the trolley."

Bree gave her mother her very best *You gotta be kidding me?* face.

"Suit yourself. That white bread is full of rubbish, you know. It will give you cellulite."

And with that, her mother powered upstairs to change out of her belly top.

Bree didn't hate her mother exactly. Especially after the whole she-birthed-her-and-it-probably-hurt thing. She didn't mean to be rude, nasty, and standoffish. But – at the risk of sounding like a massive bitch – Bree had no respect for her mother. Her mum seemed so satisfied by such shallow stuff, like good wallpaper and toned thighs, rather than her husband being around, or having a purpose to her life beyond shopping. And apart from all that inconvenient unconditional love stuff getting in the way, Bree was quite sure she didn't *like* her mother either. How can you like someone you have no respect for? The sad thing was, Bree knew her mother was equally disappointed in how Bree had turned out. She'd no doubt longed for a daughter just like Jassmine Dallington. Some perfect plastic cut-out she could get pedicures with. Instead she'd got Bree. With her embarrassing stripy tights, slammed bedroom doors and sneering judgements.

Oh well. Who didn't have issues with their mother?

Bacon sandwich demolished, Bree set out on her day's challenge. She pulled on her duffel coat and marched out towards the high street. It was a crappy day – drizzle-tastic. The sort of day that made the pretty girls squeal and hold folders over their heads and then whinge about their hair frizzing like it was the worst thing in the world, when, somewhere, children were dying of Aids in Africa. But Bree was learning that people don't find Africa and Aids very interesting. Not unless some celebrity – with non-frizzy hair – goes over there with a TV crew and starts blubbing for Comic Relief. Bree was trying to be more interesting. So she put Africa to the back of her mind and powerwalked to the local DVD shop.

Change hadn't hit their sheltered, privileged town just yet. As DVD chains closed around the country, their posh independent store continued to thrive, customers still tempted in by the decorated boxes of organic chocolate buttons and gourmet popcorn to rent the latest films.

As she pushed through the shop doors, Bree felt kind of dirty, like she was walking into a sex shop or something. She'd been here eight million times before. She and Holdo came almost every weekend while everyone else their age got pissed at parties they would never be invited to. But Bree wasn't going to their usual section – the corner dedicated to foreign films and independent cinema. No. She was going to a more shameful corner. One that, until today, she wouldn't be caught dead in.

Romantic comedies.

She was immediately overwhelmed by the bubblegum pink colour. It was on every DVD case in some form, alongside giggling airbrushed actresses. Bree pulled one case out and flipped it over to read the blurb.

"Give me an L, O, V and an E."

Angela always thought there was nothing more important than cheerleading. Until she met Kirk – star quarterback of her school's biggest rival football team. Uh-oh. Suddenly her seemingly-perfect life is turned upside down when she has to decide between her two biggest loves. But who will win her heart? Pom-poms or the Prom King?

"Oh Philip Larkin," Bree whispered. "We're not in Kansas any more."

Bree was almost ill with judgement. As she read the four-star review from *Teen Here* magazine, it practically oozed from every pore. Yet, despite the film's lack of original storyline and any semblance of three-dimensional characters, Bree couldn't ignore the other reviews on the case:

Blockbuster smash.
Cinema hit of the year.

And she couldn't forget overhearing girls at school raving about it in the corridors. In fact, if she remembered correctly, the film was so popular someone had started a cheerleading club. It had run for two terms.

People liked this stuff.

It was interesting.

Bree grabbed the DVD case and shoved it under her armpit. She spent a good twenty minutes picking out more – reading each blurb carefully before adding it to her bulging stash. Eventually satisfied, she dumped her bundle on the cashier's desk.

"You having a girly sleepover?" he asked, stuffing *10 Things I Hate About You* into one of the shop's specially-designed ink-black sleeves.

"Huh?" Bree looked around to check he was talking to her.

He pointed to the pile. "A sleepover? Looks like you and your mates are preparing for a chick-flick fest."

"Umm. No. They're just for me."

He gave her a *My, you're an even bigger loser than me* look. "Riiiiight."

Bree had never been to a girly sleepover – not since puberty anyway. She'd never played truth or dare, never rung up the boy she fancied while her friends giggled manically in the background, and never swapped kissing tips. A whole teenage-girl rite of passage whirred past as the guy rang up the register.

"They all need to be back by seven tomorrow."

"I know."

chapter eight

She exited into the drizzle and stormed home, clutching her carrier bag like it was stuffed full of stolen goods. With the films rented, she felt even more compelled to put her plan into action. She was just turning onto her long, well-manicured road when her mobile went off. She dug in her coat pocket, retrieved it, and looked at the screen.

Holdo. Well, who else would it be?

"Morning," he said. "I feel like absolute hell. Was it you who put that bucket next to me? If so, thanks. I very much needed it at about three o'clock this morning."

Bree grinned. "I thought you might."

"Who knew burgundy could be so dangerous?"

"Indeed."

"How's your head?"

As if it had overheard the question, Bree's forehead thumped dully. "Not great. Not awful though."

"God, I really was wasted last night, wasn't I? Were you? I can't even remember you leaving."

Bree grimaced. His voice sounded rehearsed and she wondered if he was lying. Was this his way of bringing up the leg-grab thing (or lack of)? Did he remember? To be honest, Bree was relieved he hadn't done anything. The thought of what could've happened made her feel a bit sick. And she didn't need to have sex with Holdo any more. Not now she had her plan.

"I don't remember much."

"Oh."

So he did remember...awkward.

"I just woke up this morning with my notepad stuck to my face..."

Holdo laughed. "Night-time drunken writing?"

"I suppose so."

"So..." Holdo started. "What you up to today?"

Bree looked at the carrier bag swinging alongside her, thought about lying, and decided against it. "Watching some films."

Holdo's voice lit up over the phone. Could voices light up? Or was it only faces? Bree's head hurt. She needed her duvet. And more carbs. Soon. Very soon.

"Awesome. Hangover day of cinema. I might join you. What you watching?"

Bree gulped.

Er...what could she say? A wide selection of chick-flicks, all featuring girls being made over and discovering that life is *sooo* much better when they're pretty and thin and beautiful and swept away by the hottest boy in school. She whispered a few of their titles, noticing they spanned several decades.

Holdo went quiet.

Then: "You're kidding, right?"

"Nope."

"Am I allowed to ask why?" His voice was angry; actually angry. Like Bree had just revealed she was planning to drown puppies or something.

"I need them for a…project I'm working on. That's all."

"What is this project? Lobotomy by Pop Culture 101?"

"Holdo, come on. I'm probably the only girl alive who hasn't watched these movies."

"And that's why we're friends."

Bree arrived at her house and punched in the security code. Hard.

"Is this something to do with your book?" Holdo asked, his voice still all superior. "Are you having some kind of meltdown because it got rejected again?"

She gritted her teeth. She wasn't ready to tell Holdo about her idea just yet. She needed to iron out the kinks first. Bree had once read that the most successful people don't tell others about their projects until after they're finished. Apparently, if you boast about something you're doing, or planning to do, people go *"Oh wow, that's amazing"*. Then you get all the self-worth and congratulations too soon and have no motivation to actually get stuff done.

But successful people – like, the really-made-it ones – stay quiet until it's finished. Bree didn't do failure, not well anyway. Therefore she was keeping quiet until she knew for sure that her plan was foolproof.

"You gonna join me then?" She only asked because he would say no.

Sure enough: "I'd rather go to an eighties-themed disco with pins sticking out of my eyes."

Bree headed up her driveway. Her dad's BMW convertible wasn't there. He was still at work then.

"Suit yourself. The offer's there."

"I think I'll work on coding my game today, and wait for your identity crisis to pass."

"You do that then."

"I will."

"Well, have fun."

"You too. If it's possible."

"Oh it's possible."

And Bree hung up.

chapter nine

The rest of the day was spent in a media-induced coma. Bree sat in bed, with her legs snuggled under the duvet and her notepad perched on her lap. She watched one film after the other after the other, obsessively making notes and adding to her list of rules, until her eyes hurt. By dinner time she had a checklist and possibly square-shaped eyeballs.

"Dinner," her mum called up the stairs.

"Coming."

Bree turned off the screen and John Travolta and Olivia Newton-John's flying car disappeared with a zap. She pulled on a grey hoodie and made her way down to a torturous hour of awkward conversation.

Her parents sat in silence at one end of their huge dining table, chewing their roast beef. Bree's dad, as always, looked exhausted. His tie was loosened, his suit crumpled. Bree sat next to him and added roast potatoes and green beans to the Quorn fillet on her plate.

They all chewed in silence and it was Bree, unusually, who broke it.

"Mum, what are you doing tomorrow?"

Her mum's forkful of beef stopped on its journey to her mouth. Out of shock maybe, or suspicion that the question was somehow a joke.

"Umm. I'm going to my body combat class in the morning."

"Can I come?"

Her mum put her fork down. "Of course you can, sweetheart."

Bree's dad looked from one to the other with bloodshot eyes – bewildered as to why his eating had been interrupted. They never normally spoke to each other at dinner.

"What the hell is body combat?" he asked. "You learning how to beat people up, huh, Paula?" He snorted at his own joke, then stopped quickly, looking knackered, like his terrible attempt at humour had sapped any remaining energy out of him.

"It's non-contact. It's just a cardio class. You sure you want to come, Bree?"

Bree nodded, ignoring her dad. "And, er, I was wondering if we could go shopping or something afterwards? Maybe go to the hairdresser as well? If any are open."

Her mum's mouth flopped open. "Seriously?"

"Yes."

"Shopping where? A bookshop or something?"

"No, like a clothes shop. Maybe that nice place in town?"

"You're honestly telling me you want to go to body combat, get a haircut, and come clothes shopping with me?"

Bree nodded again. "Is that so hard to believe?"

Bree's mum smiled. It was just a little one, so small you would barely notice it. She picked up her fork, took a mouthful of beef and leaned back in her chair. "No. I suppose it isn't."

Silence returned to the table, with only the sounds of chewing and sipping filling the air.

Until her dad perked up a bit.

He jabbed at her half-eaten Quorn fillet with his fork. "What's that?" he asked.

"A Quorn fillet."

"What in the name of Christ is a Quorn fillet?"

"It's a meat substitute. It's made out of mushrooms."

Bree's dad would probably have looked less confused if she'd told him it was made from reconstituted pigeon poo.

"Mushrooms made to taste like meat?"

"Yes." Bree took a mouthful.

"And since when have you been a vegetarian?"

Bree was just about to respond when, to her amazement, her mother cut her off.

"Oh for God's sake, Daniel. Bree's been a vegetarian since puberty, after she watched that documentary about fast food. If you were actually ever here you would've noticed."

Her dad looked like someone had just wiped reconstituted pigeon poo on his face. Bewilderment carved through his tired features. He looked from Bree to her mother, before shaking his head and returning to his meat, muttering, "Mushrooms don't taste of meat..." like a child who'd lost a playground argument.

Bree's mum caught her eye and did a mock sigh, blowing her hair up. Bree rolled her eyes back and they both fell into silent unnoticeable laughter. Her stomach glowed with the unfamiliar sensation.

She ate the rest of her Quorn fillet happily. And, in some odd sort of way, found herself looking forward to tomorrow.

chapter ten

The next morning she was shaken awake by her mother.

"Morning, love. It's time for body combat. Remember you said you wanted to go yesterday?"

Bree rubbed her eyes to dislodge the sleep from them. Her half-conscious consciousness was being ripped down the middle. Pre-The-Plan Bree would've screamed "LEAVE ME ALONE", gone back to sleep until noon, rung Holdo and then spent the remaining weekend watching the director's commentary on something. But Post-The-Plan Bree knew she needed to do this. Even though it was going to be painful.

Bree slowly sat up. "What time is it?"

"8.15. The class starts at 8.45."

"On a Sunday?"

"Yes. On a Sunday."

Bree yawned, stretched, and squinted.

"Give me a minute to get ready."

*　　*　　*

Half an hour later, Bree was in a personal hell of her own making. She had no workout gear so was wearing her school PE kit and a clumpy pair of black trainers from her earlier teenage years. She probably would have stood out less if she'd worn sexy lingerie. Everyone in the class wore belly tops, tight Lycra leggings and special workout trainers – mostly in pink – with their hair scraped up immaculately into bouncy ponytails. Everyone's limbs were perfect. Each calf was uber-defined, each buttock cheek sculpted into a perfect curve, and flawlessly toned tummies peeked out all over the place.

The instructor hadn't arrived yet but all the women seemed to be stretching out and limbering up. Bree, unsure of what to do, bent over and tried to touch her toes. "Tried" being the operative word.

She was just in the difficult process of getting back up again when some teeny tiny stick figure with French plait pigtails rocketed through the doors.

"Right, ladies," she yelled. "Are you ready to burn some calories?"

"YES!"

"That's not loud enough. I said ARE YOU READY TO BURN SOME CALORIES?"

"YESSSSSS!" Bree could hear her mum's voice over all the others.

Just as Bree was going to make some spot-on observation about the cult-like ways of this exercise class, the stick insect flipped on the sound system and Bree's life rapidly flashed past her eyes.

It was physical torture like she'd never experienced before. As everyone around her effortlessly kicked and punched in time to the quick (and awful) music, Bree could hardly keep up. Sweat dripped down her face. Her legs started to seize up, still tight from her not-fully-healed scars. She caught a glimpse of herself in the mirror and her face resembled a sunburned tomato just home from a last-minute trip to Lanzarote.

And then, as if she wasn't feeling terrible already... Jassmine Dallington arrived from nowhere. She looked brilliant – wearing some vibrant red top and tight black leggings. She mouthed her apologies to the instructor, pushed her way to the front, and joined in the routine in flawless synchrony. When Bree wasn't focused entirely on not fainting, she watched Jassmine's blonde hair swish about in front of her. Jassmine watched herself in the mirror, working through the moves effortlessly and smiling smugly at her own reflection.

An emotion stronger than exhaustion passed through Bree.

Anger.

Suddenly she hated Jassmine. Her easy life, the way everyone seemed to care about her though she'd never done one nice thing to deserve it.

Bree stepped up her effort and concentrated harder on the routine.

Hatred drove her – as she squatted, lunged, boxed and panted. It soon eclipsed the knackeredness and pain. She bobbed and weaved to the music, now keeping pace with everyone around her. Sweat still poured from her body but she wasn't aware of it.

And then, with the heavy bass as a background, something began to happen to Bree. Something...good-feeling began to rush through her veins. Her heart pounded frantically – but no longer out of protest, now almost like it was spurring her on. Her breath finally caught up with her body and adrenalin rushed through her. She'd never felt like this before. Not naturally anyway. It was the same rush she got when she locked herself in the bathroom and made red patterns on her thighs. Her head thumped in the same way. She got the same tidal wave of relief. But she wasn't bleeding. She wasn't going to scab up tomorrow. Her thighs would hurt, but good hurt. Healthy hurt.

When the music stopped, Bree was almost upset. She was just balancing in a calf stretch when Jassmine picked up her stuff and left. She passed Bree with barely a smidgeon of sweat on her forehead. A look of dim recognition crossed her face and she looked confused, trying to place Bree in her inner list of who's-worth-knowing. When she realized who she was, she deliberately curled up her lip in disgust.

I have never done one bad thing to you, Bree thought, and anger surged through her again. *Nothing about my existence affects your life in any way, and yet you deliberately make me feel like shit.*

Jassmine gave a beaming smile to the instructor and waved goodbye, before she sashayed out the room.

You don't know or care who I am. But you will on Monday. I'm going to start fighting back with the best weapon I have: words. Indelible, permanent words.

Bree's mum came over, wiping her face with a towel.

"You enjoy it, Bree?" She tossed over the towel and Bree caught it and dabbed her forehead.

"It was...hard. But good."

Her mum looked nervous. "Do you still want to go shopping and get your hair done?"

Not really. All Bree wanted to do was dollop vast amounts of Tiger balm onto every part of her and curl up with the new Booker Prize winner. But she wasn't that person any more. Well, not publicly anyway.

She scraped the last of the sweat off her face.

"That was the plan, right?"

Her mum smiled.

chapter eleven

After a long shower and clothes change in the gigantic marble changing rooms, they set off into town.

"I didn't know all the shops were open on Sunday," Bree said, looking up and down the bustling high street. Sundays had always been her writing and reading day and she rarely ventured past the security gate.

"Did I give birth to a daughter or an alien?" her mum asked, pushing the button at the pedestrian crossing. "Shops have been opening on Sundays for years. Nobody believes in God any more so we've made consumerism our new religion. Haven't you noticed all shopping centres look like churches?"

Hang on – had her mother just said something profound?

Bewildered, Bree said, "And hairdresser's are all open too?"

"Of course. They take Mondays off instead of Sundays."

"To go to church?" Bree deadpanned.

"No. So they have a chance to go shopping!" Her mother threw back her head and laughed at her own joke.

She steered them towards the "nice" bit of town and pointed to a window display.

"Oooh, those shoes would look lovely on you, Bree."

Bree looked. Her mother was pointing to a pair of chunky platforms that stood centre stage behind the glass. Platforms so stylish they would make anyone wearing them look just plain fabulous. They were black but with a bright purple undersole.

Bree looked through the glass nervously. "I dunno."

"At least try them on."

"I don't have anything to wear them to."

"What? Since when did us girls need a reason to buy amazing shoes? Come on, let's go in."

She clasped Bree's hand and half-dragged her into the store.

Bree felt out of place the moment they walked through the doors. It was like having a neon sign on her head, glowing with the words *I DON'T BELONG*. She felt the shop assistants' eyes on her as she and her mum browsed the rails of expensive clothes. She could sense them narrowing as they took in Bree's baggy jeans and hoodie. Her mother put a protective arm round her shoulder and kept up a constant stream of inane babble to cover the judgement hovering in the air like a storm cloud.

"This jumper is lovely. Ooooh, this blazer would be good

for school. It looks like it would fit in with your uniform policy but it's so much less frumpy than your current one. Shoes! We must get you some shoes too. Where are those platforms?"

Bree's arms quickly filled up with stacks of material – each item more trendy/beautiful/stylish than the last. At Queen's Hall you were allowed to wear "home clothes" once you got to sixth form, as long as they had a "corporate" feel. This stuff would fit the rules, but it was a world away from the garish frumpy stuff she was used to. When the pile was too big to add to, her mum led her through to the luscious changing rooms. They all had floor-to-ceiling red velvet curtains and spotlighting. To Bree's dismay, her mum barrelled into the cubicle with her, sat on a stool, and watched as she struggled into one outfit after another.

"That one looks great on you. Oooh, try it with this scarf. I wish I had a seventeen-year-old's body again."

It was so hard, changing in a way so her mum wouldn't see the scars on her legs. Bree jiggled and danced from outfit to outfit, her heart thumping, always ensuring the tops of her thighs were covered. Luckily her mum seemed too excited to notice Bree's odd behaviour. Or maybe Bree had been behaving so oddly already this weekend, she was immunized.

"We have to get everything," her mum said.

Bree had seen a few of the price tags. "But it's very expensive…"

"Don't worry about that."

"Maybe we should just get the shoes?"

And then to Bree's delight, shock, and embarrassment – she couldn't decide which one – her mum stood up and hugged her.

"Darling, you do realize this is the first shopping trip we've been on since you started secondary school? Financially – and emotionally – we have a lot of catching up to do." Her voice broke, like she was trying not to cry.

Wow, Bree thought. *Who knew the answer to happy families was clothes shopping?*

She wasn't sure what to think of her mother. There was a big inner conflict whirring round her ever-busy brain. On one hand, she was pissed off her mum only seemed to love and accept her when she was being a shallow consumerist mini-me. Why didn't they hug and cry when Bree finished writing her first novel? Okay, so she'd never told Mum she'd written a book, but still. Or how about when she won her first game of chess on Difficulty Level Three against the computer (which everyone knows is practically IMPOSSIBLE)? But on the other hand, she was just enjoying feeling loved. By her blood. By her mum. Even though it wasn't exactly how she wanted it, it still felt wonderful.

"I'm having a good day," she mumbled into her mum's shoulder.

Her mum pulled back and looked at her with watery eyes. "Me too. Now let's pay for these clothes."

* * *

Bags dangling off their arms like giant bracelets, the pair of them walked towards A Cut Above – home to the town's most sought-after hairdresser.

"Now beware," her mum said, as they dodged a woman pushing a double-decker pram filled with two wailing toddlers. "Damian is a bit…harsh in the way he speaks." She looked sideways at Bree's pink-tinged hair and a worried crease appeared on her forehead. "He may have a few… things he wants to say to you about your, erm, current style. But he's only looking out for what's best for you and you really can trust him. He squeezed you in as a favour to me, so he cares."

Bree shrugged. "Whatever. It's just hair."

The crease on her mum's forehead deepened.

"Dear God, don't let him hear you say that."

chapter twelve

The windows of A Cut Above were blacked out, but after pushing the intercom and giving their names, the sooty glass door opened to reveal a stark white hairdressing space-station adorned with fresh orchids. The air was heavy with expensive-smelling hairspray; wall-to-floor mirrors created a glass maze effect, and black-clad hairdressers, each with their own ridiculous haircut, danced on the balls of their feet over the foil-wrapped heads of rich customers.

"Paaaaaaaaaaaaaaaaaaaaaaaaaaaaula!" A very camp voice pierced through the fuggy air. A bald man – ironic for a hairdresser, Bree thought – strutted over with his arms flung open. "What are you doing here, darling? Your roots won't peep through for another two weeks."

"Damian! I'm not here for myself, silly. I've brought my daughter. We're having a makeover day. I rang you yesterday, remember?" Paula moved aside to showcase Bree, who stood hesitantly on the spot.

"Oh yes, of course." Damian looked her up and down and went a little pale. "*This* is your daughter?"

Bree nodded. Her mum went a bit red.

"Yes. Well, she's not had her hair cut in a while…"

"It's a mess!" he interrupted.

Bree blushed. Her hair was purposely a mess, but her whole I-deliberately-don't-care-about-how-I-look attitude seemed stupid in here.

"Well, yes, it has been a bit neglected." Her mum bit her lip nervously, like her daughter having pink-tinged split ends was as awful as bringing in a ten-year-old who wasn't potty trained yet.

Damian pushed Bree down into a chair and forcefully wrapped a gown round her shoulders. He scooped her hair out at the neck so it splayed down the black silk, making the ends look even more frazzled. He lifted it and let it drop, sighing, and watched Bree's face in the mirror.

"Okay. It's a mess. But it's a mess I can work with. What do you want, darling? Anything would be an improvement."

Bree looked up at him. "I want to look beautiful," she said, her voice authoritative. "I want to turn heads. To stand out from the crowd." She paused. "For the right reasons."

Damian chewed his lip in silent contemplation. Then his eyes lit up.

"Blonde," he said. "You need to be blonde!"

Bree tried to control the grimace her face made. Blonde.

There were so many things about blonde that she disliked. It insinuated stupidity – her worst nightmare. She quickly weighed up the other options. There was brunette. Nice, sensible, sophisticated brunette. Not exactly attention-seeking. There was black – but any Caucasian person who dyed their hair black always looked either stupid, gothic, or weird, like Chuck from English. Red. Red was definitely interesting...but was it a bit too in-your-face? A bit too desperate look-at-me-ish? Her natural colour, if she remembered right, was mouse. But who the hell ever asked for mouse?

"Blonde it is."

Damian broke into a broad grin.

"Right. We're gonna be here a while. And I'm cutting your hair off... Don't worry," he said, seeing Bree's panicked face. "Not all of it. But if you wanna turn heads, lovey, long blonde hair isn't the way to do it. No, you're getting a graduated bob and you're going to rock it."

And he leaned towards her with a pot full of purple gunk and got to work.

An hour later and Bree's head looked like a Christmas turkey. Apparently Damian had added "three different types" of blonde highlights, including "toffee", "honey", and "treacle". It felt a little bit like being a laboratory rat. But instead of curing cancer, Bree's guinea-pig status was solely in aid of beauty. Such effort for such an unworthy conclusion.

But she reminded herself that constant judgement of social norms hadn't got her very far in her seventeen years.

She wondered if Jassmine's blonde hair was natural, or if she too spent the best part of a weekend having foil plastered to her scalp. It broke the magic spell a bit. Thinking of Jassmine reminded her of that morning and the unnecessary evil she'd given Bree. She wrinkled her nose, and her mum, who was leafing through a glossy magazine, noticed.

"You okay, honey? Is it the smell of the peroxide? It takes some getting used to. I quite like the smell now."

She looked up at her mother. "Mum?"

"Yes."

"Were you popular in school?"

"Is that was this is all about? You want to be more popular?"

"Not exactly. I was just wondering."

Her mum put the magazine down and looked straight at her. "No," she said. "No, I wasn't popular at school."

"Do you think it matters? You know, in the long run?"

Her mum poked her tongue into the side of her cheek and thought about it a moment. "If I was a good mother I would tell you no, no, it doesn't matter. Not in the long run. Not in the grand scheme of things…"

"But…?"

Her mother didn't break eye contact with Bree. "But I can still remember the full names of the popular kids in my year." She listed them on her fingers. "Carly Carding, Nadine Morrison, Lauren Vegas, those were the girls. And the guys, the popular ones *everyone* fancied, were Ben Wireley and Steve Newington. How can it not matter if I still remember every single thing about them, even though it was decades ago?"

"Maybe it's just that everyone remembers the popular kids at school," Bree said, surprised at her mother's frankness. She always assumed her mother was just some Pilates-obsessed housewife. Maybe she'd underestimated her... Or just not really spoken to her before.

"That's the thing though, the thing that still makes me angry now. I can remember all their names, who went out with who and when, even what they wore to the leaving ball. I can remember every snide comment they made to me or my friends. And so can everyone else in my school year who wasn't them. But them..." She paused, and went to move one of Bree's foils that had fallen onto her forehead, before sitting back in her chair again. "They barely knew I existed then, and have definitely forgotten me by now. That just seems so terribly unfair somehow. That they're so much a part of my life, and I'm nothing to theirs. I still feel like the unpopular kid."

Bree scratched the top of her neck where the peroxide itched.

"But they might not be happy, successful, pretty and popular any more," she told her mother. "They might've failed horribly in life and are now fat, lonely and addicted to lottery scratch cards."

Her mum shook her head sadly. "Life doesn't work that

way, sweetie. They're all doing just fine – better than me probably."

"But…"

"But what? You think there should be some sort of karmic balance? That because they sailed through secondary school it's only right that they have some suffering down the line to make up for it? Okay, in a weak moment, I might have wished that to happen, so they felt a little like I did when I was at school. But what does that achieve?" She trailed off and absent-mindedly picked up her magazine again.

"So you think being popular at school is important then?"

Her mum shook her head like Bree had woken her from a dream.

"Maybe not important. But it helps. You don't carry the same scars around if secondary school was easy for you…" Then she shook her head again, almost violently, like she'd caught herself out. "No…no… You know what, don't listen to me, Bree. It *isn't* important. You know what's important? Being a good person. That's the most important thing."

Nice try, Bree thought. *But I'm not buying it.*

That evening, Bree looked at her new self in the mirror. Massive cliché, but she actually didn't recognize herself. She was trussed up in tomorrow's just-inside-the-school-rules outfit. Her hair was a buttery sheet of gorgeousness. It fell into her eyes, highlighting her perfect make-up, and shone like she'd just returned from a three-week cruise. Her face had been transformed thanks to a make-up lesson from her mum. Her spots were expertly covered, her skin glowed, her lips looked juicy and utterly transfixing – she'd never realized she'd got such good lips before.

There was no escaping it, Bree looked stunning. She tried not to smile, annoyed that looking like this made her feel so good. But a grin crept onto her face anyway and she did a little jig of joy – before remembering everything she stood for and believed in.

Finally she dragged herself from the mirror, sat at her desk, and lifted the lid of her laptop.

THE MANIFESTO ON HOW TO BE INTERESTING

Rule number one: One must be attractive

I've made this my first rule...

In order to be interesting, one must be attractive to look at.

Especially if you're a woman...

Alright, okay, calm down. Don't all yell at once. "HOW DARE YOU?" you say. Call myself a feminist, do I? Modern life has evolved past such nonsense. Attractiveness doesn't immediately place you into the winning team.

But you're wrong. Oh, how wrong you are.

Because, admit it, you're gagging to know what colour I've dyed my hair. You can't wait to see the before and after and what my figure's like now I've actually got the inclination to show it off. Hell, you're frothing at the mouth in desperation to find out how I've made my lips look this damn gorgeous.

There is something about taking something ugly and making it pretty that is compelling to us. It's a satisfaction you cannot hide from. Who didn't watch *Ugly Betty* and want to pluck her eyebrows and see what she could "really look like"? Even though that goes against the whole point of the show, you wanted her to be beautiful, didn't you? Despite, no doubt, the fact you raved on to all your mates about how great the message of the show was.

WE'RE ALL MASSIVE HYPOCRITES. We are. We want beauty. We want to watch beautiful people. We just don't like to admit that to ourselves.

And, let's face it, would you really want to follow my little experiment if I was an ugly chick? If I did all this with a face that still resembled an arse? I'm lucky enough that, apparently, I'm naturally quite a looker. Who knew? This experiment would be a little harder if I was a troll.

Oh how I wish it hadn't come to this. So quickly as well. Oh how I wish that my makeover has no effect whatsoever on my life. That everything will remain exactly the same even though I'm hot now.

But both you and I know that isn't what's going to happen.

The fact I'm attractive now is going to change things. Pathetic. Depressing. But you know it and I know it.

Let's see what tomorrow brings, eh? When I reveal my new self to a school which has no idea what's about to hit it...

Over and out.

chapter thirteen

Bree was a little less cocky the next morning.

With an unfamiliar reflection staring back at her, she started to second-guess her idea. Although she would never admit it aloud, Bree got the occasional bout of self-doubt.

She was wearing the blazer her mum had picked out. It hugged her figure – which would shape up nicely if she kept the exercise up. She'd done an exercise DVD with Mum at six o'clock that morning. Zumba – more like personal humiliation. Bree had never felt ashamed of her inability to shimmy before, but the Zumba lady somehow made it feel like a criminal offence. At least they'd been in the privacy of their own massive living room. Bree sweating like a pig on heat, her mum barely getting red and making this weird "Chooo, choooo" noise with her breathing. But the same flood of happy hormones had swamped her body like they had the day before. For an hour or so she'd felt capable of anything. She hadn't got the urge to scratch her scars all weekend, which was major news – especially with all the stress of thinking about what was coming up.

"Wasn't that fun?" her mother had said, dabbing her barely-perspiring forehead with her designer headband. "You know what? If you're serious about keeping this exercise lark up, we could get a personal trainer to come to the house. What do you think? I've always thought it was too extravagant to hire one just for me, but together it could be fun?"

Bree nodded, panting. "Sounds like it could work."

Her mum patted her on the head. "Right, I'd better get ready for Pilates with the girls. Good luck today showing off your new look..." She trailed off. "Are you okay, honey? I mean, you look fabulous, and, don't get me wrong, I've had a really good weekend with you, but it's a bit out of the blue. Is everything alright?"

Bree wasn't sure she knew the answer to that question. Was she alright? She had a writing project, one she had a gut feeling could really work. She had purpose for the first time in ages. And yet she felt a bit sick with fear at the same time.

She smiled. "I'm fine, Mum. I just fancied a change, that's all. I really enjoyed the weekend too."

There was a horribly uncomfortable moment where Bree thought her mum might hug her again. But she just gave Bree's head another tap and ran upstairs to the master bedroom.

Bree had been on a high then, but now – with her hair and make-up all done – her confidence had bellyflopped.

"You're doing this for a reason, Bree," she spoke aloud to the mirror. "Whatever happens will be good writing material. The important thing is something *will* happen, and that isn't usually the case."

She pulled at her new pair of tights. The pink stripes had gone, replaced by a daring pair her mother had picked out. There was a thicker denier at the bottom with fake seams up the backs, to give the illusion of suspenders. If they hadn't cost twenty-five quid, they would've looked a bit tarty.

"Are you sure I'll get away with wearing these to school?" she'd asked.

"Of course," her mum said, tossing a duplicate pair into her hands, in case of ladders. "If they didn't kick up a fuss about those horrendous pink things, they must allow these."

"Hey!"

Her mum smiled with her mouth closed. "Sorry."

As Bree left the safety of her home, she decided she was most concerned about the reaction of two people – Holdo and Mr Fellows. And she would have to face them both before 9.30 a.m. She was walking in with Holdo and then had English first thing.

She tottered on her new heels as she walked to the usual meeting place.

Holdo was at the corner already, off in music land, and so didn't notice her at first. His giant headphones blocked out as much reality as technology could muster. His eyes were closed, so Bree crept up on him theatrically and grabbed them off.

"What the hell?" The moment he clocked Bree his jaw fell open.

"Hi there," she said, trying not to laugh at the look on his face.

"Bree?"

"Yep."

"Seriously? Is that you?"

Holdo liked to think of himself as a feminist. He was always agreeing with Bree's heated opinions about women's rights and shared her disgust at the rugby boys' banter that terrorized the school hallways. They'd spent many an evening together staying up late discussing rape culture, glass ceilings, how strip clubs should be made illegal. But it had to be hard to be a feminist and, well, a guy too. With urges and such. Because, moral as Holdo was, Bree had once found his porn stash. In a secret folder within a folder on his laptop, labelled *Research*. And Holdo's porn tastes were, erm...well, the women weren't spending a lot of their time making intelligent comments about the Israeli/Palestine conflict, put it that way.

Evidently, Holdo was dealing with the same moral compromise as he looked at Bree now.

The full-body checkout wasn't something Bree had ever

experienced herself. She'd seen plenty of boys doing it to plenty of girls in her time. A quick up-and-down flicker of the eyes, resting a moment too long on the cleavage.

And here it was, happening to her, by Holdo of all people. You could see him fighting to look at her face, but his eyes betrayed him, dipping to her bulging top.

That was the thing about a diet of Pop-Tarts. Apparently, with the right bra, they gave you a bit of a rack.

"What the hell have you done to yourself?"

Bree shrugged and pulled her blazer shut. This new sensation of physical attractiveness was somewhat thrilling, but also somewhat uncomfortable.

"Just had a bit of a play with my appearance over the weekend. You like it?"

More inner conflict crossed Holdo's face. He was fighting between *I can't believe you've bowed down to the conformity of attractiveness in society, you are better than that* and *Hell, you look good. Please let me mount you.*

"It's…er…different…that's all."

Bree had secretly been hoping for a compliment. "Different?"

"Seriously, why, Bree?" The penis side of Holdo's brain had lost out this time. "You look…erm…good, but you also look like you're trying to be Jassmine Dallington or something. What's going on with you?"

"Nothing. I just fancied a change."

"Is this something to do with the rejection letter on Friday?"

Bree bristled. "No. Why do you keep bringing that up?"

"It is, isn't it? What? You've given up on being a writer so you think you'll just become pretty and vacant like everyone else now?"

She was losing her temper. If only he knew what she was planning to sacrifice to become a writer. If only he knew about the scary rules she'd scrawled in her notebook, ready to live out, for the very purpose of being a great writer.

"Come on, Holdo. It's just a bit of make-up. It's not like applying mascara makes your brain fall out. Plus..." She tapped her finger on his new crop of spots that had popped up around his mouth over the weekend. "Maybe you could use a bit of make-up yourself."

It was nasty. No excuse really – it was just sheer nastiness. And as Holdo's face fell, Bree felt the heavy drop of guilt blob into her stomach. He tried to cover the worst of the acne with his hand.

"Fine. You've made your point." He wouldn't look at her.

They had always bantered. She'd teased him about his skin before and it'd always been okay. He would just say, "Think this spot is bad, look at that big oozer on your chin." Or, "Well, I may be uglier but I'm much smarter than you."

Back and forth. Back and forth. Swear words and teasing and name-callings and piss-takings. One after the other after the other. And it had been fine.

Why was it different this morning? Why did she suddenly feel like a massive bitch?

And Bree realized it was because a bit of make-up, some highlights, and nice-fitting clothes had changed the power dynamic. Attractiveness puts you automatically on a higher social plain. You're immediately winning some sort of invisible game. And though Holdo was, perhaps, just as smart as her, their relationship was now unequal just because she looked better. And piss-taking about his, now inferior, looks wasn't friendly banter any more. It was downright cruel.

They walked in silence – the journey slower than usual because of Bree's new shoes. She struggled to think of something to break the awkwardness.

"You got computer science this morning?"

Holdo just nodded.

"How's the game coming along?"

"Alright."

"Watch any new films over the weekend?"

"Nothing new."

Bree sort of felt like crying. But she couldn't. Today, and how she played it, was too important. She couldn't take him along on this journey, but she hoped, oh how she hoped, he'd understand at the end. Whenever that was.

You always need to make sacrifices for your art.

They reached the school gates and Bree stared up at them like they were the doorway to another world. They were really, weren't they?

"See you at lunch?" Holdo's voice sounded hopeful. She'd been forgiven, far too soon as usual. And she was about to hurt him again. She closed her eyes and took a deep breath, feeling emotion and loss gurgle up her windpipe.

"Er…I can't. I've got stuff to do."

"Okay."

He didn't even ask what stuff and that broke her heart even more. He just swung his bag heavily over his shoulder and walked sadly away from her into the sea of students queuing at security with their cards.

Bree stared after him sadly, wondering what the hell she'd let herself in for. And how she was ever going to do this on her own.

chapter fourteen

The corridors were the worst part of Queen's Hall. It was best to run through them, head down, trying to avoid predators, until you reached the safe(ish) sanctuary of the classroom where a teacher could tell people off.

Anything of any note – good or bad – was played out in the theatrical staging of that narrow strip of carpet, overlooked by the gold-framed antique portraits of headmasters and mistresses past. It was where fights broke out and losers were deliberately tripped over; it was Jassmine's catwalk for showing off her latest "look". Hearts were broken there every Valentine's Day as hundreds of girls eagerly opened their lockers, only to discover that, no, Hugo hadn't written them a card declaring his undying affection. Drama, drama, drama.

Today, of course, the hallways were even scarier. Today it was Bree's turn to walk the catwalk. Would she be ridiculed?

Ignored? Openly embraced into Jassmine's clique just because she had perfectly-applied eyeliner?

She swung her new designer bag over her shoulder, took a deep breath, and began to walk...

An immediate difference.

People looked. Heads turned. Whispers followed her.

"Who's that?"

"Does she go to this school?"

"I think I've seen her before."

And most surprisingly: "Who's the fitty?" FROM A MALE VOICE.

Bree began to swing her hips with each step. She held her head high, flicking back her beautiful hair with a confident jolt of her head. A mate of Hugo's walked past, and she watched, almost in slow motion, as he did a double-take. Bree caught his eye, pushed down a bubble of insecurity, and gave him a sexy wink.

He walked into a locker.

It can't be this easy. Surely, it's not going to be this easy.

It felt a bit like Moses parting the Red Sea, walking towards English. Of course Moses wasn't just about to see the teacher he loved with his new look. Moses had it easy.

She sashayed her way into the classroom and set her new bag on her desk. Mr Fellows hadn't arrived yet, so she swept back her hair and practised her most *Oh? What? This old thing?* face while the class whispered around her.

Chuck's voice was louder than the rest. "Is that the twat who's usually licking Philip Larkin's arse?"

"Shh. She'll hear you."

Bree smiled.

"So? She's a loser. Just because she's wearing eyeliner now…"

"Shut up, Chuck."

Did it…? Did that just happen? Did someone just stand up for Bree? Her smile stretched. She got out her poetry anthology and hid behind it, waiting for Mr Fellows…

He strode in just as the bell was going. He whizzed past Bree's desk and she caught a whiff of his smokey coffee smell.

"Okay, okay, okay. Yes I'm late. Massive double standards on my part, I know. But that's the thing about being a teacher, we can double-standard you to high heaven. But you'll forgive me when you see what I've got in store for you today, people…" He dropped his briefcase onto his desk and whacked out his anthology. "This poem is going to make you ADORE Philip Larkin. By the end of the next hour, you're going to be BEGGING me to study him further. And brace yourself, oh those of a sensitive nature…there are swear words. Actual real-life profanities. I know! 'In Queen's Hall?' I hear you cry. Yes! Just don't tell the headmistress on me."

He was pacing back and forth, lost in his book. Bree loved it when he got all fired up about literature. He became almost manic. Like the words stoked some sort of dying ember in him and reignited it into a fire, burning, making life worth living again.

"So, if you'll all just turn to page 74... This is it. Are you ready?"

He cleared his throat.

"*They fuck you up, your mum and dad. They may not mean to, but they do...*"

And he broke off. Because he had finally seen Bree.

Silence.

Silence as he stared at her.

Bree raised her eyes above her book and met his. She lifted her chin defiantly and flicked back her blonde fringe.

"Sir?"

He barely registered the interruption. All he could do was stare. Bree ran her tongue over her top teeth, like Sandy does at the end of *Grease* before she does that "Tell me about it...stud" bit everyone in the world loves so much.

"Er, sir?"

Mr Fellows shook his head like he was being disturbed by an unwanted hotel wake-up call. "Yes?"

"The poem?"

"Oh yes...right...of course."

Stumbling over stanzas, Mr Fellows read the rest of the poem quickly before he snapped his book shut.

"So...class...what do you think?"

A silence descended on the room like a mist. This was the part where Bree was supposed to punch her hand in the air and start babbling. But the air above her remained empty.

"Anyone?"

Chuck raised his hand. "I quite liked it, sir."

Mr Fellows jumped on his answer like it was the chemical equation for the elixir of life. Anything to distract him from her, Bree thought.

"Brilliant. Why did you love it?"

"Because it had the word 'fuck' in it?"

Another hand shot up.

"Alison?"

"I like the bit about how your parents ruin your lives."

"Yeah, that's cool," someone else said.

"I'm gonna print it off and put it on my bedroom door for my mum to read."

"Ha ha. Yeah, me too."

"It's the best one by far, sir. It's like he finally gets us."

Bree fought every urge to raise her hand. Idiots! They had got it so, so wrong. It wasn't about hating your parents – it wasn't about them screwing you up, not really.

Don't put your hand up. Don't put your hand up.

She had to make do with an insolent eye roll instead, but it wasn't as satisfying as monologuing all the reasons why her class were fools.

Mr Fellows took in this sudden surge of interest with a smug grin. "So am I right in saying you LIKE Philip Larkin now?"

Chuck shrugged. "He's alright."

People nodded.

Mr Fellows blew out his breath with deliberate exaggeration. "I don't know whether to be delighted or ashamed of you all."

"Ashamed?"

"So all this month you've hated him? His beautiful descriptions of how countryside morphs into industrialization? It was boring. Miserable. You wanted to change the syllabus. But now...he's said the word 'fuck' and told you he hates his parents, and now you all love the guy?"

The class giggled.

"This is the saddest thing ever."

"I thought you wanted us to like him?"

"Yes. But for the right reasons. But, hey, I know it's a crowd-pleaser. I just wished you loved 'Whitsun Weddings' as much."

Chuck raised his hand again. He was getting much more of an opportunity to vocalize his thoughts now Bree had given up on intellect.

"Yes, Chuck?"

"Well, isn't that what we were saying last week? About what people enjoy and what they find boring? We want to hear people swearing and saying they hate their parents – it makes them...I dunno...identifiable?"

And that, Bree thought, *is precisely why I'm doing this.*

chapter fifteen

Mr Fellows stopped her from leaving after class.

"Bree? Can I have a word?"

Her insides screamed *YES!* but she kept cool and rolled her eyes. "I suppose. Why?"

He rolled his chair back, forming a barrier between her and the door. "I can't help but notice you're looking a little bit...different today."

HE NOTICED.

Bree blew up her hair. "Sir, no offence, but how is that any of your business?"

He twitched. "Well. Of course it isn't. But, as your teacher, your welfare is my business."

"And what has cutting my hair got to do with my welfare?"

He twitched again. "I'm not sure...it's just...well, you look... It doesn't seem very...you, that's all."

"You were the one telling me last week I should change who I was cos I was miserable and boring."

"That's not what I meant… You read it all wrong. Oh…" He looked at her and ran his hands through his hair. "You didn't do this to yourself because of what I said, did you?"

Bree looked at the carpet so her eyes wouldn't betray her as she lied. "No." She spat the words out. "I just fancied a change, that's all."

"Well, it suits you."

She looked up, shocked, not expecting the compliment, and his eyes met hers.

Something passed between them.

Something that hadn't passed since that balmy night outside the golf club.

Weeks of ignoring me, pretending it didn't happen, and all it takes to reignite his passion is a haircut.

Realizing what line he'd just crossed, Mr Fellows began stammering.

"Of course, that's not relevant. And I only mean that as a friend-to-a-friend comment. And, all my students look lovely as long as they're doing their coursework…" He laughed nervously. "So, yes, are we done here?"

Bree used the chink in his armour to pounce.

"Sir, would it be alright if I started doing creative-writing club again? I know I've not done it since Year Eleven, but I've got lots of ideas and, well, it would look good on my CV."

He nodded, still looking flustered. "Yep. That's fine.

Of course. Next meeting is in a week or two. Christ! The bell. Don't you have a class to get to?"

Without saying goodbye, she stalked out of the classroom, smirking.

So Holdo and Mr Fellows had seen her. Now it was time for Jassmine and the perfect posse.

So you're dying to know how it went, aren't you? My first day as an attractive – and therefore interesting – person.

I'll be honest with you. I didn't think it would be like the movies. I'm not a thicko and I know Hollywood and books and love songs on the radio are responsible for spreading the most atrocious lies about life on a daily basis. Egotistical bad boys falling in love and changing their chauvinistic ways because they meet a ditzy girl who falls over sometimes. Or some under-appreciated policeman saving the world from certain destruction at the very last moment. Or a massive weirdo loner undergoing a makeover and suddenly everyone's like, "Oh wow. You're pretty now. And you don't wear glasses any more. I'm going to forget immediately that I've spent the last five years of our school career telling everyone you have rabies and sticking Kick me notes to your back, and suddenly respect you, make you popular and completely change the way I relate to you." For ever.

Life doesn't work like that.

Or so I thought.

Here were my predictions for today. People might notice, sure. But I'm still me. I'm still that loser they've hated for years. Why would that change just because I'm pretty now? I expected MONTHS of snazzy new outfits before I even got a "Hello".

How wrong I was.

Because, today, walking down the school corridors, it felt like pop culture crap is actually onto something. People moved out of the way for me. Me! I heard whispers of excitement about me. Me! Some guy – who until this week has only spoken to me once, and that was only to say "Out the way, you're blocking the vending machine" – actually SMILED at me. ME!

I became somebody in the time it took to walk from the school gates to my first lesson. I became important and interesting from the moment I applied thirty-quid mascara this morning. Years of torment have been forgotten in a quick outfit change.

How screwed up is that?

At first I was confused. It CAN'T be this easy, I thought. The world can't be so vacuous. Looks can't alter your life so drastically and so quickly.

But then I thought about it. And – I'm not sure why – but yes, becoming attractive does do that.

Imagine your school and then imagine the loner-iest weirdo social outcast there. You've thought of one, right? Every school has one. They usually have some kind of...issue, making them the weirdo they are. Usually it's because they're fat. Or noticeably ugly. Or just plain weird. Or smell funny. It doesn't take much. And they've got a bad attitude, haven't they? They're PERFECT for winding up, because they react. You get what you want. Their hatred for you for being so much higher on the social food chain is so obvious, that you kinda enjoy flicking them the odd nasty comment. Sniggering behind their back just loud enough for them to hear. Asking guys at school questions like "Would you shag so-and-so for a million pounds?" and then laughing hysterically at the disgust on their faces.

Until today, that person was me.

Now, imagine if, one day, your outcast waltzed into school looking bloody fabulous. Better than you, in fact.

In theory it shouldn't make a difference. In fact, it should just add fuel to the bullying fire, shouldn't it? "Oh, look, bless, you're trying to BE like us."

But attractiveness doesn't work like that. It's power, it's currency. And if you've spent your whole school life treating this suddenly-gorgeous girl like total crap, if the power shifts, then you're in trouble.

Everyone's in trouble.

Because there is a whole lotta karma heading your way.

So, yes, I was wrong. About how quickly this plan would work. But it's working, right?

So now I'm onto phase two.

"What's phase two?" I hear you cry.

Every school has an outcast and – because nature always has to balance, doesn't it? – every school has a popular group too. A gang of people you know every single detail about – though they probably struggle to remember your name.

Got them?

Good. Because I've got those people in my school too.

And I'm coming to get them.

chapter sixteen

Breaking into the perfect posse wasn't going to be easy. Bree knew that. But in just three days a number of notable things had happened.

1) She and Holdo no longer walked to school together

Nothing was said. No guns were drawn. But, after Bree's spiteful comment and decision not to eat lunch with him, Holdo hadn't waited at the school gate to walk home with her. She'd walked back alone – her new shoes rubbing blisters into the backs of her ankles. Holdo never stayed mad at her for long though, and the next morning he stood at the corner, nervously shuffling his shoes in the leaves.

Bree: "Hi."

Holdo: "Hi."

And that was the extent of their dialogue for the rest of the journey. All their usual topics of shared hatred failed to stimulate conversation. So they kicked leaves and looked down at the ground, as the silence strangled them and their friendship. Lump after lump swam up Bree's throat and she struggled to swallow them down.

The next morning – just to avoid the sheer awfulness of it all – Bree left for school earlier than normal. And Holdo didn't wait at the gates at home time. And so, very quickly, Bree was all alone in the world.

The second thing was:

2) *Hugo gave her his famous shag-me eyes*

Bree had plans for Hugo, but they weren't due to start for a while yet. So she was surprised when they were put in motion for her early.

By him. And his groin.

Just before a form-time dedicated to pushing the Duke Of Edinburgh gold scheme like it was crack, Hugo and his disciples blocked the doorway once again.

"How's plans going for your eighteenth, dude?" Seth was red-faced again. It was definitely just how his face was naturally, all the time.

Hugo smiled, and tapped his nose. "All under control, gentlemen. All under control."

"Are you really holding an actual festival in your garden?"

He laughed. "I could do. I could erect a tent especially for drunk girls and call it the Gash Palace."

Or you could call it the Questionable Consent tent… Shh, Bree. Stop being a feminist, just for now. It's not part of the plan.

Bree stood there patiently waiting to get past, tapping her shoe as they all hiccupped with laughter.

"Gash Palace. That's brilliant!"

"It should have turrets."

"Made out of thongs, condoms and hardened lube."

"I could be the king of Gash Palace and wear a crown," Hugo said.

More insane laughter.

"Ahh, man. If that's the case, let me be in your court!" Seth said, almost dribbling.

Bree cleared her throat and they all looked up, not the least bit embarrassed to have been overheard.

Last Friday, they'd ridiculed her. And now, despite the earth only spinning a measly five times, everything was completely different.

Bree gestured to the door. "Can I get by? You're all kinda in the way?" She giggled.

I've just giggled. And said "kinda". Please, God, make this all be worth it.

If her film marathon was anything to go by, giggling was an intrinsic part of breaking into a popular gang. Giggling, along with quick sassy comebacks, a bitch-eat-bitch mentality, and a kindness lobotomy. This was the first time she'd really tried it out.

Hugo stared at her in confusion, like he was trying to place her face. Then he smirked, stood back, and bowed with a hand flourish – like she was a princess.

"This way, madam."

The guys guffawed, getting the joke. Bree fought the urge to smash their heads together.

"You can bow all you like, but I won't be going into your Gash Palace, Your Highness." She needed all her acting skills to make her voice sound playful and confident. She was dying on the inside.

"OOOOOOOOOOOOOOOOOOOHHHHHH!"

They jumped on her comment in delight, pissing themselves with laughter.

"Whoa. The Gash Palace backlash has already begun."

"DENIED."

Bree, hating herself, let out another giggle. She stepped past them, flicking her heavily-mascaraed eyes up at Hugo as she did so.

He just stared at her.

Bree had heard about Hugo's legendary eye-shag. His deep-set blue eyes, framed with luscious completely-wasted-on-a-boy dark eyelashes, were apparently irresistible when he gave you "the look". She'd heard girls who'd fallen foul to it drone on about it in the loos.

She was quite sure she was getting it now. Her knees went buttery and her heart did this weird dive thing, as all sorts of hormones flashmobbed through her blood.

It was a bit too soon. She couldn't conquer phase two – the perfect posse – with Hugo eye-shagging her. So, trying to remain unflustered, she broke eye contact and sauntered straight past him.

3) Some girls at school had started wearing the same tights as her

And not even ironically, like the time Jassmine and the

perfects had all worn pink stripy tights and walked behind Bree, sniggering.

By Thursday, she'd spotted at least four other mock-stockings and heard grumblings from her Latin teacher that they broke uniform rules for not being corporate enough. Bree planned to keep the trend changing. Her mum had deposited yet another clothing bundle on her bed which included two new pairs of tights. One was sheer apart from perfect black velvet polka dots. The other had miniature stepladders on them. Bree didn't know much about fashion – apart from that ponchos were bad – but even she knew these tights were cool. Her legs were getting a lot of admiring looks these days. From boys – enjoying her showing off some leg. And girls – wanting to see what she wore next.

Things had certainly changed in a few short days. People had upped and noticed. However Jassmine etc. weren't acknowledging her rise from loser to looker. They still ignored her. When she'd breezed past them earlier that day, they'd been busy congregating around Gemma's phone, whispering and screeching with delight.

"Noooo, Gemma, you can't send that around."

Gemma shrugged. "Why not?"

"How did you even get it? Oh, it's awful! Look at the size of her nips."

Gemma shrugged again, her eyes glinting. "Danny left

his phone in my form room by accident. I picked it up to see whose it was, found this picture of his girlfriend, and sent it to myself."

"You are just evil," Jassmine said, poking her with delight.

"I'd rather be evil than have burger nipples."

"*Burger nipples*," they all whispered and dissolved into laughter.

Bree wasn't entirely sure what was going on, but she felt like someone's life was about to get ruined.

She needed to be in that huddle. To find out what was going on. How was she going to break them?

During Latin, Bree sat in her usual spot, doodling in her notebook, as she'd already conjugated the verbs set for that week. Latin was a very full class – it looked good on the UCAS form. And Bree would do anything to ensure her place to Cambridge. In her head, she saw herself frolicking through the cobbled streets with a gang of lovely smart friends, trading intellectual comments with one another…

Anyway, Latin was so crammed, her scribbling went unnoticed.

Bree wrote down everything she knew about the perfect posse.

The perfect posse
Jassmine Dallington
Aka The Queen.

Why? The usual reasons. Tumbling mane of perfectly coiffed blonde hair. Perfect body, combined with that weird power some people have that makes everyone desperate to be liked by them.

If rumours were true, she wasn't utterly perfect though. She was nicknamed "Apple Tits" behind her back, because apparently her boobs looked like two halves of an apple stuck onto her body. And she seemed to have an utter weak spot where Hugo was concerned – letting him mess her about like an abused puppy.

Apart from that, there wasn't much there with Jassmine. She was pretty vacant, like personality would damage her reputation or something.

Gemma Rinestone

Gemma was mean. Soulless mean. Like, you wouldn't be surprised if she laughed watching *Schindler's List* mean. Anytime Bree had been teased by the perfects, Gemma had been the orchestrator. She'd been that way since they were little kids, yelling "LOSER" the loudest through the gap under the toilet cubicles in Year Seven when she knew Bree was hiding in there.

The weird thing about Gemma was that she wasn't actually very pretty. At all.

She was also blonde, but her hair was frizzy and she had a weird gummy smile with too-big clown lips. Plus, the foundation she shovelled onto her face didn't hide the thick layer of acne on her chin.

That said, when Gemma Rinestone started putting her hair up in a bun with rainbow clips – a fashion nuke bomb for anyone else – a week later the whole school was doing it.

And though attractiveness might not be a currency she was wealthy in, Gemma was filthy rich in the currency of evil. These were some of the mean things Bree had seen her do:

- Lifted up some random Year Seven's skirt for five whole minutes while the poor kid just stood there, crying.
- Personally stolen Bree's graphics coursework, dumped it in the canteen bin so it was irrevocably ruined by spaghetti hoops, then boasted about doing so.
- It was she who'd started Jassmine's "Apple Tits" nickname, during some intensely complicated fight with her about something to do with somebody else's ex-boyfriend and a sexual experience on a bench at a party... Jassmine still didn't know.
- She was the "editor" of the Year Eleven yearbook and tampered with the *Most likely to be...* results. She invented a new category called *Most likely to eat their way through the school canteen* and made the winner this poor fat girl called Matilda, who'd never once spoken to Gemma or anyone else for

. that matter. When the yearbooks were handed out, Matilda broke down into silent tears, ran from the school and was never seen again. Gemma laughed and said loudly to anyone who was listening – which was everyone – that "some people just can't take a joke". She also changed the results so she won *Most likely to be a model*. Bree knew this because she'd helped on the yearbook and was in charge of counting up the votes.

Gemma hadn't even made the top twenty.

Jessica Rightman
Jessica was convinced she was going to be a Hollywood movie star. And so was the rest of the school. She'd been the lead in every school play for the past four years. She sang throughout every lesson in her TERRIBLE nasal voice. She'd got some God-awful brother, Drew, in the year above, who also believed he was some sort of acting genius. Their parents had to be pushier than Stalin.

Aside from the annoying singing habit, Jessica also practised her vocal skills by making snide comments to anyone she considered beneath her. Which was everyone. Like she was permanently pissed off that she had to share oxygen with other people.

Jessica also wasn't that pretty, definitely not as pretty as Jassmine. Everything on her face was right. Two eyes (blue), a nose, okay lips, cheeks, etc. But the way they were put together wasn't quite correct. Everything was too angular and pointy. But Jessica believed herself to be a goddess and threw herself at all men, expecting them to drop dead with gratefulness. Her victims tended to either use her, or shrug her off their laps. At which point she'd laugh, screech "You're such a tease!" and toss her hair back with a big swoosh of inner denial.

And then there was the hanger-on.

Emily Nashville
If anyone needed an example of vacuous air, they should just point to Emily. She'd sacrificed her personality, on a metaphorical temple like a slaughtered lamb, in order to get in with the perfect posse. Her opinions were Jassmine's opinions. Her jokes were Gemma's jokes. Her put-downs were Jessica's put-downs. She laughed at anything any of them said, clutching her sides like she was trying to hold in her guts.

So that was the four. The four Bree needed to infiltrate somehow.

Bree's concentration was interrupted by a flurry of vibrations echoing around the classroom. Phones rumbled on silent simultaneously under people's desks. Her Latin teacher, Mrs McQuire, who was oblivious to any technological advance from the twentieth century onwards, didn't notice.

Well, she didn't notice until the whispering began.

"Oh my God." Someone psst-ed next to Bree, shoving their phone into their neighbour's lap. "Have you SEEN this?"

Bree, whose phone, oddly enough, hadn't gone off, strained her neck to catch a glimpse of the screen.

She caught her breath.

It was a photo of a girl from their year, Natalie. Topless. A selfie, from the looks of it. She was pouting naively at the camera, but Bree's eyes ignored that, and went straight to her chest. Someone had manipulated the photo in Paint, pointing a massive red arrow to her boobs, with the words BURGER NIPPLES scrawled underneath.

So this was what Gemma had been talking about. This was the life the perfect posse had decided to ruin that day. For sport. Some poor girl they hardly knew, whose only sin was to be naive enough to send a photo like that to her boyfriend.

The poor, poor girl.

"Quiet," Mrs McQuire said. "What's going on? No talking."

The class ignored her.

"It's Natalie – jeez, have you ever seen areolae that big?"

"Where did it come from?"

"Gemma's phone."

"Poor Natalie."

"What a bitch."

"Have you sent it to anyone else?"

"QUIET, PLEASE!" Mrs McQuire yelled, and they settled – for now. But the buzz of silent gossip hung heavy in the air, the vibration of received texts punctuating their verb conjugations.

Bree looked at her notepad and felt a bit sick. She noticed her hand shaking and lay her pen down.

Why?

She picked up her pen again and wrote the word down, underlining it twice.

Why would those girls do that?

Why was she trying to break into them?

Why do people find them so interesting when they do things like that?

This wasn't about revenge... Well, maybe it was a little bit. She'd wasted many hours of her life fantasizing about how to get revenge on them – especially on the days she was their victim. But it was more about her writing – getting good stories, good material, stretching who she was and noting what happened along the way. Could she make it a bit about revenge too? Would she even be able to? For the sake of the perfect posse's victims – herself included – shouldn't she try?

She stared at the list, trying to work out what to do. Who to approach. And how. How does one go about making oneself popular? What was the secret ingredient?

Everyone in the circle of perfects offered something, she realized – brought something to the stockbroking table of popularity.

Jassmine was their high-roller. Oozing confidence and beauty, she was the sort of person who made perfection look effortless. You can't learn that. It's a gift usually bestowed on people who don't deserve it. Yet she played her ace card well – keeping the school infatuated with her and Hugo's relationship, living out a real-life soap opera. Being just nice enough for people to want her to like them. Not having any obvious flaws.

Gemma brought the nasty side. The fear factor. The lack of soul needed to dominate a school. She was smart. She got people – how they worked, what they wanted, needed, how to break them. Bree had heard she was amazing at maths and the teachers were priming her for a life as a merchant banker. She could imagine Gemma used those skills in her social life as well. Weighing up and calculating the risks of a nasty comment. Predicting market shifts in popular culture and Queen's Hall's collective opinions. Having the guts to go on her instinct made her a force to be reckoned with. None of the others brought that.

Jessica, well, she brought deluded self-confidence and apparent star power thanks to the school plays. School plays, in Queen's at least, were cool. Achievement – including dramatic achievement – was another form of currency here. And what better way to showcase such currency than for every student and parent to part with twenty-five quid twice a year to watch seventeen-year-olds hurling themselves round a stage shrilling "I Feel Pretty" in the school's three-hundred-seat, red-velveted, state-of-the-art theatre? Around the time of the play, Jassmine always got a tad twitchy as Jessica's celebrity soared. Jessica would start wearing sunglasses to "hide her dark circles from all those late-night rehearsals" and glow whenever an eager Year Seven told her how good she was. There'd been an infamous moment last year when Jessica got cast against Hugo in *Cyrano de Bergerac*, which had meant they would have to do a kissing scene.

But Hugo mysteriously dropped out right before rehearsals began. Funny that...

So, what could Bree offer them?

She was smart. That was an asset. But she was a bit too smart. Geek smart. And she was probably a bit richer than them. But money wasn't really an object for any of them. Then there was the fact that they were definitely a little scared of her transformation...but how could she use that to her advantage?

"Bree?"

Maybe set up a rival posse? But then who would she recruit? That would require a whole evening of list-making and she needed to strike while the makeover hype was still hot.

"Bree?"

"Huh?"

She looked up to find Mrs McQuire staring at her.

"The bell's gone, Bree."

The chairs around her were empty and the hubbub of student noise echoed out in the corridor. It was louder than usual, as the gossip and photo spread from person to person like a YouTube viral. In fact, the photo probably already was viral by now... She looked at her notebook. It was crammed full of illegible scrawl. For the best really, as her teacher was eyeing it disapprovingly.

"You'll need to work on your handwriting for the exam. No one will be able to mark that mess."

"Sorry...I was..."

And, without explaining herself properly, she dashed out the door. She folded her notebook into her new designer satchel and made her way to the quieter toilets in the chemistry block to reapply her lipgloss and, most importantly, to think. Yet when she pushed through the doors she heard she wasn't alone.

Someone was in the far cubicle, crying.

Not just crying, but sobbing to the point of hysteria.

"Are you okay?" Bree called out. She wasn't usually one to get involved, but this wasn't the kind of crying you ignore.

Her voice didn't stop the torrent of wails.

"Hello?" she called out again, tentatively.

Silence. Except for the odd gulping and sniffing noise.

She bit her lip, wondering what to do. After a second or two, she went into the neighbouring cubicle, climbed onto the toilet seat and peered over.

She could distinctly see the top of Natalie's head.

"Hey, Natalie, is it?" she said gently.

Natalie didn't even look up. "Leave me alone," she coughed out.

"Are you okay?" Bree asked, ignoring her.

"Please, just LEAVE ME ALONE!" Natalie shouted at her with such ferocity, Bree imagined her hair being blasted back.

"Are you sure?"

"Please…" And it was said so desperately that all Bree could do was get down off the toilet and go to her next lesson.

chapter seventeen

She spent the rest of the day ruminating. And the evening. She ate her dinner in her usual mute state while her mum's hyper-babble filled the silence. But her mum must have noticed something was up, as she was standing outside Bree's bedroom door later on.

"What do you want?" Bree asked, annoyed that her mum was blocking the entrance.

"I got you this today." She stuck out her hands, and opened each palm to reveal two black tubes.

"What is it?"

Her mum started jumping up and down with a scary smile on her face, squealing through her teeth.

"Seriously. What is it?"

"Open one and see."

Bree took a black tube and popped off the lid. "It's a lipstick." She twisted it and a Disney Princess pink twirled elegantly upwards.

"IT'S NOT JUST A LIPSTICK!" Her mum looked like she was about to wee with excitement.

"What is it then? Does it recite poetry?"

"Don't be silly. Don't you see?" Her mum twisted out the other one. "This is the Marvel limited edition Pink Princess lipstick. Sold out everywhere. Worn by every beautiful woman who matters. And apparently suits everyone who tries it on."

Bree tried not to roll her eyes.

"I got you two! One to wear, and one to carry around to marvel at its beauty. Marvel – get it?"

"Great." She couldn't keep the sarcasm out of her voice.

Her mum shot her daggers. "Bree, you're missing out on how important this lipstick is. It's the only plus side of your dad working so many hours and leaving us alone all the time – the freebies he gets from the cosmetic industries he represents. I could have given these away to the girls and been worshipped for ever. But I saved them for you instead."

Bree held her hand up. "Wait. Dad works for a... cosmetics company?"

Her mum roared with laughter. "You don't know what your own father does for a living?"

She shrugged. "Whatever it is, it makes him grumpy. And never here."

"He looks after the legal interests of major corporations and specializes in the patenting of new products. He's in charge of the Marvel brand relaunch. He is basically God of lipstick. And he will be around more soon…well in five years anyway, as he's promised to retire early."

"Huh?"

"Here." She shoved both tubes into Bree's hands. "Just take them and wear it tomorrow. All the girls in school will be queuing up to talk to you."

Bree wasn't sure if she could trust this information. She twisted the pink lipstick back into itself and eyeballed it suspiciously.

"Why do you think I want girls queuing up to talk to me?"

"Come on, Bree. It's not rocket science. Girls need friends. Girlfriends. It can hardly be stimulating spending all your spare time listening to Holdo moan on about his computer gadgets."

Hearing Holdo's name made Bree's heart hurt. She pushed the uncomfortable feeling to one side and looked at her mum. "Thank you."

"Any time. I've booked the personal trainer to start next week."

"Great."

Then Bree escaped into the sanctuary of her bedroom to have a think.

She did apply the lipstick the next morning. It couldn't hurt, after all. Plus, it was a Friday and teachers were always a bit lax about make-up rules on a Friday. She matched her pink lips with another pair of statement tights – these ones had tiny flecks of hot pink in them. She hurried to school, still trying to work on her break-in plan.

What do I have that they don't?

There had to be something.

It was freezing. Winter was hurtling towards them and soon all the trees would be bare. It was a shame really, that she was so alone. This was a fun time of year to have a social life. Halloween, Bonfire Night…annual events geared towards the misbehaviour of under-eighteens. Apparently Hugo was planning a massive firework display for his eighteenth. She really needed to wangle an invite to that. Soon. She'd prefer it not to come from Hugo himself though. That would definitely piss off Jassmine Incorporated.

Holdo would think she was crazy for wanting to go to a Hugo party. She and Holdo always used to watch classic horror films on Halloween… God how she missed him.

She didn't listen in English. There was nothing Mr Fellows could tell her about Philip Larkin that she hadn't already taught herself. Class went much slower without her answering all the questions. He kept flicking her anxious looks, like a puppy wanting attention from its owner.

He was all "What do you think, Bree?" this, and "Bree, come on, you must know the answer" that, now she wasn't making her crush blatantly obvious any more.

She couldn't work out how it made her feel. Most of her felt warm everywhere with the thought that he cared; inside her head she was fist-punching in triumph that he was finally showing her attention again. But the cruel voice that always popped up to say *hi* whenever she felt good was saying: *He couldn't get you out of his classroom fast enough when you were a frumpy loser.*

After yet more Latin, it was time for lunch, and Bree went to the ladies to reapply.

She put her make-up bag in the sink and leaned forward towards the glass to examine her reflection. Just as she was retrieving the Princess Pink, as if it were fate, Jassmine and Jessica sauntered in.

They gave Bree an unfriendly look and took a space two sinks down, jabbering inanely to each other.

"Oh my God," Jassmine said. "I can't believe there's still, like, two whole lessons to get through until it's the weekend. I just wanna get drunk and let my hair down, you know?"

Jessica nodded furiously, while looking at herself in the mirror. "Totally. At least I've got drama this arvo. But double Latin? Poor Jassmine."

Jassmine wrinkled her nose. "Tell me about it. It's so completely boring. Why do I need to talk like dead people who wore togas? My parents INSISTED I took it though. My teacher is such a div. She dresses like – I'm totally not kidding – like a cat lady on crack. I swear, everything she wears is crocheted. By herself. Probably while sobbing on a rocking chair, surrounded by pussies."

Jessica almost giggled herself to death. "Oh my God, Jass. You are sooooo hilarious."

Jassmine plumped her hair and smiled at her reflection. "I know."

Bree twisted up the tube of lipstick. She leaned further forward and carefully smeared some on her top lip. Then her concentration was interrupted.

"No...effing...way."

Jassmine was at her side.

"That's not the limited edition Princess Pink you've got on, is it?"

The first time you ever speak to me and it's because I have lipstick?

Bree didn't miss a beat. She looked down at the tube like she was almost surprised at it being in her hand. "What, this? Oh yeah. I suppose it is."

"But it's a rip-off, right?"

Bree gave her most confident *Oh please* face. "I don't do fakes."

She didn't even do lipstick this time last week, but last week could've been ten million years ago judging by the ecstatic look on Jassmine's face.

"Can I try some on?"

Bree shrugged. "Sure."

A high-pitched yelp escaped Jassmine's mouth and the lipstick tube was swiped from Bree's hand. Within seconds, Jassmine had a matching pinky pout.

"I can't frickin' believe you have this." She kept making kissy faces in the mirror, turning this way and that. "Where did you get it? Did you rob someone?"

Bree maintained her aloof delivery. "Er...no. My dad's kinda, like, a big deal in the cosmetics industry. He's helping with Marvel's relaunch."

Like. She had just unnecessarily used the word "like". Just as the films had subliminally told her to.

"No frickin' way."

She nodded. "Way."

Bree watched Jassmine struggling to digest all this new and confusing information. It must've been hard for her. Until Monday, Bree had been easily categorized and plonked on the "loser geek" shelf. Not to be worried about, concerned with, or really bother acknowledging. Now she was a trendsetter with the ultimate "in" to a prettier world.

"Didn't I see you in my body combat class?"

Yes. You saw me and looked at me like I had leprosy.

Bree made her eyes wide. "Was that you? I thought I saw someone I recognized."

Jassmine nodded like a bobbing dog, while Jessica swung her head from side to side like she was watching a bewildering tennis match.

"It totally was you! I arrived late, otherwise I would have come over and said 'hi'."

Like hell you would.

Bree batted away the comment. "Ahhh. It's alright."

"Do you go to that class regularly?"

"Not really. Usually I just work out with my personal trainer..."

It wasn't quite a lie.

"No way? You have a trainer? I've been begging my mum for one for yonks."

"I actually work out with my mum."

"Really? That is so cute."

There was an awkward silence and Bree waited for Jassmine to fill it. She couldn't get over how right her mum had been about the lipstick. This was better than anything she could've planned herself. She must make it up to her somehow...

"So. What you up to tonight?"

Nothing. Sitting at home and blogging about how horrible you are.

Another shrug. "I'm not sure yet...I've not made up my mind."

"Do you..." Jassmine hesitated. "Do you wanna come over to mine? We're having a girl's night in. I would love to raid your make-up bag."

Bree pretended the thought bored her. "Erm...maybe... I could do, I suppose..."

"Come on. It will be fun!"

"Alright then."

Jassmine gave her a big beaming smile. A rare sight for anyone other than Hugo. "Brilliant. Here's my address..." She grabbed an eyeliner and scribbled on Bree's hand. "Come at seven. No need to bring drink." Then she turned back to her reflection. "God, this colour really is amazing. They say it suits everyone, you know?"

"I know."

Jessica was still reeling from the display of utter unlikeliness. She stumbled on her words for the first time ever.

"Er…Bree, is it? Could I try some of your lipstick on too?"

Bree confidently tossed her hair back, made a face, and made her voice sickly sweet – the sort of sugar-rush sweet reserved only for the bitchiest of comments.

"Oh? Really? I would but…well, it's kinda special and I don't wanna use it up too quickly. You get that, right?"

Jessica looked like her world had just fallen in. "Right… of course."

"See you at seven? I've got some old lipsticks I can bring for you to play with?" And, with that, Bree scooped up the contents of her make-up bag and sashayed out into the corridor – a lifelong power balance completely reversed in one toilet break.

Her Princess Pink lips couldn't stop smiling.

chapter eighteen

Bree took aaaaages getting ready. What do you wear to a girl's night in? She had absolutely no experience of such things. In the end, she swallowed her pride and asked her mum.

It took a while for the excitable shrieks to stop.

"Ouch. Mum. Eardrums, remember? They're prone to perforation?" she said, unable to keep from smiling at her mum's obvious delight.

Her mum ran into her bedroom uninvited, flung open her wardrobe and started tossing random articles of clothing over her shoulders.

"Right…where are those jeans I got you from Diesel? Here they are. Oh my God, Bree, you've not even taken the label off! Well, these are perfect…" She ripped off the tag and chucked them over. They hit Bree's chest with a thump. "And you need a nice jumper – not too tarty, mind.

It's only girls. Where's that gorgeous cashmere I got you last Christmas?" She ripped open another drawer. "This has the tag on too. Seriously, honey, I don't understand you."

An hour later and Bree was walking the short journey to Jassmine's house. Most Queen's students lived in the same area, where a collection of privately-owned roads were surrounded by the best of the suburban countryside. A few students lived "out in the sticks" – to have even more land – and were driven in each day by their mothers in blacked-out four-by-fours. Hugo's home apparently had numerous acres, an actual boating lake, and he was always whingeing about how much he rinsed on taxi fares. But Jassmine's was only five minutes away.

And, this time last week, an alternative universe away.

Not any more.

Bree's house was bigger. She noticed that straight away and it surprised her. There was no security gate here either. It was also a little bit tackier – all fake columns this and lion statues that. But none of it made ringing the doorbell any less daunting. She took a couple of deep breaths before yanking the ornate chain.

Remember why you're doing this. Even if tonight's awful, it's material.

It took a few moments of anxious waiting – was this a trick? – before Jassmine opened the door.

"Bree. Hi. You came."

Bree switched personalities and gave a beaming smile. "Yeah, of course. You invited me, remember?"

Jassmine laughed and stepped aside to let Bree in. "Come on in."

The tackiness was emphasized indoors. Everything was painted a shiny white; there was marble everywhere and blown-up professional canvas prints dominated the staircase. There were several of Jassmine, posing with her hands under her chin or flicking her hair back while pouting.

"Oh no. I can't believe you've seen these," Jassmine said, as they walked upstairs. "How embarrassing."

Her humiliation was totally fake. She looked incredible in all the photos. No matter how cheesy they were.

"Wow, Jass," Bree said. "These are gorgeous. You should totally be a model."

Jassmine looked delighted but at least pretended to be bashful. "Shut up. No way. I'm not tall enough."

"I still think you'd have a great chance."

Jassmine beamed. "The rest of the girls are already here." And she held open the door to her bedroom.

Jassmine Dallington's bedroom. The inner sanctum. How many boys and girls had dreamed of accessing this place?

It was just as tacky as the rest of the house. The walls were bright purple. And there were fairy lights over the bed. Bree bet Jassmine thought she'd had an inspired design moment coming up with that idea. The worst bit was the stencilled mural on the focal wall. Someone had carefully painted: *"Dance like nobody's watching, love like you've never been hurt, live like it's heaven on earth."* It was in a garish calligraphy script and took up the whole wall.

The perfect posse were all there already. Sitting on the four-poster bed. Staring.

"Hi, guys," Bree said confidently, giving them a half-wave.

None of them smiled.

Undeterred, Bree gestured towards the wall. "Wow, Jassmine. I love that quote!"

"Isn't it the best? It was on the front of a birthday card I got for my super sweet sixteenth and I just read it and got, like, tingles, you know? And I just thought, *What a wonderful message for living your life.* So Daddy hired some local artist to paint it on my wall."

"What a clever idea. You want to be an interior designer?"

"I dunno. Maybe. I got a B in Art GCSE."

Bree had got twelve A stars. "Wow. That's amazing."

The others were still staring. Gemma looked like she was chewing a lemon covered in salt. Jessica was snarling, still stung by the lipstick denial earlier. And Emily just looked utterly confused – like she couldn't handle the sudden reversal in instructions from *Laugh at this girl* to *Make friends with her.*

Bree pretended she wasn't completely terrified and sat on the bed next to them. Jassmine followed.

"So what's the plan?" she asked, looking around.

The posse didn't seem to appreciate Bree taking the conversational lead but Jassmine wasn't bothered.

"Same as we do every Friday night. Get drunk and gossip."

"Sounds fascinating." She struggled to keep the sarcasm from her voice.

"It's our tradition," Jessica spat, giving Bree angry eyes. "It's only ever been us until tonight. Nobody else has complained."

Ignoring her, Bree dug into her pocket. "Oh. I just remembered, Jass. I brought this for you. I had a spare." She handed over her extra Princess Pink lipstick. Jassmine went nuts and Bree gave Jessica her own look over Jassmine's shoulder.

Screw you.

"THIS IS INCREDIBLE, THANK YOU! Girls, you have to try it."

Bree still couldn't explain the power of the lipstick. But it thawed the girls. Even Jessica cheered up when she was allowed to try it out. And soon, Jassmine had pulled out a collection of spirits and juices from under her bed and they started making cocktails.

chapter nineteen

Three cocktails later, and the primary activity appeared to be dressing up in Jassmine's clothes, putting make-up on each other, and taking photos.

"Make sure you get my legs in," Jassmine yelled at Emily, who was head photographer. "I don't do all those squats and lunges at body combat so you can miss them out of the frame."

Bree was trying very hard not to laugh. She'd been put in a see-through top, applied about eight coats of the new lipstick and had her hair backcombed. She was posing on the bed with Jassmine like they had been friends for ever.

"Why are we doing this again?" she asked through the gritted teeth of yet another smile.

The flash on the phone went off. Then flashed again.

"What's the point of being fabulous unless you rub it in everyone's faces?" Jassmine replied, beaming at the lens and bending a leg forward to make it look even slimmer.

"But what are we doing with these photos?"

"Posting them online, duh. I bet hundreds of people look at them tomorrow morning and cry because they weren't here."

"Riiiight."

"Come on. Say 'Wogan' really slowly when Emms takes the next photo. It's what models do to get a really good pout. One – two – three…"

"WOGAN," they said together.

Forgive me, Virginia Woolf, Bree thought to herself, *for I have sinned.*

The whole evening seemed utterly bizarre to her. Bree had spent most Friday nights either alone, writing, or drinking overpriced wine with Holdo. She'd heard people talking about Jassmine's "crazy" girls-only parties. And, no doubt, desperates at school would look at these photos and get the wrong impression that this was fun and their life wasn't. That Jassmine and co. were cool and they weren't. But it was just a huge illusion.

After they grew bored with squeezing their cleavages together, the girls turned to jumping on the bed and singing along to music Bree didn't know. It was at this point that Jessica took a leading role – pushing everyone to the side and launching into a solo.

"Oh no, Emily. You totally aren't filming this, are you? I'll be so embarrassed."

So embarrassed you've checked to see if the camera is on twelve times.

Bree was bored. And a little let down, to be honest. To compensate for her disappointment, she drank more cocktails.

Now cocktails were something she HAD missed out on. They tasted so damn good. If only Holdo would get over himself enough to try one.

Holdo… Her tummy wiggled uncomfortably.

More songs. Bree's head got swimmy and she found it increasingly difficult to contain her real personality.

They were now in a circle, all a bit pissed, bitching about people who weren't there.

Jessica's cocktail swirled around dangerously in her ornate glass. "Don't get me wrong," she said, taking another slurp. "Sara is, like, one of my best friends. But sometimes I worry about her, you know? She's just so…easy."

The other girls nodded animatedly.

"And I just worry, cos it's not like she has to be. She's soooo pretty. Isn't she pretty?"

"Oooh yeah."

"Gorgeous."

"Stunning even…"

"That's what I'm saying." She drained the cocktail and looked surprised that it had gone. "She's gorgeous. But she just gives it out, you know? It's like, 'Hello. You fancy me, right? Brilliant. Let me just open my legs and present to you my vagina…'"

The girls sniggered.

"I mean, if I didn't know her…and if she wasn't one of my best friends… Well, I would think she was a total slut. And that's what everyone else thinks, especially the boys. I know she *says* she doesn't cheat on Ethan, but I think she's lying to me. And it's such a shame, because we're mates and we wouldn't judge her, would we?"

"No." The others shook their heads determinedly.

"I dunno. I love her, but she's just a slag, isn't she?"

More sniggering.

Bree was still trying to work out what system they used to define girls as "sluts". She thought maybe the golden rule was: *Every girl who has sex once, with anyone, is a slut…unless you are in the perfect posse.* It was like playing double-standard bingo. She felt sick.

Gemma took over.

"Okay. Fair dos. Sara, bless her, is a total slut."

More hilarious laughter.

"But at least she's not a scary psycho like Natalie! Did you *see* her come up to me today? The idiot actually cornered me after bio and said she was going to kill me! Can you believe that?"

They all gasped.

"I know. It's not my fault she's got burger nipples."

The girls all burst out laughing again, and Bree's nausea got worse.

"I still can't believe that photo. It TOTALLY serves her right for getting together with Danny," Jessica said. "I mean, she knew how you felt about him, Gem."

Gemma had the audacity to look sorry for herself. "I know… Bitch," she added as an afterthought.

Bree had managed to get through up till now with lots of head nodding and shaking, while looking around her to ensure she was nodding or shaking at the right time. Sometimes she muttered pointless stuff like "Yeah, scary", or "Oh no, wow", but it was half-hearted.

In truth, she was drunk, tired, and finding this whole experience very unpleasant. She downed the rest of her Sex on the Beach and focused on focusing.

"What about you, Bree?"

"Huh?"

Gemma was staring at her over the top of her pink Martini glass.

"You talking to me?"

"You're just very quiet over there."

Bree's head wasn't quite sober enough to decipher the hidden meaning in those words. All she could tell was that nastiness may be heading in her direction.

She shrugged. A nice safe shrug.

"What's your story anyway? Last week you were Twatty McGeek and now you're here sipping cocktails with us."

Was that a question? The grammar in that phrase was all out.

Another safe shrug. "I was invited."

Gemma laughed a huge fake laugh but her eyes remained narrow.

"I know that, stupid. But what happened? Where did you come from?"

"I've been going to school with you lot since I was a kid."

"Yeah, but you've always been hanging round with that computer freak. Sir Acne of Loserdom."

The others giggled.

"Holdo?"

"Oh yeah. I forgot about his stupid nickname. Like he's even read *Catcher in the Rye*."

Holdo had. At least twice a year since puberty.

Her brain was struggling. She still wasn't sure what she was supposed to say. "What about him?"

"Well, what's the deal? Were you guys shagging or something?"

The circle drew nearer, their faces garish. The sweet smell of alcohol on their breaths was putrid and overpowering.

Bree made a face. "Ergh. No! I don't want to catch his terminal acne!"

That was apparently the right thing to say. They all threw back their heads and laughed viciously while she felt sick with guilt. It didn't stop her continuing though.

"Our parents are just friends, that's all. But he's such a geek. He, like, alphabetically organizes his pornography into different files."

More laughter.

Bree had never really made anyone laugh before. Not a roomful of girls anyway. She supposed it was meant to feel good, to be responsible for Jassmine's mouth hanging open, her white teeth vibrating in hilarity.

It didn't feel good.

It felt terrible.

Sorry Holdo, sorry Holdo, sorry Holdo.

chapter twenty

The drinks continued. Bree experimented with drinking away the guilt. The girly shrieks got louder. The phrase "terminal acne" got yelled a lot.

And as the minute hand of Jassmine's glow-in-the-dark pink clock inched round, Bree felt worse and worse about her betrayal.

Two drinks later, she was rescued.

Jassmine's mother – who was shockingly "earthy", all woolly-jumpered and make-up free – came into the room, clapping her hands.

"Come on, my gorgeous girly girls. Home time."

They picked themselves off the carpet, staggering here and there, mumbling thank yous to Jassmine's mother.

Downstairs, Bree found herself hugging them all goodbye. The squeezing only made her feel sicker. She was desperate to get out and grateful for the cool night air that hit her on Jassmine's doorstep.

"Bye, everyone." She waved backwards.

"Bye, Bree," they chorused.

Luckily Jessica, Gemma, and Emily were walking in the opposite direction, so Bree could be alone with her thoughts as she stumbled home.

Her stomach bubbled with guilt. Her head drowned in self-loathing. And her entire body itched with the whole… anti-climax of it all. She'd expected a wealth of knee-jerking discoveries about these girls. A glimpse into the hidden brilliant-ness of what made them so powerful. But they just seemed like normal, average girls, who were just a bit luckier (and more evil) than everyone else.

But, mostly, more than anything, she felt horrible about Holdo.

It took her a while to walk up her hill. The pavement kept moving and she stumbled into the road. It was late and there were no cars around – just as well, otherwise Bree would've been run over multiple times.

Holdo…

They had been through so much together and this was how she repaid him. Tossing him aside on some literary whim, like an unworkable two-dimensional character. And now she'd just profited personally from ridiculing him. Who was she? How could she make it up to him?

She thought of last weekend and moving her leg onto his.

She had an idea.

I know what I can do…

* * *

Holdo didn't expect to find Bree at his front door after midnight, especially as they hadn't spoken since that awkward walk to school.

"Hello, dear friend." She launched herself over the threshold and swaddled him in a suffocating, alcohol-fumy hug.

He was too surprised to reply.

"Come on, let's go to your room." She grabbed his hand and pulled him up the stairs.

"Bree, wait."

She crashed into his room, an eager smile on her face, delighted with her problem-solving abilities. She looked around. There was an almost-empty bottle of red on his desk. *The Godfather Part II* flickered on pause on his television. And some pornography was still playing on his laptop. The faint grunts echoed round the room.

"Hang on." Holdo dived across the room and smashed the laptop screen closed. Bree opened her mouth to laugh hysterically – but, as soon as she did, she found she'd forgotten what was funny. The porn memory had been vanquished by the power of vodka and cranberry juice.

She pulled Holdo onto the sofa. He looked scared and embarrassed. Mostly scared.

"So how are you, Holdo?" she asked in a breathy voice.

He looked over both shoulders, subconsciously checking she wasn't talking to anyone else. "I'm…fine. And you?"

Bree flicked her hair back and laughed again. "Oh, me? I'm brilliant. Perfect in fact."

"Well, that's good to hear."

Bree stared at Holdo's mouth. It wasn't entirely un-kissable. It might even be enjoyable. "So what have you been up to?"

He pointed at the screen. "Just, you know, watching the best film out of *The Godfather* trilogy."

Bree pushed him against the sofa arm and snuggled into his chest. "Great. I'll watch too."

Holdo was too shocked to object.

They watched in silence for a few minutes as Al Pacino mumbled his way through scene after scene. Bree had watched the trilogy with Holdo multiple times but still never really understood what was going on. The actors never seemed to pronounce anything properly, but she didn't consider that a cool enough thing to say. Instead of concentrating on the film, she decided her plan was still brilliant. The perfect karmic balance for her despicable behaviour earlier.

"Holdo?" She tried to make her voice sultry again.

"Huh?" He looked down, half-distracted by the film.

"I don't feel like watching a movie right now…"

He pressed pause on the remote. "You want to watch something else?"

She shook her head. It felt like a tidal wave was rushing from side to side. "I don't want to watch anything right now."

She leaned over and kissed Holdo full on the mouth. It took him a moment to respond – maybe he was too stunned. But after a second or two, his mouth reacted. Spurred on, she pressed her body against his, pulled his face to hers and pushed her tongue into his mouth. He responded some more.

It wasn't so bad really. Her third kiss. With her eyes closed, she couldn't really tell it was Holdo. He could be just about anybody. In fact, in her imagination, he was Hugo for a while. And then Mr Fellows. And then Al Pacino had a turn. Why not?

Bored of kissing, she decided to move things up a notch.

She grabbed Holdo's hand and pushed it up under her cashmere jumper so he was cupping her boob. He groaned – a sort of puppy-like yelp of pleasure – and squeezed it so hard it hurt a bit.

It was actually okay. Having Holdo cup her boob. Again, with her eyes closed, he could be just about anyone.

With new confidence, Holdo moved his other hand up to her other boob all on his own. Bree analysed the sensation with detached interest. She decided it felt a bit like her boobs were two stress balls and Holdo had had a really hard day at the office.

Well, that's a new metaphor. See? This "make your life interesting thing" is turning out to be fruitful after all.

But she needed more. The stress-ball boob-grabbing and sloppy tongue-kissing weren't absolving her guilt fast enough.

She leaned back on the sofa and pulled Holdo's body weight on top of her. They fell on each other clumsily but he kept his mouth on hers. Wiggling to adjust her position so she didn't get squashed, she ran her hands down the front of his scrawny chest, the way she'd seen people do it in movies. Then she moved her hand so it was stroking Holdo's groin.

He jumped away from her, eyes wide. The kiss broken. "What are you doing?"

Bree pretended she didn't feel complete and utter humiliation. "I was just, you know…?"

Fear raced all over Holdo's face; the blood drained from it.

"What? You want us to have sex?"

"Sure? Why not?"

It was a bad choice of wording.

"It's not a big deal for you?" He looked confused now as well as scared. And maybe a bit hurt. She thought back on what had happened in the last two minutes and tried to work out why. But she couldn't get her brain to make any sense.

"It's just sex, isn't it? It's what people do. It's what everyone else our age does. Why shouldn't we do it?" She ran her hand through her new blonde hairdo and it stayed slicked back with sweat. She could still taste Holdo's tongue in her mouth. Mixed with cranberry juice. And a little bit of vodka.

Holdo's face was going through an extraordinary range of emotions very quickly. "Erm…Bree? What did that kiss just mean to you?"

Think, brain, she thought. *Say something clever.*

"I thought it would be a nice gift. To make up for being such a dick recently."

His expression turned into just plain hurt. "You mean... you didn't want to kiss me?"

"No...I mean...yes. You're my best friend."

"But you didn't want to kiss me?"

"Well...'want' is a confusing word."

"No it's not, Bree. It's a simple verb."

"It can also be a noun, you know?"

"That's beside the point. Why were you just about to have sex with me, Bree? Why? Because lust apparently hasn't come into it." His voice was choking. Tears? No. Boys didn't cry, did they? This had gone so horribly wrong. She had to make him understand.

"Because I wanted to make it up to you. It's what everyone does, isn't it? And, well, I know you won't really get the chance unless I do it with you. And I wanted to make it up to you..."

Sense that was. Perfect sense. *So why is he almost crying?*

He didn't speak. Bree used the time to pull herself upright on the sofa.

"Holdo?"

He wouldn't look at her. His hands were in his hair and he stared vacantly at a nondescript bit of carpet.

"Holdo? I'm sorry..."

He said something, but his voice was so quiet she could barely hear him.

"What was that?"

"I think you should leave," he repeated.

Her eyes widened. Never ever in the history of their friendship had Holdo ever asked her to leave his company. Not even when she said she thought the *Lord of the Rings* trilogy was a bit overrated.

"Holdo? Come on..." She tried to laugh it off.

"Please, Bree. I don't know who you are any more. Whatever it is you're doing, whoever it is you're trying to be, I don't wanna know her. Please leave."

Stunned and sobered up (almost), Bree stood. She hovered for a moment, waiting for him to say something that made it better.

There was nothing but silence.

Silence and a bit of wheezing – Holdo wheezed when he got emotional. She knew that because they were best friends. *Were...*

She stumbled out of his room and the door swung shut behind her.

The urge started in her fingertips as she ran the short distance home. She clenched and unclenched her fists, hoping to contain the feeling there. But it spread up her arms and down through her chest. Her heart hurt. It was suffocating in the negative energy building around it. The feeling spread round her body like an infection.

She needed to get it out somehow.

Bree never cried. She didn't know how. She was broken

somehow. She *wanted* to cry – because how brilliant it would be if she could cry right then. If she could let all the poison out with healthy, scar-free tears. She tripped over her feet and let out a yelp. She tried to turn it into a sob, trying to teach herself to cry, like a child shakily learning the alphabet. But she was emotionally dyslexic.

The poison hurt worse and worse. As she stamped in the security code on the gates to her home, it had settled in her stomach like an unlit bomb. With every step, another awful memory of that night flashbulbed into her brain.

Left step. *The look on Holdo's face just now.*

Right step. *Laughing about him with the perfect posse.*

Left step. *Sucking up to Jass and feeling sick about it.*

Right step. *Deliberately not letting Jessica borrow the lipstick.*

Bad person. Bad person. You're a horrible useless awful bad person.

By the time she let herself into the kitchen to get a glass of water, the decision had been made. She floated up the stairs and quietly let herself into her room. The urgency built and built.

Bree walked into the bathroom and locked the door.

Half an hour passed, maybe an hour, before the bathroom door reopened. A calmer teenager emerged, who winced when she sat at her desk and opened her laptop.

Bree began to type.

Rule number two: One must make friends with other attractive people

So I'm attractive, therefore you now care about me.

Therefore it only makes logical sense that I'm to befriend other attractive people so we can trade exploits like Pokémon cards.

I've thrown myself into the lion pit. And the lions have perfectly kept, highlighted manes, straightened with GHDs.

Here's the thing. "Interesting" has another meaning: "popular". Because one isn't popular without being interesting and one isn't interesting without being popular.

I've been told that we'll all grow out of this, of course. When we "mature" and all that bollocks. Soon, one beautiful day, we'll all grow the hell up and emerge into the real world, rubbing our eyes and realizing that the quiet computer geek is actually much more interesting than the popular people at school.

But this is puberty, folks. And the most interesting people are the ones you wish you could be.

Come on. You all have them. That group of people who have grown into their faces five years before the rest of us. The ones who wouldn't know a real problem if it Cossack-danced right in front of them. The teenagers who know how to work people, who ooze confidence, and have this seemingly perfect and exciting life that you'll never have an admission ticket to. I bet you can name them. Right now. There'll be at least four names you can list immediately. Four people you know all about, and yet, to them, your existence isn't something they've given any thought to. Unless it's while they're torturing you.

Got that list of four names?

Good. Because those four – I've infiltrated them for you. I'm your mole. Your heavily-made-up mole. I'll report back everything you want to know about these people. What do they really do? What are they really like? And, most importantly, what are their flaws?

It doesn't matter that my gang isn't your gang. My list of four isn't your list of four. Because here's the really depressing thing – they're all exactly the same. Secondary school is just a bunch of clichés repeated over and over, day after day, all over the world. There are, everywhere, in every corridor, popular people strutting about, flaunting their perfect lives to make you feel more miserable.

And I'm going to expose them for the fakes they really are.

chapter twenty-one

The weekend passed and the cuts scabbed over. By the next week, Bree was fully immersed in her new double life.

She and Jassmine met at the corner every morning and gossiped on the way in.

School was different. Walking through the corridors used to be a nightmare. She would get bashed into, and would have to dodge and weave her way into safe tributaries, taking the odd nasty comment. Now people parted when she walked to class. And it wasn't just there either. Bree could enter any toilet and suddenly one of the mirrors – prime school real-estate – would become free so she could reapply her make-up.

There was no queuing in the canteen either. Although it wasn't like the perfect posse ate much anyway. So far acceptable food consisted of chips, salt and vinegar crisps, gum, mineral water, and apples. Bree began to realize that her previous tuna sandwich binges may have been part of her original downfall. When they weren't sharing a bag of crisps (between FIVE – so hungry!), they would bitch about anyone who wasn't sitting at the same table. It was odd really, how many different ways Jassmine and her friends could be offended by other students' behaviour. Especially as those other girls spent all their time trying to please the posse.

"Like, oh my God, did you see the size of Rachel's skirt today? It's like, love, I'm not your gynaecologist. Put your flaps away."

"Tanya's voice annoys me so much. It's just so screechy. I swear she does it on purpose to get attention. Especially as no one cares about her any more now her dad won't let her throw those insane house parties."

"I heard Kimmy let Russell's big brother touch her up at Abi's seventeenth birthday party at Pizza Express. UNDER THE TABLE. I don't know if that makes her a slut. Or him a raving paedo."

Their hatred for others was what gave them their power. Disdain won them cool points. And they were all protected because they had something to offer. Bree vaguely remembered Tanya had used to be pretty friendly with them. But apparently not after her dad's party prevention inadvertently expelled her from the popular gang.

Luckily, Bree's mum kept up a steady supply of must-have beauty products, so her current account with the perfect posse was well in the black. She hoped she was in favour for more reasons than that…though she wasn't sure. She struggled to keep up the levels of enthusiasm needed to partake in their false exchanges, and occasionally let out the odd eye-roll or snort of contempt. At first she tried to cover them up, until she noticed her judgemental behaviour stopped Jassmine and the girls in their tracks. They would look at her nervously, waiting for her to join in again.

Perhaps, because Bree had such universal disdain for everyone – including them – she was the strongest of them all.

Either way, time with the posse was invaluable. She'd already learned that…

1) Everybody, yes, every single person had a nickname

Jass and the girls had an incredible ability to create harshly accurate names for everyone in their school year. They had brought Bree up to speed while queuing for chips in the school's five-star cafeteria. There was Aaron Brown, aka "Spunk Fingers", a football obsessive who was once caught wanking in school over an issue of *Nuts* magazine. Poor Rebecca Knightly, a shy but lovely hockey girl, was known as "Hell Face". Okay, so she had spots…but she had a really nice personality.

"Anyone who is described as having a 'nice personality' is minging," Jassmine informed Bree when she pointed this out. "It's linguistic spin. Like everyone fat in the world gets described as 'bubbly'."

Chuck from Bree's English class was called "Personality

Hair". A whole girly gang who Bree had thought were on good terms with the perfect posse were called the "Pleaselikemes".

Bree put a vitamin water on her tray. "So what was my nickname? You know, before you realized I'm actually amazing?"

Jassmine looked down and Jessica giggled nervously. Gemma, however, wasn't embarrassed.

"I told you at Jass's. You were 'Twatty McGeek'."

"Right... Er, why?"

"Cos you were a twat...and a geek."

It was surprising how much hearing it hurt her feelings.

Brazen it out. Keep them scared.

"Fair enough. Well, I'd rather be known as a geek than 'Bitch in the Ditch'."

Gemma furrowed her eyebrows. "What's that supposed to mean?"

Bree shrugged, like it was nothing. "You guys aren't the only ones who come up with nicknames. Us underclass 'twats' can make things up too."

Gemma looked a bit scared by that. "Okay. I get the bitch part. But what does the ditch part mean?"

Bree reached the till and handed a tenner over to the canteen lady. "It's where the rest of the school wishes your dead body would be found."

The others cracked up while Gemma looked temporarily terrified. "No way."

"Yes way." She was lying of course. But Gemma didn't need to know that.

2) They trolled people on the internet

Seriously. It took up about fifty per cent of their time. There was this national website – Dirty Gossip – where you logged onto your own school's page and posted rumours about your classmates. Their head teacher had been on national news trying to get it banned. Bree had clicked on it once and read all sorts of awful and simply implausible things about fellow students.

With glee, Jassmine etc. would make up random crap (*Hannah Jayden got fingered by Seth but then her fanny sneezed on him*) and post it via their phones – though they swore to Bree it was all true. Either way, she'd heard crying in the same toilet stall Natalie had used, looked underneath it, and saw Hannah Jayden's shoes. Bree considered making a poster for the cubicle, like the ones you see on the backs of toilet doors in cafes and stuff for domestic violence.

Are you a victim of Jassmine Incorporated? You're not alone. Call our free helpline service on 0800 LIFE'S UNFAIR to talk to a trusted advisor.

That was the weird thing. The posse really knew everyone – like, *everyone*. Who they were, who they fancied, how rich they were, what their parents did. Bree had always assumed they found everyone else irrelevant. But, in fact, no one went under their radar. They kept tabs on the somebodies, the nobodies, and the inbetweeners, while simultaneously spreading malicious rumours about them. Bree had always thought their perfect lives were just down to luck. But luck had nothing to do with it. Other students' lives were harder because they made them harder. Because they kept them down where they belonged. Like the captain of a pirate ship making crewmates walk the plank so there wasn't a mutiny.

3) *They were OBSESSED with what they looked like*

Bree wasn't sure if it was just them, or all girls. But these girls piled make-up on like it was running out. Bree had already started getting up an hour earlier to get ready for school, yet she reckoned her new "friends" took double that. They all wore fake eyelashes. Every day. They all GHD'd their hair into perfect ringlets or flicky waves, securing the style in storm clouds of hairspray. And they were always on the lookout for the latest miracle product. It was only now she realized the true power of her lipstick.

It was tiring though – living life as one big photo shoot. Wherever she turned, the word "Smillllllllllle!" was yelled at her and a phone camera lens would be shoved in her face, the picture immediately uploaded onto whatever social networking site was in that week. Every outfit was documented. Every "look". Every style. Every pound of weight lost.

These girls were their own PR and marketing gurus, plugging their product of "me" at any given opportunity. Only up-close were the flaws visible – like Monet paintings. Gemma, for instance, had spots. Jessica had the world's largest forehead, carefully hidden under her sweepy fringe.

Emily was so pale she couldn't find a foundation white enough to match her skin tone.

It was only Jassmine who was visually perfect. Isn't that always the way? There has to be one that's naturally gorgeous – just to add that extra pull of envy.

Bree documented these discoveries on her blog, typing out everything each night. Exhausted. It felt like extracting poison from a wound.

Material. It was all writing material, she supposed.

chapter twenty-two

It was her first creative-writing club since Mr Fellows had agreed she could come back.

She stood in front of the half-empty classroom with two top hats nicked from the drama cupboard, one in each hand.

"Right," she told the small class. "In my left hand you've got your subject. It's a hat full of nouns. Please don't ask me to explain what a noun is otherwise I will bash you to death with a Collins dictionary."

The cluster of Year Sevens and Eights chuckled.

"Good. Now, in my right hand is a hat filled with stuff that could happen to your noun." She reached in and grabbed a piece of folded paper and opened it up. "Like this one says *Gets lost in a storm.* I want you guys to come up here, pick something from each hat, and then use the combination of the noun slip and the action slip to write a short story."

The miniature people, all looking too small in their businesslike school uniforms, nodded enthusiastically.

"Brilliant. You've got until the end of the lunch break. Up you come."

They scampered over, grabbing bits of paper and opening them up like Christmas presents. *"Oooh"*s and *"What have you got?"*s filled the room. When they were all quiet again, Bree leaned back, put her feet up and sighed. Her shoes were killing her.

"Feet hurt?" Mr Fellows pulled up a chair next to her. Bree ignored him at first and looked at her teeny students, frantically scribbling in their exercise books in pencil, snapping the lead in their excitement.

"You know what's really depressing?" she said, gesturing to them. "Is that, in two years' time, they'll swear on their mother's life that they never used to come to this club."

Mr Fellows gave her a small smile and lazily propped his chin on his palms.

"Strange, isn't it? Secondary school. You think *you* find it hard? I'm here year after year, watching eager children bounce up on their first day, rucksacks rigidly on their backs, desperate to read. And then I have to watch their slow deterioration into adolescence. You know, when I became a teacher, I had all sorts of daydreams that I'd be like Robin Williams in *Dead Poets Society*. I thought I'd dazzle students with my knowledge of words, get them to love books as much as I do, and at the end of term we'd all get matching *Carpe Diem* tattoos or something." He sighed, and looked over the desks. "But, no, year after year, you all grow up and get hormones and I'm just the saddo teacher harping on about poetry."

One girl, JoJo, caught Bree's eye. Her nose was so close to the table it was almost rubbing it. She'd already filled a page of her book.

How long until she finds boys and it all goes downhill?

"Why do you do it then, sir?" Bree twisted in her wheelie chair and fixed him with a stare.

"You get the odd student who makes it all seem worthwhile." He stared back and time slowed a little.

Then he chucked a book at her. Bree almost missed it, distracted by searching for the meaning in his words. She caught it just in time though and looked at the cover.

"Franz Kafka?"

"I thought it was about time you were enlightened."

Bree grinned and chucked the book back at him. "I've read it already."

Mr Fellows missed the book and it landed, splayed open, on the floor.

"You're kidding! I didn't find Kafka until I was at university."

"Yes, well, I'm probably smarter than you were at my age."

Mr Fellows returned her smile. "As I said, some students make it all worthwhile."

It felt nice in there – in his classroom, with the little ones. She'd forgiven him for all the pretending-he-didn't-kiss-her bollocks. Now she'd lost Holdo, Mr Fellows was the only person left with whom she could be Bree. He was her mini-break from her double life.

As if guessing her thoughts, he said: "So what do your new mates think, then? Jassmine and her crew – I've seen you with them. Are they impressed that you're running the creative-writing club?"

Bree smirked. "They think I have detention."

"Extra-curricular activities aren't cool, then?"

"Sir, this is Queen's Hall, the only school on earth where extra-curricular activities *are* 'cool', as you so out-of-touchly put it."

He picked up the Kafka book and put it away in his desk drawer. "So why the lies then?"

"There are extra-curricular activities, and then there's running the creative-writing club."

"So creativity isn't cool?"

"Please stop saying 'cool', sir."

He held up his hands. "Point made. So these new friends of yours? They can't be good friends if you're lying to them."

Bree turned to watch the students again, all of their heads off in a world created by their imagination. A million mystical miles away from the reality of school.

"This is secondary school. Everyone lies to everyone. The earth would stop rotating if someone under the age of eighteen in this place said something that wasn't utter bullshit…"

She stopped herself and thought of Holdo. Was that true? Was she being fair? He never spoke bullshit…in fact, he was unpopular because he was so open about what he believed. Did he care? He didn't seem to… Was it only Bree who cared?

When she side-glanced, Mr Fellows was giving her another look. A look that said he got it. Similar to the look he gave her outside the golf club. She felt heat rise up her body.

"Bree…"

"What?" She flicked her new blonde "do" round to face him fully.

"I—"

"FINISHED!"

Enthusiastic JoJo banged her exercise book on the desk between them.

Bree jumped. "Wow – already?"

She nodded, her ponytail bobbing.

"What was your noun and action combo?"

"Peanut butter sandwich and the storm one."

"Tough one. What did you come up with?"

"A teddy bear's picnic that gets out of hand," the girl said confidently.

"Riiiiight. Wow. Original. I never would've thought of that."

The girl glowed from the praise – it was like a light bulb illuminating her from inside. She leaned forward. "You're friends with Jassminc Dallington and that lot, aren't you?"

Her voice was full of awe, like Jassmine and co. were Pulitzer Prize winners or something.

Mr Fellows noticeably bent in to hear Bree's answer.

"Kinda, yeah."

The girl leaned in further. "What are they like? You know…in real life?"

Bree was so tempted to say, *Well, why don't you visit* www.themanifestoonhowtobeinteresting.blogspot.com *and find out that they're all actually dull bitches?* but decided against it. Now was not the time to blow her cover. So much still needed to be done. So many words still needed to be written. Good ones. Interesting ones. Not like old-Bree ones.

"They're just people, JoJo."

"They're not… I think Jassmine looks like an angel."

Bree shrugged the comment off, a bit annoyed. "This looks like a good story," she said, changing the subject. "Do you want another combo?"

"Yes please."

She held out the two hats and JoJo grabbed more slips and ran back to her desk.

Mr Fellows chuckled. "Wow. You hear that? You're friends with angels, Bree."

She was more annoyed now. This was supposed to be her time to escape all that crap. "You know, magic tricks are never that interesting once you know how they're done."

"What's that supposed to mean?" he asked.

Bree looked out of the window in the door and watched students trickle past in big clumps. "I dunno. It's just not so exciting, is it? Once you know it's just a hanky stuffed up someone's sleeve?"

He got up and sat on the desk, blocking her view of the corridor.

"Why are you suddenly close with them, Bree? What's going on? You're a completely different person from the girl I spoke to a couple of weeks ago."

"You're the one who told me to live my life, sir."

"I said 'life'. Not 'a lie'."

She stood up, really annoyed now. The heat from her body shotgunned up to her face.

"So me being pretty and popular is a lie then?" she whispered at him angrily.

He held up his hands. "Whoa. No," he whispered back.

"Well, you're suddenly talking to me now. You weren't so interested in that different girl two weeks ago, were you?"

Mr Fellows glanced over his shoulder to make sure the students weren't listening.

"I don't know what you mean," he whispered.

But he did, she could see it in his face.

"I think it's you, Mr Fellows, who's lying."

And, for the first time ever, she left creative-writing class early, banging the door behind her.

chapter twenty-three

She was in such a rage she didn't look where she was going and smacked right bang into Hugo's rugby chest.

"*Doooph.*"

"Ouch. Walk much?"

She looked up, rubbing the arm which had taken the brunt of the collision. Recognition dawned in his face as their eyes made contact.

"Hey, it's you," he said. "Where are you leaving in such a hurry?"

"Detention."

Hugo raised one of his perfectly-formed dark eyebrows. "Detention? Already? You're not starting out well, are you?"

"Huh?" Bree tried to fight all the internal urges swimming round her belly triggered by the eyebrow raise.

"It's just, you're new, aren't you? I've seen you with Jass. Isn't it a bit soon to be getting detention? Especially at

Queen's Hall…you'll be down on the 'naughty list' straight away."

It was just as well she'd decided that "nonchalant" was the way to win him over. She bristled with anger. "Hugo. I've been in your form room since Year Seven."

He ran a hand through his gorgeously spiked hair and smiled mischievously. "No way."

"Yes way."

He laughed. "Well, that's embarrassing."

"For you. *I* know who *you* are."

He puffed out his chest proudly. "Well, everyone knows who I am. Look at me."

She knew she was supposed to giggle, but – thank GOD – she didn't think he worked that way. Not really. Maybe when he was part of a boy herd, but not now, just the two of them. So she rolled her eyes and – bingo! – he unpuffed his chest. Just like her research movies had told her he would.

"Have you really been in my form room since Year Seven? I'm sure I would have noticed you – I mean, look at you."

She tried not to blush. Or smack him round the face.

"I honestly have…" She didn't want to tell him she'd just been a weirdo loner until a few weeks ago. "So what's happened? You run out of girls to hit on and now you're opening your eyes to potential new victims?"

He laughed again and mock-pushed her.

She was right. He liked having the piss ripped out of him.

"Tell me what you really think, why don't you?"

"I'm sure I'm the only person who ever has."

"Woooooaaahhh. Personal attack. I'm offended."

"*You're* offended? You didn't acknowledge my existence until sixty seconds ago." She blew up her fringe and looked bored.

"Okay. I'm sorry. I can't believe I've never introduced myself. I'm Hugo." He reached out his hand. "Nice to meet you. What's your name?"

She shook his hand. "I'm Bree."

"Bree? Hang on…your name does ring a bell."

"Yeah, right. Stop lying."

He smiled another gorgeous grin. Ignoring it, she tossed her bag over her shoulder.

"I'd better get going."

"What? Now? But we're only just getting to know each other."

"You had your chance in Year Seven."

He laughed again. "You're not going to forgive me very easily, are you?"

She shook her head and looked up at him through her eyelashes. "Nope."

"Aww, man." He threw his head back in defeat. Then: "I know. You forgive me and, in return, I'll invite you to my incredibly amazing eighteenth. It's gonna be more like a mini festival than a party."

The invite! The invite she so desperately needed.

Bree wrinkled her nose, never missing a trick. "What? The Gash festival?"

"Oh. You heard about that? It's only a laugh, you know, with the lads."

"The rugby lads?"

"Yes, well, you know what it's like...*tally-ho* mixed with rampant chauvinism."

She actually let out a real laugh. "When did rugby players get so self-aware?"

He ignored that. "So you coming to my party?"

"Maybe."

"That's the nearest I'm gonna get to an answer, isn't it?"

"Maybe."

"Okay. Come if you like. Don't come if you don't like. I'll only cry myself to sleep..."

"Using another girl's knickers as a hanky."

He completely burst out laughing at that. "Maybe. It is *my* birthday. But I'll make you the Queen of the Gash festival if you come."

"And they say romance is dead."

More raucous laughter. "You have BANTER, girl."

Bree resisted the urge to visibly shudder. "I'd really better go." She walked past him.

"Wait!" he called after her. "So is that a yes?"

She spun round. "Okay then. I'll see you there."

"Brilliant. I'm texting round the details – you'll hear about it. See you there...Bree. See? I remembered."

"Congratulations," she called behind her, knowing he was watching.

Well played, Bree. Well played.

chapter twenty-four

Jassmine dropped the annoying bombshell on the way to school.

"Bree, you'll never guess what? Hugo and me. We're back on."

She was almost too shocked to notice the grammar mistake. *Hugo and I, HUGO AND I.* "Huh? What? I thought you were still on a break? Where did that come from?"

Jassmine giggled and hid behind her hair. "Last night. I invited him round after rugby practice to, you know, just catch up. And then he just came out with all this deep stuff. Like how he missed me. How rugby practice wasn't the same without me cheering him along from the sidelines. And how he wants us to get back together."

Or he was tanked up on testosterone after the match and wanted to expel it.

"Wow. Jassmine, that's amazing! I'm so happy for you."

Crap crap crap crap crap crap.

Seducing Hugo – the next rule on her list – was going to be painful enough, but if he had a girlfriend? *Ethics alert. Ethics alert.* Fair enough, ethics hadn't exactly been oozing out of Bree recently, but a girl's gotta try.

"I know. I'm so happy for me too. I really missed him, you know?"

"Yeah, I know."

It was warm, not really a winter day at all. Both of them had their blazers tossed over their shoulders. Bree had invited Jass over that morning to work out with her personal trainer – always worth upping your collateral. She could just about keep up with Jass, and her mum now. Lunges had become a routine part of life, alongside jogging on the spot while waiting for the kettle to boil. As a result, her body had slowly morphed into something she hardly recognized. Limbs were gradually being sculpted, and she couldn't poke her cellulite dimples with her finger whenever she sat on the toilet any more. She'd started to actually look forward to her morning workout. Not so much because she cared about her body, but more, with all the new-life madness around her, it was the only time she felt entirely in control. Well, then and when she tucked herself up each night with one of her favourite books, easing away the stresses of not-being-her all day with soothing, beautiful words.

"So…did you and Hugo talk about that girl at Seth's party?"

Jassmine flashed her a look and launched into an overly-prepared speech. "He said nothing happened. It was just a silly rumour. I trust him. We're in love."

With yourselves.

"Aww. That's so romantic."

"I know, right?"

"Hugo's just such a great guy."

"I know. Isn't he? I'm so lucky."

They turned the corner and there he was. Waiting for Jass, leaning against the school gates in an oh-so-cool James Dean way. Jassmine ran over.

"Hello, you."

She leaped into his arms and they launched into a passionate snog, perfectly timed so all arriving students got a full view.

"Wow. Look at that."

"They must be back together."

"But I thought he cheated on her?"

"Didn't she cheat on him?"

"They look so good together."

"Such a sweet couple."

"I wonder what happened?"

The whole school was enthralled. It was all Bree heard about in lessons. Jassmine this and Hugo that. Blah blah blah blah. People were behaving like the two of them were A-list celebs who'd just announced their engagement. And in a way they were – the A-list of Queen's. It was depressing how excited everyone was when, really, nothing of interest had happened at all. Boy meets girl. Girl meets boy. They fall in lust. Have an argument. Boy cheats on girl. Girl forgives boy. They live happily ever bloody after until a) they start uni, or b) – the more likely option – boy cheats on girl again.

HOW WAS THAT INTERESTING TO PEOPLE?

But Bree didn't make the rules. If she did, everyone would be raving on about how Holdo would be a self-made millionaire before he hit twenty-five. And how Bree was likely to get a book deal before she graduated uni. How Hugo obviously had a severe case of narcissist disorder. And that Gemma Rhinestone was, in fact, evil. And Bree's life could go on as normal and she could wear shoes that didn't hurt her feet, and a face that didn't need to be plastered on every morning, and she could raise her hand in English and say, *Actually, I think one could argue that Christopher Marlowe is a technically better writer than Shakespeare, but his untimely murder meant he wasn't able to evolve to produce his best work,* and everyone would go, *Yes, but of course,* and lift Bree onto their shoulders, chanting her name.

Or whatever.

But instead she clopped after Jassmine in her heels, yelling, "Wait up!"

An annoying side effect of the Jassmine/Hugo reunion vom-a-thon was that the girls now sat with Hugo and "the lads" at lunchtime. Time not spent groping through school jumpers was time wasted. So, the next day, Bree found herself in the company of complete cavemen. It was hot again, a final gasp of sunshine before the full force of winter hit, and everyone was making the most of it by "sunbathing" while trying not to shiver. They had prime spots, on the sloped bank next to the lacrosse field, which caught the most sun. Hugo lay with his hands behind his head and Jassmine on his lap. The other girls arranged themselves carefully in a semicircle facing the blokes, tucking their skirts around themselves.

Matty Boy – usually known as Batty Boy when the "lads" were teasing – gave them all a full-on perv.

"You see," Matty said, lying back in an imitation of Hugo, "this is what I love about the sunshine. All you gorgeous things get your skin out. Mmmm, loving your legs, Gemma." He winked at her.

Gemma grabbed a tuft of grass and chucked it at him. It fluttered to the ground aimlessly and Matty laughed.

"Oooo, I'm really scared of some grass."

"You should be, you perv," she said, half-scowling, half-smiling.

"Your legs are a bit hairy though."

"Hey! My legs aren't hairy."

"Hmm, hang on, let's check." He reached over and quickly stroked them.

"Get off!"

"I was wrong, Rinestone. You're a Gillette Goddess."

"And you're a sex offender."

He smiled. "Guilty as charged."

Bree could never work out why Matty Boy was popular. On all aesthetic points, he shouldn't have been. He was short. A bit chubs. GINGER. He had freckles all over his face and almost-white eyelashes. Plus he had a tendency to dress like a wannabe gangster, all gold chains this and baseball hats that, which looked ridiculous on his Caucasian-as-HELL skin. But he was a cocky little gobshite and that appeared to be his salvation. Never, on any account, underestimate the power of egotism. Bree had heard him referred to as "fit" and "well hot" by actual girls with actual working pairs of eyeballs.

"Now, Bree, I'm most disappointed by your lack of efforts in showing some skin today."

Bree had been busy thinking about how Shakespeare invented the word "eyeball", so did that cartoon looking-around thing before she realized Matty was talking to her. For the first time ever.

Her legs were clad in a sweaty pair of tights covered in tiny lipstick prints today – her scars still needed to heal up.

She looked at him over the rim of her designer sunglasses. "Excuse me, do I know you?"

Hugo laughed and Jassmine's head bobbed up and down on his stomach.

"Yeah, Batty Boy, where are your manners?"

Matty wrinkled his nose. "I'm only polite to girls who've got their legs out."

"Well, I'm only polite to boys who don't need to dye their eyelashes."

Hugo pissed himself laughing, so much that Jassmine's head lolled onto the grass. The boys clocked his reaction and all laughed too. Then the girls joined in.

Bree dug into her bag and chucked a mascara at him. "Here, you can borrow this if you'd like."

More laughter.

Matty lobbed the mascara back at her. Quite hard. Luckily, she caught it before it hit her face.

"Oooo, calm down. Someone's got man PMS."

The laughter continued.

"Who *are* you anyway?"

Bree held out her hand. "Lovely to be introduced to you, Matty. My name's Bree."

He looked at her hand like it was dirty but shook it anyway.

"There. That wasn't so hard now, was it?"

The laughter died down, with Seth the last to quieten.

"Damn. This new girl has proper banter," Seth said.

Bree beamed inside. Her planned transition from flirty to backchat seemed to be working. They respected her lack of fear. She lay back next to Jessica and relaxed behind her glasses, glad the conversation was no longer about leg-showing. Jassmine reclaimed her spot on Hugo and kissed his cheeks while he ignored her. Jessica and Emily both looked a little lost without her guiding them.

"So what are the latest plans for the party then?" Seth asked.

Hugo batted Jassmine away.

"My dad's hiring some kickass DJ and a massive marquee. It's going to be epic. Like, apocalyptically epic."

Jassmine ignored the rebuff and started stroking his hair.

"Man, I'm so excited I might get an erection," Seth joked.

"Really? Cos Batty Boy here told me you had trouble getting it up in your shower session with him last night..." Hugo raised an eyebrow.

The laughter Bree had generated was nothing compared to this. Jassmine and Emily cackled the loudest, making shrill shrieking sounds.

"You're hilarious, Hugo!" Emily shot him an admiring look but was instantly stared down by Jass. "I mean...ha ha. Seth, you're not really gay, are you?"

He blushed pink, while trying to look like he didn't care. "Why? You're not coming onto me, are you? Cos I think if you did, I definitely wouldn't be able to get it up. Yuck much?"

Emily's face recoiled into itself, her eyes blinking madly to hold in sudden tears. Seth looked round eagerly for hilarity. He got none.

"Seth, you are such a dickhead," Jass said. "Like Emily would shag you anyway."

"Yeah, mate. Calm down, no need to make it nasty."

"I'll happily shag you, Emily," Matty Boy piped in.

"Oooo, thanks, I guess," Emily muttered, and everyone giggled.

"What's with the tension today, boy?" Hugo said. "This is our last chance to catch some serious vitamin D before, like, next century. Can't we all chill and stop being mean to each other? I've decided that the following topics of conversation are the only things acceptable: the Rugby World Cup, Jassmine's tight arse—"

"Oi," she said, slapping him playfully.

"As I said, her tight arse…erm…my clungefest of a birthday. And did I say Rugby World Cup?"

Bree rolled over onto her tummy. "Wow, Hugo. Way to buck the trend of rugby meatheadness there."

He smiled and caught her eye, then gave her a knowing look. "Do you want to give head to my meat, Bree?"

She was glad her sunglasses hid most of her face as she was irritatingly impressed with his quick way with words. The others cheered.

Bree couldn't think of a very good comeback. "In your dreams."

"Be careful, Bree. My dreams often become a reality." And he did the eye-shag thing again. Her stomach went a bit funny…until she caught the look on Jassmine's face. The murderous look.

"This isn't an allocated topic of conversation. Don't you guys need to discuss kicking a pig skin around or something?"

Her aloofness saved her. Jassmine stopped evilling her and began harping on about England's chances. This gave Bree time to think.

Hugo wants me. This is interesting.

chapter twenty-five

The tension in Bree was building, like a slow-cooker meal of crap and stress. She'd never believed in fate – but she felt somehow, somewhere, inside her bones, or her heart, or whatever, that Hugo's party was going to be a dramatic event in her life. One of those nights forever etched onto your memory. Usually for the wrong reasons...

There were a number of complicating factors to her master plan. The first being that she'd forgiven Mr Fellows and now spent ninety per cent of her time wondering what his face would look like at the end of a church aisle on their wedding day.

You know, as you do.

Creative-writing club was her oasis from bitchiness, her holiday home from Shallowsville. It just so happened that it had become an after-school club, so it was less obvious now to Jassmine and company when she kept slinking off.

This also led to a few late nights in Mr Fellows's classroom afterwards, spending a little too much time tidying away pencil pots and thesauruses. It was gorgeous, every last moment. They explored his extensive bookcase, delving into old volumes of poetry and reading their favourite stanzas out to each other. Or had disagreements over who should win the next Pulitzer...which she really needed. She missed Holdo's yearly sweepstake.

It was all completely inappropriate. Of course it was. The situation had veered into dangerous territory many times. He spoke in far too much detail about his personal life. She heard all the clichés about his unsatisfactory relationship with his wife. How he couldn't bear being with someone who didn't read. How he'd rushed into marriage with the first girl who'd showed an interest in him at university. He once even hinted that they hardly had sex any more.

Each word, each held look, moved them further and further into HE'LL-GET-FIRED-AND-JAILED land. But, as organic as their developing friendship seemed, it also contained a tidal wave of emotions she felt were too strong to control. Bree was being pushed along by the current and it felt good, so good. Being with him made her brain go quiet and the edges of reality go fuzzy.

They hadn't kissed again or anything.

It was all in control, she thought.

Maybe.

Nothing would happen. It was fine.

*　　*　　*

Another issue was that, sometimes...only occasionally...
well, sometimes a bit more than that, Bree found herself
quite...*liking* some of the perfect posse. When they weren't
torturing people for no reason, that was. Though that had
calmed down considerably since Jass had got back with
Hugo, as she was too distracted following him everywhere.
Plus, Bree prided herself on coaxing Gemma out of posting
some of her most barbaric rumours on Dirty Gossip. Ironic
really, as Bree was blogging about their every move.

She walked in with Jass every day now and they chatted
in the way she'd always imagined girls chatting. Jassmine
wasn't utterly shallow all of the time. She had moments of
genuine insightfulness when she wasn't discussing Hugo,
her appearance, or who was a loser at school. Her intellectual
revelations were never earth-shattering, just:

"Sometimes I worry about all the crap they put in make-
up. What if I'm just applying cancer to my face every day?"

Or:

"Do you think Gemma might have some undiagnosed
personality disorder?"

Definitely not reinventing gravity, but there was more
there than Bree had initially thought.

The others weren't so bad either. Gemma was so
consistent in her nastiness it actually made Bree kind of
respect her over time. It had to be hard work to keep up
such constant levels of aggression towards everyone. Jessica,

especially, had grown on Bree ever since they'd both drunk too many apple Martinis at Gemma's house and sung Broadway songs the ENTIRE way home.

They'd covered every Andrew Lloyd Webber song they could remember, stumbling into the road, so the walk home had taken three times longer than normal. Then Jessica had confided that sometimes she thought Jassmine was selfish and that when Hugo pulled out of *Cyrano de Bergerac*, she'd cried herself to sleep for two nights running.

Emily was just harmless. Pathetic? Maybe a little. But harmless. And who could blame her for attaching herself to them like duct tape? If she was hanging onto their coat-tails for an easy ride through school, then why not? Bree's life had certainly become easier since she'd got in with them.

She supposed that this was what *she* found interesting about people. How, as you get to know someone, it's not so much their good points that warm you to them, but the eccentricities, the confessions of self-doubt, the flaws you only realize when you get close up – like the pores on your nose in one of those ghastly magnifying mirrors. She didn't believe there were many great life lessons out there for her still to learn. But perhaps this was one of them. That, by letting people in, even seemingly shallow nasty people like Jassmine, you learn something. Something you can only get through intimacy.

Then Gemma would call her Twatty McGeek again and all this candyflossy insight would fall right out the window.

Little by little, piece by piece, the inner sanctum of Queen's Hall was revealing itself to Bree, like peeling a large onion – that smelled of Coco Mademoiselle. Each quirk and admission of secret yearning was noted and blogged about, and Bree had begun to think she sort of "got" most of them.

Apart from Hugo.

Hugo.

What an enigma. The boy didn't reveal ANYTHING. It was all bravado, bravado, bravado mixed with odd signals Bree just didn't understand. Like opening his eyes mid-snog with Jassmine to wink at her. Or randomly smoking one day after school in an alleyway and then deliberately burning Seth's arm with a cigarette butt. Or putting his hand up in Bree's philosophy class and saying the most profound thing about Plato she had ever heard…then making a fart noise with his armpit and blaming it on the teacher.

The boy was a mystery – one she was keen to unravel. If only she could think of a way to do it other than The Bad Way. The way she was certain was the only way. And a way that made her stomach churn like batter being stirred.

chapter twenty-six

"Mum, I need your help."

They'd finished dinner. It was just the two of them. Again. Her mum's attempt at a meat-free spaghetti bolognese had tasted of wrong. Just plain wrong. So most of it was now churned up by the garbage disposal and her mum had ordered in Thai. The boxes lay scattered between them on the carpet, a stray noodle hanging out onto the rug, where it would sit until morning, when the cleaner arrived.

"Of course, Bree, what is it?"

"I've kind of been invited to a party. A big party. And I have no idea what to wear. I was wondering if you could—"

"GO SHOPPING WITH YOU?"

The leftover box of pad thai was hurled to one side in her excitement. Bree couldn't help but laugh.

"Well, yeah. That's what I was gonna ask."

"Again? You'll let me go shopping with you again?"

"Sure. Why not?"

"I thought last time would be a one-off. Like, a lifetime one-off. Unless maybe one day you decided to get married, and needed a wedding gown, and every other person on earth was dead – I hoped maybe we would shop again then."

"Hey, Mum. I enjoyed it last time."

"You did?"

"Sure."

"But you scowled the whole time."

Bree laughed again. "Well, I wasn't so used to that sort of thing back then. I'm more into it now." She gestured to today's outfit. A pair of skinny jeans with a dusty pink see-throughish jumper, garnished with different-sized pearl necklaces. "See this? I picked this out all by myself this morning."

"And you look lovely."

"Thanks. But I've never been to a party before."

"Is it Jassmine's party? She's an…interesting girl."

Jassmine. A guilt surge squidged in Bree's stomach. Hang on, *interesting*? What did her mum mean by that?

"It's not Jass's party, but she's gonna be there."

Her mum clapped her hands together. "This is so exciting! Your first massive party. Why don't you go shopping with Jassmine though? Surely it's more fun to shop with her?"

Bree looked at the stray noodle on the lush cream carpet. "Yeah. Maybe. But I kind of wanted to spend time with you."

She made an *oomph* sound as her mother flung herself across the rug to hug her.

Her mum took the finding of a dress very seriously. Like, military-operation seriously. She dragged Bree out of bed before the sun was even up, despite it being a Sunday, and within an hour they were on a train whizzing to London.

Bree yawned. "I still don't see why we couldn't shop in town."

"And risk someone potentially turning up in the same dress as you?"

Bree hadn't thought about that.

"What kind of party is it anyway?"

"Sort of like a mini festival, I think." Bree blitzed through the rumours in her head. "It's in this guy's garden. But I think his garden is more like a country than a garden."

"Grass?"

"I assume so. Unless his whole garden is tarmacked."

"You'll need wedges, otherwise your heels will sink into the grass."

"Wedges? What are wedges?"

"Just trust me, darling."

They got a taxi from Victoria station ("I don't do the tube, darling") and were spat out onto the bustling streets of London. Right in front of the gold revolving doors of their destination: Selfridges. Or *The Mother Ship* as her mum kept calling it, laughing hilariously at her own joke.

They were soon engulfed by the thick air of the cosmetics counters. Each one displayed a rainbow palette of every conceivable beauty product, surrounded by perfume bottles sculpted into ornate glass oddities.

It was a different universe.

"We need floor three." Her mum steered her past assistants spraying all sorts of overpriced water at them. "Womenswear."

They fought their way to the lift and emerged again into a different and equally puzzling world. There were clothes EVERYWHERE. Rails and rails of them; it was overwhelming.

Her mum was utterly undeterred. In fact, she ran out onto the shiny floor and draped item after item over her arm.

"This could work. Oooh, I love this one. Hmm, the colour's great but the hemline would need to come up..."

Bree could only follow behind her, watching the pile build.

"Mum. I don't think it's physically possible for me to try all that on before the end of this century."

"Don't be silly. Let's go get a spot in the changing rooms."

Bree's very limited experience of changing rooms consisted mainly of cramped cubicles with mirrors that made everything evil, curtains that never closed properly, and lighting that took sheer unadulterated joy in highlighting every imperfection of every atom of her skin.

Selfridges' changing rooms were quite different. They were ushered through to something called the Personal

Shopping zone, where they were given their own little suite – complete with beautiful mirrors that made everything in this beautiful world even more beautiful, as well as sparkling glasses of champagne to drink. They were left entirely to their own devices as Bree struggled in and out of stuff, grateful for the curtain separating her from her mum so she didn't have to worry about Mum seeing her scars.

Her mum provided a constant stream of commentary.

"No that one won't do, you look like a headmistress. What is it with fashion these days? Doesn't anybody have a waist any more? You should definitely show off your legs, they're your best feature. Red, honey, I'm thinking red. What do you think? You may as well stand out, you're so pretty. If only it were summer, looking good is so much easier in the summer."

The pile of discarded clothing on the floor grew. Nothing was quite good enough. Nothing was "the one".

"Matching an outfit to an important event is like trying to find a soulmate," her mum said, digging through the other (much smaller) pile of stuff left to try on. "It takes hard work, belief, and instinct."

"Mum, it's just a dress."

"It's never just a dress, dear. It could be the dress you're wearing when you get your dream job, or when you meet the love of your life. The cloth, the way it's cut, how it makes you feel, this all has an impact, you know. It can be life-changing… I still remember exactly what I was wearing the night I met your father."

"Dad?"

"Yes. It was a red dress – far too short really, but I was young then, and you got your legs from me. I was so silly, running around London, all tarted up, desperate to find a banker to take care of me…" She picked up a dress in bright blue silk and chucked it over. Bree caught it and pulled it over her head.

"I still have it you know. Hanging up in my wardrobe. I sometimes get it out and wonder if he'd still have come over if I'd worn the yellow crop top I'd been planning on. Whether he would have bought me that life-changing bottle of champagne if I'd worn jeans…"

Bree turned round to show her the dress and Mum instantly stopped talking.

"Ta-daa!"

"Oh, honey. I think that's the one."

Bree turned back to her reflection and did a mini double-take. All the other dresses had been too short, too tight, too baggy, too…just *ergh*. This dress was special, though. Despite it being silk, the dress casually hung off the shoulders. It had a wide white ribbon that tied at the back, making it almost little-girl-at-a-birthday-party-ish – if only it weren't so short. It skimmed the tops of her thighs lightly, just long enough to hide her scars.

If clothing could be soulmates, Bree had just met the One.

"It's…good, isn't it?"

Feverishly, her mum said only two words:

"Get it."

Bree turned this way and that, imagining all the future circumstances in which her dress would be there to hold her hand. She thought of its past life – sewn carefully by some determined fashion graduate, working late to impress her new boss. Maybe the dress had been waiting for a few weeks now, wondering who would come and claim it... what its future might hold. It might have even unwrinkled itself this morning and said to the other dresses, *Today is the day, I can feel it in my ribbons, I'm going to get BOUGHT today.* And now they would voyage to Hugo's party together and experience whatever it was that they'd experience there.

Her mum interrupted her thoughts. "So who's the boy then?"

Bree turned round, flustered. "Huh?"

"The dress...it's obviously for a boy."

Bree went red.

"That blush tells me everything."

Bree went redder. She turned to examine herself from the back, trying to dislodge the shame.

"Mum?"

"Yes."

"Was there a boy at your school? You know...one that everyone liked?"

"You mean, did my school have a Mr Dreamboat?"

"No one says 'dreamboat' any more, but yeah..."

Her mum lay back against the leather sofa and mock-fanned herself. "Was there ever? Francesco Biaggio. Parents were Italian. He was, as a result, GORGEOUS. He knew it, of course. They always do, don't they? Mainly because every single girl in my class was violently in love with him and flung themselves against him, usually without clothes, at every available opportunity."

Bree screwed up her face. "Classy."

"I can't talk. I was one of them."

"Mother!"

Her mum laughed and put her face in her hands. "God, it was so awful. I threw a party for the sole reason it would give me an opportunity to seduce him. I thought somehow if I slept with him he would magically fall in love with me. I was so nervous I ended up downing a bottle of red wine before anyone arrived. When he turned up – late of course, though still sober as it was only, like, eight – I dragged him upstairs to my room. I told him to go into the en suite to "freshen up", then I got a batch of tea lights and lit them all…only I was too sloshed to place them around the room. When he re-entered, he just found me half-slumped on the floor, my entire body surrounded by candles like chalk round a dead body at a crime scene, grinning at him manically."

Bree stifled a laugh. "No way! What happened?"

Her mum laughed too, her eyes rejoicing in the memory. "Well, oddly enough, he turned down my request to 'Make love to me and look into my eyes and tell me that you love me and look like you mean it'. He made a polite excuse to leave. At which point, I burst into hysterical tears and he put me to bed, and rocked me while I cried about how ugly I was."

Bree had to sit down next to her on the sofa, she was trying so hard not to laugh. "Seriously, Mum?"

"Oh, how I wish I was joking. The memory still haunts me some nights."

"Oh no, really? I was hoping all my teenage humiliations would become nothing worse than funny anecdotes over the passage of time."

Her mum patted her adoringly on the cheek. "I'm afraid not, honey. Teen humiliation haunts you for the rest of your life. But it's good for you – it's important in life to learn how to laugh at yourself. Everyone needs a slice or two of humble pie."

"So what happened with you and Francesco?"

She sighed, took a sip of champagne. "God, nothing. He slept with practically everyone else in my class but me. Last I heard, he'd become some hotshot banker. Don't they all really?"

Bree nodded.

Her mum put an arm around her. "So, this guy? The one you've got the dress for…"

"I never said it was for a guy."

"Bree. Come on… I'm your mother."

She rolled her eyes. "Okay. So there's a guy… Is it some sort of scientific population requirement to have an insanely attractive guy in each school?"

"Let me guess." She ticked the qualities off on her fingers.

"Far too handsome for his own good, devilishly charismatic, annoyingly intelligent, and suffers from some sort of narcissistic disorder but everyone ignores this due to the handsomeness and charisma?"

Bree realized at that moment where she got her cynical streak from. "Something like that. Why is there one in every school? Are they all the same? What's their purpose?"

"To screw you up for life."

"Nice, Mum." Bree reached over and took her mum's champagne glass for a sip. "Sugarcoat it for me, why don't ya?"

"It's true. Why else do you think I remember Francesco's name?"

"Not everyone gets drunk and tries to seduce the most popular boy in school with a candle show."

Mum raised an eyebrow. "True. But I bet every girl I was at school with still remembers his name. And what his favourite colour was – green, by the way. And what his hobbies were – violin and football. And what part of their class timetable enabled them to cross paths with him in the corridor for two seconds – Wednesdays, incidentally, just after I finished biology. He would have biology after me in the same classroom and I would walk past him on my way out. Sometimes I would fantasize about him sitting in the same seat I'd just sat on. That our bottoms were somehow in tune with each other and how this obviously meant we were soulmates."

Bree laughed again. Her mother, making her laugh. It was happening more and more.

"So – other than the fact that you're a PSYCHO, how does the most popular boy in school ruin every girl's life?"

Her mum thought about it for a bit, picking up a few stray dresses and reacquainting them with their hangers.

"I think they teach you, at a young and impressionable age – and yes, I know you think you're really mature but you're not the fully fledged you yet, not quite – that attractive men don't fancy you. Because the most popular boy in school is almost always the ONLY really attractive boy in school. And they never go for you because you don't live in a Hollywood movie." She pulled another discarded dress back onto its hanger. "And so, when you grow up, and grow into your features and become the you you're going to become…well, then whenever an attractive man shows any interest in you, you're so damn grateful, you put up with their shit out of sheer adoration of the situation. *Wow, you are attractive and you fancy me. Yes it's fine that you cheated on me, of course you did.* Because attractive men – and now, honey, this really is a life lesson…" She waggled her finger at Bree. "…They haven't usually had to eat those slices of humble pie I told you about, and that can make them not very nice people. You see, they've never once not got the girl, so they're never scared of *losing* the girl. And if they're not scared of losing you, then they'll screw you about. Find a *nice* guy, Bree…not too good-looking… They make good husbands."

Bree couldn't decide if her mum was a genius or deranged. She thought about her parents' marriage, for probably the first time ever. Was her mum happy? How could you be happy with someone who was never there? Maybe Dad was just really super-nice when he finally got home...

"So this guy the dress is for – is he the going-to-wreck-your-life-for-ever guy?" her mum asked, interrupting her thoughts.

Bree smiled. "He's a rugby player..."

Her mum threw her arms up. "And that's all I need to know."

Bree went back behind the curtain, shrugged her way out of the dress and clambered into her jeans, putting the silken garment lovingly on its hanger.

"It's okay, Mum. I'm in control. I know what I'm doing."

"That's what *I* thought, kiddo. But the candle wax stains still haven't come out of my parents' carpet," her mum called through the material. "Be careful, love."

chapter twenty-seven

"I can't frickin' believe Hugo's party is actually tonight."

Jassmine's head was tipped back as she pressed up against the mirror to apply yet another coat of mascara.

"I know." Bree began to backcomb her hair. "We're gonna blink and it will be Christmas."

"Ooooh, I LOVE Christmas. Baileys is, like, the only alcoholic drink where the taste is totally worth the calories." She dabbed at her lashes again. "Bree, this mascara is, like, INCREDIBLE. I don't think I'll need to wear falsies ever again. I can't believe the swag your dad gets."

Bree looked at the cosmetics littering Jassmine's bed. Her father had certainly outdone himself. He'd just secured a new load of Marvel in their spring/summer range. She wasn't sure what that meant, but she did know that Jassmine was pretty close to licking her face in appreciation.

"It's awesome, isn't it? You look like Bambi. Bambi on MDMA."

Jassmine giggled.

It had been Jassmine's idea to get ready together and, oddly, she hadn't invited the others. They were meeting them at the party. It seemed like Bree had won the position of right-hand man. Well, woman. Girl? Right-hand girl? Either way, it was just the two of them. Bree had brought the make-up. Jassmine had brought the cocktail shaker and collection of spirits. They'd made cherry cocktails, topped up with Diet Coke, and were already on their third. Which explained...

"Ouch, I just got myself in the eye with the brush." Jassmine blinked madly and tears poured out of one eye, carving a trail through her foundation like pioneers.

"Eeech!" Bree winced. "Are you okay?"

"NO!" she wailed. "I'm wrecking my make-up."

"Keep looking upwards. Hang on, I'll get a tissue." She grabbed a cleansing wipe from her toiletry bag and held it under Jassmine's eye. The top of it tinged black with her mascara-ridden tears.

"Just keep blinking..."

"Frickin' mascara..."

"Hey, watch it. That's Marvel you're talking about."

"Okay then. Frickin' cherry cocktails making me crap at applying mascara."

"That's better."

Jass kept blinking and Bree could see the worst was over.

She mopped up the last of the oozage, brandished a powder brush and covered up the tear trail on Jassmine's face.

"Thanks, Bree."

"Don't mention it."

Recovered, Jass took a medicinal sip of her cocktail and stared at Bree over the rim of her glass. "You're actually quite nice, aren't you?"

No I'm not. I'm horrible and I'm going to hurt you and try and seduce your boyfriend and I'm sorry but I have to.

"Don't tell anyone, will you?" she deadpanned.

"I'm being serious."

Bree couldn't look at her. The wretched feeling bubbled in her tummy again. She'd never got ready to go out with a girlfriend before. It was yet another social rite of passage that had passed her by while her head had been stuck in a Sylvia Plath book. It surprised her how fun it was – savouring the anticipation of a big evening, making it part of the event. In fact, she would rather this *was* the event. Then she wouldn't feel sick with guilt. And fear.

"Hugo talks about you a lot..."

"Huh?" Bree's thoughts were interrupted by the curveball comment. She tried to look nonplussed, though her heart started banging like a rock concert. "It's only cos I give him hell."

"No...it's not just that. He says you're 'different'." The cautious way Jassmine spoke revealed that this hadn't been casually brought up. It had been planned. Engineered.

Tread carefully.

Bree flipped open a hand mirror and closed it again, making it click. "Well, I'm new to your group, aren't I?" She had to look in Jassmine's eye now, otherwise it would be so obvious.

Judas, Judas, Judas...

Jassmine isn't Jesus, Bree. You're not stabbing someone saintly in the back. Just the most popular girl in school. Who trolls people on the internet.

She changed the subject as carefully as she could. "What have you got him for his birthday? Men are so hard to shop for!" Although she'd never struggled with Holdo's birthday presents. He was always ecstatic with his book tokens.

Jassmine's face relaxed. "Aren't they just? I've been panicking for weeks. What do you get Hugo? I mean, the boy's got everything. But I think I've cracked it. Do you wanna see?"

Bree nodded.

"It's a bit cheesy."

Really, Jass? With your purple bedroom and fairy lights.

"I'm sure it's lovely."

Jassmine scampered over to her bedside drawer and yanked out a small velvet box. It was a lush deep purple and had some silvery logo on it.

"Oooh, looks posh."

"It is. I owe my parents money until, like, 2095."

Bree took the box and carefully opened it. A thick silver chain with a heavy pendant was nestled like a snake in purple silk.

It was vile. So vile that Bree instantly felt sorry for her. For her lack of taste and for how much she obviously cared for him.

"Wow, Jass, it's so tasteful."

"Isn't it? Look, there's an inscription."

Bree turned the pendant over, trying not to smudge the polished metal – although frankly, any sabotage would improve the thing.

It said: *I love you more today than yesterday but less than tomorrow.*

Dry heave.

"Jeez, Jass, that's so thoughtful. Did you think that up all by yourself?"

Jass looked proud, like she'd crafted the damn thing herself. "No. I wish. I just Googled *nice love quotes* and this one came up and I thought it was really clever. It is, right? It makes you think for a bit and then you get it and think, *Wow, that's so clever and so sweet.*"

And so likely never to be worn on Hugo's neck EVER.

"Hugo will adore it."

No, he wouldn't. Jass didn't know him at all. He'd pretend he loved it, and then ruthlessly rip the piss behind her back so his mates wouldn't do it first.

"You think?"

"Yeah. And it will be a great way for him to remember you when you both go to uni."

"Oh…that." Jass flopped down on her giant bed. "Don't remind me. I think I'll actually die from a broken heart."

"Long-distance relationships work out all the time."

Jassmine gave her a look. "Yeah, especially with guys like Hugo." She stared into the blackness out the window and drained her glass. Bree watched her thin throat gulp. How many had Jass had already? It wasn't even seven o'clock.

As a distraction, Bree turned up the volume on the entertainment system and started singing along, pulling a silly face. Not one to ever be down for long, Jass giggled and quickly joined in. They sang as they curled Bree's hair with GHDs, while they drowned themselves in a napalm cloud of perfume, and hit incredibly high notes, fake-opera-style, as they put on their outfits.

Bree wore stockings with her dress – to update her tights look a bit, make it sexier for the evening. Unfortunately, they weren't the easiest things to put on, especially when singing opera pop. She hopped around on one leg before crashing backwards onto the bed, on top of Jassmine.

"*Oomph.*"

They both cracked up laughing.

"Bree, you've just crushed at least ten of my ribs."

"Sorry. These stupid stockings."

She rolled off and began yanking the stockings up again.

"Fucking hell, Bree, what's with all those cuts on your legs?"

The room went cold. Ice rushed into her head like drinking a slush puppy too fast. Bree looked down. Her dress had ridden up in the fall and her scarred mess of a top-thigh was exposed. It looked angrier and nastier than usual.

She whipped her skirt down. "Nothing," she said abruptly.

"Bree." Jass sat up. "What happened? Show me! Are you okay?"

Bree's ears were thudding hard and she tried to keep the tremor out of her voice.

"Oh that? It's nothing. Honestly. I just…er…" Her brain couldn't think of an excuse. Humiliation coursed through her. She crossed her arms. "Leave it, Jass."

"Why won't you let me see?"

"There's nothing to see."

"Did you do that to yourself, Bree?" Jass asked quietly, moving nearer on the bed.

"No."

"It's okay. You can tell me." Her arm appeared round Bree's shoulder. She shrugged it off.

"Please just leave it." Bree's voice betrayed her and wobbled. She scratched her arms, focusing on the sting over the embarrassment.

How had she allowed this to happen? How had she been so stupid? The plan could never work now. Who would want a stupid self-harming freak in the perfect group? Jass was going to tell everyone and then everyone would know her awful little secret. And her parents might find out, and there was no way her dad would understand…or her mum…and then what?

She felt her throat go tight.

"Bree. It's okay. I understand…" Jassmine paused. "I used to do it too."

The words didn't quite go in at first.

"What you do to yourself...I used to do it too."

"Yeah, right."

"It's true." Jass squeezed her hand, before tipping her head over so her hair spilled onto Bree's lap.

"What are you doing?"

"See? Can you see it?"

Bree's mouth dropped open as she leaned in to get a better look. "Jass, I never noticed. What happened?" She prodded the bald patch with her forefinger. It felt smooth.

Jass righted herself and her hair fell into place. The bald patch was hidden again, like a rabbit in a hat.

"I told you. I did what you did." She spoke so calmly and matter-of-factly. For the first time ever, she sounded wise.

"But I don't do that. Pull out my hair, I mean. It's totally different."

Jass gave her an almost-patronizing half-smile. "Self-harm isn't just about cutting, you know. People do all sorts of things."

Self-harm.

She'd just said it, just like that. Like it was a really common word, like *postbox*, or *bin* or something. But to Bree, who'd done it for three years now, never told a soul, and hated herself for every moment, the word felt almost too twee. It didn't come close to how she felt about it when she did it.

"No one's ever called it that to me before," she admitted.

"Does anyone even know?"

She shook her head. If she'd been a crier, she would have been sobbing by now. Instead she just continued to scratch her arm. "No one understands."

"Understands what? That sometimes you feel like a boiling kettle, getting hotter and hotter, and the only way to let it all out is to do this – like it's erupting steam all over the place? Or that sometimes, when you're really low, it's just nice to feel…something, any kind of physical sensation… and pain is the sensation with the most powerful pull? Or that, maybe, it's a way of proving you're alive? *I must be, there's blood coming out of me, this proves I exist.* Or, *Look, I've got an entire tuft of hair filling my fist – I must be here, I must be real, I can prove it.*"

The walls of Jassmine's room had somehow disappeared and Bree felt like she was floating above the situation.

One of her favourite quotes of all time was one by Alan Bennett, from his play, *The History Boys*. It was something the English teacher, Hector, said about reading:

The best moments in reading are when you come across something – a thought, a feeling, a way of looking at things – which you had thought special and particular to you. And now, here it is, set down by someone else, a person you have never met, someone even who is long dead. And it is as if a hand has come out, and taken yours.

She'd felt that beautiful sensation so many times in her lonely life. So many authors' hands had metaphorically leaped from the page and snatched her heart, leaving her breathless. And she would read the magical passage again and again, laughing to herself. Then she would get out her notebook and write it down to return to in an inevitable lonely time in the future.

It had never happened with a real life person though. Let alone a real life person who also happened to be the most popular girl in school. Someone who Bree, on principle, hated. But right then, in that moment, with the red of shame still on her face, Jassmine's hand had metaphorically and literally grabbed her and articulated how she'd always felt, but could never find a way of expressing.

Her consciousness found its way back into the bedroom. She looked over at Jass in confusion.

"I don't understand. You, your life, it all seems so…"

"So what? Perfect?"

"Well, yeah."

"It is mostly. But only recently. Dad lost all his money in the crash. We didn't think he was gonna get another job. They were talking about selling this place, and even sending me to the free college down the road. Then, of course, that was the time Hugo dumped me…" She trailed off.

"I never knew. You always seem so…together."

"That's weird," she said, smiling. "Cos that's exactly what I would say about you."

A warmth grew in Bree's heart as they just sat there, staring at each other, giggling. It was the warmth of attachment…of friendship. It felt like the world was hugging her.

What the hell was she going to do?

"I've never noticed it – your hair, I mean."

"It's fine if I don't wear a ponytail. Luckily they're not in vogue at the moment."

"Do you still do it?"

She shook her head. "No. I've found other ways to let it out. Why do you think I'm always in body combat class on a Sunday morning? I feel like I've mostly outgrown that need now, maybe. Anyway, Dad's got a new job now. We're rich again. Hugo and I are back together. Maybe it was circumstantial?"

And with that it was easier to hate her again…

"You should get some help though," Jass told her.

"I'm fine, thank you."

"Seriously, Bree."

"Lay off, Jass. Can't we just forget it and have a good night?"

Jass looked like she was going to protest but decided against it, and broke into a wide smile.

"Deffos. Come on, more cocktails are needed!"

chapter twenty-eight

By the time they arrived at the party, Jassmine was already a bit too drunk.

"Whoops," she said, flashing some side boob as she swung out of the taxi onto the ground. "Oh no, I've got mud on my playsuit."

She held up her hands like a toddler wanting a carry. Bree sighed and hoisted her to her feet.

"Your mate alright?" the taxi driver asked, looking worried.

"She'll be fine. Won't you, Jass?"

But Jass had already stumbled away across the field. "Wow, Bree, have you seen anything like this before?"

Yes. A field. The field was the dropping-off point for Hugo's bash. Everyone was climbing over a stile and walking a hundred metres or so towards two massive illuminated marquees. The way was marked with tea lights, making all the half-pissed teenagers look sophisticated as they avoided muddy puddles.

"I'm so frickin' glad I've got wedges on," Jass said, stumbling again. "Though I can't believe Hugo's making us walk in this weather."

The place looked like a summer music festival, even though it was November. And therefore freezing and pitch-black already. Bree crossed her arms over herself, wishing she was old enough for a coat to be fashionably allowed again. They shivered their way past the candles, drinking it all in.

"Jesus, Jass, your boyfriend is in a different realm of wealth."

She nodded a bit too enthusiastically. "I know. Just wait till you see the boating lake."

As they got nearer, Bree could make out more of the set-up through the dark. The main house was huge, naturally. All Ye-Olde-style, but obviously modernized to within an inch of its life. There was another, smaller, building to the side, just off the drive.

"The servants' house," Jass informed her. "Though they don't have any now. Hugo just uses it as a house party venue…"

It wasn't really a garden, it was practically a National Trust landmark. Okay, Bree's garden would have made most regular eyes bulge, but at least she didn't have marble statues dotted around. Or a maze.

"We had sex once in the middle," Jass informed her as they passed it, Bree all agog.

The party was already humming but it was a struggle to work out where to go first. The biggest tent had a live band playing and shedloads of people were crammed in, sweating all over the place, and generally moshing…which Bree had read about once but never actually seen in real life.

Mosh pits. Holdo had a whole lot to say about mosh pits. *"It's not appreciating the music,"* he would have said if he was here. *"It's just showing off. You should have to pass an IQ test before you're allowed to listen to certain bands live."*

But Holdo wasn't here. He didn't have an invite. Whatever test you needed to pass to get into Hugo's eighteenth, he'd failed it. Not that Holdo would care.

The smaller – but still huge – tent had a DJ pumping out noise and guests were dancing madly, a throbbing mass of bodies as the strobe lights hit them. Then there was a bar tent – free bar, naturally. A toilet block tent. A tent that had obviously been erected for the sole purpose of people exchanging bodily fluids – there were pillows and cushions everywhere. There was even a tent full of shisha pipes.

"Where do we start?" Bree called over to Jass, yelling a little to ensure she was heard over the pounding music.

"Er…duh, let's go to the bar?"

"You don't think you need to take it easy for a bit first?"

Jass wrinkled her nose. "Er. No? Loser."

And she stumbled off across the field. Bree sighed again and followed.

The bar seemed to be home to everyone who was anyone. Gemma, Jessica, and Emily were all already there and screamed when they saw them.

"You guys, you're so fashionably late!" Jessica rounded them up into an overexcited group hug. "Bree, that dress is awesome."

"Thanks."

"We had a few cocktails at mine first." Jass giggled. "Where's Hugo?"

"Oh, he's around here somewhere. Pretending he's King of the Universe," Gemma said. She was wearing some weird neon lace dress. It didn't look great. But, of course, because it was Gemma, the whole world was tricked into thinking she looked hot.

"That's my boyfriend you're talking about."

"Chill, Jazzy Spazzy, you know what he's like when he gets a lot of attention."

Jassmine's eyebrows furrowed. "Are girls throwing themselves at him?"

Bree gulped. Scared for those girls. Scared a little for herself...

"What do you think?"

Jassmine straightened out her playsuit menacingly. "Right, let's find him and sort this out."

"Chill, Jass," Jessica said, her eyes wide and nervous. "Have a drink first."

"Okay."

That didn't take much persuading.

As Jassmine's sort-of friend – bar the about-to-backstab-her part – Bree thought it best if Jass didn't have anything else to drink. The others didn't agree. In fact, they tipped alcohol down her like it was water.

"Raspberry mojitos!" Gemma yelled, pushing a straw into Jassmine's mouth like she was a baby bird. Jass sucked obligingly. "It's always good to get her just that little bit more pissed when she gets psycho jealous," she muttered to Bree. "Otherwise innocent girls' eyes get plucked out."

"Riiiiiight," she replied. "Jass? Do you want a shot of sambuca?"

Jass nodded.

They stayed at the bar for a while, checking everyone else out, sneering at people they didn't think should've been invited. Emily was far too grateful to be there, it was almost pathetic. She squealed and pointed at every single detail. A few shots sorted her out though. Bree hadn't done shots before, and she couldn't help but think of the disdain that would no doubt be on Holdo's face if he could see her now... downing shots of tequila and licking salt off Gemma's chest, plucking a piece of lemon out of Jass's mouth – all as men looked on helplessly, their pupils (and trousers) bulging with lust.

"Now this is what I like to see," said Hugo as he and his mates arrived out of nowhere just as Bree was halfway through sharing a lemon slice with Jessica. "Bree, I didn't think you were the type."

Bree wiped her mouth delicately and looked him straight

in the eye. "Well, this party's so crap, there was nothing for it but to get drunk."

"I know," he said, looking around at the hundreds of people dancing on the lawn, laughing, snogging. "It's really flopping, isn't it?"

"HUGO!"

Jass launched herself at him like a missile, winding all her limbs around him at once.

"Jass? How much have you had to drink?" He sounded annoyed.

"Not much," she said, her false indignation ruined by a stray hiccup. "Anyway, it's your eighteenth, I wanted to make sure we celebrate it in style."

Matty appeared from behind Hugo and spotted Bree.

"Bree, you made it." He high-fived her. "We didn't know if you girls were coming."

"What? And miss the sight of you all pissing in Hugo's lake?"

"Oi," Hugo said. "No slashing in the garden. There's a toilet block for a reason."

Seth swayed out from behind Hugo, a strong contender for someone drunker than Jass.

"Guys, when the hell are we gonna start dancing?"

"Good point," Hugo said. "Come on, to the dance tent."

And the gaggle of them left the bar and entered the strobe-y glow of the dance marquee.

chapter twenty-nine

There must, Bree thought, *be a correlation between popularity and one's ability to dance without looking like an absolute twat.*

And as she had only recently become popular, this stint in the dance tent was possibly her biggest test yet.

Hip hop was playing. Actual hip hop. And in true, upper-middle-class Britishness, this meant that all the girls had temporarily forgotten their ethnicity and were dancing like they had the right body parts to shimmy.

The other girls, though, were just about pulling it off.

Gemma played the part of the pole, and the other girls gyrated around her. If they weren't tossing their hair, they were either stroking their boobs or crotch.

Bree supposed with popularity came confidence, and it takes confidence to grind down to the ground, open your legs, and shimmy back up again, while maintaining a nonchalant look of disinterest and being watched by an entire rugby team.

She didn't know what to do. She couldn't dance, no one had ever taught her. She'd once been dragged to a cousin's fancy wedding and managed to get through by pointing her finger in the air. If she tried to be sexy in the conventional way, she would fail instantly. There was nothing for it but to brazen out some kind of invented move and hope people thought it was the new thing.

She shrugged her shoulders mechanically and jolted her body about in time to the music. She then added in a little step-tap, step-tap. And then decided to look completely and utterly bored by the whole process.

"Wooooahhhhhhhhhhhhhh, go Bree!" Gemma yelled.

When the girls subtly altered their dance moves to look more like hers, she knew she'd pulled it off.

The music was thumping, the beat infectious – although Bree would still never listen to it anywhere else. Hugo and the lads were jumping on top of each other's backs, spilling beer over each other, or doing lame attempts at dancing too. Jassmine was getting more and more disorientated. She kept flicking her hair back. It wasn't falling into place any more though – instead it was becoming more dishevelled. And once she noticed Bree getting attention, she took action. She hurled herself into the middle of their makeshift circle, grabbed Hugo and pulled him towards her. She turned her back to him and grinded up against him, using her arse. She'd obviously picked up a few tips from that recent documentary, *Lap Dancing Uncovered*. Bree thought Hugo would love it, but in fact he looked a bit uncomfortable. Each time Jassmine flicked her hair back, it whipped him in the face. She didn't notice. She was too determinedly channelling her inner stripper.

Distracted, Bree felt something rub up against her bottom. Something…bulgy. She whipped her head round.

It was Matty. Grinding on her.

"What the hell do you think you're doing?"

He grinned. "Come on, it's just dancing."

"No. It's sexual assault. Get your bollocks off me. Now."

Matty laughed and did as she said.

"COCKBLOCK!" Seth yelled, his face all sweaty.

Everyone laughed. She caught Hugo's eyes and a moment passed between them. A shiver ran down her back. She lost her balance on the grass in her wedges and tripped a little.

"You okay?" Jessica caught her and pulled her up.

"Yeah I'm fine."

"Matty SO fancies you." She sounded almost wistful.

"Nah, he just got horny watching the Jass and Hugo sex show."

She looked back at them but Hugo had disappeared. Jass stood with her arms wrapped round herself looking confused and upset.

"He. Just. Left!" she half-screeched, punching her fists towards the ground like a child on the verge of a tantrum.

"Abort the tent. Abort the tent," Gemma yelled cheerfully

into Bree's ear, and the girly gang bustled Jass out of the marquee, leaving the rugby boys behind.

She was wasted. Losing it. Bree had never seen Jass like this before.

"Where's Hugo?" she yelled into the darkness. A group of passing girls stared at her. Bree steered her away by the shoulders.

"Come on, let's get you some fresh air away from the tents."

"Do you know where he is?" she demanded. "I bet you do. You've always fancied him, haven't you?"

Bree was about to protest but Gemma put her hand on Bree's shoulder.

"Ignore her. She accuses one of us of shagging him every time she gets really drunk." She turned to Jass. "Come on, Jassy-min. Bree doesn't fancy Hugo. And even if she did, he's only got eyes for you."

They coaxed her towards a quieter bit of the party – a pond with a water fountain lit up by sparkling lights. Away from the music and fuss, Jass appeared even more wasted. She slumped on a bench and slid down to one side.

"HUGO?"

Christ – she sounded nuts.

"He's coming. He's just saying hello to all the guests."

"Hugo. I LOVE YOU!"

"And he loves you too, sweetheart."

"You. Bree! She wants to shag him – well you can't, HE'S MINE."

"Jass, I don't want to shag your boyfriend."

"Okay then."

She was momentarily satisfied and closed her eyes. The lights lit up her face and, it had to be said, Jass had looked better. She was sticky with sweat, she'd smeared half her make-up off, and her hair was sticking to her head. Jessica and Emily came and crouched round their Queen, offering noises of encouragement.

"Jassmine, are you okay?"

"Don't worry, Hugo will be back soon."

"You look so pretty tonight."

Gemma rolled her eyes at Bree.

Jassmine smiled, her eyes still closed, then she opened her mouth to talk again...

"...I'm gonna be sick."

"Quick," Bree yelled, "into the pond."

It was too late. Jass vomited – gross, cherry-smelling vom – all over the perfect patio stones.

Nobody really knew where to look. It was like seeing Her Majesty the Queen blowing chunks all over Buckingham Palace. Bree scooped back the majority of her hair and patted her on the back.

The puking went on for a while.

"Jass, you okay?"

She spat onto the paving stones. "I'm fine, thanks. I'm just going to lie down here for a moment."

"No, not in the puke!"

And hats off to Gemma, she grabbed her away just

in time. Jass collapsed on the bench and promptly fell asleep – a big grin on her face.

Everyone looked round at each other. With Jass unconscious, Bree gave the instructions.

"Okay. We need to get Jass somewhere warm. Do you reckon you guys could carry her to the chill-out tent?"

Gemma nodded in agreement.

"But Jass won't want anyone to see her like this," Jessica protested.

"She also won't want hypothermia. Will you help walk her?"

"Okay then."

"It's pitch-black, no one will see. Just put her in a quiet patch until she sobers up."

Gemma began tapping Jassmine's face.

"Jass, wake up, honey."

Jass batted her away with her eyes still closed.

"Go away. Bad baby."

"Jass, do you think you can get up and walk with us to the chill-out room?"

"I think you're a poo-poo head." And then Jass opened her eyes and threw her face back laughing.

Gemma smiled wryly. "Ladies and gentlemen, she's back with us."

"POO-POO HEAD, POO-POO HEAD!" Jass laughed manically.

"Bree?"

"Yeah?"

"She still looks a bit pasty. Do you mind going into Hugo's house and finding a medicine cabinet? There must be one in one of the bathrooms. Hopefully there'll be those diarrhoea sachets in there – you know? The powder you add to water they give dehydrated people? Diro-rite or something? Well, they're also brilliant at sobering people up. Do you mind having a look?"

"Not at all. Is she okay, you reckon?"

"She's always fine after she's sick. Bloody Hugo though. She only ever gets like this when he's not treating her well. I told her not to go back there but she…well, it's Hugo, isn't it? Who wouldn't?"

Bree couldn't disagree.

"Which one's his house?" she joked.

Gemma smiled. "Oh, it's quite hard to find. It's a very modest little place – shall I draw you a map?"

Between Gemma and Jessica and Emily, they managed to heave Jass up and did a stagger-sway walk back towards the party.

Bree walked on ahead, scared she would trip in her massive wedges over a branch or something. It was so dark, but the lights from the party beckoned her towards the big house. As she got nearer, she could tell by the vibe that the party was peaking – peaking into a drunken hedonistic mess. There were couples everywhere, snogging against tents, groping each other with that unabashed lack of insecurity that alcohol gives you. She dodged more than a few puddles of sick. It was hard to get anywhere quickly as everyone she passed seemed desperately pleased to see her, trying to embrace her in a group hug, or pull her towards the music tent to watch "the totally awesome band". The noise was deafening and disorientating.

She finally got to Hugo's house and slid a glass door to one side, closing it behind her. She leaned against it and savoured the quiet for a moment, sighing. She'd felt okay with drunker people around her…but in the quiet warmth of Hugo's kitchen, she realized she was pretty wasted too. It took a moment or so to calm her thoughts and stop her head spinning. She looked around. It was a very nice kitchen… black everything, with every state-of-the-art mod con the world had invented.

Right, medicine cabinet.

She walked down a long cream corridor, cautiously opening doors and hoping she wouldn't find anyone behind them. She wasn't sure where Hugo's parents were, but he'd been pretty insistent that his house was out of bounds during the party. Perhaps they were holed up in their bedroom somewhere? Watching nervously from behind the curtains and wincing whenever they heard a smash. If that was the case, she didn't want to be the one who disturbed them. But room after room was empty. She found a gym, a sitting room, a dining room with a chandelier and enough seats for the UN summit, and at least five spare bedrooms. It didn't take long to find a bathroom with a hopeful-looking cupboard. She found the Diro-rite amongst the usual paracetamol and antidepressants. She grabbed two sachets and was about to make her way back into the party when she spotted an unexplored room, the door ajar. Through the gap she could see a sleazy poster.

It had to be Hugo's bedroom.

She knew she needed to get back. That Jassmine needed looking after. The kind, sensible side of her brain told her to take the sachets, give them to Jass, and help cover up her drunkenness like a good popular citizen. But the bitter side of her reminded her that Hugo was the next big rule to tick off on her manifesto list. That he was a key part of this social experiment. And that any scrap of information about him would help her piece together the weird puzzle of who he really was.

Plus what girl on earth didn't want to have a prod around Hugo's bedroom? Or Francesco's bedroom? Or <insert your secondary school crush here>'s bedroom?

So she widened the door and walked in.

It was blue, obviously. What teenage boy's bedroom wasn't blue? With a king-sized bed and smart chequered duvet cover. It smelled of Hugo's aftershave, with an underlying hint of boy-smell. She was disappointed to see Hugo's choice in posters was as clichéd as his choice of girlfriend.

Generic uninspired poster no. 1: Reservoir Dogs. I.e. *I have watched one decent macho film and am therefore cool, deep and amazing.*

Generic uninspired poster no. 2: That black-and-white shot of two girls in their underwear lying on a bed, tonguing each other. I.e. *I fancy women, WOMEN, get it?*

Generic uninspired poster no. 3: A shot of Jonny Wilkinson and co. winning the Rugby World Cup in 2003. I.e. *I AM rugby*.

She blew her fringe up and browsed his bookshelf. Usually the highlight in anyone's bedroom. Hugo's was, again, disappointing. Only GCSE set texts, a few toilet books that were obviously unwanted Christmas presents and a Guinness Book of World Records left over from childhood.

Bree's eyes made her way to the top of his bookcase where there were a few framed photos. One of his family, all smiling on a luxury yacht. And one of Hugo holding up the inter-school cup the rugby team had won last year. She picked up the frame and traced the outline of his face. It was annoying how fit he was...

"Having a good peek, are you?"

Bree dropped the photo. It fell onto the carpet with a thud. "Hugo! I...umm..."

He stood in the doorway, leaning against the frame with a smile on his face. He was rosy-cheeked and his hair was a bit sweaty. "I always knew I would get you into my bedroom eventually but I thought you'd make it a bit harder for me."

Still stunned, she said, "I was just, er, looking for this..." She held up the medicine packet.

"Diro-rite? You got the squits, Bree?" He wrinkled his nose.

Bree looked at the packet and made the connection. "NO! God, no, it's not for me. It's for Jassmine."

He screwed up his face. "Jassy has the squits?"

Bree fought the urge to say yes out of spitefulness. "No. She's just a bit, er, sick, that's all. Gemma said drinking one of these will help."

He walked in. With every step, Bree's heartbeat thumped harder.

"Is she wasted?"

Bree rocked her hand from side to side and Hugo rolled his eyes in reply.

"Has she been sick?"

"A bit, yeah."

"Ahhh, she'll be fine then. She's always fine after she's vommed."

He walked past her to his desk and fiddled about on his laptop for a bit. Bree, unsure what to do, picked up the fallen photo and put it back on the shelf.

"Anyway...I'd better go...see how Jass is."

Music came out of Hugo's speakers.

"I'm not letting you go that easily."

And, before she knew what was happening, he was in front of her – right up in her face.

"Hugo, what are you doing?"

She'd never been this close to him before; she could smell the alcohol on his breath. It wasn't gross, more overpoweringly sweet.

He took a step closer. "Nothing."

Another step.

"Sexual harassment is illegal, you know?" Her heart

started to beat so fast it hurt. She swore his eyes had special powers – and those eyelashes…

He touched her cheek softly and her face automatically leaned into it.

"The thing about harassment, Bree, is that it's only harassment if it's unwanted."

She carefully removed his hand. "And what makes you think I want you to touch me?"

He answered her by kissing her. Full on. With no build-up or introduction or anything. It was an aggressive kiss; his tongue conquered her mouth and he tasted how he smelled – sickly sweet. It was like sipping honey.

Bree kissed him back for a bit – she didn't mean to… well, she did – but managed to stop herself after a second or so. "What are you doing?"

He grinned mischievously, grabbed her arse and pulled her into him. "What do you think I'm doing?"

He kissed her again. It annoyingly felt so nice that it took another few seconds before she found the willpower to stop again.

"Hugo. You can't just go around kissing people."

"Why not?"

"What about your girlfriend?"

He actually looked confused for a moment, before realization dawned. "What? Jassmine?"

"Yes – Jassmine. Girlfriend. Remember?"

He dismissed the objection. "Well, aren't you supposed to be her mate?"

"I've not been kissing you back."

"Yes, you have."

"No, I haven't."

"You want to."

"No, I don't."

"Yes, you do."

She sighed. This was what was supposed to happen. She knew she'd played him just right. The trouble was, maybe it was the alcohol, or maybe it was Jassmine being a surprisingly good friend earlier, or maybe it was because that good friend needed looking after, or maybe it was because she was supposed to extract vital blog material about Hugo's character before any of this happened, but it was all suddenly going too fast and she was scared stiff. She felt guilty, and also a bit...aroused.

"Hugo, just because I'm a girl doesn't mean I automatically want you."

"Doesn't it?" And he burst out laughing.

"You're so full of it."

"And you're so fit." He put his mouth on hers again and it was so hard to resist this time. *Fit.* An actual boy had just called her "fit". The word turned her brain to candyfloss. Yes, that shouldn't matter. And yes she wanted her thoughts and feelings to be recognized, and they were OBVIOUSLY more important than how she looked...

And yet...no one, not one person had ever called her fit before. Or pretty. Or attractive. Or that, ever-so-rare but gorgeous word...beautiful. They were adjectives reserved for other people. Other girls. Until tonight.

She felt herself being pushed backwards onto Hugo's bed. She sank into the Egyptian cotton with her eyes closed and got lost in the sense of being kissed by someone. Someone who really knew how to kiss a girl. She could feel the weight of Hugo on her, pinning her down, his hands sliding up and down her waist. He let out a small grunt, and his hand slid down her leg, and then back up again, but back up under her skirt.

Her eyes flickered open. Her scars – he'd find them, feel them.

"Wait."

He didn't stop. Just made another guttural sound as his hand climbed higher.

"Hugo, wait."

He broke off and looked down at her, annoyed. "What?"

"What's your favourite book?"

He looked even more pissed off. "Huh?"

"Book. As in reading. What's your favourite one?"

He wiggled his eyebrows. "I dunno. *The Kama Sutra?*"

She sighed again. "Are you actually thick? Or do you just pretend to be to fit in with all the rugby players?"

"I'm horny."

He pushed her back down again. His hand went straight to where it had been before. Bree gasped. He hadn't noticed her thighs, and his hand had already bypassed right by them. Upwards...

"You like that, do you?"

She couldn't tell if she was turned on or terrified. Her heart now felt like a hummingbird was crashing inside her chest and she couldn't really breathe properly. This was the plan, right? So why did it feel like it was going so wrong?

Hugo got more aggressive. His tongue was so invasive there wasn't much space for her own tongue. She was trying not to gag. His hands grabbed random parts of her flesh and squeezed them so hard it hurt. Was this what foreplay was like? And if so, was this what sex would be like? Was she going to have it? She needed something – a look, a gentle caress, a small whisper – to reassure her that she wasn't just meat, that he did *like* her.

"Hugo?" She tried to get the words out but was muffled by his large exploring tongue. He groaned again, sounding more and more like an animal. She felt a tickle between her legs and realized he had expertly slid down her knickers. She lurched up and broke free from his mouth.

"Hugo?" she said louder.

The look on his face was uber-mad now. She didn't know what to do. She'd lost control somehow.

"What?!"

She was almost too ashamed to ask the question. It shouldn't matter anyway; she wasn't doing this for love. But she had to hear the answer. The tiny part of Bree left that had self-respect, that didn't want to sacrifice everything to the cause, needed to hear it.

"Do you like me?"

It sounded stupid the moment she said it. So dumb. So needy.

Hugo grinned. "Of course I like you."

She looked down at the chequered duvet. "Yeah, but what do you like about me?"

His face softened. Finally – a streak of humanity. He made his eyes wide and nudged her face with his head. "I dunno, but you're just amazing. You're not like any other girl I've met before."

The words floated down to her belly button where they melted like throat lozenges.

"Really?" She hated the way her voice sounded.

"Really."

He kissed her again and she kissed him back for all she was worth, running her hands up into his hair. Hugo pushed her back down and showered her face and neck with more kisses.

And that was where the romance ended.

chapter thirty

Afterwards Hugo went into the en suite to "have a piss". Bree lay there, pulling her dress down, and listened to him peeing. It went on for a long time.

Had he needed that the whole time they were...you know? It would explain why it hadn't taken very long.

Thank God.

The trickling stopped and Hugo emerged from the bathroom. "You good to go back to the party?"

Her head jerked back in shock. "What? Now?"

He walked over to his computer and turned off the music.

"Er, yeah. It's my eighteenth, remember? I appreciate the present and all" – he said it in such a leery way that she flinched – "but I need to get back out there. Plus, Jass will be wondering where we are." He tapped his nose like they'd just shared a hilarious secret. A secret that didn't involve the blood in Bree's knickers, the aching between her legs, and the ballooning shame and disappointment in her stomach.

"I just thought we could...you could..."

"What?"

Let me lay my head in your lap while you stroke my hair and tell me all your feelings? Tell me how special I am...how special that was? Acknowledge the fact you've just ejaculated inside me and how big a deal that is? Say you love me...that you've always loved me? Reassure me that it won't always hurt, that we'll take it slower next time, and you'll light candles, and whisper in my ear how beautiful I am throughout so I feel like a human? ANYTHING OTHER THAN THIS.

A lump caught in her throat. "I dunno. Forget it."

Hugo stretched his hands out behind his back. "Cool. See you out there. Feel free to use my bathroom to clean up."

He left.

He left. Just like that.

chapter thirty-one

Bree tidied herself up.

Her exterior was spic and span after a quick mopping session in the bathroom, but her interior screamed and writhed in confused, mangled pain.

The cold air hit her the moment she stepped back out into Party Central. She stepped over a couple lying horizontally on the patio, their lips almost surgically attached.

They're going to get piles of the entire body, she thought to herself. And felt proud of herself for making a joke.

The music tent had become been-there-done-that in the short time she'd been away and everyone was crammed into the dance tent. She peered in. Glow paint had been distributed and neon teenagers jumped together as a heaving singular organism. She didn't know the song at all, but apparently everyone was very excited by the singers taking their brains to another dimension. She caught a glimpse of Hugo. He was dead central in the hedonistic mass, jumping up and down with his finger pointing in the air, his head thrown back in ecstasy. Everyone had their arms around him. She felt sick. The strobe lights made it worse. She couldn't make out Jassmine or any of the others in the flickering, jarring blue light, so continued to the chill-out tent.

"BRRRRRRRREEEEEEEEEEEEEEEEEEEEEEEEEEEEE!"

Jassmine flung her arms round her before she'd even got into the tent properly.

"Hello, Jassmine." She hugged her back.

Gemma appeared behind them.

"What the hell took you so long?" She was suspicious. Of course she was.

Bree waved the Diro-rite. "I got lost in his stupid mansion, didn't I? I bet that place has its own postcode."

"You've been almost an hour. Jass was sick again. I had to hide the cushion she vommed on in the rowing boat."

Only an hour? And so many undoable things had happened. Jass did smell a bit sicky, but Bree felt so guilty she kept hugging her anyway. Like guilt was something you could squeeze out.

"I'm here now. Let's give her this medicine. Which, by the way, Hugo saw and so he now thinks I'm leaking poo."

Gemma's eye's narrowed. "You've seen Hugo?"

Damn, maybe mentioning him to show she wasn't scared

of mentioning him meant actually she did look suspicious rather than if she hadn't mentioned him at all.

"He helped me find my way out of his house."

And took my virginity and now I want to die.

"He's not come here ONCE to see if Jass is okay."

Ahh, *that* was why she was snooping.

"Really? That's pretty low."

Bree released Jassmine and told Jessica to fetch a glass of water to dissolve the medicine into. She lay back on a cushion, her brain tired and lost...and not expecting Jassmine to lay back with her.

"Bree?" she whispered. The faint whiff of sick was on her breath, and her eyes were wide and childlike. "Have you seen Hugo?"

At the mention of his name, more emotions tumbled into her belly. "Briefly, why?"

Her wide eyes got dewy with new tears. "He's barely seen me all night. I've not even had a chance to give him his present."

"I saw him in the dance tent, why don't you go find him?"

She shook her head stubbornly. "No. He has to come to me. That's the only way I'll know."

"Know what?"

"That he does actually love me."

A wave of nausea hit Bree – she felt like she was on a ferry, about to capsize in a storm.

She couldn't do this. She had to leave.

Now.

She hobbled to her feet.

"Bree? Where you going?"

"I, er, I don't feel very well."

"Have some of my diarrhoea medicine."

At that moment, Jessica returned with the water.

"Here you go. Do you want to add the stuff?" Bree pushed past her, shoving the packet into Jessica's hand.

"Bree? Where you off to?"

"I don't feel well. I'm gonna go home."

"What?" Gemma said. "Just have a lie-down. We've got Jassmine sorted now, and she's twelve times more pissed than you are."

"No. Thanks. I just want to get home."

And she ran out of the tent into the blackness.

As she waited for her taxi, ankle-deep in mud, Bree tried to think of things to stop the gloom spreading through her bloodstream like a lethal injection.

Reasons why losing my virginity to Hugo wasn't so terrible after all

1. He used a condom

So there was no chance of producing a mini-Hugo as a lifelong reminder of what a horrible, disgusting, despicable thing she had just done. Plus there was no chance of catching some gross STI, which he no doubt had.

2. No sexual encounter will ever be as disappointing

Which would be nice if she planned to have sex ever again, which she really didn't. If that was sex, it could go do one. It wasn't anything like she'd read or seen about sex before. Even literary books that won awards for their "realism" had the girls writhing in orgasmic bliss. What a con! She'd endured the whole experience trying not to vocalize her pain and therefore couldn't even think about having one of those orgasms everyone goes on about. From her own measly experience, orgasms were figments of women's imaginations – used as some kind of deluded fantasy to gift-wrap the fact that, when it really comes down to it, men just mount you like lions do on the Discovery Channel.

3.   He said "That was great" afterwards, which, even though she shouldn't care, must have meant she wasn't particularly bad at sex

Which, again, was futile. As she never wanted to put this "skill" to use ever again.

4.   It's material, it's material, it's material

The reason why she did it. She could write about it now. Losing your virginity is always of interest. But she wasn't sure if she could relive the last hour in her brain to put it into words. It would make it more true, more dirty, more horrid, horrid, horrid.

Yet, if she didn't write about it, then what? What had she done it for?

She didn't sob the whole cab ride home; she still didn't know how. Instead Bree stared out at the winter sky and felt the inky blackness fill her entirely. It sank through the windows and into her like vapour. She felt the dark grow inside her, killing off everything like a toxic gas.

Sometimes, when she got this low, she didn't want to hurt herself.

Not because she wasn't down, more the opposite. She was too down to even bother spending the time on herself.

Tonight there was only numb left.

There was no desire to do anything other than creep into her house quietly and lie flat on the bed, her eyes on the ceiling, staring indefinitely, thinking nothingness.

The next morning, after sleep finally found her, the numbness was still there. There was ice in her veins, hardening up her blood, making her arteries bulge like milk smashing its bottle when left outside in the snow. She was vaguely aware of her mum coming in, talking some nonsense about the party, asking how it was, whether she wanted to come to body combat or not. Bree just turned over in bed and stared out the window.

Her mum left.

The sun moved from one side of Bree's window to the other.

Her eyeballs filmed over from lack of blinking.

Still there was nothing but numb.

Maybe it went quickly, or maybe it dragged on for ages, but eventually the sun left and the dark sky came back.

She got up only once.

To sit at her desk and type slowly and lethargically at her computer.

Rule number three: One must have sex with other attractive people

So I'm attractive.

I'm mates with other attractive people and have been drip-feeding you all of their secrets. What's next on the list?

Why, I must have a love interest, mustn't I?

And, in the spirit of the living-the-teenage-dream cliché, who better to have "a love interest" with than the most attractive and popular member of the opposite sex? And by "love interest", I mean "sex". Because we can flirt and kiss all we want, but that's not what interests you, is it?

There's always one, isn't there? That special someone when you're growing up and surviving school. That one person who shines a little brighter than the other pennies.

But they're not just your special someone. They're the whole school's special someone.

We all fall for them at the same time like Lust Lemmings, catapulting ourselves in their direction, sprucing ourselves up each morning for that one chance encounter in the corridor. Everybody wants to be the person they pick, the one they choose to live a perfect couple existence with.

You've got their name in your head?

That's nice, because they probably don't know you exist. Let alone that you think about them constantly.

Well I did it. I got him.

Oh yes, I ignored romance and self-esteem and saving-yourself-for-love and all the other nonsense that you shouldn't really ignore if you can possibly help it... That special guy in my school...I just gave him my virginity.

How I wish I could tell you all the gory details – and I know this is probably the most interesting thing I've done so far – but I just can't, readers, I can't.

You'll want to know if it hurt, probably. What he said. How we did it. What positions. Was it romantic? Has it changed me as a person?

All I can say is that I've sacrificed a lot in the pursuit of being interesting, and I just took it too far.

Worse than that, I took it to a point where I can't undo it. Virginity loss isn't something you can Tippex out, or erase with a rubber and blow away the dusty bits.

And while some of you may be gagging with jealousy that I lost it to the captain of the rugby team, I can honestly say I'd be very happy to swap places.

Because here's the thing. We don't KNOW these love obsessions of ours. If you're a loser like I was, you don't chat with them, you don't spend time with them, you usually only admire them from afar. And the problem with attractive people is that you can project an attractive personality onto them.

In my case, that personality wasn't there.

I tried for you guys, and for myself, to worm some information out of him. To glean an insight into his mind, his heart, his soul. I wish I could tell you that he opened his heart up to me afterwards. That I lay my head in his lap and he told me everything about his overbearing parents, and his favourite book, and what his childhood was like, and how much pressure there is on him to be the most popular guy in school…

But he just pulled up his zipper and left.

And though that might be interesting news to you, it's kinda heartbreaking for me.

So. I'm sorry, folks, but that's it. Rule three is finished as quickly as it started.

chapter thirty-two

"Bree?"

She didn't hear him.

"Bree?"

Huh?

"Bree? Are you okay?"

She could see Mr Fellows's mouth move. And yet his words were garbled and nonsensical, like she was underwater.

She half-nodded her head.

"I said, are you okay?"

Bree heard him that time. She nodded properly. Her head felt like it weighed ten tonnes. "Yes. I'm fine."

Mr Fellows bent down so his face was level with hers.

"Seriously? Are you alright? You've barely spoken all session."

It was Monday afternoon, after school. The big Monday

after the big party and she was running the creative-writing workshop. Well, her body was. Her mind was elsewhere entirely. The truth was, no, Bree wasn't really okay at all. She'd blown Jassmine off that morning, couldn't bear the thought of seeing her. Or pretending to be a good friend. She'd sent a text saying she felt sick then skulked around school all day like a ninja, making sure nobody saw her.

Listening in on corridor conversations though, she learned that Jass had successfully fed everyone a brilliant lie that she'd had her drink spiked at Hugo's party. It was a genius cover-up for such a public spectacle – now nobody could take the piss out of her trashed behaviour. And the rumour was that Hugo and she were even more in love after he helped her through the "ordeal".

Hugo… Bree had spent the whole of yesterday with the duvet over her face, half-smothering herself, counting to a hundred and back again, a hundred and back again, to pass time. She didn't get this dark often, thankfully, but when she did it was terrible. Worse than when she hurt herself. At least then she felt something, not just nothingness. But this was like the universe was treacle and she was stuck in it. Just moving was effort. The treacle piled on top of her head and made everything hurt and her brain turn to sludge. She'd bumped into Holdo on her way to Latin and he'd seen it in her eyes immediately. Despite the fact they never talked any more, he'd stopped her.

"Bree? Are you okay?" He went to grab her hand but stopped himself. "You look…you know."

He'd always been so great when she got like this. No questions. No pushing her. No "snap out of it"s. Holdo would just silently put on one gruesome horror film after another and let Bree lie on his sofa, watching them sideways, until it passed.

But that was then and this was now, and so Bree just muttered "I'm fine" and pushed past him. Not able to handle the sympathy in his face. She didn't deserve it. She didn't deserve anything.

Lessons over, here she was in creative writing, a bunch of overeager Year Sevens scribbling away at an exercise she couldn't even remember giving them, and Mr Fellows's face in her face.

"Has something happened? No offence, Bree, but you look...well...not great."

She stretched her arms up and yawned. She'd not bothered with her appearance today, just like the good old times when she was nobody and Hugo's body parts hadn't been inside her. She exhaled dramatically. "I'm...fine. Honestly. It's just...you know."

Mr Fellows sat next to her. "No. I don't know."

"It's just, what's the point? That's it. What's the point? In anything?"

It exhausted her just getting those words out. She closed her eyes for longer than she probably should have but it felt nice.

"Bree. Has something happened to you?"

"No. Yes. I dunno."

She couldn't talk to him here. Not with all the kids around, trying to listen in. Could she talk to him anyway? He was a teacher. And he liked her. And he wouldn't like her if he knew what had happened. What she'd done wasn't a Bree thing to do. It would ruin his view of her – and his was the only view that really mattered.

"Why don't we chat after creative writing is finished?"

She found herself nodding.

Half an hour later, Bree sat on Mr Fellows's desk, rolling a yellow pencil back and forth.

"So are you going to tell me what's wrong?"

She rolled the pencil off the table by accident. It landed on the carpet without making a sound.

"Is this in your job spec, sir? Or am I supposed to go to the school counsellor or something?"

He sighed and rubbed his face. "A student's welfare is my business, Bree."

"Is that all I am? A student?"

She expected him to get mad. Defensive. Like he always did when she pushed the boundaries. This time he didn't. He just moved a little closer.

"You know you're more than a student, Bree."

The darkness lifted a little.

"You're a friend... And friends tell each other when something's up."

She couldn't tell him. It would wreck her in his eyes.

"It was just…Hugo's party."

"What happened?" he asked. "You're worrying me."

But she couldn't say. He wouldn't get it.

She stood up. "Just forget it."

Bree went to leave but he grabbed her arm.

"Stop."

She looked at where he was touching her. He didn't let go.

"What are you doing tomorrow?" he almost whispered.

"Huh?"

His face looked urgent. Conspiratorial. "Tomorrow."

"Umm, coming here. As always. Why?"

His touch on her softened but he didn't remove his hand.

"How would you feel about going on a field trip? An educational one. Just you and me?"

It was against all the rules. Logic, as always, pinged straight into her brain, listing all the reasons why this was wrong. But that's not how you live, is it? Through logic. So, like unwanted dinner guests, Bree pushed the thoughts from her brain to make room for spontaneity. And excitement.

She nodded. "That sounds…perfect."

And it did.

She saw in his face that her answer had prompted the same moral battle and she watched as it raged within him. But his brain obviously came to the same conclusion because he gave her a beaming smile.

"Shall we meet at the train station? Say, ten o'clock? I'll call in sick."

"Yes."

He let go of her and sat back. "It goes without saying, I guess, but you shouldn't tell anyone about this."

Bree smiled for the first time all day.

"Sir?" She was afraid to ask the question, but she needed to. "Why are you doing this?"

He scratched his head, pushing his hair back from his forehead. His entire face looked soft, like a velour teddy bear.

"Because sometimes it's just your turn to be there for someone, Bree. And I don't think you'll let anyone other than me be there for you right now."

Dangerous words. Dangerous, true words.

"Thank you."

"I'll see you tomorrow."

chapter thirty-three

Just as she felt able to breathe again, just as she felt safe again…she bumped into Hugo in the corridor. Literally bumped. Like bumper cars. When she saw who it was, all the suffocating black matter rushed back.

"Well, well, well, look who it is."

He did a full body scan. She resisted every urge to shudder and run. The collar of his polo shirt was thick with mud – rugby practice. She'd been stupid to think she was safe after school.

"Hello, Hugo."

He held his hands up. "Ooooo, so formal, Bree. That hardly seems appropriate, does it?"

Sick. Sick feeling in her stomach.

"Shh. Are you completely stupid?"

He ran his tongue along his top teeth. "I'm completely up for a repeat performance."

So much sickness and yet she couldn't tell him to slam his penis in a fridge door. He was too dangerous.

She lowered her voice to a hiss. "Aren't you supposed to lose interest now you've got what you wanted? Isn't that how you work?"

He laughed. A proper throw-your-head-back laugh.

"Aren't you supposed to become all clingy now and ask me to dump Jassmine and marry you?"

"Keep your voice down. Someone will hear."

He looked around. "So?"

"So? Do you want to piss on Jassmine's heart?"

"Mmmm. Kinky. I didn't know you were into water sports, Bree."

She couldn't bear to be near him. "You're disgusting." She turned on her heel to leave but he grabbed her wrist. Hard.

"Where are you going?"

His face was angry suddenly. Aggressive. Fear replaced the nausea.

"Away. Before you say something stupid. Loudly. And screw everything up."

"I hope this doesn't mean the end of our time together?"

"Jassmine is my friend." Bree stuck out her jaw. Maybe reasoning with his soul would work? He must have one somewhere, buried inside all that testosterone.

Hugo let go. "Funny…you weren't acting like her friend the other night."

"And you weren't acting like her boyfriend."

"Touché." He smiled. "And this is why we're so good together."

Bree mustered all the strength left in her drained body, grabbed his hand, and placed it on his own crotch.

"No. You and your hand are what's good together. And I really don't want to come between such a special relationship."

She stalked off down the corridor, leaving him laughing behind her.

The moment she got back into her empty home she got into bed. Her mum must've been out shopping, or yoga-ing, or wondering why her new perfect daughter had turned back into her old crappy daughter. Bree pulled the duvet over her face and allowed all the emotion she'd repressed since seeing Hugo to seep out of her. She bit her fist until tiny specks of blood emerged and she could taste the iron in her mouth. This brought back the nausea. She dragged her bin to her bedside and dry retched into it, spitting and gurgling up nothingness onto the top of a celeb magazine Jass had brought round. After that pleasantness passed, she stared at the ceiling, counting to a hundred and back again, trying not to think about the sharp objects in the en suite.

Hugo was dangerous. She'd known that from the start and that this part of her plan wouldn't be easy. What she hadn't counted on was a) growing more of a conscience and b) a sexual experience so awful that she couldn't bear even entertaining the thought of doing it again. This threw an oversized spanner into everything.

How could she keep him placated enough so he would leave her be, without being actually sick? He loved the chase, she knew that. But she could only fight him off for so long before he got frustrated and wanted to play a different game.

The darkness crept back in again. It started in the top corners of the ceiling and she watched as it edged down the walls. She could see an actual shadow creeping down towards her, ready to penetrate through her skin, pour through her veins and head straight to her heart. Making it all numb.

Bree had no will left to fight it.

But then, just as the blackness was about to reach her, she got out of bed and went to her special bookshelf. To let the books rescue her, like they always did.

She took out her copy of Jane Austen's *Persuasion* and flicked through to her favourite quote at the end.

"I am half agony, half hope."

The book fell open to the page, the quote still decorated with pink biro hearts Bree had intricately drawn all round it when she first read it many years ago. It was a quote about love, written in a letter to the heroine at the end, after a story of patience and longing and things never going as they should.

To Bree, it was a quote about her life.

Half of it was agony, the simple agony of being Bree, of seeing herself as the world saw her. Weird. Pointless. Nasty.

But the other half of her life was hope. Hope that it would all be worthwhile in the end, hope that she'd eventually stop hurting all the time.

Hope that the agony would produce words and sentences as beautiful as that one.

It was also a quote about love.

Mr Fellows...

She had a whole day with him tomorrow.

It was like a match being struck.

And the bad retreated as she fell asleep properly – for the first time in two days – a small smile on her troubled face, and the book clutched in her hand.

chapter thirty-four

Her legs wobbled as she walked to meet him at the station. Her knees, in fact, had grown a will of their own that didn't agree with the other parts of her lower limbs. It was like trying to run a marathon on tranquillizers.

Then, of course, there'd been the issue of what to wear.

Bree knew he wouldn't care. Not really. He'd kissed her in that awful champagne clingy mess at the leavers' ball. He'd seen her vast collection of neon stripy tights. Witnessed every statement hair colour. And…it wasn't even a date, was it?

Plus Bree had a brain. A brain he was interested in. She laughed as she realized it was kind of like her brain was going on a day trip today – like a witness protection person being allowed a restful day by the sea or something. She was allowed to say intellectual things today. She could talk about the books she'd been secretly reading. All this was wonderful, and yet it would be so lovely if she could just look…well, fantastic at the same time.

In the end she'd plumped for dark skinny jeans and a lacy black jumper, with a big faux fur cropped overcoat that made her feel like a glamorous spy. A touch of red lipstick and just a brushing of mascara finished the look off.

Oh – and she'd accidently-on-purpose hidden a Kafka book in her bag which she planned to accidently-on-purpose drop on the floor and say *"Oh, oops, silly me. Have you read this one?"* before looking up at him through her eyelashes, the very face of intellectuality, sexuality and innocence.

Well, that was the plan.

She pressed the button at the pelican crossing and waited for the green man to flash. She was only about twenty metres away from the station entrance and caught sight of Mr Fellows waiting for her. Her heart went into overdrive. He was here! She watched, amused, as he paced back and forth outside the sliding doors. He repeatedly checked his watch, looking troubled.

He hadn't seen Bree yet.

She crossed the road and walked up to meet him, her eyes on him the whole way. He kept turning his head from side to side, jumpy, looking for spies from school or something. And then, finally, he saw her.

She watched a conflicting range of emotions cross his face. Fear. Shock that she'd come, maybe? And then relief. His eyes softened and he couldn't help but smile as she walked up the steps.

There was an awkward moment when they didn't know how to greet each other. They performed some weird hug-kiss-dodge dance, before quickly and silently deciding on a polite British peck on the cheek.

"Bree, you came."

She grinned. "You sound surprised."

"No. Yes. Well, I didn't know if you would." Nervous energy poured out of him. His voice sounded crazed.

"I said I would, didn't I?" she said in a soft voice, trying to calm him.

"Yes of course. I've got you a Travelcard. Although I couldn't use a Young Persons Railcard to get a discount. Because of course I don't have one, do I? Cos I'm an old bugger. Not like you. So I just got you a regular one. Is that okay? That's okay, isn't it?"

"Sir. It's fine. Do you want some money for it?"

He flinched. "Oh God. You just called me sir. What are we doing, Bree?"

Away from the classroom, Mr Fellows seemed completely different. There was no authoritative desk between the two of them. He wasn't wearing his normal navy-blue suit, but a grey V-necked jumper and jeans, with a beanie hat covering most of his hair. It made everything even odder. Even more wrong. Yet, when Bree thought about how his eyes had looked when he'd seen her, she felt the happiest she had since she'd started this stupid project.

"I don't actually know your real name, Mr Fellows."

It was the stupidest thing to say. He sighed and put his hands over his face.

"Of course you don't. Oh God, seriously, Bree, what are we doing?"

She reached out and gently removed his hands, forcing him to look at her.

"We're not doing anything wrong."

"It's illegal."

"No it's not. I might just be bunking off school because I'm a seventeen-year-old who hates my life. You might be pulling a sickie to go for another job interview. We've bumped into each other at the train station by chance. No one can prove otherwise."

He stared at her. "But that's not what we're doing, is it, Bree?"

"I'm not sure what we're doing but I know it doesn't feel wrong."

A smile crossed his face. "Exactly right as always." His voice was happier now. "Anyway, it's not like we're hugging or kissing or anything, is it?"

"No." Bree managed to keep the disappointment hidden. "You're just cheering me up, right?"

"Right."

They grinned at each other.

"So when's the train leaving?" she asked.

Mr Fellows looked through the glass of the sliding doors at the announcement board. "About fifteen minutes."

"Brilliant. Plenty of time. I'm just going to buy a bottle

of water." She moved to go to the little shop attached to the station but he called something out, making her stop and turn round.

"Logan," he said.

"What?"

He looked right into her eyes, so intensely that she really couldn't breathe. Only savour...

"My 'real' name. It's Logan."

Smiling, she said, "Nice to meet you, Logan."

He smiled back.

"Nice to meet you too."

chapter thirty-five

That was the end of the awkwardness for most of the day. Whatever moral hump Logan needed to overcome, it was done. It was a blissful train journey up into London. With rush hour over, half the carriage was empty, leaving plenty of room to devour the broadsheet paper Logan had bought.

It was like being in a couple. The sort of couple Bree had always wanted to be one half of. They rode up in companionable silence – talking only to swap sections or read out bits they thought were good, or funny, or wrong. They occasionally put their papers down and stared vacantly out at fields of green speeding past, which became lines of offices and traffic-clogged roads. Bree made a passing comment about how getting the train into London always reminded her of Larkin's *The Whitsun Weddings* poem and Logan gave her one of those looks that made her feel like she was the most special thing in existence.

She wished the track would spread on infinitely so they could stay in that carriage for ever – that God would build more railway line like Scalextric so she could stay this happy always. But God was obviously too busy pretending to solve world hunger and wars, and so, much too soon, she felt the train slow and grind to a halt in the city at Victoria station.

"Where are we going?" she asked, as they picked up the bits of newspaper they'd inadvertently strewn all over the carriage.

"It's a surprise."

Bree made a face as she folded up the *Life and Style* section to put in the bin. "I hate surprises."

"Well, you'll like this one."

They disposed of their rubbish and navigated their way down to the Underground. The tunnels were warm with leftover body heat from the earlier rush hour. Bree took off her fur coat and fanned herself with her hand while they waited for a tube. One arrived shortly and they hopped on, each holding onto a pole rather than sitting.

"I love the Tube," Bree said, as they whizzed through the darkness. "It always reminds me of those photos from World War II, crowds of people sleeping down here, using the stations as giant bomb shelters."

"I'm not a huge fan," Logan said. "I don't like thinking about what would happen if we got stuck."

"We'd suffocate slowly?"

"Exactly."

"No we wouldn't."

"Well, maybe we wouldn't die. But I would definitely have some kind of mental breakdown."

Bree elbowed him playfully. "Oh, because bunking off work and taking a student up to London isn't having some kind of mental breakdown?"

Lead balloon.

His face went blank.

"Come on, I was joking."

"Not funny, Bree," he muttered towards his shoes more than to her face.

"Well, I know that now."

The silence lasted two whole stops.

"So which stop are we getting off at?" Bree asked eventually.

He didn't answer at first. She felt a little guilty, but mostly a bit pissed off. Why couldn't they joke about the fact that what they were doing was totally forbidden? It was too weird pretending it was normal.

"The next one."

She looked at the Tube map along the top of the carriage. "King's Cross St Pancras?"

"That's the one."

"Are you taking me to Paris?" Her face lit up.

"Er…no."

"Oh…of course not…right."

They rode on in another fuggy silence. Bree was a bit annoyed, but she couldn't quite put her manicured finger on why.

Well, okay, she could…

He hadn't declared his undying love for her the moment they'd got on the train. He hadn't entwined his fingers with hers, stared into her eyes and said, "Bree. Let's run away and grow old together in a caravan, writing poetry and reading it to each other by a roaring fire."

They got off at their station and rode up the escalators together, avoiding being whacked in the ankles by tourists wielding wheelie suitcases, and emerged into bright winter sunlight.

"Where now?"

Logan looked about to get his bearings and sidestepped to a map. "Er…right, I think."

It was a quick walk past bustling traffic before Logan stopped and said, "We're here."

She looked up at the imposing red modern building.

"Where are we?"

"You don't know?"

She shook her head.

"It's the British Library."

All her annoyance dissipated.

"Seriously? This place?" She took in the wide paved courtyard of red and cream squares and the crimson bricks of the building. Everything looked neat, tidy and, most oddly of all, new.

"What? What's wrong?"

She turned on the spot, just gazing at it. "No. I'm fine. It's just, well, not what I thought it would look like at all."

"You've never been here?"

"Never."

He looked proud of himself. "What were you expecting it to look like?"

She shrugged. "I dunno. More like Hogwarts. It's so… modern."

"They moved it from the old British Museum Reading Room, so it used to look more like Hogwarts. It's got a copy of every single UK book published, you know?"

This fact made Bree very excited. "Really? Every single one?"

It looked even more swanky and un-library-ish on the inside. Security guards checked their bags and Bree practically floated up the giant marble steps.

"I can't think of a happier place for a book to live," she said, to no one in particular.

Logan laughed. "So you're over it not looking like Hogwarts?"

She half-nodded. Everyone around them looked like the sort of person Bree could be friends with. They each had their head in a book, or several. They weren't wearing stupid fashionable clothes, but rather comfy stuff for a day of study. And the quiet thing was taken seriously.

"Maybe one day my book will be in here," she murmured.

"Are you working on a new book?" Logan – she would never get bored of knowing that was his name – looked at her with a mixture of admiration and anxiety.

She grinned to herself. "I'm working on something. I'm not sure what it is yet."

"It's great that you've kept on writing, Bree."

"Well, there are no more girls chucking themselves off piers, you'll be relieved to know."

She could see him struggling not to laugh.

"That's…a shame." His non-smile got bigger.

"Hey!" She smacked his arm. "That was an amazing piece of prose!"

"It was quite an accomplishment…to make one suicide attempt last for 110,000 words."

He burst out laughing and she flew into a mock rage and chased him up the giant staircase, much to the displeasure of everyone around them. Out of breath, she jokingly punched him again in his (rock hard) stomach and they sank onto a bench.

"So what is there to do here?" she asked, looking up at the high ceiling.

He scratched his head and looked uncomfortable. "Well, you have to apply to get into the reading room to see all the actual books."

She wrinkled her nose. "What sort of whacko library is this? You can't just walk in?"

"Nope."

"So can we apply to get in?"

He looked even more uncomfortable. "Well. You have to be over eighteen."

Bree nodded slowly. "Riiiight."

"There's something I brought you here to show you though."

"Is it age appropriate?"

It was supposed to be a joke but it didn't sound like one. Their age gap, and all the reasons they shouldn't be there, hung around like cheap perfume.

"Come on, it's this way."

He led her back down the stairs, past a giant glass column filled with proper antique books. She pointed to the towering shelves, encased in glass.

"See, that's what I thought the British Library would look like."

"It does pack a bit more of a visual punch than a computer database, doesn't it?"

"So where are we going?"

"It's just at the bottom of the stairs."

He led her through a dark doorway and they emerged into a deep purple light. The air was cool in that museumy way that immediately demands good behaviour. Everyone pored over backlit glass cases.

"What is this place?" Bree whispered.

The tranquillity of the room calmed Logan's face. He took her hand and squeezed it.

"It's the Treasures of the British Library. I thought if anything was to cheer you up, this would be the place."

Bree squeezed his hand back. Hard. Then dropped it to go discover the treasure.

It was like a literary equivalent of pornography.

Everything she saw made her happy. There were original printed works of Shakespeare, an important ancient document called the Magna Carta, which she pretended to know about to impress Logan, and handwritten song lyrics penned by John Lennon himself. She spent an age in front of each exhibit, her breath steaming up the glass as she lost herself in the history. She imagined all the different people who'd held these artefacts before, what their lives were like, what had been happening to them.

Logan trailed after her, smiling. "You enjoying yourself?"

She nodded. "Yes. Loads."

"I've saved the best till last." He held out his hand. She took it tentatively and he guided her past more exhibits before stopping in front of a central glass case. "It's Jane Austen's writing desk," he said, stepping back to give her a better look. "And her teenage diary as well."

He may as well have said: *Here is everything. I am perfect for you.*

"No way." Bree pressed her entire face against the glass. "How did they even get this?"

"Family donation."

"You mean Jane Austen has descendants that breathe the very same air as us?"

"Yeah, I suppose so…but she never had kids obviously, so I wonder how it passed down the line. Maybe it was…"

Bree had stopped listening. She and the desk were having a moment. She smushed her forehead against the glass to get as close as possible.

Jane Austen wrote at this very desk.

Jane Austen.

Bree's ultimate idol in the universe.

She took in the dark wood, the little nooks and crannies where Jane may have stored ink, or parchment, or whatever she used back then. Her very own skilled fingers had touched it. If there wasn't glass separating them, Bree could have touched the very same spots.

The diary was displayed next to the desk, sprawled open at a random page. Her handwriting. Jane Austen's actual handwriting was there – right in front of her. Bree closed her eyes briefly and imagined how that page had once been blank. How it had been just moseying about in the nineteenth century waiting to be doodled on, or ripped out for someone to jot down a phone number...not that they had phone numbers in those days. Yet, one day, Jane Austen had sat down and filled that page with her thoughts and feelings, and history was made. Neither Jane nor the page had known that – in a couple of hundreds of years' time – Bree would be looking at that very entry. She thought of her own faithful laptop computer. Would some mixed-up girl, someday, hundreds of years in the future, smush their face into a museum exhibit to look at Bree's stuff? She could only wish.

She sighed and Logan looked at her.

"You okay? I think I lost you for a moment there."

"I'm so okay. God, though, it was so much more romantic back then, wasn't it?"

He looked confused. "What? Falling in love? I don't think Jane had a very romantic life."

Bree shook her head. "No. Not falling in love. Writing. Writing's much more romantic when it's pen and ink and paper. It's..." She searched for the word. "More timeless. And worthwhile." She gestured towards the desk. "Think about it. There are so many words gushing out into the universe these days. All digitally. All in Comic Sans or Times New Roman. Silly websites. Stupid news stories digitally uploaded to a 24-hour-channel. Where's all this writing going? Who's keeping a note of it all? Who's in charge of deciding what's worthwhile and what isn't? But back then..." She closed her eyes again and pictured her idea of the olden days, which, funnily enough, looked a lot like the BBC version of *Pride and Prejudice*. "Back then, if someone wanted to write something they had to buy paper. Buy it! And ink. And a pen. And they couldn't waste too many sheets cos it was expensive. So when people wrote, they wrote because it was worthwhile...not just because they had some half-baked idea and they wanted to pointlessly prove their existence by sharing it on some bloody social networking site."

She stopped herself and was about to get embarrassed and defensive when she caught how Logan was looking at her.

He was really looking at her.

His face was transfixed, like she was some kind of magical ranting fairy who'd bewitched him with her whingeing.

His smile was lazy. All his hair had fallen into his eyes and he'd not bothered to scrape it back. She felt naked.

"What?" she said, all self-conscious.

He still didn't answer.

"What is it?"

He half-shook his head. "It's nothing."

"Tell me," she insisted.

He opened his mouth. Closed it. Then opened it again.

"It's just sometimes I forget you're only seventeen. And, well…" He stared at her again. "I really need to remind myself sometimes before…" He trailed off.

Her heart warmed up like it'd been shoved into a microwave, and the heat spread down to her stomach. "Before what?"

Logan took a step towards her boldly, like he'd made a decision.

"Before I kiss you again."

He leaned his head in and Bree moved to meet him, enjoying that sweet anticipatory relief that comes just before a delicious kiss. Every centimetre of her skin tingled.

But the kiss didn't arrive.

She was expecting his warm lips and instead got an angry elbow jolt. She looked behind her.

"Hey."

An angry old lady wielding an overpriced gift shop copy of *Sense and Sensibility* pushed past and evilled her. "Sorry. I'm just trying to get closer to Jane's desk," the woman barked at them, clearly not sorry at all.

They'd been standing in front of it all this time. Bree shook herself back to reality to see that their romantic encounter had created a disgruntled queue behind them. They both went red. Logan coughed and stepped away.

"Erm, yeah, sorry, we didn't mean to hog the exhibit."

It was like reality had grown a humongous hand and was tapping Bree on the shoulder with it.

He was married. He was her teacher. It was wrong. So very wrong.

Even Jane Austen must have thought so. If she'd agreed with it all, her spirit would've no doubt let them snog each other senseless in front of her writing desk. But she obviously didn't approve if she'd sent a narky OAP in to break things up.

They stood, both determinedly looking at the carpet, as the line of people trickled past them, taking their own turns with Jane's desk.

"So, what next?" Mr Fellows asked, all formal.

"I'm not sure, sir." She deliberately emphasized the "sir", though she wasn't sure why. "It's you who planned this trip."

He looked at his watch. "Well, er, it's still quite early, but we can head back home if you like. My…umm…wife won't be expecting me back until seven though."

The word "wife" hit her like a bullet. She supposed it was just that – a verbal bullet. Payback for the "sir". She couldn't leave it like this though, not after it had been going so brilliantly. She racked her brain for something to do. Something unkissy. She remembered something.

"I know somewhere we can go. I don't think it's too far away."

He looked dubious – somehow their mutual trust had vanished. It felt awful.

"Really? Where?"

"It's free."

"What is it?"

"You'll find out when we get there." Her attempt to make things jokey again instantly face-planted, but she persevered nonetheless. "You'll like it, honestly."

"Alright then."

They rode the Tube in more silence. Each stop punctuated the awkwardness, making the situation feel even more screwed up. But Bree hoped that getting away from the scene of the non-kiss might make things normal again. Well, as normal as a teacher and student playing hooky to go stare at some dead woman's writing desk can be.

"We're here." She strode out of the carriage, leaving him to follow. They emerged into weak sunlight shining directly into their eyes – the sort of low winter sun that painted everything gold. Bree already felt better. Mr Fellows looked around him – taking in the tourists, the pigeons, and Nelson's Column.

"Trafalgar Square? What are we doing here?"

She pointed over the heads of about ten thousand tourists photographing the fountain to the grand staircase of the National Gallery.

"We're going there."

He followed her finger. "The National Gallery?"

She nodded.

"You're into art?"

"No. Not usually. But probably the only painting I care about in the whole world is in that gallery."

And for the first time since the Jane Austen desk incident, he smiled. "Now I'm intrigued."

She smiled back. "Well, let's go in and satisfy your curiosity."

They made their way past huddled groups of tourists, not even glancing up at Nelson's Column as only London-regulars could, and climbed the ornate staircase. The moment they entered the gallery, the hustle and bustle of the city was replaced with whispers. The air was cool. Bree hadn't been there in years and had forgotten how beautiful the entrance hall was. She crossed the turquoise mosaic floor and stared up at the glass domed ceiling. It was stunning.

She felt Logan by her side.

"Whoa, that's pretty."

"It is indeed."

"So where's this favourite painting of yours?"

"Erm. Straight ahead, maybe?"

"You don't know? I thought it was your favourite painting in the world."

"I can look at it online whenever I want."

He smiled again. "That is so sad."

chapter thirty-six

They got a bit lost. Bree ended up having to ask directions and the gallery guy looked a bit surprised at her request.

"Erm, that painting?" He scratched his head. "Room Five, I think."

She followed the signs and, soon, there it was. In a small red room with nobody else in there. Bree sat down right in front of it and grinned when she saw the look on Logan's face.

"This?"

"Do you like it?"

"It's grotesque! What? I'm so confused."

"It's called *The Ugly Duchess*."

"It's a bloke in a dress."

"It's not a bloke, look, she's got boobs."

Logan wrinkled his nose. "Ergh. I missed those. They're like shrivelled balloons. It's horrific."

Bree watched all the emotions play out on his face, still smiling, before turning her attention back to the painting. She'd never really "got" art and how people could "get lost" in paintings. She'd often thought people only pretended enthusiasm to make themselves appear more cultured and interesting. But, with this one, she got it. Just staring into the brushstrokes coaxed her mind into a quiet spot it very rarely visited. She examined the duchess's wrinkled face, her intricate headdress and the small red flower she clutched in her hand like her life depended on it.

Who were you? Bree thought.

Logan sat next to her, a bit too close.

"Okay. So it's…different…but why is this your favourite painting? It's not exactly easy on the eye."

"That's what I like about it."

"Why?"

Bree thought back to the day she first saw this painting and all the thoughts she'd had, right on this very bench, all those years ago.

"How many portraits of pretty blonde women with their perfect boobs out did we walk past to get to this room?"

"I dunno. Every other painting, I guess."

"That's exactly why I like this one. She's gross. Horrendous to look at. Her breasts are all deflated, her face is like a nightmare, she makes you recoil. And yet…somebody, somewhere, a long, long time ago, thought this woman was worth the time – the *days* – needed to paint her picture. To make her place in the world more permanent."

"Why?"

She moved even closer to him on the bench. "That's precisely why I like it. I don't know. But she obviously had some story to tell."

"You think she was interesting in some way other than the way she looked?"

She looked at him. "Exactly."

They sat there for a while, just looking.

"Bree?"

"Yes?"

"I like that this is your favourite painting…"

"But…?"

"But…well, you wouldn't put it on your bedroom wall, would you?"

She laughed. "No. I suppose you wouldn't."

"Bree?" His voice sounded a bit nervous.

"Yes?"

"Why are you so obsessed with people being interesting?"

That was a question and a half. She felt herself get ruffled and defensive, her skin itching the way it always did when someone hit a bit too close to her private thoughts. This was Logan though…

"What do you mean?" She stalled for time.

"Well, this painting, and all the new things you're doing at school. Why? Why aren't you happy just being you?"

Bree stopped looking at the painting and instead assessed her feet.

"I want to be a good writer. And you're the one who said I had to lead a more interesting life."

He looked worried. "I think you took what I said too literally, Bree. I never told you to change who you are."

"I want to be a writer, more than anything," she protested. "And you were right, I didn't have anything to write about. But now I do."

His eyebrows furrowed together in concern. "What? What are you writing?"

She considered telling him about the blog. About the rules. But the words got wedged somewhere inside her before they were even near to her throat. Much as she had fallen for him, this…thing, whatever it was she was doing, it was just for her.

"Nothing. Just, you know, scribbling in my diary. The normal sort of crap seventeen-year-olds write about."

"I'm sure it's not crap."

"What if I told you I was writing *The Pier* sequel?"

He spluttered with laughter despite himself.

"See!"

"Sorry, Bree. Honestly, I'm sure whatever you're working on is brilliant."

She looked back at *The Ugly Duchess*. "I dunno. Life is so bloody hard. I don't want the whole struggle to be pointless. If I'm going to get crap thrown at me from great heights my whole life, well, I want to damn well make sure I leave a mark on this world in exchange for all the misery. I *need* to be interesting, Logan, I need to be someone. Because…

otherwise…I'm just sad and lonely and confused and it's all for nothing. And she" – she gestured towards the painting – "she might have been a total minger, but she was interesting enough for someone to paint her. And now, here she is, hanging on a wall in the National Gallery. She probably had a horrible, lonely life and has been dead for hundreds of years, but now, technically, she's immortal."

Bree finished her speech with a tight voice. Logan was quiet for a moment, before cautiously putting his arm around her.

"It gets better, Bree. Life, I mean. You will never be more miserable than you are aged seventeen. Not because life itself gets easier – it's always going to be hard in some way. But you know yourself better, and you don't care what people think as much."

She shrugged him off, not wanting to get confused again by the will-they-won't-theyness between them. "Oh yeah?"

"Yeah. I hated school. I don't think there are enough adjectives in the English dictionary to describe how awful I felt throughout adolescence. But now…" He tailed off.

"Now you're so happy that you've pulled a sickie from work and lied to your wife so you can spend the day in London with a teenager?" she finished for him.

Well, someone had to say it. Eventually.

He didn't stand up to leave, not like she thought he would. He just shook his head a bit.

"I'm not sure what we're doing, Bree. But I know that, so far, we've not done anything wrong."

So far…

"All I know is that, for some reason, we need to see a bit of each other at the moment. For both of us. I've had such a great day."

She looked over at him and nuzzled her head into his neck to try and get him to put his arm back round her.

"Really?"

He grinned and obliged. "Really."

Their intent attention on *The Ugly Duchess* meant all the silly tourists crowded round them, queuing to get close, and taking pictures on their phones – tricked into thinking it was *The Mona Lisa* or something. Bree's elbow got jostled by one enthusiastic American wearing not one but two bumbags.

"Ouch."

Logan manoeuvred her more into him so she was out of the way of the stampede.

"Have you had enough time with her? Maybe we could grab some food?"

"That sounds great."

And, getting their elbows out ready to fend off sightseers, they barged their way out of the room.

The next hour was spent stuffing their faces with afternoon tea in a place Logan knew. Bree happily sampled every flavour of teeny tiny sandwich, all the scones, and the two types of clotted cream on offer. Although nothing would ever compare to the joy of a strawberry Pop-Tart.

They waddled out, feeling pretty sick, into London rush-hour traffic and tried to navigate their way to Victoria station in a sugar-induced haze. The entire city appeared to be heading in the opposite direction from them so it was like swimming upstream in an endless torrent of grey suits and glazed-over eyes. They were banged into and jerked about by seemingly everyone – too busy being busy and important for manners. In the end, Bree turned it into a game, and yelled "I'M THE SALMON, I'M THE SALMON" whenever they accidently stepped into another crowd of incoming walking traffic. Logan took it a step further, adding a fish face and flapping his body about limply, while the swarms of people rushed past, deliberately ignoring their attempts at humour. Exhausted by giggling, fish impressions, and the day in general, they collapsed onto their train and rode home quietly. Bree leaned on his shoulder as she watched the grey buildings whizz past and turn back into meadows and mansions.

It got awkward though when they came to say goodbye. Logan kept looking around anxiously.

"So, I guess I'll see you tomorrow," Bree said, so sad that the day was over. She felt rejuvenated and free, and like herself for the first time in ages.

"Yes, I've got you first thing, haven't I?"

She nodded.

"You'd better have done your coursework." He waggled his finger.

It was supposed to be a joke but Bree could almost hear a klaxon honking.

"When have I ever not done my coursework?" Although admittedly it had been a struggle to get it all done recently, what with her blog, her workouts, playing pretend with Jass... She'd only just made her Latin deadline last week, when usually she handed coursework in two weeks in advance.

"Yes...right... Oh, is that the time?" He looked at his watch. "I'd better..."

Bree looked at the time on her phone. "Yeah, me too. I'd better..."

They stood in silence.

Finally, she said, "I had such an amazing day, Logan – sorry, I mean, sir. It was just what I needed. Thank you."

He readjusted her scarf, a proud look on his face. "You do seem a lot happier than yesterday."

"I am."

"Is it back to being the most popular girl in school again tomorrow, then?"

She rolled her eyes, not really wanting to think about Jassmine and Hugo just yet. It was so rare in her life to have moments to truly cherish, she wasn't going to wreck it with bad thoughts.

"Yep. I guess so."

"Okay. Bye, Bree."

"Bye, sir."

He turned and walked away first. She watched him

become smaller and smaller, until he was ant-sized. Then she turned on her own heels to go home.

Rule number four: One must fall in love with somebody forbidden

So we're off sex – probably for ever – and now we're onto its much less exciting, but oh-so-much-more important relative: love.

L.O.V.E.

It's what we're here for, folks. To find someone. To have them find you. To have a warm burning in your belly that makes you want to kiss the world for making you feel so wonderful, and also throw rocks at it because you hate how vulnerable it's made you.

And when we're not desperately searching for it ourselves, we're hunting for stories of other more successful seekers. Is there any story more beautiful to listen to than how a couple got together? Even boring couples. Even ugly couples. Even imaginary couples. We read books about people who don't exist, who are only a collection of character strokes on a page, and actively YEARN for them to be together.

These tiny dramas of first moves, missed opportunities, and misread signals make up the very best of human life. If it were possible, we would cover ourselves with superglue and roll around until we were covered in love story after love story, like a protective blanket from everything else that is shit.

Love is interesting.

Falling in love is interesting.

Being in love is interesting.

Falling out of love is interesting.

But it is so unimaginably more interesting if that love is forbidden.

You aren't supposed to be together.

This particular love isn't allowed.

Is there anything more potent than that?

I can't fake all of this, you know. My hair's fake for you guys. My clothes are fake. For at least seven hours a day, every word that falls out of my lipsticked mouth is fake.

Most of this project is planned down to the letter. It has to be. How else are you going to follow my lead?

But this...this rule you can't fake.

I have something to confess to you.

I am in love. And it is forbidden.

He is my teacher at school. He's married.

There are laws, actual laws stopping us from falling in love. We cannot be together in any way, or under any circumstances.

And yet I love him.

I love him so much that my heart does this weird

hip-hop-type dance in my ribs whenever I see him. I measure time by when I'll see him next. It drags for every second he's not there, then whizzes right past me when he is.

I love the me I am when I'm with him.

I have thought about what our children would look like.

So here's an unexpected bonus for you all. An added surprise element as part of our expedition to become interesting. Aren't you dying to know if we get together or not? It doesn't matter if you approve or not, you still want us to...just to see what happens.

I wish I knew what happens.

Because here's the real killer...I'm quite certain he loves me too.

chapter thirty-seven

A new day and it was time to go back to the double life.

"Breeeeeeeeeeeeeeeeeeeeeeeeeeeeeeeeeee!" Jass pulled her in for a hug when they met at the corner. "I missed you."

Bree couldn't help but smile a bit. She'd never been missed before.

"It was only three days," she said into Jassmine's armpit.

"God, really? But so much has happened. How are you? Are you feeling better? Gemma said you left Hugo's early cause you were sick but we all thought you were just a lightweight. But you really were sick?"

Bree untangled herself. "As a dog."

"You lucky thing. I love getting stomach flu. I'm always so thin afterwards."

They walked in step towards Queen's Hall. An overnight frost had coated every grass blade in a beautiful icy outfit that scrunched as they clopped over it.

"So what have I missed then? Any fallout from the party?" She was still too scared to say Hugo's name in case her voice gave her away.

Jassmine's face went all serious. "Well, did you hear my drink got spiked?"

Like hell it did.

"Oh no! Seriously?"

"Awful, isn't it? Hugo's parents are looking into it. The police say there's not much they can do."

"The police?"

"I begged Hugo not to tell them, said it wasn't worth it, but he insisted. He felt terrible that it happened in his house."

Or he was just trying to distract you from his cheating…

"Wow, Jass, are you okay? I mean, you were pretty out of it…I just thought you'd…"

"That I'd drunk too much? No. You got ready with me, remember? I barely had anything beforehand."

Apart from so many cocktails you couldn't get out of the taxi…

"Yeah, of course, how scary."

"It's really scary." Jass didn't look scared at all.

"So what else did I miss?" Bree asked, deliberately veering into a big patch of untouched grass to make footprints in the frost.

Jassmine clapped her hands together. "Ooooo, I shouldn't say…"

"What? Come on."

"Alright. This is so exciting. Matty Boy is TOTALLY in love with you!"

Bree looked up from her footprints. "Huh?"

"Matty Boy. He loooooooves you. He got really pissed after you left and said he thought you were well fit."

Bree tried not to wrinkle her nose. "Seriously?"

"Yep. Isn't that amazing?"

"Er..."

"So..." Jass tilted her head towards her. "Do you fancy him?"

Bree hadn't prepared for this development. Bloody hell. Where had all this male interest come from? She never thought she'd complain but...well, now she really felt like complaining. "Who? Matty Boy?"

"Duh."

"Not really. Why? Am I supposed to?"

"I think you'd be really good together."

Of course you do. You're probably hoping it will cockblock Hugo.

"Hmmmm."

"'Hmmm', you're interested?"

Bree made another face. "Jass, he's funny and all, but he looks like a demented snowman."

Jass snorted, trying to hold her laugh in. "Oh, Bree, you're so mean."

She hunched her shoulders. "It's true."

"He's not entirely unattractive..."

"Jass, please, stop it."

They were almost at school. Fellow students began joining their path, some of the younger Year Sevens taking it in turns to skid on the ice. They all silently made room for Jassmine and Bree though.

"That's a shame. He's been so cute these past two days. He's all like 'Where's Bree?' 'Is she better?' 'Have you heard from her?'"

Her heart bled. Not. It might have oozed a teeny bit if Matty Boy had been the slightest bit interested in her back when she was a nobody.

"Aww, cute," she deadpanned.

"So you really don't think he has a chance?"

"Jassy-min, I *know* he doesn't have a chance."

"Christ. Do you fancy *anybody*?"

Bree winked. "Only you, love, and you're taken."

Jassmine let out another unattractive snort of laughter. "Right, well, he's gonna be disappointed. Do you want me to tell him you're not interested?"

Bree thought that was a weird thing to ask. Jass obviously wanted to elbow in on the non-existent drama.

"Nah, it's okay. He'll work it out soon enough."

"I really don't mind."

"Honestly, I'll handle it. Thanks for telling me."

"Any time." Jass paused for a moment. "It's nice to have you back, Bree."

That was a phrase she never thought she'd hear.

"I missed you too, babe. Now I'd better get to English and showcase my new tights."

"Yeah, I was gonna say, they're gorrrrrrrrrgeous."

"Why, thank you." She stuck out a leg to show them off. Her mum had bought them as a present when she was in her depressive hole. They were the same fake-suspender style, but vibrant red. Racy as hell. Totally against school rules of course. But Bree had Mr Fellows first lesson and wanted him to remember everything that had gone down yesterday.

"I bet the headmistress has confiscated them by lunchtime."

Bree yawned. "Probably. Right, I'm off to English. What you got?"

Jassmine curled her lip. "Sociology."

"Meet you at lunch?"

"Of course."

chapter thirty-eight

A fizzy bubble grew in her stomach as she strutted through the school halls. She'd missed him the moment he'd left yesterday and time had dragged and then some since. Now they had to spend the next hour pretending they hadn't snuck off to London together. That they were just a normal student and teacher – one learned, one taught, nothing more. Apart from the fact that they'd run off together.

How frickin' hot is that?

She entered precisely one minute after the bell so everyone else was already there and seated. Her skirt was deliberately hiked up to show off her legs.

"Bree, you're late," Logan said, sounding a bit pissed off.

Huh? Why was he in such a bad mood?

"Sorry, sir."

"Just sit down and get your book out, everyone's waiting."

She sat down quickly, pulling her skirt down in shame

and digging out her book. She turned to the front like a robot model pupil, disappointed.

"Right, as you're late, you can remind us all of where we were up to."

He gave her the teeniest tiniest wink, a knowing one, and everything was better again. Her belly unleashed a torrent of ADHD-suffering dolphins that dived about in her gut.

"Er..." She couldn't think or talk. Her brain was stuck on the way he'd looked at her yesterday in front of Jane Austen's desk. She couldn't even remember what book they were reading.

"We were getting to the rude bit of *The Handmaid's Tale*," Chuck volunteered, saving her.

Logan turned his attention to Chuck. "Oh, is that right?" he asked, putting a finger over his mouth.

"Yep." Chuck shook his personality-hair back and looked proud.

"How would you know that unless you read ahead?"

The class laughed – Logan too – and Chuck slouched down into his chair.

"Everyone flicks straight to the filthy bits in books, sir," he protested.

"Well, if you read it properly, I'd be surprised if you were aroused by it. It's not the most pleasant of sex scenes."

Bree flicked through her copy. Remarkably, she hadn't read ahead for this lesson. She'd been too preoccupied. She scanned the sex scene page and grimaced. The book was weird – all these fertile women were trapped in rich men's houses and forced to shag them to help save the failing population. In this sex scene, the rich guy's wife was there too and they engaged in some odd threesome.

Ick.

"Judging by Bree's face there, she's just got to the 'sex scene'." Logan made the quotes with his fingers. "What do you make of it, Bree?"

He stared her straight in the eye. Her breath deserted her and ran off into someone else's body to ask for asylum. It should be illegal for men as good-looking as Logan to stare like that and say the word "sex" at the same time. She made an overdramatic grossed-out face to compensate.

"It's weird. Why did she even include it? I hate sex in books, it's disgusting. Why can't the author just allude to it? Like in the old James Bond movies?"

"That's an interesting point, Bree. The thing about Margaret Atwood is..."

And he was off, back to being a teacher again. A good teacher, one who managed to teach them important parts of the syllabus the day they read a sex scene in class. As he got more animated, his hair flopsied into his eyes and he pushed it back haphazardly, each time making her belly bubble more. There was no doubt about it, he was a good-looking man. Yet he was so much more than that too. His heart was good, he had an actual functioning brain, and he got Bree. Understood her. No one else, male or female, had managed that feat before. He was careful for the rest of the lesson, making no more than two small glances in her direction. She was a bit gutted but knew it was important to maintain the illusion that they were just pupil and teacher.

The time flew – as it always does when you're within a five-metre radius of someone you're falling for – and soon she was daydreaming her way through Latin. It was like a virus had hacked into her brain, erasing all other thoughts but Logan, Logan, Logan.

She didn't even mind seeing Hugo again at lunch.

"Hello, stranger," Jessica said, as she approached them all in their prime spot in the school canteen. "We missed you."

Hugo had his arm slung lazily round Jassmine, looking bored. Gemma was copying Emily's homework, and Seth was cramming as many chips into his mouth as possible, making Jassmine squeal with disgust.

"Bree." Matt stood up, then sat down, and glowed red.

Oh yeah…that. Bollocks.

"Hi, everyone." She waved, then took the only seat left, next to Matty Boy – what a surprise! She took a crisp, and popped it into her mouth. Matt moved closer to her.

"You feeling better? Were you very sick?" His face was all concerned.

Argh. This was gonna get awkward.

"I'm fine, thanks." She took another crisp.

"Did you enjoy Hugo's party?"

"Yeah, Bree. Did you enjoy my party?" Hugo gave her a knowing eyebrow-raise.

Even now, being so blatant and disgusting, he couldn't penetrate the happiness in her tummy.

"It was…satisfactory, I suppose," she quipped back.

"Only satisfactory? I should've tried harder to be a good host for you."

Jass picked up on the conversation, leaving Seth with a gob full of chips and no audience.

"You didn't like Hugo's party, Bree?"

"I was joking. It was great," she said, keen to stop this before it got dangerous.

"Great, eh?" Hugo danced his eyebrows some more.

Innuendo. The humour of idiots…

Jass looked at each of them in turn, frowning. She pulled Hugo tighter, like he was a dog on a choke lead.

"Hughie?"

He reluctantly looked at his girlfriend. "What?"

"Have you talked to the police any more about who might've spiked my drink?"

Bree was pretty sure fifty per cent of the table rolled their eyes. But she wasn't expecting what came next.

"Er, no, Jass. Cos I reckon you were just in a drunken state cos you drank too much. Your own fault, no one else's."

From across the table, Bree saw tears appear in Jassmine's eyes.

"What? Hugo? I don't understand what you mean."

"Yes you do." He pushed her off his lap so she fell sideways onto the chair next to him, all awkward and uncomfortable.

Nobody knew what to do.

Hugo declared he wanted more chips and left, while everyone watched Jassmine teetering on the edge of an emotional outburst. Bree tried to smile kindly at her but she got a glare back.

"What you looking at?"

"Whoa, nothing. Jass, are you okay?"

Everyone was quiet. Even Seth – always good at saying inappropriate stuff – had his mouth shut, trying to swallow all his chips.

"Yes, I'm fine, why wouldn't I be?" Her voice was sharp and spiteful.

Bree backed off. "Just checking."

"Well don't."

Gemma gave Bree a *Don't bother* look.

Jass looked round the table for her next victim. Her eyes stopped on Emily.

"Emily, your new hair really doesn't suit you," she said, for no reason at all.

Emily's hand went to her fringe in shock and shame. It was her turn for tears to well up. Was this how it worked? Did Popular Land have a reverse version of "Pay it forward" with nastiness dripping down the hierarchy like sloppy leftovers?

Jassmine pushed her chair back. "I'm going to go see if Hugo's okay. He's always so grumpy when he's got a rugby match coming up."

The rest of them looked at each other as she strode off – scared she'd come back.

"I think your new fringe is gorgeous," Bree whispered to Emily. "Ignore Jassmine. She's just taking relationship stuff out on you."

Emily looked like she was gonna fall over from the endorsement. "Really? You think?"

"Yes. Makes your face look uber-skinny. Don't take it personally. It was just Russian roulette who she was going to vent on. You were the unlucky one today."

"Well, that was awkward," Gemma announced and they all dissolved into giggles, the tension in the air evaporating.

"They've been fighting so much recently," Jessica said. "Especially since the weekend. It doesn't help that he keeps refusing to wear that necklace."

"I wonder why…" Seth said ponderingly, and they all pissed themselves again.

Equilibrium restored, lunch continued. Bree took another crisp. Matt moved up nearer to her, close enough she could feel his breath tickling her neck.

"Hey, Bree."

She swallowed. "Hey, yourself."

"I just wanted to apologize, you know, for my behaviour at Hugo's." He twisted his hands in his lap and his pale face was bright red.

"Your behaviour?" She didn't understand.

"Yeah, I'm sorry. I was out of line…"

"Matt, I honestly don't know what you're talking about."

He turned even redder, if possible. "Well, you know, when I tried it on, on the dance floor. You weren't very happy."

"Oh, that."

He'd grinded on her in the tent. She'd completely forgotten. Jeez, out of all the bad behaviour various people – herself included – had indulged in that evening, Matt's grinding practically made him a nun. Could you get male nuns? Never mind.

"Yeah, that. I'm really sorry."

"Matt, it was nothing. I'm over it. I was never under it."

"Oh." He looked disappointed.

"Don't worry about it." She was about to turn to Gemma but he got another line in.

"I'd like to make it up to you."

She bit her lip. "There's no need."

"No, I really want to. Sorry. I was so drunk."

"Honestly, it's fine. Just buy me a drink next time we're all out if you really want to."

He leaned closer. She could smell ketchup on his breath.

"I could take you out for a drink? If you'd like?" All his normal brazen confidence had disappeared and he'd morphed into a vulnerable, adorable boy. An adorable boy who was about to get his heart rugby-kicked.

Bree wasn't sure what face to make, or what to say.

"Just us?" he said hopefully, like her silence was her not understanding.

"Erm…I'm not sure, Matty. I really like that we're mates."

His face fell, then went hard. The adorable boy abruptly vanished. "Yeah, well, I was only asking to be polite. And I only grinded you cos I was wasted." He budged over to sit next to Seth.

Bree sighed and turned away. "Gemma," she called. "What's up with Hugo and Jassmine?"

Gemma blew her hair up, looking bored. "He's been nasty to her since his party. She's convinced he cheated on her."

For the first time that day, horridness shot through her happy bubble. She prayed to every god available that her face gave nothing away. "Seriously?"

"Yeah. Don't know why you look so surprised."

What did that mean? Did she know?

"What do you mean?"

"Well, it's Hugo, isn't it? I would be more surprised if he'd stayed faithful."

She was safe. Thank you, all the available gods.

As if they knew they were being talked about, Jassmine and Hugo reappeared at the table, arms round each other and nuzzling.

"Oh great," Gemma muttered. "They made up...again."

"So, guys," Jassmine said, like no drama had occurred only minutes before, "we have exciting news."

Seth clapped his hands together. "Mate, have you got her preggo? Thought you were looking a bit tubby, Jassmine."

Everyone laughed, until they saw Hugo and Jassmine's faces. They stopped.

"Shut up, dickhead. At least I have the sperm count to get a girl pregnant."

Seth didn't speak again.

"Anyway," Jassmine continued, "we just saw some saddos putting the posters up. Queen's Hall is having a Christmas party in two weeks' time. Fancy dress!"

This, apparently, was welcome news.

"Wicked," Matty Boy said, leaning back in his chair. "I'm going to get some of those fit Year Elevens under the mistletoe and show them what a Christmas present really is."

Bree tutted. "How respectful. And what if you're not on any girl's 'Dear Santa' list?"

The look he gave her made it clear Matty's short-lived crush had passed.

"Where is this party?" Jessica asked.

"Right here. In the school hall."

Everyone made "Aww, what?" noises.

"That's pathetic," Gemma said. "Couldn't they hire out a boat on the Thames or something? I mean, our parents pay for us to go here."

"I think the whole point is that it's...rustic."

"Sounds a bit naff to me."

"A party's a party."

"Two weeks. God, is it Christmas that soon?"

"Fancy dress?" Gemma spoke again. "What the hell are we all going to go as?"

chapter thirty-nine

"The nativity scene," Bree answered, as she pressed the button on the photocopier.

Logan raised both eyebrows. "The nativity scene?"

"Yes, I know. Look, it was the best I could do. Have you not seen *Mean Girls*? Saying the words 'fancy dress' to girls like Jassmine is like hiring an aeroplane to spell out *Go on, show us your tits* in the sky. Getting them to give up their lifelong dream of wearing sexy Santa outfits was pretty damn hard."

The photocopier fired up and started whirring.

He gave her an impressed nod. "I can't believe you've got the most popular people in school to dress up as the nativity."

"Yeah, well, it's kinda backfired..." She picked up a pile of warm photocopies and folded them in half, before handing them over to Logan to staple.

Logan smiled with his eyes. "Backfired how?"

Bree sighed and picked up a spare stapler to help.

"Well, the last I heard, Jass and Gemma were discussing how to 'sex up' their nativity costumes. See-through tops were mentioned, so this may be the very first Christmas we get to see Angel Gabriel's lingerie…" She sighed again. "I don't know what's more offensive: the sexualization of Santa's wife, or the sexualization of the Bible."

"The Bible," Logan said, smiling properly now, not taking it seriously. "Definitely the sexualization of the Bible."

"Oh God, what have I done?" She rested the cool metal of the stapler against her face and exhaled.

"Oh God? You're blaspheming already?"

"Shut it."

He bit his lip, trying to hold in his amusement. "So what character have you got?"

Oh yeah…that.

"A…sheep," Bree said.

Logan put his papers down and burst out laughing. "A sheep?"

"Yes."

"Why?"

"It was lucky dip! Don't worry, I'm sure I'll look more like a stripper than a sheep by the time they're done with me."

He looked her up and down, taking in the new blazer she'd bought the other weekend that nipped in her waist. Not in a leery gross way, but just in a nice appreciative way.

"I bet you will."

And it was there again. The sexual tension. She was surprised all the inanimate objects in the supply cupboard didn't come to life and start rubbing themselves.

They were photocopying the new edition of the creative-writing club's magazine, read only by members and their parents. It was gone five, most of the school had left, and they were holed up in the supply cupboard with a good stack of photocopies still to get through.

"So what's it like?" Logan asked.

"My sheep costume? Umm, cotton-woolly…?"

He shook his head. "No, not that. What's it like to be part of the most popular group in school?"

The photocopier whirred and beeped as Bree had a little think.

"It's not that great. I just feel like I'm leading some kind of double life… I suppose I am really."

"What's that supposed to mean?"

"Nothing."

The machine ground to a halt, announcing its finish with an angry beep. She lifted up the top to replace the sheet. When she closed it Logan was right there, up in her face, his expression all wild and intense.

"What is it?" She felt all self-conscious under his security-light gaze.

"Nothing."

He stepped even closer so that his taut stomach touched hers. The contact sent electric ripples up through every part of her; her breath caught. Logan's face was so tight she thought for a moment he was going to cry.

"I was a nobody at school," he half-whispered and she could feel his breath on her face. The smell of it, coffeeish and chocolaty, was thrilling. More electrical surges danced up her spine.

"I find that hard to believe."

"It's true. I was skinny and awkward and spent all my time hiding in the stinky toilets writing bad poetry in a bound leather notebook. Not one girl fancied me. I didn't even have my first kiss until I got to university."

He got even closer, if that was possible, and ducked his head so their lips were almost touching... They were going to kiss...it was going to happen again...she couldn't wait.

But then an unwelcome thought pinged straight into the mailbox in her brain, marked with a red "high importance" exclamation mark that she couldn't ignore.

"Logan?"

"Hmmm?" He was staring at her lips, just centimetres away now.

She turned her face to give herself more time. "I read once, a newspaper story, about teachers who fall for their students."

She hadn't read a newspaper story, she'd researched it the other day when she was supposed to be updating her blog. She'd googled *Student teacher relationships*, along with *Are they illegal?* and *Do they work out?* Instead of finding the answers she wanted – *No, go for it*, and *Yes, they always work out* – she'd stumbled across some upsetting psychological research she couldn't stop thinking about.

"Huh?"

He jerked back and she panicked. She didn't want to lose him, to ruin this moment, but she needed to know.

"Hear me out." Her voice shook and she grabbed his hand. "It's just…they quoted this psychologist who said the most common reason it happens is because the teachers themselves hated school. Like you just said. They couldn't get anyone to fancy them at school and they were a loner and unpopular and, well, these affairs – I mean, the proper love affairs not the sleazy paedo affairs—"

"Paedo?" His mouth gaped open in horror.

"No, that's not what I meant, sir!"

"Bree—"

"Please! Listen! It's important." Her voice was so close to breaking; surprise tears had sprung into her eyes. "These relationships…they usually happen with the popular students at school. This psychologist thought it was the teacher's way of living out some kind of fantasy… They're so flattered by the attention…and their self-esteem is all low because their own school years were so full of rejection…that they fall for the fantasy, not the student."

Logan looked so shocked she was sure she could pop ten grapes in his mouth and he'd just choke rather than chew.

"So I'm scared, Logan. That this is all this is…that I'm just a fantasy…"

If she was gonna cry she was gonna cry now and so she focused on breathing. Yet, in a second, he was by her side once more, cupping her face in his big wonderful hands and forcing her to look at him.

"Bree, aren't you forgetting something?"

His eyes were welling up. Her teacher's eyes were welling up.

"What? What am I forgetting?"

A small tear cracked out of his left eye but his face was beaming with happiness. She couldn't keep up.

"Bree, I loved you when no one at this school knew your name. I loved you when you dyed your hair purple and it washed out into some sludge colour. I loved you when your skirt clung too tight, you wore those terrible neon tights and put your hand up to answer every single question I asked the class." He smiled again. "I love you, Bree. Popular or not. I love you."

And then words failed them both. His mouth was on hers and she actually let out a groan, it felt so good. He pushed her against the photocopier so that every part of their bodies was smushed together and she was so lost in his kiss she didn't notice the angry beeping sound the machine made in complaint. Logan's kiss was the complete opposite of Logan himself – urgent, strong, overbearing. He aggressively pushed his tongue into her mouth – yet it wasn't like kissing Hugo. This was wanted. Her own tongue reciprocated, tasting him, trying to memorize every centimetre of his mouth. His hands tangled up in her hair and hers in his. It was so wonderful. She knew it was wrong, so wrong, and that made every millisecond so charged and so good. Somehow they found their way onto the floor, lying side by side, their legs entwined, their backs scratching against the grey industrial carpet. They didn't once break the kiss. His hands stroked up and down the side of her ribcage, each touch making goosebumps erupt on her skin. Their feet smashed up against the cupboard door, subconsciously keeping it shut against intruders.

It was everything Bree dreamed a kiss could be. It was a kiss that would be etched onto each of their memories for all time. A kiss to relive in boring periods of their future lives. One of those rare moments where every single other thing in life relinquishes its importance and becomes backing vocals. When they were finally done, they lay in each other's arms, stunned by the magnitude of how brilliant it was. Logan's face glowed as he nestled Bree's head into him and stroked her hair and face, like he couldn't believe his luck that he got to touch her.

Some people spend their whole lives hoping they'll be looked at the way he's looking at me right now.

Nothing had ever really felt good before. Her whole existence until that moment had been grey after grey after grey with the odd moment of black chucked in. Today – now – she'd finally met white. The colour of light and brightness and hope and redemption and purity and…and… oh, screw the descriptions, she wanted to kiss him again. So she did.

Eventually, exhausted, they broke apart and reallocated their time to just staring at each other in wonder.

Logan was tracing his fingers across her face again, drinking in every bit of her.

"Hey, you," she said shyly.

He grinned lazily. "Hey, yourself."

"Do you really love me?" It really couldn't hurt to hear it again. Multiple times. Preferably on a loop over and over.

"Yes, Bree. I love you. For so long."

Her smile matched his.

"You do realize you've not said it back, don't you?" he half-joked and, at that moment, she saw the insecure boy he once was. And probably always would be, a little bit.

"I haven't?"

"No."

"I thought it kind of went without saying."

"You've still not said it."

She sat up a bit straighter and readied herself. She'd never said those words to anyone; they were utterly alien to her. She'd read them a million times in text, seen them printed in black ink, or announced by actors on the telly. She'd heard people around her saying them – Jassmine, occasionally Hugo when he wanted Jassmine to stop being mad at him, her dad that one time he drank too much at Christmas. But her own mouth had never formed that particular string of shapes. She had never clicked her tongue off the roof of her mouth for the "l" of love and then followed it up by pursing her lips for the "you".

She spoke uncertainly. "I love you too, Logan."

His already-broad grin stretched across every part of his face. "That wasn't so hard."

She wanted to say it again. "I love you."

He threw back his head laughing. "It's great, isn't it?"

And then – as always – a dark thought came along to gatecrash the party. *This isn't the first time he's said those words…*

And then the dark thought rang up all its dodgy mates and told them to come along and smash stuff up… *He probably says it all the time to his wife.*

And then reality turned up in a police car and told everyone at the party to clean up and go home.

Bree untangled herself from him. "Logan, what are we doing?"

He noticed the change of tone in her voice; she could tell by the way his face tightened. He knew her so well, this gorgeous man. "What do you mean?"

She didn't want to state the obvious but now was the time. How could she not ruin this? It was only the most perfect thing that had ever happened to her. She wouldn't be Bree if she didn't vandalize it.

"You're my teacher."

The words fell like cluster bombs, their gravity pushing their bodies apart.

"I know that, Bree," he said quietly.

"You're married."

"That I am."

She only had one word left. "How?"

"How what? What are you asking? How is this going to work?"

She nodded, too scared of what the next five minutes would bring.

Logan sighed and used his hands to push himself up against the side of the photocopier.

"This is serious, Bree, what we've just done. I could lose my job. Jeez – if I slept with you, I could go to prison."

Bad words, bad words, bad words.

"But do you not think I've already thought of all this? That I haven't gone over it and over it, all the reasons I shouldn't love you, all the reasons I need to stay away, why I shouldn't go there. Do you not realize how much those thoughts plague me every bloody day?" He sighed again and looked exhausted. "I can't not kiss you though, Bree. I can't not love you. It would be like telling myself not to breathe. And I'm not sure how we're going to do this, how it's going to work, how we can work out being together…"

She stopped him by putting her finger over his lips and making a hushing sound. She'd seen someone doing it in the movies once. Logan ceased talking.

Bree didn't need to speak or hear any more words. For once, her favourite things were completely unwanted.

She leaned over and kissed him again until time lost all meaning and there was only feeling and sensing and love and light and love and light and love.

*   *   *

That night's blog was a short one.

I kissed him. I love him. He loves me. I kissed him.
I love him. He loves me. I kissed him. I love him. He
loves me.

She typed it again and again, and each time she smiled
from a deep place inside of her that she never knew existed.

chapter forty

There were some noteworthy aspects to being in love. And Bree wouldn't have been Bree if she hadn't taken the time to note them down.

Note them down and publish them online...

Things that are awesome about being in love

Everything is happy

Not the most eloquent of sentences, she knew, but it was the simplest way to describe it. That ever-elusive state – happiness – now followed her wherever she went, whatever she was doing. It was like her heart had turned to gold and thumped molten glowing goodness through her veins.

Smiling was easy. Effortless.

In fact, it was harder not to smile. She didn't walk, she floated. Life's tediums – Jassmine crying in the loos about Hugo again, getting an A– in her Latin coursework, the guilt she felt whenever she ignored Holdo in the corridor – didn't affect her at all. Well, maybe a bit, but then *LOGAN* would pop into her brain and she was off again, listing all the things she loved about him to herself. Just the mere whisper of a thought of him made everything and everyone good.

I...like myself

Self-esteem. Bree had it in spades when it came to her intelligence. But when it came to other parts of herself – appearance, character, humour – she'd always ticked the *self-loathing* box.

In truth, in her entire life up until last week, she'd hated who she was. Why else would she have scratched open her skin as punishment for the simple crime of being Bree? And yet now she was beginning to realize she wasn't that bad after all. Logan saw things in her she'd never seen. He complimented her on stuff she didn't know you could get complimented on.

Like: "That's what I love about you, Bree. You're so dry in everything you say. It's a gift."

Really? Terminal cynicism can be a gift? Not just a defence mechanism?

Or: "The way you roll your eyes, it just kills me."

Apparently rolling your eyes could be sexy. Rather than nasty.

And: "You're a much kinder person than you give yourself credit for," Logan told her one evening, when she'd revealed her ruthless abandonment of Holdo.

The Bree he saw was so different to the one she knew. But, with a constant supply of complimentary analysis, she was beginning to see the Bree he saw.

Yes – it was awful. Self-esteem shouldn't be an egg that hatches and grows because some guy says he loves you. She was mad at herself for being so ethically floozy. But there's nothing like being loved by someone who chose you entirely of their own free will. Especially when there were so many others out there available for love too. She'd been chosen. Her. And not because she was the last option, like in PE lessons. But because she was her. It was such a comfort. Such a warm, cosy, morally-wrong-but-she-didn't-give-a-flying...comfort.

You live for the moment

Bree had always envied those live-for-the-moment people.

The type of people who saw life as one big adventure after the next, shooting head first into anything exciting that rocked along.

Whereas her life and thoughts revolved around two major narratives:

- Reliving and analysing every single regret of the past, on a loop, until she felt sick with cringing and remorse.
- Worrying methodically about the future and every little thing that could potentially go wrong.

While she was busy doing that, life passed her by. Moments whizzed past, unnoted. Memories were left unmade. Time was wasted in such a vast way it was practically insulting.

But not now she was with Logan.

For once, "Now" was all that mattered. She stepping-stoned from one "Now" to another, hopping on and off brilliant moments without a care for the last one or the next.

It was probably just as well. The past was just embarrassing. How they'd both behaved was almost funny when they dared talk about it. The future was…not worth thinking about. If she hadn't been so intoxicated on love, she would have been worrying about:

- His wife.
- Being found out.
- Logan losing his job.
- His wife.
- How were they ever going to stay together?
- Going to university in a year and a half and being away from him.

- The age gap.
- His wife.
- Sleeping with him.
- Logan getting arrested and jailed.
- The awkwardness of the "how we met" speeches on their wedding day.
- His wife.
- Yet right now, all these were only fleeting thoughts, because she was living, living, living and loving, loving, loving.

Her mum spotted the change first.

"You're different," she declared one morning. One rare moment when Bree's dad was eating with them too – though he was hidden behind a paper, his hand only emerging to pick up his extra-strong freshly-ground coffee.

It was blunt. But – to be fair – Bree was *humming* as she ate her organic porridge with fresh fruit and honey from next-door's bees. Recently, she just hadn't felt like Pop-Tarts.

She swallowed. "What?"

Her mum crossed her arms. "What's going on with you?"

"Nothing."

"You keep…smiling."

Bree giggled and her mum gasped and pointed.

"See, you just giggled! Since the day you came out of my womb you have never once giggled. Has she, Daniel?"

Her dad lowered the paper enough so she could see

the dark workaholic circles under his eyes and stared at her bemusedly.

"No," he said cautiously, like he wasn't sure if he was being tested or not. "Bree doesn't usually giggle."

She didn't really know how to respond to that. Yelling *How would you know? You're never here?* didn't seem appropriate.

"What's happened? Have you met someone?" her mum continued.

Hating herself, Bree felt her cheeks grow warm.

"You have? A boy?"

"Mum, leave it," she warned, though her voice was too full of joy to sound threatening.

Her dad's eyebrows rose above the top of his paper. "I trust this boy isn't a loser," he said. "You're worth more than that."

Bree evilled him. "No, Dad, he's not a loser." *He's just my teacher.*

Her mum squealed. "Well, well, well. My little girl...in love."

"MUM." Bree sounded scarier this time.

"Okay, okay, don't tell me anything. It will save me dying from shock."

To her credit, her mum did leave it, and instead started questioning Bree's dad about when he could next take some time off. Although she kept giving Bree little smiles for the rest of breakfast.

* * *

Jassmine noticed it next.

"You're being less mean to everyone recently."

Never one to mince her words, Jassmine. It was one of the things Bree liked about her. Though she was sure Jassmine's respect for words was unintentional.

Bree examined her lipgloss in the mirror. Marvel's newest addition to the range – 4D lipgloss. Her dad had been boring her to tears explaining the formula.

"What you talking about?"

"You. You're being less sarky than normal."

"I am?"

"Yes."

"Hmm."

They were having a between-lessons make-up reapplication gossip. Usually this happened only twice a day. But, with new products and the upcoming dance to discuss, it'd become a between-every-lesson occurrence.

"You just seem a bit…distracted is all." Jass wasn't giving up.

"You'd be distracted too if you were spending every spare waking minute individually supergluing cotton-wool balls onto a playsuit."

Jassmine laughed. "See! That's the first time you've snapped all week. I've missed it."

Bree blotted and dropped the paper towel in the bin. "You miss me being a bitch? Do you have self-esteem issues?"

"It's just weird… You seem happier."

"I won't be happy when I'm wearing that sodding sheep costume."

Jass rifled through Bree's make-up bag and picked out glitter eyeliner. "Why are you doing this to yourself again?"

"Sheep is what I pulled out of the hat."

"I'm sure you'll make it look good."

"Says Miss Angel Gabriel, who only has to put a bit of tinsel on top of her head. It'd better not rain though, otherwise the cotton wool is going to absorb all the water and I'll expand horizontally."

They giggled together, just like friends.

"So why are you so cheerful then, Bree?"

"God, you're not giving up, are you?"

"I'm interested, that's all… Have you met someone? You NEVER talk about boys."

"That's cos I can't get a word in edgeways when you're always moaning about Hugo."

It was supposed to be a joke but Jassmine's face scrunched up.

Again.

It had looked that way all week.

"Sorry, Jass, it was supposed to be funny."

Jassmine blinked desperately so the newly-applied eyeliner didn't smudge and make glitter tears. "Am I really that bad?"

Bree gave her a hug. "It was a joke."

"A joke based on truth," Jass sniffed into her shoulder.

"Are things really that bad between you?"

Hugo had been treating Jass like utter crap since his party and Bree couldn't help but feel partly to blame. He kept putting Jass down, blowing her off, and flirting outrageously with Bree and others in front of her. And Jass kept coming back for more. It was painful to watch, but what could any of them do? Jassmine seemed determined that they *were* the perfect couple and the school would stop revolving if they broke up.

And Jassmine didn't even know about the torrent of texts Bree had been getting from Hugo since she ill-advisedly gave him her number to shut him up in the corridor one day:

When's the rerun then?

If you're playing hard to get, it's working. I'm hard...

Come over to mine? My parents are out. So is my penis.

She'd ignored him but life was just a game to Hugo and ignoring him seemed to spur him on.

Jass grabbed a wad of toilet tissue and carefully caught a stray tear. "No, it's fine. Sorry, must have PMS or something."

Bree patted her shoulder. "You do know relationships are supposed to make you happy, right?"

"We *are* happy," Jass snapped. "If you knew what he was like when it's just us two...he's really sweet."

"Hmmm."

"Anyway, you've still not told me why you're so cheerful." She blew her nose into the tissue and chucked it into the bin.

"Can't I just be full of Christmas joy?"

"Is it Matty Boy? Have you two got together on the sly?"

"No," she sighed. "He asked me out but I said no."

"Ahh."

"What is 'ahh' supposed to mean?"

"Well, it just explains why he's been telling all of us that he thinks you're a lesbian."

"He hasn't?"

"He has."

"The bastard... God, some guys just can't take rejection, can they?"

"Nope."

"I'm gonna get him." What an arse. Bree tipped her newly-cut hair upside-down to revive its deflating 3 p.m. volume.

"I'd like to see that. When?"

"I dunno. At this stupid dance."

"You could spike his drink and yank his trousers down or something."

"Or I could get the DJ to turn on the UV light – he's so pale, his whole body will glow in the dark."

And they both pissed themselves. Jass gave her another big hug and Bree knew she was a) feeling better and b) going to let Bree off the hook.

"It's so annoying it's on a school night. Queen's is so lame."

Bree began packing up her bag ready for next lesson. "At least after it we only have one day of school to get through before the Christmas holidays."

"Yeah, I suppose. We can all go in hungover together."

The bell went.

"S'laters."

"Laters."

chapter forty-one

"Everyone keeps asking me why I'm so happy."

Logan grinned over his newspaper. "Oh, do they now?"

She nodded.

"I can't think why."

"Me neither," she said back, smiling.

It was Saturday, the last weekend before the end of term. Logan had picked her up from the end of her road and taken her for coffee two towns away. She didn't know what he'd told his wife and didn't ask. They'd pulled over on a country lane on their way there for an enthusiastic kissing session. He'd reclined his driver's seat and she'd ended up on top of him as they groaned into each other's mouths, his hands running up her body. Now, with their hair still messy, they sipped gingerbread lattes on a soft leather sofa in a coffee chain, trying to ignore the cheesy Christmas carols playing in the background, and sharing the weekend supplements like an old married couple.

Christmas had exploded that week, as it always does halfway through December. Shops were crammed, younger students wore tinsel in their hair at school, and everywhere smelled of either pine or cinnamon. The night before, Bree's dad had come home brandishing a two-and-a-half-metre Christmas tree. Her parents were up late decorating it and, by the sound of all the popping corks, getting wasted at the same time. When Bree had tiptoed past the living room that morning she'd peeked in and found the tree lopsidedly daubed with baubles and three empty champagne bottles on the floor.

Logan folded his paper and put it on the coffee table so he could scooch closer to Bree. She cuddled into him instinctively and took his hand. They squeezed each other's fingers.

"So you're happy?" he murmured into her ear. Just his breath on her neck was enough for her to lose the ability to think coherently.

"Deliriously so, and you?"

He squeezed her hand tighter. "Bree, you have no idea."

They stayed like that for a while, just gently nuzzling each other, oblivious to the odd disapproving look flung in their direction, until Bree broke free to take another sip of coffee.

"God, I love Christmas," she said. "Everything tastes so good. Who would've thought gingerbread and coffee would go so well?"

Logan pulled her back to him. "I wouldn't have thought you were a Christmassy person."

"I wasn't...until this year."

"Oh, is that right?" He pulled her in tighter. "Does this mean I'm going to have to get someone a present?" He kissed her all down the side of her face.

"Perhaps...nothing big. Maybe just a first edition of *To Kill a Mockingbird* or something?"

He nodded. "Of course, of course. And maybe the original manuscript of *The Catcher in the Rye*?"

"Well, it *is* Christmas."

He kissed her more and she leaned into his mouth, savouring how good it felt. How everything felt. The kisses on her neck, the sweet taste of gingerbread on her tongue, the smell of cinnamon in the coffee shop. She'd already got Logan's Christmas present; in fact, she'd made it herself. She'd given herself a blog holiday and focused on writing him a short story instead. Although she hated to admit it, she'd struggled to write it. Words were harder to find when she was happy. Regardless, it was called *The Story of Us* and she'd even illustrated it herself with funny cartoons of them. The old Bree would've hated something so sentimental and sickly, but New Bree thought Old Bree was a sad lonely girl who just needed to be loved.

A group of adults walked in and Logan tensed instantly. He ducked and hid behind Bree, who sat up to get a better look.

"Do you know them?"

"Shit. Maybe, I dunno. That guy – I think I might know him from somewhere."

A hard knot twisted in her intestines. Logan buried his face into the sofa.

"What are you doing?" she whispered.

"What do you think I'm doing? Hiding. If he knows me then he might know Carol."

Carol. Her name. The Wife's name. He'd never used it before. The knot twisted in on itself and Bree's whole stomach cramped.

"We're miles from home – what are the chances it's someone you know?"

"Hang on. Let me go to the toilet so I can get a closer look."

And he was up, acting like he didn't know her at all. He walked to the men's toilet slowly, trying to look at the group naturally.

Bree slurped her coffee sullenly. She stared into the dregs of her cup and felt the Christmas spirit leak out of her. When he returned, two minutes later and smiling, she wouldn't let him put his arm around her.

"What's up?" he asked, trying again, but she shuffled across the sofa.

"So you didn't know him then?"

He grinned. "Nope. False alarm."

"Brilliant news."

"Why are you being like this?"

"Like what?" For the first time in her life, Bree really sounded her age.

"Like this." He gestured towards her crossed arms and pouting face. "All sullen, like a teenager."

"I am a teenager, remember? That's why you just publicly disowned me."

"Publicly what? Bree...what? Oh, that? You really think that's what I did? I just panicked, that's all. Come on, you can't blame me for that. I am kind of putting myself in a dangerous position for you." He scratched his head, looking exasperated.

Bree thought she was in a pretty dangerous position too. Her heart was his, and he could stamp on it whenever he wanted.

"Are you ashamed of me, is that it?" she asked, annoyed at her own insecurity.

"Of course that's not it."

"Then why did you just go hide in the toilets?" Her heart...hurt. She didn't know organs could get cramp, but that's what it felt like.

"Bree...come on, that's not what happened."

"That's what it felt like." She didn't care that she was being immature – she was seventeen, she WAS immature.

He tucked a bit of hair behind her ear. That thawed her a little and she hated herself.

"You know things are...complicated between us."

"They don't have to be." She sounded like a small child.

"What do you suggest? That I leave my wife and run off with you?"

It wasn't a *bad* idea.

"You're not even eighteen yet. I'd go to prison. I could even go to prison for this…they call it an abuse of trust."

"I don't want you to go to prison… You're the only one I do trust…"

God – things were serious. She'd been so busy falling in love she hadn't wanted to think through the Real World consequences.

"I turn eighteen next September. It's less than a year away." It was something…

"What do you suggest we do, Bree? I wait for you to finish school and then we run off into the moors like Kathy and Heathcliff?"

He was making a literary joke about their relationship. She knew she was supposed to laugh but it really wasn't funny.

"I don't know."

And she didn't. She really didn't.

"Let's just see where life takes us, shall we? How does that sound?"

It sounded like a cop-out, to be honest. A get-out-of-jail-free card. But what choice did she have? She didn't have the strength to give him an ultimatum…that would risk losing him. And Logan was the only person left in her life right now she could be herself with. If she lost him, who would she be? Would she morph into popular Bree for ever? Like, if the old Bree fell over in the forest and no one was there to hear her then did she make a noise?

She found herself nodding.

"That's my girl." He squeezed her so tight she almost couldn't breathe. When he released her, she really looked at him. Just the beauty of his face – the slight wrinkles around his eyes, the strong arch of his nose and slight dimple in his chin – made it all forgotten. For now at least.

"Now…why don't you tell me more about this sheep costume? I can't wait to see you in it on Thursday."

chapter forty-two

They got ready for the dance at Jassmine's, naturally.

It was insanely festive in her bedroom. She'd taken fairy lights to a whole new level; they were draped over every available surface and the place stank of festive-scented candles.

"ALCOHOL!" Jass announced, as she came back from the kitchen carrying a tray of odious-looking drinks.

"What the hell are those?" Gemma asked, her face glimmering. She'd picked *First wise man* out of the hat. Gold. So, obviously, Gemma wore a revealing gold dress and had covered herself with body glitter. Bree was impressed with her make-it-sexy-somehow expertise. There wasn't a false beard to be seen.

Jass carefully put the tray down on her desk, which was overflowing with discarded clothes.

"IT'S EGGNOG! Well, I didn't know what eggnog was so I just tipped some Baileys over some sambuca. Look – they're like mini Guinnesses!"

Bree eyed them apprehensively and Jass caught her.

"Don't worry. I'm not going to get wasted again like at Hugo's."

"Er…I thought your drink got spiked?" Bree asked innocently.

Jass tipped a glass of fake eggnog down her throat, winced, and picked up another. "Oh, come on, we all know I just drank too much."

Gemma stood on the bed.

"LADIES AND GENTLEMEN, SHE'S FINALLY ADMITTED IT."

They all clapped and cheered and Jassmine joined in. She looked pretty. She'd got some twisty floaty white dress and cinched it in with gold braid. A delicate halo made of thin gold tinsel shone off her honey-blonde hair. It was surprisingly demure, especially in comparison to Gemma, and Bree was grateful not all of them were going to offend any Christians at the party that night.

"Yeah, yeah, okay…well, it was a good cover-up."

"Good?" Jessica said. Also an angel. Although for some mysterious reason (Jassmine), she'd been downgraded from gold tinsel to silver. "The police filed a report."

Jass handed out the other glasses. "Who cares? It's not like any real crimes happen round here anyway… Bree, I can't talk seriously when you look like that."

Bree looked down at herself and pretended to be confused. "Like what?"

"Like a sexy sheep! How the hell have you managed it?"

She stood up and twirled to show everyone her costume again. It had all come together somehow – her playsuit covered entirely with stuck-on cotton-wool balls. The VERY short playsuit...although adequate cotton wool had been applied to hide her thigh tops.

"You look almost...cute. But then also really filthy. I'm in awe," Emily said. She was dressed as King Herod, wearing a tiara instead of a crown.

Bree opened her arms. "Do you want a hug? I'm so comfy."

"I want one!" Jass yelled and launched herself on top of her. They both fell backwards, laughing like tipsy teenagers. Probably because they were tipsy teenagers. Jass stroked her belly. "You're so soft. I can't stop stroking you."

"Back off, lezzer."

Bree hated to admit it, but she was having fun. The impossible had happened and the perfect posse weren't taking themselves very seriously. Okay, so each nativity costume had a sexy twist, but at least they'd been up for it.

Jass picked up yet another glass and stood on the bed. "I want to make a toast."

"Oh, no. She's getting wasted again," Gemma muttered. Loudly. Deliberately.

"Shut up, Gemma."

And she did.

"Christmas is about the year coming to an end. And I don't know about you, but at the beginning of this year I never thought Bree, aka Twatty McGeek, would be here, drinking with us, and making us dress up as nativity characters."

Bree felt herself go a bit dark peach.

"But, for whatever reason, Bree, you somehow got a life. Joined our friendship group. And, I don't know about you guys, but I'm really glad you did." And, to Bree's utter shock and despair, Jass's voice broke. "Bree, you're, like, brilliant. We all love you, don't we, girls?"

The others chanted their agreement and Bree's face went peachier and peachier.

"So Happy Christmas, everyone. Now let's go and make Queen's Hall wildly jealous that they're not us."

They all clinked their glasses before necking their drinks. Then Mariah Carey's "All I Want For Christmas Is You" came on Jassmine's massive stereo and they all whooped and danced like strippers. Bree couldn't join in. She was still stunned by what had just been said. And a little touched. She'd done it. She'd actually done it. Bree, total loser extraordinaire, had successfully hacked into the inner circle. Not only were they scared of and influenced by her, they actually liked her.

Bree wasn't used to being liked. It felt so great she felt instantly vulnerable.

Would they still like her if they knew the truth?

chapter forty-three

The school looked fantastic. Any worries about it being a dowdy school dance evaporated when they saw all the upside-down Christmas trees blinking with fairy lights and hanging from the ceiling.

They made their entrance together. The boys and the girls.

"No bloody way."

"They've come as the nativity."

"That's so…random."

"That's so…awesome."

"LOOK AT ME!" Hugo yelled at everyone, his face already pink from being half-drunk. "I'M THE VIRGIN MARY."

He yanked out a toy doll from nowhere, and held the mini-Jesus above his head like it was the FA Cup.

By the response he got, you would have thought the guy had just won an NME award.

"That is siiiiiiiiiiiiiiick."

"Woooooah, go Hugo!"

"I can't believe Hugo's come as the Virgin Mary. Virgin? Hugo?"

"I can't believe Seth's come as Joseph."

Seth, keen to show off, ran after Hugo to share in his glory, but tripped on his dressing gown. The room cracked up.

Matty Boy, a shepherd, shuffled over to Bree with a shy smile. "Aren't I supposed to be looking after you?"

"It's okay," said Bree, still a little pissed off at him for telling everyone she was a lesbian. "I'm a very independent sheep. Plus I'm a lesbian, apparently. Which if you think is an insult means you're one very shallow-minded shepherd."

"Sorry."

"What was that?" She leaned towards him overdramatically with her hand to her ear.

"I said I'm sorry."

"Oh yes. Brilliant. About what?"

"Erm. About being a bitter bastard and spreading rumours about you?"

"Oh, that. Well, you should be sorry."

He grinned. "Will it make it up to you if I tell you you've somehow made a sheep costume very sexy?"

She was about to rebut but Hugo jumped over, picked her up and squeezed her tight.

"Well, call me Welsh, but I may have to become a sheep-shagger by the end of the night." He spun her round while she tried hard not to grimace. Even through her protective layer of cotton-wool balls, his touch turned her stomach. "You look so hot," he whispered, his mouth right in her ear, making her shudder.

She pushed him off and looked around. Everyone was watching, especially Jassmine, who looked quite rightly suspicious.

"Don't you need to be looking after your child? He is the son of God, after all."

"Who, this?" And he was about to drop-kick the baby Jesus across the dance floor when Jassmine ran over and grabbed it off him. She shrieked with fake laughter and used Hugo's hilarious behaviour as an excuse to stand right between them.

"Hugo. You can't treat the son of God like a rugby ball. You'll upset people."

"I can do whatever the hell I want."

"Oh yeah?"

"Yeah."

And then Jass was upside down, her dress falling over her head, showing off her white thong. He ran with her to the bar, her tinsel halo falling to the floor as she screamed. Loving. Every. Moment.

Bree took the moment's peace to analyse her surroundings. They were all being stared at by jealous faces. Somehow, from the outside, this soap-opera existence looked appealing.

For what was effectively a school disco, the place really did look pretty damn good. As well as the trees hanging from the ceiling, there was a chocolate fountain, and a huge four-metre right-way-up Christmas tree covered in candy canes. A giant ball of mistletoe hung suspended over the middle of the dance floor and some students were already using it to maximum effect. She looked for Logan, wondering what he made of it all, and located him standing behind "the bar", guarding the punch from a-spiking. He wore a suit, but scruffily – just how she liked it. His hair poked out from underneath a Santa hat. His eyes met hers at the same time and it passed between them again – the sexual tension – careering across the giant room. He nodded, silently acknowledging her and what they were. Her heartbeat went nutso and she was relieved when Gemma grabbed her round the waist and pulled her towards the bar.

"Come on, we need to hit the punch while it's still spiked."

"How's it been spiked? It's being guarded."

"Yeah, but it's being guarded by that pathetic 'I'm down with the kids' English teacher. He deliberately turned a blind eye when Hugo poured in half a bottle of absinthe."

"Absinthe?!"

"Yep. For massed pissed-ness, one needs to spike punches with absinthe."

Gemma's description of Logan dented Bree's pride. He wasn't "down with the kids". He just had a soul, unlike every other teacher. Her Latin teacher, in charge of distributing sausage rolls, was wearing tweed, for God's sake!

When they got to the bar, Logan dipped a cup into the punch and held it out to Bree.

"Punch, girls?"

God – he was so good at this.

She took the plastic cup and took a sip. It was definitely alcoholic. "Thanks, Mr Fellows."

"You girls go easy now," he said, handing one to Gemma. "Too much fruit juice can make you hyper."

"I'll bear that in mind," Gemma said sarcastically.

"See," she whispered as they walked away sipping. "He's so cringe!"

Bree felt like a porcupine that had just put all its prickles up. "He's not. He's cool..." She saw the look on Gemma's face. "For a teacher, anyway. Shall we dance?"

After Bree's second glass of punch, things got a bit hazier. She remembered them playing a LOT of Christmas songs, especially The Pogues, her absolute favourite. Then, at her suggestion, the lot of them cleared a space on the dance floor and re-enacted the entire nativity scene. To music.

It was ridiculous. But cool because it was them doing it. Jassmine was surprisingly hilarious, grinding up against Hugo and fake-flying about the place. Gemma demanded the DJ play the eighties tune "Gold" for a dance solo. And Bree spent a lot of her time running away from Matty Boy, who kept catching her with his shepherd's crook. She could tell the evening was peaking when "Merry Christmas

Everyone" came on and the nativity scene wrapped their arms around each other and bellowed along.

She had to admit it – it was fun. This wasn't the ice-cool, perfect, popular crowd she'd loathed from afar. These weren't the twisted vindictive people she'd hated. This group of people were intelligent, up for a laugh, self-deprecating... and she couldn't help but feel just a little bit responsible for the change. Well, she was definitely responsible for the decrease in bullying levels. Gemma had even closed her "Dirty Gossip" account the other day.

Maybe Bree wasn't so uninteresting after all. Maybe she was an...okay person? Maybe it was the absinthe. Maybe it was the Christmas spirit. But, for once, Bree was really actually proud of herself and who she was.

She also needed a wee quite badly.

She made her way to the toilets blearily, stopping to chat to people as she passed. It was only when she sat on the loo seat that she realized she was a bit drunk. So she sat there until her head stopped cartwheeling and took a while washing her hands too. Looking in the mirror, she saw her sheep costume was getting a bit tatty but she still looked awesome. She smiled at her reflection, dried her hands under the dryer and walked out, only to bump straight into Mr Fellows. He was leaning against the wall, his Santa hat all askew.

"Logan."

"Shh," he whispered, with a wicked smile. "Is there anyone else in the loos?"

Miraculously – for a girl's toilet – it was empty. Although she had, for some unknown reason, staggered to the "crying toilets", like a homing pigeon, which were further away from the hall.

Bree shook her head.

"Brilliant." He grabbed her hand and pulled her back into where she'd just left.

"Logan, what are you doing?"

He didn't answer at first, just pushed her into a toilet cubicle and locked them both in. He pushed her against the wall and frantically kissed her, every inch of his body pinning her to the door. He tasted like absinthe.

"Logan," she giggled into his mouth. "Have you been drinking?"

"You. Are. So. Gorgeous," he replied, between kisses.

She closed her eyes as the sensation of his lips took over all rational thought. "Logan, we'll get caught."

"I don't care."

She gave up and kissed him back. More than that, she jumped up slightly so he was holding her weight and wrapped her legs around his waist.

"Oh my God, Bree."

She took that to mean he liked the leg-wrapping. He let out a man-sigh and slammed her body back. Everything was a blur of hazy lust and hormones. She loved the taste of him, she loved the way they could be caught at any moment, she loved that she felt so…wanted. There was only kissing and touching and stroking and groaning and all the other "ings" that happen between two consenting adults – but not so much between student and teacher.

Eventually, Logan broke off.

"What?" she said, suddenly all shy as he gazed at her adoringly.

"You're really something, you know that, right?"

She looked down bashfully. "What do you mean?"

"Did you see everyone in that hall? How they looked at you? How they circle you?"

"Don't be stupid."

"It's true."

He hugged her tight. "I can't believe I'm kissing the most popular girl in school…"

Bree's trouble-detector kicked in. "What? Is that why you came in here?"

"I was just joking."

"Oh…" The words still jarred with her. "That's not why…is it…?"

"SHHH," he whispered urgently. "Somebody's coming in."

The bang of the door made adrenalin surge through her. The clip-clop of heeled shoes racketed off the lino floor.

Oh no oh no oh no oh no. Logan's hand clamped over her mouth. She could feel the frantic beat of his heart pressed against hers.

If they got caught…

"Jassmine Dallington looks like such a tart," a voice said. Bree didn't recognize it – just someone from their year, maybe. The smell of the girls' collective perfumes wafted under the gap at the bottom of the door.

"At least she's tried to look sexy. Have you seen the state of Bree? A sheep's costume!"

"I know. I don't get why they're mates with her."

"Such a weirdo."

"Always has been. And suddenly we're all, like, supposed to forget, just because Jassmine had a lobotomy or something."

"Hold my bag, will you? I'm dying for a wee."

They listened, both their hearts thudding, as one of the girls clopped into the cubicle next to them and started peeing like a carthorse.

"Hugo looks so fit, as always," the girl called through the cubicle door, mid-wee.

Despite the urgency of the circumstance, Bree couldn't help but roll her eyes.

"And doesn't he bloody know it," the girl's friend replied.

It was so hard to breathe quietly. Bree had never noticed before just how noisy an activity it was. Or how her heartbeat appeared to have an amp attached.

Logan wasn't much quieter, his breath was quick and rasping. His hand over her mouth was shaking so violently, she was surprised it wasn't making tap-dancing noises against her teeth.

The girls argued amongst themselves a bit longer, discussing the physical merits of Hugo, Seth and Matty Boy.

God, Bree thought, *girls really do take ages in the bathroom.*

Finally, after an eternity, they left, the door swinging shut heavily behind them. Logan and Bree stayed in silence, listening out for any stray noise that may indicate someone had stayed behind

There was nothing.

Logan let out a big sigh of relief, so loud it could've been heard from the dance floor.

He didn't say anything though. Just removed his hand from Bree's mouth and stepped away from her like she was toxic all of a sudden.

"Well," she said, wanting there to be noise to erase the tension. "That was terrifying."

His face had gone white. He wouldn't look at her. "Shit," he muttered. "What if they'd caught us?"

She cupped his face and tried to get him to look at her. "They didn't. We're okay. Come on, look at me."

But he wouldn't. "I could've lost everything." Logan took off his Santa hat and wrung it.

Bree tried again to reach out to him. "But you didn't. Everything's still the same."

"How am I even going to get out here without getting caught?" He looked round the cubicle in panic.

"I can go out first," she suggested tenderly, "and check that the coast is clear."

"Would you?"

"Not until you stop being weird with me."

"I'm not being weird."

"You are. You really are."

More silence. More tension. He gave her a weak smile.

"I'm sorry… That just scared the crap out of me. What are we playing at?"

"I don't know," she replied shyly. "But I like this game."

He didn't reply and she bit her lip, wondering how to calm him down.

"Do you want me to go check if it's okay for you to get out now?" she asked.

"Not really. I'm terrified."

"Don't you have to guard a punchbowl?"

"Oh that…yeah… I don't think I'm very good at my job, Bree. I keep breaking all these rules."

"Is it worth it?" she asked quietly.

And he came back to her again. That led to one more kiss, and another, and another. Eventually, Bree crept out of the cubicle, looking left and right repeatedly like she was crossing a busy road. Nothing. All the sinks stood empty. She tiptoed cartoon-style to the door, opened it and looked up and down the corridor. It was dark. And empty. Delightfully empty.

"Logan," she whispered behind her. "It's all clear. Go, go, go, go, go."

And like a lightning bolt, he was out of the door. Stopping only to graze his lips against hers in the darkness before he was swallowed by the beating sounds of the music down the hallway.

chapter forty-four

Bree stayed in the corridor, leaning against the door, letting her exhalation of breath take with it all the tension of the past twenty minutes.

"Well, well, well, so this is why you're not replying to my texts."

The voice came from nowhere, like a ghost. She immediately knew who it was. Every hair on her arms stood on end.

"Hugo?"

He stepped out from a crevice of darkness that had hidden him so successfully. Cold-blooded fear ran through her brain.

How much had he seen?

"The English teacher, Bree? Seriously?" He stepped nearer.

Bree tried to step away, but she was backed up against the wall. "What are you on about?"

Even she could tell her attempt to sound blasé had failed.

"You puzzle me more and more as I get to know you better," he said, his eyes scanning her face for a reaction. "I find it hard not to think about you."

"This is lovely and all, but I'm going back to the dance." She turned to leave but Hugo slammed his hand in front of her face, blocking her exit with his arm. The violence of it made her jump.

"What if I tell someone?"

More dread ricocheted into her bloodstream, like someone had just squeezed a UV drip filled with the stuff. "Tell them what?"

He couldn't prove anything. Could he?

"That wonder girl Bree is boning a teacher."

"Don't be ridiculous, Hugo. I'm not boning him."

That, at least, was true.

"Really? Am I a tough act to follow then, is that it? Does poor Mr Fellows not think he can live up to me?"

Judging on Hugo's one measly performance, Bree was quite certain a slug on Viagra could outscore Hugo's sexual expertise. Although she didn't think this was the time to tell him that. Every neuron in her brain was in think-quick mode. She attempted to push past his arm, expecting him to drop it, but he stood firm and slammed the other one on the other side of her – utterly pinning her in.

Alright, she'd admit it, she was actually quite scared.

"Hugo. What are you playing at?"

He leaned his face so close to hers that if anyone walked

past it would've looked like they were snogging. Not good. Nothing about this situation was good.

"I'm getting bored of you pretending you don't want me, Bree," he said, in what he probably thought was an alluring way. "Let's just skip forward to the bit where I do filthy things to you again. If you've got a thing for teachers, I can teach you a few things..."

There are times in life when you really should do the sensible thing. This moment was one of them. The sensible thing was to pretend she fancied the pants off Hugo, make some false promise to shag him later, and launch into some big speech about how she and Mr Fellows weren't doing anything, she was far too much in love with Hugo instead.

But recently Bree hadn't been doing the sensible thing.

In fact, Bree was getting a thousand words of material every day out of not doing the sensible thing.

And Bree had just about lost her temper.

"FOR FUCK'S SAKE, HUGO!" she yelled into his face, so loudly that he recoiled, giving her a bit more room. "When are you going to get the message? I don't fancy you. I NEVER want your hands, or anything else, anywhere NEAR me again. Do you get that? That night at your party was the worst experience of my life. It was crap. YOU were crap. And you wanna know why? Because you're full of crap. I hate you. I hate everything about you. I think you're a nasty, vacuous, arrogant, chauvinistic bell-end. How you treat Jass is despicable. How you treat EVERYONE is despicable. You wanna know why I slept with you?" She stood up straight, high on finally saying what she felt after months of suffocating. "It was an experiment. That's all. And it was a gross one at that. So please, let me go, cos if I have to spend another SECOND near your teeny tiny penis, and teeny tiny brain, I will scream for help and then projectile vomit onto your smug, self-satisfied face."

If she were in a movie, people would've appeared out of the darkness and started a slow applause that built to a crescendo.

If she were in a movie, Hugo would have burst into tears, run off into the distance, and gone to get a job as a bin man or something.

If she were in a movie, Logan would have chased after him, smacked him in the jaw, then run back to Bree, scooped her up into his arms and they'd have ridden off on a perfectly white horse that appeared out of nowhere.

Life isn't a movie though, is it?

Hugo stepped back. He cocked his head to one side and gave her a wink.

"Careful, Bree. I'm not the sort of person you should piss off."

"Shut up, Hugo. You're not in the bloody mafia."

He smiled. He wasn't supposed to be smiling.

And smiles aren't supposed to fill you with dread.

"I'd better be getting back to Jassmine. She'll be wondering where we both are."

"Can I suggest you keep her wondering? She's my friend, I don't want to hurt her."

That was the point when Hugo lost his temper. He got right up in her face, and spat as he talked.

"YOU don't tell me what to do, Bree. Got that?"

If he was trying to intimidate her, it was working. Her hands shook uncontrollably and she scrunched up her face to blink out the spit splatters.

"You've dropped your baby Jesus," she said, and pointed shakily to the floor.

He followed her finger, saw the doll discarded on the lino, and burst out laughing. "Oops."

Then, just like that – just like nothing had happened – he picked up the baby Jesus, winked at her again, and sauntered back towards the music.

While Bree slid down the wall and hunched up on the floor, desperately trying to get her breath back.

chapter forty-five

She was woken by the delicious smell of hot buttered toast.

"Wake up, Miss Hangover, you've still got one day of school left."

Her mum put the breakfast on her bedside table and yanked open the curtains. Dull grey light from the drizzly landscape outside half-arsed its way into her room.

She sat up, rubbed her eyes and blinked. "Ergh. What time is it?"

"Half seven. You've not got too long."

Bree turned her achy head to look at the side table. She saw the toast, plus a glass of orange juice. "Mum, you are an actual legend, you know that, right?"

She smiled and sat down at the end of Bree's bed. "I was young too once, believe it or not. I know from experience that carbs and vitamin C are the way forward."

Bree took a bite and moaned. "Definitely the way forward."

"So, did you have a good time? I found your sheep costume at the bottom of the stairs this morning. It's pretty ruined."

Bree tried to remember the end of last night. Ahhh – it had been raining on the way home. Her sheep costume had absorbed everything and doubled in size. Jass had found it hilarious and walking home – well, staggering home – had taken double the time because she'd kept cackling and taking photos.

Jassmine... Oh crap, Hugo. The thought of their conversation filled her with dread again. But he'd acted like nothing had happened once they both got back to the dance. She'd arrived in time for the last two songs and they'd all put their arms around each other in a circle and yelled "*Happy Christmas*". And Hugo had just been normal – well, as normal as a six-foot rugby player dressed as the Virgin Mary can be.

What else had happened...?

Oh yeah – Gemma had got a bit too sweaty doing sexy dancing to "Santa Baby" and dripped puddles of gold glitter all over the place. That was brilliant.

It'd been a good night. She never would have thought that lot were capable of fun, but sometimes, just sometimes, Bree was willing to admit she was wrong.

And now there was only one day left until two weeks off. She planned to scale back her Manifesto duties over Christmas – spend more time reading important books, watching a few art-house DVDs. She thought she might even see if she could rekindle her friendship with Holdo on the sly… She missed talking about…life stuff with him. She missed…just him, so much.

"Yeah, it was fun." Bree sipped the beautifully thirst-quenching juice. "The costume got rained on, but other than that I had fun."

"Did you kiss anyone under the mistletoe?"

"Mum!"

"What? I'm just asking. I know you're hiding a boy from me."

Logan. The horror of Hugo seeing them smacked into her again. But she was sure he hadn't said anything the rest of the night… So she bit down on her worries for now.

She was meeting Logan after school to say goodbye for Christmas and to exchange gifts. Well, she hoped he'd bought her something. She still didn't quite understand why they weren't allowed to see each other over the holidays, but he'd brought up all sorts of reasons – mainly family commitments, and having to go to Scotland to see in-laws, which made her jealous as hell.

"I need to get dressed," she told her mum.

"Yes, yes, yes. You never tell me anything," Mum answered as she swished out of the room.

Bree didn't spend a large amount of time on her appearance that morning. Just plastered foundation with reflective particles all over herself to hide any signs of hangover, plumped on some red lippy and scraped her hair into a high ponytail. It took a few attempts to get the buttons right on the security gate but, other than that, she felt relatively functional.

She was only two minutes late to meet Jassmine at their usual corner, but Jass wasn't there. She played on her phone for a few minutes, expecting to see a Jassmine-shape strutting down the pavement from a distance. But no Jassmine-shape materialized.

She gave it another five minutes.

Still nothing.

She texted her.

Where are you, waster? I've made it to the corner okay, so you better. I'm waiting five more mins then I'm off without you.

No reply.

After ten minutes, still nothing. Jass was either asleep or vomming down the toilet, Bree reasoned. So she set off on her way.

Waiting for Jass had made her late. She ran to school, sweating off her light-reflecting foundation and ending up a red mess. There was only a minute to get to the form room so she didn't have time to meet up with the others for their usual post-party toilet gossip.

The moment she walked down the corridor she felt something was up.

Eyes, all of them, were on her. Students actually rubbernecked as they passed her. Whispers whizzed round her ears, making them tingle.

What's going on?

It was hard to check herself subtly. Did she smell? She angled her head down and tried to sniff her armpit. She didn't think so. Was her red half-melted face that bad? She dug out her compact mirror and checked her reflection. Nope. She looked okayish…not spectacular… but okay.

She kept hearing the same word.

Potatoes.

Seriously, what the hell was going on?

She made it to form room just as the bell was going. Everyone was already sat down, including Hugo, Seth and company. The moment Bree walked in the door they burst into sniggers.

"Be quiet, the bell's gone," Mr Phillips commanded.

This made them laugh harder. Bree sat down and gave them all a *What the hell?* look but none of them would return her gaze. Apart from Hugo. He smirked and stared at her as she pulled out her chair and took a seat. She repeated her questioning look and he made a face that made her blood turn to ice and harden up her arteries. She couldn't even describe what face it was. A mixture of a wink, a nod, and a Cheshire-cat grin.

It was bad.

Oh God. Had he told? What had he done?

"POTATOES," Seth yelled and the whole class erupted in laughter.

The whole class minus Bree.

"Enough of that," Mr Phillips said, before launching into a lecture about revising over Christmas.

Bree didn't hear a word he said. She was rationalizing for all she was worth. Was it about Mr Fellows? Surely Hugo wouldn't have told everyone about that? It was just an empty threat, something to lure her back into that crusty bed of his. If he'd told, she'd be in the headmistress's office, frantically making up lies. Had he told about what had happened at his party? She shook her head to herself... No...it wouldn't make sense. He would lose Jassmine, and he liked having her for his own screwed-up reasons. Plus, would anyone really believe him? Everyone knew Bree wouldn't do that to Jassmine... Well, everyone thought that, anyway. So what was it? *Potatoes?*

She came to the conclusion that he'd just made up some silly joke rumour about her as punishment for her outburst. She'd find out from the girls at lunch and laugh it off, just in time for Christmas.

That had to be it...

She didn't bother talking to the guys after leaving the form room. They kept saying "potatoes" anyway, again and again – each time seemingly more hysterical than the last. She got to Latin super-fast – funny how easy that is, when a whole school parts in the corridor for you. She was getting impatient and double Latin didn't really help matters.

The clock hands trudged wearily from second to second, apparently stopping at scenic pubs on the way to have a pint. Time dawdled and backtracked its way to lunch, while Bree tapped her foot so hard she almost wore a hole in the carpet.

Finally, FINALLY, the bell went. Bree shot out of her chair like a bullet covered in olive oil and jogged to the usual bathroom. The girls would be in here. They always were. She'd finally know what was going on.

The moment she pushed open the door she could hear wailing from the end cubicle.

"How could she do this?"

"I don't know, honey. Please stop crying, they're not worth it."

"She's such a slut."

"She is, and everyone knows that now."

"But how…"

Bree's breath caught. It was them. Jassmine was crying. He'd told. The sonofabitch had actually told.

She was gonna have to lie a LOT to get out of this one.

"Jass?" she called, as quietly and sympathetically as she could.

The cubicle made "Shh" noises and went quiet.

"Jass, I know you're in there. I can hear you."

Still silence. Well, silence with a few added shushes thrown into the mix.

Bree sighed. "I don't know what Hugo's told you… but please don't believe him… I'm not sure what's going on but we need to sort this out... You're my best friend..."

The door slammed open and Jassmine appeared. Her face was so scary Bree took a step backwards.

"How dare you?" she hissed.

Jassmine had been crying so hard that her face looked as if it had had an allergic reaction to her own tears. Every centimetre of it was bright red and sodden. Her eyes were swollen, her hair matted. Grief oozed out of every pore. But there was anger there too. No, not anger, fury. Actually, not fury... What's worse than fury? This was it.

"Jassmine," she protested weakly. "Don't listen to him. He's lying. Whatever he said, he's lying."

"STOP LYING TO ME!" she yelled, and Bree's hair almost flew back with the ferocity. "How dare you? HOW DARE YOU? Not only have you taken the one thing – the ONE THING – that's good in my life and ruined it, you now, as someone who CLAIMS to be my friend, have the AUDACITY to lie about it? I hate you. I HATE YOU. Get out. Get out NOW. You're finished in this school, got that? FINISHED."

She burst into tears again and slumped to the ground, howling and hiccupping.

That's when Bree got it.

She'd been trying to ignore it for so long, but Jassmine was a human. A real person. She wasn't just a character, a cliché, a popular bitch. There were emotions and insecurities and history and a life being lived by a *person*, a vulnerable human, just like everyone else.

Who could get hurt. And betrayed. And humiliated.

And she wasn't just a human. She was Bree's friend. A friend who'd been so amazing about Bree's scars, who'd welcomed her into her world. Yes she'd been awful to Bree in the past, but that didn't make what Bree had done to her right. And bitterness wasn't an excuse for anything.

Out of a natural overwhelming instinct to care for her, Bree tried to get to her side to make it better. But Gemma, her face so full of spite it was even uglier than usual, stepped in front of her.

"Get away from her."

One by one, the perfect posse stood in front of Jassmine, stepping forward to protect their queen...their friend.

"I don't...know..." Bree tried to talk but words failed her. Words never failed her.

"You heard what she said," Jessica said. "Get out."

There was nothing else Bree could do but turn and walk out. The door slammed shut behind her, and Jassmine's renewed wails echoed down the halls, painting the air with utter heartbreak.

chapter forty-six

Bree needed to talk to Hugo.

What had he done? If she knocked some sense into him – preferably repeatedly with an iron bar – he'd realize how stupid he was and they could backtrack. Tell Jass it was a lie. A joke that got out of hand.

Where would he be?

There was only one place he would want to play out this spectacle so publicly.

The canteen.

The moment Bree pushed open the double doors, everyone fell silent. Dozens of heads turned in her direction in unison. Her heart thudded so loudly it was like a drumbeat. A death drum. She walked slowly and purposefully towards Hugo's table. He and the others were the only people not watching. They all stared instead at Hugo's stupid tablet, laughing like hyenas.

How could he? When his girlfriend was a sobbing mess only a hallway away.

As she passed tables she heard mutterings. Names being called. Each and every one meant for her. It was the longest walk of her life but she held her head high and strode with purpose. She got to his table.

"Hugo?"

Thank GOD, her voice sounded as self-assured as she needed it to sound.

He didn't look up.

"Hugo?" she said again. Louder, and with even more authority. "We need to talk."

This was hard, what with two hundred people watching every moment.

He still ignored her.

"Hugo, come on, stop being a dick—"

Hugo held up one finger and broke her off. Then he slowly and deliberately brought it to his mouth.

"Shh," he said, and his face made her tremble. "I'm watching something."

The tablet. He just as slowly and deliberately turned it round. A video was playing, full screen. It had been filmed in night vision, so Bree couldn't make it out at first.

There was a toned white arse, glowing in the green artificial light. It was moving up and down on top of someone.

No…

It was Hugo's arse.

And there, screwed up in pain, was Bree's face. Under him. Her hair flicked over her face every time he thrust into her. Her eyes were clenched shut and she was whispering to herself.

It brought back every stabbing memory of that horrid, horrid moment.

Her body began to jitter like she was plugged into an electric socket. The video wouldn't stop. It kept on playing. She stared at herself. Nausea welled up in her stomach, twisting it into a knot that would never be untied.

"You...filmed us?" Her voice was so weak that everyone in the room leaned in to hear.

Then all the pennies dropped.

Just before they did it, he'd gone to his laptop to put music on. Or so she thought. But he'd actually been turning on his webcam.

In that moment she was certain no one would ever be as evil as he was. Her whole body was screaming.

Hugo grinned – utterly indifferent to the life he'd just destroyed.

"I thought it would be fun," he said smoothly. "You know, to make a memento of our time together? Little did I know you would be crap in bed. Look at you. It's like shagging a sack of potatoes."

Potatoes.

Just the mention of the word made Seth and Matty Boy piss themselves laughing again. And, from person to person, table to table, it spread. Until it felt like every single person in the cafeteria was laughing at her. Just like always. But, this time, it was so much worse.

There was only one thing to do.

Bree turned round and ran.

chapter forty-seven

She knew he would be in his classroom. He always was. Every lunchtime. Said he hated all the politics in the staffroom.

Wonderful, dependable Logan. The man who loved her. He could make this better. He could take her into his arms, and smooth down her hair and say grown-up things and suggest adult solutions, like "Let's run away together, right this moment".

Bree had never needed another person before. Now she needed Logan more than anyone had ever needed anyone. Ever. Ever. Ever.

The halls were empty. Everyone was in the cafeteria, gorging themselves on the feast of gossip. There was so much to discuss, to dissect; not to mention the video footage to watch.

She was at his door in less than a minute. Looking

through the glass, there he was, and already things felt a little better. Her heart lurched in her ribcage. She bashed through the door, her face wild.

"LOGAN!"

It would've been obvious, even to a more conventional teacher who didn't touch up his students in stationery cupboards, that something was seriously wrong.

And yet Logan didn't really react to her dramatic entrance. He just closed the book he was reading and turned to face her.

"Yes, Bree, what is it? Do you have a problem?"

It was like they hardly knew each other.

"Logan. Something awful has happened. I need your help."

"I'm your teacher, Bree. You will therefore call me Mr Fellows."

What?

"Logan?"

"Bree. I'm warning you." His face was utterly passive, his lips drawn tight. He wouldn't look at her.

"What's going on?" She went over and kneeled down, trying to get him to look at her. But his eyes went left, right, up, down, anywhere but to her eyes.

"I don't know, Bree. You're the one who came into my classroom."

"Seriously, what's going on?"

He picked up his book and turned a page over. "I don't know what you're talking about."

Then she got it. He already knew. Of course he did. Every person in the school knew, it was all they were talking about. Salacious gossip moved faster than an Olympic sprinter and would've been heard by everyone – teachers, TAs, students – probably by the time Bree was rushing to form room.

She pushed the hair back that had sprung free from her ponytail, unable to compute that this day was capable of getting any worse. She focused on getting through each second, one at a time, without screaming or curling up into a ball.

"Logan…I know you know."

"Know what?" He turned another page even though he wasn't reading.

Seriously? He was acting like a child. But she was too desperate to be angry. She couldn't lose him too, that was unthinkable.

"Logan…it happened before us. It was…it meant nothing…it was just this thing I'm writing… It was the most awful thing that's ever happened to me…and he filmed it, Logan, he *filmed* it. And now everyone's seen…" Her voice broke, wavering like a shrill opera singer on a closing note. She was drowning in the enormity of how horrific everything was.

He looked up at her. Thank God. He was making eye contact.

"Logan…" She tried again, but he broke her off. His voice was full of nothingness.

"Do you know how it felt?" he half-whispered to her. "To find out like that? To hear the kids talking about it, all through every class I taught this morning? Do you know how it felt?"

She pleaded desperately. "I'm sorry I didn't tell you. It meant nothing. It was awful. It was before we even got together."

He carried on. "I can't believe you slept with him. Hugo, the guy everyone calls Mr Popular. The guy everyone wants to be. And you didn't even have the courtesy to tell me yourself... You just knew the news would get to a sad loser like me eventually, is that it?"

"Sad? Loser? Logan, I don't get what you mean. Or why you're angry."

He stood up, his eyes red. "I felt like I was seventeen years old again, Bree. And I didn't like it. I didn't like being seventeen back then, and I didn't like it today."

"I DON'T LIKE IT EITHER!" she yelled back, not caring who saw or heard. "HOW DO YOU THINK IT FEELS FOR ME? DO YOU NOT CARE ABOUT HOW THIS FEELS FOR ME?"

"Don't yell at me, Bree. I'm your teacher."

"You are NOT my teacher. You're my boyfriend."

It was the first time she'd dared use the word. Funny how losing everything gives you such courage. The choice of word didn't go down well though. He flinched.

"I am not your boyfriend, Bree. Stop being so silly."

"Then what are we? Where are we? You said you

loved me. That you've always loved me... And now the worst thing that's ever happened to me has just happened – why aren't you helping to make it better?"

"We're nothing," he said quietly.

And her heart, her fragile heart, combusted – spraying ash and dust down through her stomach. "You don't mean that."

"I'm sorry. But we, this, it was a mistake. I don't want to see you any more."

There was no emotion on his face. No pain in his eyes. No wobble to his beautiful lip. She couldn't take it. She would rather him be angry than emotionally defunct.

"I can't believe you're doing this," she said, a bit of anger in her voice now. "I've not done anything wrong."

"Bree. Let's leave it now."

"No I will not leave it. So I had sex with someone...big deal. What about your wife, Logan? What about your fucking wife? Don't you have sex with her? Why is that okay? And it's not okay for me?"

"Bree, stop," he pleaded.

"No, I will not stop. You can't do this. You can't just let me fall in love with you and tell me you love me back and then do this. Not when everything is so wrecked. Do you really love me? Did you ever?" She sounded hysterical now but she didn't care. Her voice was so high it was almost a squeak.

He looked at the carpet instead of her and she knew then that she'd lost him.

"No, I didn't. I don't…I don't know what I was doing."

Trauma. It doesn't eke itself out over time.

It doesn't split itself manageably into bite-sized chunks and distribute itself equally throughout your life.

Trauma is all or nothing. A tsunami wave of destruction. A tornado of unimaginable awfulness that whooshes into your life – just for one key moment – and wreaks such havoc that, in just an instant, your whole world will never be the same again.

Bree didn't know there could be hurt like this. It felt like her ribs were breaking. Snapping open with the explosion of her heart. And with the hurt came rage. Rage at school, rage at being a stupid pointless teenager, rage at Hugo, rage at life, but, most of all, rage at Logan.

"You're a disgrace," she said, clenching her fists.

He didn't respond so she picked up his book and threw it at the wall.

"Do you hear me? You're a sad pathetic disgrace. I could tell everyone, you know? I could tell your wife. The school. Everyone. I could ruin you in a moment. Tell everyone what a pervert you are. Give me one reason why I shouldn't do that. Give me a reason not to, Logan…please…"

This was the moment when she hoped, despite it all, that he would say: "Because I love you and I'm sorry."

Hope. A silly word. A David of a word against the Goliath of trauma. A David with no slingshot.

Instead, in this reality of realities…on this day of all awful days…

All she got was…

"No one would believe you."

His eyes were still fixated on the carpet. The eyes she knew so well, the face that had looked at her with such adoration just the night before.

"Yes, they would."

"No, they wouldn't."

"Well, let's see then, shall we? I'll go and tell them now."

Logan rolled his eyes. He actually rolled his eyes. In that moment she understood why love and hate were considered such close mates.

"They won't. They'll just think you got a sad, pathetic crush on the only person who showed you kindness."

She closed her eyes, like the act would shut out every bit of hurt that pierced her.

"I hate you."

Words were all she had left to fight with.

Words. Her friends. The only friends left.

But Logan didn't want to fight.

"Bree. Just go. Stop embarrassing yourself."

If there'd been any hint of regret in his expression… If there'd been even a glimpse of bittersweetness behind his stretched smile… If there'd been anything, anything at all, left in him that even betrayed an atom of care for her, she would've forgiven him.

There was nothing.

Bree, apparently, was nothing.

chapter forty-eight

Bree went home.

Bree got inside her house without her mum hearing.

Bree went up to her bedroom.

Bree ran straight to her en suite.

Bree opened the bathroom cabinet.

Bree took out what she needed.

Bree huddled against the wall, rocking her body back and forth.

Bree thought about the look on Jassmine's face.

Bree remembered how the whole school cafeteria had turned to look at her.

Bree replayed the video footage in her head.

Bree thought about Logan.

About their day in London.

The time in the stationery cupboard. Meeting for coffee. And all the brilliance in between.

Bree heard his words echoing round her broken brain.
We're nothing.
Bree didn't even wince when the razor met her skin.
Bree made it all go away.

chapter forty-nine

"Bree, oh my God, my darling, what have you done?"

"Bree? Bree? Can you hear me?"

"Hello? Yes, it's my daughter. She's done something. There's blood everywhere. I can't...I don't know...help me...what do I do?"

"Bree. Come on, darling, stand up, we're going to the hospital."

She was moving. Her body was moving. Step after step after step.

Inside.

Outside.

Inside again.

Car engine.

"Bree, stay with me. Let's talk, shall we? Bree, darling, I love you. Come on, it's nearly Christmas. Bree? Bree?"

Shouldn't it be hurting more than this? All she felt was calm.

"Almost there, darling. Come on, keep your eyes open."

Blurs were happening outside the window. Blur after blur after blur into one big smudge.

She closed her eyes. The sky was too bright.

"No, Bree, open them, keep them open. BREE, KEEP YOUR EYES OPEN NOW, DO YOU HEAR ME?"

The Darkness engulfed her. It hugged her up and swallowed her whole.

And Bree smiled.

chapter fifty

Reality doesn't wait for you to be ready for it. It doesn't go away when you tell it to. It's like a persistent mosquito, determined to suck your blood and leave you with a bumpy itch that you can't stop scratching.

Bree wasn't ready to face reality yet. But it was ready for her.

"Bree, nice to see you with us."

It was a doctor. She could tell by the uniform and the folder of notes clutched in his hands. If he was a doctor, then she must be in some kind of hospital.

She looked down at her body.

She was lying down, in an uncomfortable bed, wearing the ugliest gown known to man.

Yep – Bree was in hospital.

Why?

She looked round the sterile bright ceiling for triggers.

And it all came back to her. The bathroom, the cutting, the blissful feeling of it all going away. Then, her mum's voice. Her mum's frantic voice.

What had she done?

Her body erupted into trembles, like ten million earthquakes were hitting her at the same time. What had she done? What had she done? What had she done?

"Where's my mum?" she asked urgently. Her mother. Her poor, poor mother. How much more could she fail her?

"Shh, Bree, they're outside," a doctor said, trying to calm her. "You're okay. Your parents are outside and they're very worried about you, but you're okay."

Her breath kept catching in her throat and she struggled for air. "What happened?"

"Do you remember, Bree?"

Not really. Then… Oh God, the video. The awful, horrible video. And Logan. Logan! Her heart shattered all over again as the memories whizzed, one by one, back into her brain. She rocked herself back and forth in the hospital bed to try and soothe the trembles.

"I did something stupid, didn't I?"

"I'm not sure if stupid is the right word…unwise perhaps?" He gave her a nice, warm smile and she felt a bit calmer. Like his smile was medicine.

Bree took a breath and lifted her gown. Yep – it was real. There was a huge white bandage across the top of one leg and there wasn't one bit of her that wanted to write about it. She gasped, and more earthquakes erupted through her blood.

"You're very lucky to be here, Bree. You almost hit a major artery."

"I did?"

That hadn't been the plan. The plan wasn't to...was it? No. No! Okay, maybe, on her worst days she'd considered it...but that was so different to actually doing it. What if her mum hadn't found her? What if her mum *had* found her, but too late? She had to make this doctor understand.

"You don't think I tried to kill myself, do you? I didn't. I wouldn't..."

The doctor perched on the side of her bed, and again, there was something about him that soothed her.

"What do you think happened, Bree?"

"I wouldn't...I don't think...I just wanted it to go away."

"What's that, Bree? What did you want to go away?"

"School."

"School?" He looked surprised.

"Don't you remember being seventeen, doctor?"

She won a small smile.

"Yes, and it wasn't *so* bad. Now, I'm going to need to ask you some questions."

She rolled to make herself more comfortable and as she did she saw the doctor's ID tag. She ground her teeth.

Dr Karl Thomas, Psychiatric Unit.

For once, Bree realized she couldn't smart her way out of this one.

"So," she said, and her eyes filled with wetness for the first time in for ever, "what do you want to know?"

chapter fifty-one

So Bree talked to the doctor. She talked and talked and talked. She told Dr Karl Thomas absolutely everything, after checking ten million times about his confidentiality obligations. She told him about her book being rejected, she told him about the blog idea, her makeover, losing Holdo, sleeping with Hugo, falling in love with Logan, and then all the horror that had happened most recently. It was liberating really, being able to tell someone all about it. And psychiatrists are such good listeners. He let her get it all out, nodding only occasionally and making notes on his pad, his eyes sympathetic but not in a patronizing way.

"...So, yeah, after all of that, I just maybe took the whole self-harm thing a bit too far. I guess."

Dr Thomas gave her a small smile.

"Do you have *any* idea of the potential severity of what you did?"

"I do. But I didn't mean to…" She paused, biting her lip. "Why do people do it, doctor? You must see young people like me all the time. And maybe you see some that don't have mums that find them in time. But why?"

Dr Thomas sighed, a sigh filled with sadness at having heard that question asked so many times before. "We don't know yet. They're usually just very sick and see this as the only way out…and then…"

"And then what?"

"Nothing."

"Please?"

He mulled over his words, staring into some vacant nothingness just over the frame of his glasses.

"Well, sometimes, in cases like yours for example, they just do it," he said, and looked up at Bree. "They weren't planning it and they don't think about what it really means. They do it out of anger, to prove a point usually. You mentioned school – school really is hell for some people. I don't doubt that. Ever. But what they don't get is that death is permanent. Whereas every other problem in their lives usually isn't. And if they're trying to make a point, they won't be around to see the point being made. There's no coming back from…that. I wish I could make them understand it before. I wish I could tell them. This is for ever…you're never coming back. You'll never have this chance to live again."

Bree winced as she pulled the blanket further up her shaking body.

"I will always try to live," she told him, and her voice stopped shaking and rang out clear around the curtained walls. "From now on, I promise, I will always choose to live."

chapter fifty-two

A nurse came in and checked a chart at the end of her bed. Bree waited until she'd left, then she asked the doctor her next question.

"You're not going to lock me up in a padded room, are you?"

He turned over a page on his clipboard. "No…we're not. But, what you've just told me…are you going to tell anyone else about it? Open up a bit more?"

"I am telling people. Sort of. I write a blog every day."

"What about telling real people? Like your parents? Or that nice friend Holdo?"

Bree pulled a face. "Holdo will never speak to me again, and he's right not to. I treated him like crap. And my parents…" She stuck out her tongue. "Are you kidding me? I doubt they care. Especially my dad."

"You'd be surprised, Bree… Both of them were in

quite a state when you were brought in."

"Dad's only annoyed he got called home from work early."

Dr Thomas noted that down on his pad, then flicked all the sheets back to the front and stood up, holding it against his chest.

"Maybe I can talk to him about the importance of spending more time together, if that's an issue. But, tell me, do people always live up to the awful expectations you impose on them?"

That was a question and seven eighths. Did she really do that? Bree stuck out her lip.

"Anyway…" His voice switched to breezy and Bree knew the worst was over. "What bits can I tell your parents? I really suggest you tell them everything, but I understand it may take some building up to. Whatever you decide, I'm not going out there and telling them their daughter hacked her leg to pieces for no reason."

Bree started to panic again. "Not the blog…they'll make me stop and it's all I have." She'd come so far, she couldn't stop now. Plus, if they took away her writing, what did she have left?

"That's not true—"

"Shh," she interrupted. "I'm bargaining. And not Logan… my dad will go mental."

"Quite rightly…"

"You promised not to tell." Part of her still hoped she'd be able to sort things out with Logan after Christmas.

Even after what he'd said. Her heart didn't have an on/off switch – maybe his didn't either.

Dr Thomas held up his hands. "I know I said I wouldn't tell. Though the guy has broken the law and, personally, I feel should be held accountable. But, come on, your parents need to know something. You can't shut everyone out, Bree."

Bree lifted her blanket up and peeked at her leg again. She was already dreading the day the bandage would come off, and what her leg would look like underneath.

"Okay…" she said quietly. "The video, you can tell them about the video. That's enough reason for now."

"I'll tell them for you." And there was sympathy in his eyes again. The video – that awful video – it would make anyone feel sorry for her. Well, anyone who wasn't a student at Queen's Hall. "You'll need a few follow-up appointments, I'm afraid. I'll chat to your parents about setting up some talking therapy sessions for you. Unfortunately, it will take a few weeks for the referral to come through."

"What? I have to go the therapy? But I've told you everything!"

"Bree, stop arguing, please. Telling is just the beginning of what you need. Remember why you're here. Remember what you've just promised. I'll go bring your parents in."

He pushed through the curtains and Bree heard him start talking to them in a quiet calming tone.

Bree was scared about seeing them. She rearranged herself in the bed multiple times. First she sat up with a fake beaming smile. Then she experimented with slumping low, her head lolling on the pillow. She wasn't sure what they wanted to see. Just as she was readjusting once more, the curtains flung open and Bree's mum hurtled onto the bed.

"Oh Bree, my darling." And she clutched at the blanket and sobbed.

Bree's father strode in nervously, sat on the chair, and looked at everything other than Bree.

"Bree, why didn't you tell me? I could've helped you, stopped you...oh God...I thought you were going to die." She was off again, tears making blotchy marks all over Bree's scratchy blanket.

"Muuuuuuum," Bree tapped her back awkwardly. "It's okay. Stop crying."

Mum answered with fresh tears. Bree and her dad exchanged a look, though he still didn't say anything.

"Mum, I'm okay. Please calm down, come on, this isn't like you."

Her mum hiccupped then sat up. She appeared to get a grip on herself and wiped the make-up rivers away from under her eyes. "Sorry...I'm just in shock, that's all. I never expected..."

"For your daughter to be so messed up?"

She grabbed her hand. "Oh, sweetie. You're not messed up. You're wonderful. We're going to get you help."

"Mum, I don't want help. I'm okay."

"Honey, you're in hospital. Because of what you did to yourself. You need help."

Bree pouted and looked back down at the blanket. "Sorry."

"Sorry for what? You don't have to apologize. I'm just glad you're alright, that's all."

"No. It's not that." She could hardly bring herself to say the next words, but talking earlier to the doctor had helped. Maybe now was the time to start being more open. "I'm sorry for not being the daughter you thought I'd become. All together and pretty and popular. I'm still just a loser mess, like always."

Her mum's grip tightened on the blanket. As Bree peeked out from beneath her hair, she saw Mum's mouth drop open.

"You don't honestly think I care about all that, do you? I love you just the way you are."

"No you don't." Bree's voice was shaking. "You're just like everyone else. You didn't care about me when I had pink hair and ugly clothes and was a massive loser. You were ashamed of me. And then I got all pretty and popular and suddenly you couldn't get enough of me. Well, sorry I'm such a disappointment, but this is how I am."

She was met with silence.

"Bree. Look at me. That's not how it is."

Bree wouldn't look at her. "That's what it feels like."

Her mum grabbed her chin and pulled it up. "I've always cared about you, Bree. I've always loved you. But, these past few months, you've finally let me care for you. You've finally let me love you. It's not to do with your hair or your clothes or your workout sessions or who you hang round with at school – that's not why we've got close. We've got close because, for once, you've let me in, Bree. And I jumped on it – it's the first chance you've given me since adolescence, I think…" She trailed off.

Bree did a long hard think. "Is that true?"

"Of course it is. You're my daughter, I love you."

"But I'm a loser. I'm nobody."

Then her mum hugged her so hard her ribs hurt. Bree's dad watched on, still silent.

"No you're not. You're smart and pretty and kind and wonderful and so much better than you've ever given yourself credit for. So people don't get you at school – so what? So you're not popular and you're a bit bitter about it – so what? None of it really matters, honey, as long as you love yourself."

Bree thought about school and instantly felt sick.

"I can't go back, Mum, don't make me. The doctor must've told you what happened…" She went bright red. Oh, the humiliation. Every time she remembered the video clip, it was like being doused in an icy cold shower of fresh humiliation. And her parents knew about it now – that she'd had sex. The embarrassment churned through her stomach. "…He…he filmed it."

There was nothing her mum could say. The pity in her eyes was excruciating to see.

Mum hugged Bree tight. "Don't worry, love, you don't have to go back there. It's okay."

"Really, you promise? Dad?"

It was then that her father finally spoke. "Bree, you will go back."

Bree and her mother sprang apart and stared at him.

"You can't run away from your problems."

Bree was too stunned to talk.

"You heard what happened. How can we let Bree go back there?" Her mother stood up.

"It's exactly why she should go back there." He stood up too, his chair making a horrible shrill screeching sound on the hospital floor as he pushed it back. "Bree, I can just about handle a psychiatrist telling me he's not going to section you after all. I can maybe learn to deal with the memory of taking tonight's phone call from your mother. All this I can handle. But what I won't tolerate is my daughter, my only daughter, letting herself be a victim. Letting herself get kicked down the stairs by people who are not half the person she is. I won't take it. I know I'm not around very much because of work, and I'm sorry I've not been there, but I'm here now and I'm telling you this. We didn't raise you to be like this. We raised a fighter. Now where is she?"

Silence was the most appropriate response to that.

Her dad, taken aback by his own dramatic outburst, sat back down, looking exhausted. A hint that he cared, that he was worried.

Bree did another long hard think.

So much had changed. Her looks, her life, her love. And,

yes, it had ultimately made her that bit more interesting, but she'd paid quite a price for it. Along the way she'd lost her ethics, her morals, her virginity, her dignity, her old best friend, her new best friend.

All those weren't a tragedy, not completely. Let's face it, most people lose all of the above at some point.

But the one thing she had lost, and that she really missed – though she hadn't realized it until now – was not caring what people thought. She didn't used to give a holy crap. And *that* was power.

Her mother, worried by her silence, jumped to her defence. "Don't be so unsupportive. Let's look at good schools she can transfer to. Or how about home schooling? I'm not letting her go back there."

Bree cut her off. "Dad?"

"Yes, honey?"

It was the first time he'd ever used a term of endearment.

"How do you propose we fight this?"

The exhaustion left his face, and an energy fired up behind his eyes. For the first time, she saw him for the powerful man he was, rather than the knackered mess they saw at home.

He smiled.

"Well, there's a reason you and your mother never see me. It's because I'm a lawyer. And I know lots of those evil lawyers that everyone hates…"

chapter fifty-three

And so it came to be that Bree and her family managed to get on for a while. She was discharged the next day, with a change of bandages and some stern words from Dr Thomas.

"Don't get all cocky now, thinking you're all better just because you and your family had a chinwag. There's still lots you've not told them. And I still want to book you in to talk to someone."

"I talked to you, didn't I? Didn't that cure me? And are doctors allowed to say the word 'cocky'?"

"See, you're being cocky. Life's tough, Bree. I think you need to work on your coping mechanisms."

She made a face. "Maybe Santa will give me some for Christmas?"

He shook his head. "Nope. Not that easy, sorry. Coping

mechanisms take a bit of work... I'll be ringing in the New Year."

When she wasn't thinking about Logan, or Hugo, or Jassmine, or Holdo – or anything else resembling her life for the past couple of months – Bree, at first, was surprisingly chirpy in the lead-up to Christmas. Being a social outcast gave her more time to do all her favourite things. Like reading *Ulysses* (by James Joyce) and pretending she understood it. Writing emotional poetry about what her feet looked like in the bath. Revising for her exams that weren't for another two months. And watching reality television for the sole purpose of tutting at it (but secretly loving it).

They stayed in their unexpected version of happy families through the entire festive period. Dr Thomas gave Bree's dad some stern advice to be around more and so he took Christmas Eve off and took them up to London for a posh meal, before whisking them off to Selfridges for some last-minute shopping. He let them each pick something and Bree chose a key necklace, the most beautiful thing she'd ever seen. She promised herself she'd wear it whenever she needed strength. They got home in the early hours of Christmas morning and watched *It's A Wonderful Life* until silly o'clock.

The next day the mass effort of "being happy together" continued. They wore Christmassy jumpers and oooed and aahed over each other's gifts. Bree's dad even bought something called a "Tofu Turkey" with a meat-free wishbone and everything.

Unfortunately the fake turkey tasted of sawdust, and her dad complained so much that her mum drove to the 24-hour petrol station to buy him some bacon. The day ended with her mum drinking too much brandy and snoring lightly on the sofa, while Bree and her dad discussed the upcoming legal proceedings against Hugo. It was a bit of a sour end to a nice few days and the bitter taste was still there when she woke up on Boxing Day.

Bree's dad went back to work ("But I'll be home by seven, I promise"). Her mum began stressing about her Christmas calorie consumption and wouldn't shut up about detox juicing. Days and days of utter loneliness spread out before her.

A few days after Christmas, a letter was left in their postbox.

It was typed and hand-delivered. Logan obviously didn't trust her not to blab. Her hands trembled as she read it, and she sank down onto her bedroom carpet.

Bree
I don't know where to start.

I am so sorry. I am so sorry for what I have done to you. You are just a child and I am sorry.

I'm leaving Queen's Hall so you won't see me again. I am sure you'll be glad about that after how I treated you.

You made me feel young again, Bree. In a good way. You were the dream I never had when I was your age, and I was selfish and cruel to act on my impulses. You also made me act like I was your age, which is the only explanation I can offer for my behaviour on the last day of term.

You are not like anyone I've ever met before. There is something there, Bree, something very special that, with time, you'll see more of yourself. And someone worthy of loving you will see it too.

I'm moving to a school in a bad area of inner city London. The pay is worse, the kids are definitely going to be worse, but I have to stop kidding myself that helping rich teenagers get into Oxford is making a difference.

My wife and I are working on keeping things together. I would appreciate it if you didn't try and contact me in the future.

Again, I am so sorry.

Yours,

Logan.

There were so many potential reactions to such a dung heap of a letter.

Bree could've laid on the carpet and cried until nothing was left. She could've ripped the letter up and burned the pieces. She could've taken it to her mum and told her everything, and built on their new foundations of "sharing".

All Bree really wanted to do was let out every emotion using a sharp instrument.

She reread Logan's writing over and over, a sadness building in her guts and breeding through her intestines. Rejection. Rejection from an utter gobshite, but still more rejection. She slowly walked with it over to her bookshelf and carefully stabbed the letter onto the clogged nail.

The urge to go to her en suite was overwhelming. Even though her parents had removed everything sharp (thinking she wouldn't notice) she was sure she could fashion something. But Bree remembered what she'd promised the doctor.

She went to the dresser and put on her key necklace and made her way quietly to the kitchen. She pressed a pint glass calmly against the ice machine and listened to the loud clatter of it being filled. Then Bree returned to her room, locked herself in the bathroom and, one by one, clenched the cubes of ice in her hands until they each melted.

Just like they'd told her to do.

The pain from the ice wasn't quite the same but it did hurt. In a different way. She clenched until her hands were so numb she couldn't pick up any more cubes.

It wasn't quite enough.

So Bree told her mum she was going for a walk, wrapped herself up in all sorts of woollen things and walked from her house to the nearest park. Then, from the nearest park, she walked into town. Then, from town, she walked to the next town. Then to the next park. She walked until her face was red raw from cold and her legs felt like they were molten iron being whacked by a blacksmith. On the return journey, at some points, she wasn't sure if she had enough energy to get home. But she carried on walking, her feet crunching over frosted grass, her breath heavy and even.

With each step she felt a little better.

When she eventually got home, she had to calm down her frantic mother because she'd stupidly forgotten to take her mobile. Once she'd promised for the millionth time that she'd never hurt herself again, she stumbled upstairs to her room.

The nail was still pride of place under the bookcase.

Bree smiled. She knew just what to do.

When she fell asleep that night, every single rejection letter lay destroyed at the bottom of her father's office shredder.

Including Logan's.

chapter fifty-four

The next day was New Year's Eve. A night when it's universally impossible to have fun, no matter what you attempt.

When Bree woke she still felt terrible inside. A scalding hot bath didn't help. Probably because she had to hold her bandaged leg out of the water. Neither did watching her mum doing her workout, squatting across the carpet like she needed a dump.

"Mum, I was thinking of going to London today. Is that okay?"

Her mum put down the towel she was rubbing her face with. "Of course, sweetie. Let me just get showered and then we can get the train together."

"I'd rather go by myself, if that's alright?"

A horrified look passed over her mum's face – as it often had that last week. "Bree…I think I should come with you."

Bree wondered if her mum would ever stop worrying now when she went out alone. And she felt so guilty for causing that.

"Mum, I promised Dr Thomas, and I'll promise you... I won't do anything like that again. I really truly promise. I get why you're scared, but, please, let me go. I'll text throughout the day, if that helps."

Her mum sighed, and Bree watched an invisible battle parade through her brain. Finally she said: "It's New Year, it's going to be busy."

"I know. I'll come home before night-time."

"Alright then. But the texts need to be regular. Otherwise I'll worry."

It was freezing outside. Grey and depressing, like the clouds of frizzy rain knew Christmas was over. Bree wore her big fur coat, like she had the time she went up with Logan. On the way to the station she passed Holdo's house and stood outside for a bit. They'd always spent New Year together – watching Jools Holland and whingeing about how crap all the bands were while drinking red wine.

The train to London was quiet, everyone having lie-ins to ready themselves for the night's forced fun later. The city itself was packed though – full of sales shoppers exchanging Christmas presents for stuff they wanted more. She hopped on the Tube, glaring at anyone who dared look at her. Not many people did. Her contagious bad mood radiated outwards and no one sat next to her the whole way. When she got off at Trafalgar Square it was a miserable scene – all grey, grey and more grey. She picked her way past dilapidated pigeons and marched straight into the gallery. She didn't stop at the Rubens, or the *Water-Lilies*, or any of the other priceless paintings tourists queued for hours to see.

Bree went straight to *The Ugly Duchess*.

The room was empty – nobody cared about *The Ugly Duchess*. Bree sat before it, taking in every brushstroke and remembered the day she'd first seen it.

The day the obsession with being interesting began, if she really thought about it.

She was eleven. Year Six school trip. That last year of primary school, when the bullying from Jassmine and co. was really bad.

Jassmine was popular, even back then. And Bree was a loser, even back then. She'd sat at the front of the coach, next to the teacher, while her classmates had the time of their lives behind her. At least three different boys "asked out" three different girls, using a complicated courting method of passing notes between the seats. The back row was, of course, dominated by the social elite, like the grand box at a ballet. Mini Jassmine and mini Gemma decided which songs were sung, which dares were dared, which notes made it to their intended owners and which were opened and read aloud while their writers turned red.

Bree, her body heavy with puppy fat, pretended to read

To Kill a Mockingbird until she got coach sick and vomited into a paper bag.

The smell stunk out the entire coach and the whiny noises of children shouting "Breeeeeeeeeeeeeeeeeeee, you reeeeeeeeeeeeeek" was the overriding soundtrack until they pulled up outside the gallery.

Everyone ran off in different directions the moment they were let loose. Mini Jassmine and mini Gemma found mini French exchange students to flirt with in the cafe. Mini Bree paced the gallery alone, as always.

She wasn't tough back then. In fact, she'd been quite the crier-in-her-teacher's-skirt. Loneliness is horrible for anyone, but it's particularly awful to be a lonely child. Mini Bree tried to lose herself in the paintings but didn't really "get" any of them. Room by room, her clumpy shoes trod the wooden floors, painting after painting passing her by.

It was only by accident that she found *The Ugly Duchess,* when she was looking for the toilet.

At first, she was drawn in because she was a kid and looking at ugly people was funny. Then she started feeling sorry for the ugly lady in the painting. She wondered what her life had been like, why someone had chosen to paint her portrait. Was it an elaborate joke to ridicule her? Had everyone else in court been laughing at her?

That was when mini Bree had her first thought that began to turn her into the Bree she was today.

It didn't matter if it *was* a joke. It didn't matter if they'd been laughing at her because she was so ugly. What mattered was that the Ugly Duchess stood out enough that someone felt the need to put paintbrush to canvas. And now, hundreds of years on, here she still was. Existing and having an impact on someone.

Bree decided to be like the Ugly Duchess.

One day, she thought, *I'm not going to be eleven any more. I'm going to be old, like seventeen or something, and I won't be miserable any more because I'm going to work really hard and make sure I'm interesting and people will want to know about me. And I'll come back here, and look at this painting, and feel a little bit sad that I was so sad when I was eleven but also really happy because that's not who I am any more. I'm going to come back here and I won't have any troubles any more. I'll have loads of friends and be really happy because I'm so cool and interesting.*

Time can be strange sometimes. It can leave imprints in particular places, leave ghosts of memories trapped. Right then, on that cold New Year's Eve, Bree felt the ghost of mini Bree all around her. She was sitting exactly where she'd sat all those years ago and yet nothing had changed. She was still lonely. She was still a nobody. Age and experience hadn't done what it had promised. It hadn't made the world fair or right.

Bree made a silent apology to her child self for letting her down.

She let one lone tear escape.

Her misery was interrupted by a Japanese couple taking her photograph. Twice.

She stood up, furious. "What are you doing? This isn't the Tate Modern; I'm not an installation piece."

They ran off, their camera bag shaking behind them. She wiped away her tear and flicked it off her finger.

There were more ghosts here, of course. The ghosts of her and Logan, their romantic trip. She could practically feel the happiness trapped in the wood of the bench where her bottom had sat only a month or so ago.

She missed him.

He was an arsehole…but she missed him.

She guessed that was mostly how love worked.

Rule number five: One must lose all sight of oneself, get into a huge emotional mess, and break down as a person

Ralph Emerson apparently once said that life is a journey, not a destination. You may have heard that a few times before. It's the sort of saying people buy as bumper stickers and put on their cars to pretend they're all deep and meaningful.

Ralph Emerson was right about so many things.

This was one of them.

I've – hopefully – held your interest throughout this process by doing superficial things like tinting my hair and shagging some guy at school.

But you ultimately want more than that.

You want to see my emotional journey, don't you?

I have to mature and progress in order to remain interesting. And part of that process is having a complete mental breakdown, losing everything I hold dear...and then let's see if I can magic up some happily-ever-after in Act Three.

It's in every basic narrative you're told. As predictable as getting a cold in winter. Think of films... Maybe the girl won't get the guy after all, she's getting on a plane to Timbuktu, he doesn't realize how much he cares, or does he...? Hang on...is he running through the airport after her?

YES, YES HE IS.

These moments of ultimate redemption and satisfaction aren't a pay-off if your protagonist hasn't suffered first.

The thing is, I knew this would happen. I knew things would get messy. How could they not? I pretty much planned it in.

What I didn't plan for was just how wrong things could go and just how awful it is being where I am right now.

Because, as clichéd-story-making as all this is right now, this is my life and in life you're not guaranteed a happily-ever-after.

I'm interesting now, sure. I'm also so sad and lonely I'm surprised I still have a reflection.

This is my journey, this is what I'm doing for me, to make me a great writer, to make me an interesting person. But I'm warning you, the path to being interesting isn't an easy road.

That guy I slept with? He filmed it. Couldn't have planned on that. Couldn't have planned on him broadcasting it round the whole school either.

Interesting development. Not a fun one though.

That teacher I loved? Turned out this great love of mine was a bit one-sided. The more I think about it, the more I realize he was just using me to address some kind of sad self-esteem issues hangover from his own awful teenagehood.

Those awful girls I befriended? Turns out they weren't so bad. Mean and horrible sometimes, yes, but human and sincere too. They're not my friends any more though.

I have no friends, no one.

Do you want to know what I'm scared of? I'm scared I won't be able to give you the redemption you crave. I'm terrified that my journey won't tie up all the loose ends nicely. Because this is a life, not just a story, and life doesn't always go the way stories tell you.

What if I don't have a happy ending?

That is what I'm really scared of.

chapter fifty-five

Bree celebrated New Year with her parents, who missed some spectacular at the local golf club as part of their new "let's be a proper family" pilot scheme.

When your parents feel sorry for you, you know you've failed some kind of societal entrance exam.

And she still hadn't told them the half of it yet. She couldn't bear to.

They'd all dressed up and opened some dusty bottles of expensive champagne her dad kept in his wine cellar.

In a moment of champagne braveness, Bree had fired off a text to Holdo.

Hey, you're welcome round mine tonight if you fancy taking the piss out of Jools Holland with an old friend?

She'd been ultra-careful with her grammar out of respect for his needs.

He didn't reply.

Of course he didn't.

As Big Ben struck midnight, they drunkenly clinked glasses and sang a pathetic version of "Auld Lang Syne".

Bree's mum stood on the sofa, swaying and spilling her champagne. "To new beginnings," she declared. Not waiting for the others to clink her, she gulped back her glassful and hiccupped.

"To new beginnings," Bree echoed, and drained her glass too.

She wondered if anyone, anywhere, was getting the night they wanted.

Hugo was having a massive party. He'd called it "Gash Fest Revisited".

She wondered what lucky girl he'd slobbered on at midnight.

She wondered if Jassmine and the others had gone.

She wondered if Logan had thought of her as he kissed his wife when the clocks struck twelve.

She wondered if Hugo's legal papers had got to him yet.

Bree might not have redemption guaranteed to be heading her way, but she sure did have shit in one hand, and a fan in the other.

chapter fifty-six

On January the fifth, Bree stood in front of her mirror and nervously surveyed her reflection while her mum gave her a pep talk.

"Just keep your head down, honey." She was actually brushing Bree's hair, like she was five. "People will forget soon enough. You'll be old news soon."

"Old news doesn't stay on amateur porn sites until the end of time."

"You know your dad is blocking it from being reposted. You're lucky to have such a powerful father – lots of girls are in this situation and can't do what we're doing."

"Did you just call me lucky?"

"Of course not. No. I didn't mean it like... Oh, Bree." She looked more scared than Bree. "Are you going to be okay today?"

"I'll be fine."

"Are you sure you don't want me to drive you? I can miss Bikram yoga."

"Mum, honestly, I'm fine. Thanks for being so sweet."

They tried one of their new hugs – they'd been practising those a lot lately.

"Well, you look…under-the-radar."

Bree laughed, though in her tummy she felt like she had the norovirus mixed with gastric flu. "That's what I was aiming for."

She was wearing grey woolly tights, with a grey blazer and grey school skirt. She'd tied her hair back in a low ponytail and just put on a bit of mascara… The only item of any note was her new key necklace. Her warrior necklace.

If she ever needed strength, she needed it today.

"Let me know how you do. I'll have my phone on me all day. And we need to talk about arranging those appointments Dr Thomas recommended."

Therapy.

Bree tried not to make a face so as not to upset her mother. But she'd been successfully dodging making an appointment all holiday. She'd chosen to live, yes. Wasn't that enough? Did she really need to open up and let all the pain come flooding back and be pressured to tell her parents and make them hate her too? She was hardly holding herself together as it was. What else would unravel if someone prodded about in her brain? And would Dr Thomas and his mate make her stop writing the blog?

*　　*　　*

Timing her walk to school was a treacherous business. She didn't want to leave too early in case she bumped into Holdo, who always left early. But she also didn't want to leave too late because Jassmine always left late.

She hopped from one foot to another outside her security gate, trying to shake the jelly from her legs.

School – can't be that bad… It's just that everyone hates you and has seen you naked.

She shook her head. That was not the attitude of a warrior.

She didn't bump into anyone in the end. The urge to bunk off was intoxicating but her dad was right. She wasn't going to be a victim.

Not today, not any day.

Although it's hard not to feel like a victim when you walk down a corridor and absolutely every single person stops talking at exactly the same time.

"I can't believe she's come back."

"I wouldn't, I'd be too ashamed."

"Jass is going to go off her nut."

"I heard she was transferring, what is she doing here?"

"Why is she wearing all grey?"

Despite the whispers, nobody spoke to her, nobody moved out of her way, she was socially invisible. She got to her form room early and sat in her old seat near the front, and waited.

The class filled around her. They circled her, gawping. When Seth came through the door, his mouth fell open, like in a cartoon. She could see him about to say "Breeeeee" in greeting, before he remembered. Instead, he just walked right past. Like everyone else.

Everyone but Hugo.

The temperature dropped before he even walked in. She was ready for him. She held her eyes to the door, ready to meet his, not willing to blink in case he saw it as a sign of weakness.

He swaggered in in his usual fashion, all relaxed, until he clocked Bree. Then his eyebrows pulled together, his face went red, and he pulled his sleeves up.

Everyone in the room went quiet.

Hugo marched over and slammed his bag on her desk. Bree, expecting hostility, didn't even jump.

You are not a victim. You are not a victim.

"How dare you?" he yelled. Yes, yelled. Right in the middle of school.

Bree pretended to look bored and examined a nail. "I don't know what you're talking about."

"You had the police come to my house and arrest me for being a PAEDOPHILE."

Audible gasps escaped around them, like they were surrounded by a live studio audience.

"Oh," Bree said dryly. "That."

Hugo picked up his bag and slammed it down on her desk again. Everyone else in the room jerked back. Everyone but Bree.

"I'm not a paedo," he said.

"Actually, Hugo, the law disagrees with you there," she replied, smiling. "I am still seventeen, which meant I was under eighteen when you filmed me. In legal terms, that makes it a paedophiliac image. In legal terms, by turning on your webcam – without my permission, I might add, you utterly incomprehensible dickhead – you were effectively 'making' a paedophiliac image. When you uploaded it onto your computer, that immediately counted as 'possession' of a paedophiliac image." She counted the charges on her fingers. "Oh? And showing the whole school? That counts as distribution."

She leaned back in her chair, trying to look satisfied, even though inside every part of her was a jelly factory.

"You little bitch."

"Careful now, Hugo… You don't have to say anything, but anything you do say will be held against you in a court of law."

He clenched his fists and got right up in her face. "There's no way in hell this is going to court. My dad's getting the most expensive lawyer in the country to fight this. I don't even know how you managed to bring those charges, but they'll be dropped within days."

"That's weird," Bree said, stroking her chin. "Because my dad's best friend probably is the most expensive lawyer in the country…and, oddly enough, being my dad's best friend, he's kind of on my side."

"This is ridiculous. I'm not a paedophile. I'm only eighteen."

Spit flicked into her face and she resisted the urge to wipe it off.

"It's not ridiculous, Hugo. It's just not been tested in case law yet. This is a majorly topical legal issue – arseholes like you uploading images of underage girls onto the internet… They may well want to make an example of you. Hmmm, I wonder what Oxbridge will make of that?"

And then Hugo went for her. She was expecting this, so ducked and he missed.

"You *************************************** *********************!"

Bree hadn't known it was possible to use so many expletives.

Seth dived across the room to hold Hugo back but he wasn't strong enough. More boys joined in to restrain him.

"You'll regret this," Hugo yelled at her over the wall of bodies separating them. "You'll regret this, you slag. People don't mess with me."

"Oh do shut up, Hugo."

And, in disbelief – at her, at the charges, at her blasé attitude towards the most humiliating thing that could ever happen to anyone – he shut up and sat down. Just as Mr Phillips came in and asked what the hell was going on.

chapter fifty-seven

English was the next hurdle to jump over.

Stupid as it was, Bree couldn't help but fantasize that Logan would be sat at his desk, like always.

As she walked through the door, the teacher's chair was empty. Still hope then.

She got out her poetry anthology and pretended she couldn't hear all the whispers.

"Did you hear? Her dad's got Hugo charged with paedophilia."

"No way."

"Yep."

"Is that even possible?"

"Is she not...scared of him?"

Bree smiled. She couldn't have played it better. Her dad was right. If you didn't act like a victim, people found it difficult to treat you like one. Everyone buzzed. For most of them, this was the first Bree-sighting since before Christmas – they were eager to analyse her every facial expression.

"Right, everybody settle down."

Bree didn't even have to look up from her notepad to know it wasn't him.

She hated herself for how much her heart dropped.

"Sit down, class."

Bree came up from her anthology to match a face to the voice. Their new English teacher was a fifty-something woman with alarmingly large nostrils and a matching pearl necklace and earring set. Nobody knew she was their new English teacher yet though, apart from Bree.

"Where's Mr Fellows?" Chuck asked.

"Mr Fellows no longer works at Queen's Hall, he's moved to a school in London. My name is Ms Masoon. I'll be teaching you from now on."

You could feel the disappointment oozing out of everyone's pores.

"What?"

"But he was the only decent teacher here."

"Is this because he let us spike the Christmas party punch?"

"Does this mean we're not doing Philip Larkin any more?"

"What about our coursework? He was halfway through marking our Shakespeare."

Ms Masoon answered everyone's questions as best she

could – apart from the one about the punch, which she became temporarily deaf for. Bree didn't listen to any of it.

She still couldn't believe he'd left.

Because of her.

"Now, if everyone will open their anthologies, I'd like us to pick a new Philip Larkin poem. I know you were doing *This Be The Verse*, but I'm afraid the headmistress isn't keen on you all reading vulgar language in the classroom."

There were a few groans and then everyone got on with it.

Mr Fellows was forgotten by the end of the lesson. By everyone but Bree, of course.

The next hurdle – see Jassmine and the others again for the first time. She had her "I'm sorry I slept with your boyfriend" frown plastered across her face all day, just in case they bumped into each other.

She had spent a rather depressing lunchtime telling the creative-writing club that it was no more – unless they could find another teacher to do it. Their faces had drooped like melted chicken nuggets; one had actually started crying.

She'd forgotten how young eleven was.

"But where are we supposed to go at lunchtime?" one asked, her lip all wobbly-woo.

"I dunno. The canteen?"

The way they all jumped at the word, she might as well have said "Hades".

"I can ask the librarian if she'll let us hide in there," one whispered to another.

"Hide?" Bree repeated loudly. "What on earth is there to hide from?"

They all gave her a look like she was the stupidest person on this planet.

"From all the bad stuff that happens to everyone who ever goes to the canteen."

"Yeah, like what happened to you."

They were the first people besides Hugo to mention it directly to Bree's face. She was taken aback.

"Thanks for the reminder," she said quietly.

"Sorry, Bree." The girl who'd said it looked petrified. "Are you okay? You're not cross, are you?"

They were the first people to show her concern and she gathered them into a hug.

"Not cross, just sad. Sad you guys feel you need to hide in the library. I'll chat to the librarian, if you really want me too. But remember, you're all kind, lovely, intelligent people who are going to do just fine in life. You shouldn't be scared to go to the canteen."

They beamed at her like she was Mother Teresa.

"In the meantime, go forth and read books that will make you feel better. May I suggest *The Catcher in the Rye*, *The Perks of Being A Wallflower* and *To Kill A Mockingbird*? Mr Fellows didn't feel you were ready, but I think differently."

More beaming. They all hugged until Bree saw Jassmine walk past.

"Oh, guys, gotta go."

She ducked out into the corridor just as the back of Jass's head bobbed away round the corner. She would be headed to the English block bathroom to apply lipgloss, like clockwork. When she hadn't been overhearing rumours about herself, Bree had heard Jassmine had got with some uni guy on New Year's Eve on a boat on the Thames.

Hope always dies far later than it should. Bree hoped that this romantic development might somehow defuse some of the situation bombs between her and Jass. What she couldn't work out was whether she wanted forgiveness because she needed Jass for her blog, or because she actually missed her as a friend.

She followed at a safe distance and – well, whatdoyaknow? – into the bathroom Jass went, digging her make-up out of her bag as she swung through the door.

Bree waited half a minute and then swung in herself.

Jass jerked when she caught sight of her in the mirror. Then she recomposed herself and continued reapplying lipgloss.

"Jassmine."

No reply.

"Jassmine, I am so sorry."

Jass smacked her lips together, chucked the gloss into her school bag and walked out. She didn't even look at Bree. If it wasn't for the initial flinch, Bree might have doubted her own existence.

When she saw the whole perfect posse together, before the end of school, she got the same treatment.

Bree had gone from social obscurity to a queen of the school, to most despised student, and back to social obscurity again.

Her mum picked her up in their giant jeep.

"So, how was it?" she asked, as Bree got into the car.

"It was…school."

"That bad, eh?"

Her mum pulled out a bar of chocolate from her coat pocket. She gave Bree a warm yet watery smile and handed it over.

"How did you know?"

"School is school."

Bree's dad came home halfway through dinner which, for him, was like coming home mid-afternoon. The grin on his face stretched from thinning patch to thinning patch. He clunked his briefcase on the dining room table and some of Bree's peas rolled off her plate.

"Guess who made Hugo d'Felance cry this evening?" He wiggled his eyebrows, looking a bit like Danny DeVito.

Bree stood up, knocking more peas off her plate. "Really?"

"Like a baby."

"Does it make me a bad person that this information makes me happy?"

"No, love. It makes you my daughter."

So Bree was a bit like her dad then. It was nice to finally have the time with him to figure this sort of thing out. "Nice" didn't really cut it as an adjective for how she felt about that really. If Bree and her dad did hugs, a hug would've been done there and then. Bree's mum did the honours instead, knocking his briefcase over.

"Oh, that's great news, Daniel."

"That's not all." He shrugged off his coat and sat down at the head of the table. "Hugo brought his computer in and I got my IT guy to run tests on it. The only copy of the video is there. He never uploaded it onto any sites – just showed his tablet to whoever wanted to see it. It was all just bravado and winding you up. Which makes you the luckiest girl in the world. I made him sign a legal document stating that this was the only copy and that if another one resurfaces we can basically take every single penny from every member of his family until the end of time."

A lightness filled Bree, from her toes up to the tip of her head. "That's amazing. Thank you so much."

Her mum started rubbing his shoulders. "That really is brilliant news, darling. What about the charges?"

He made a small face. "They're a bit harder. Basically, Bree, we can try. But it's a long shot and we've scared him enough, I reckon."

"So…?"

"So, my legal advice would be not to bother." He rubbed his hands together. "But my fatherly advice would be not to tell Hugo that for a while."

The beginning of a grin twitched on Bree's face. "How long can we play him for?"

For the first time ever, you could see the resemblance between Bree and her dad. They both had exactly the same smile.

"I can eke it out for a month or two."

"Did he really cry?"

"Kept sobbing that he was sorry."

"He's not said sorry to me yet."

"Oh, don't worry, he will. Soon. I'll make sure of it."

Hugo corned her after school the next day to beg for forgiveness.

"Bree, I'm so sorry. Please drop the charges."

She'd never seen him look so desperate. She was surprised his face even had the muscle memory to look that way.

She crossed her arms. "Are you sorry that you filmed me without my permission, broadcast it to the entire school and tried to ruin my life? Or are you just sorry that someone actually stood up to you for once?"

Hugo kind of lurched at her, like he was about to grab her, but he stopped himself and just scratched his arms like a crazy homeless person or something. "I'm sorry for everything."

"I don't believe you."

"Please! This could wreck my life."

"You tried to wreck mine."

"I know. I'm sorry."

"You're not though, are you? You just know using that word might make things go away. This is what you're like Hugo, that's the problem. You've never once had to be accountable for who you are. Well, I'm sorry, but you picked the wrong girl to mess with."

chapter fifty-eight

February the fifteenth.

A whole month had passed, the school had calmed down and Bree had settled back into social obscurity.

A whole month had passed and she'd managed to dodge and weave her parents' desperate attempts to get her into therapy. Too scared that she would be forced to open up and made to tell her parents everything, ruining her again in their eyes.

A whole month had passed without having any friends, or anything to do except write her blog.

But there was nothing to write about.

February the fifteenth.

A nothing day, usually. In fact, before this particular February fifteenth, the only thing of any note was people comparing Valentine's Day stories. Lucky people getting cards and going on dates. Unlucky people wallowing in their misery and checking their post eighteen times a minute, just in case.

So far, so not shocking.

But February the fifteenth was about to become a date of massive significance for students at Queen's Hall.

It would be a date pupils talked about for many years to come; titbits handed down through the year groups via hushed whispers in toilet cubicles and cafe queues.

Of course, Bree didn't know the significance of the day when she got up that morning. Most days blur past, punctuated by the odd life-changing moment.

She didn't know, that for her especially, this was going to be one of the big days.

Bree didn't know as she decided what to wear – another stylish, if a bit blendy-in-y, blazer and sheer tights. Bree didn't know as she brushed her teeth. She didn't know as she – yet again – checked her mobile with the stupid notion someone might've called.

She hadn't had one text message since before Christmas. Her mobile was a forty-quid-a-month alarm clock.

The first inkling Bree had that something was up was when she was waiting to get through security at school.

There were whispers. Everywhere. Again.

Bree could almost feel the excitement in the air as she unwound her scarf and took off her woolly hat. The atoms inside the building fizzled like fireworks.

Groups of people stood with other groups they didn't usually stand with. Swapping stories. Audible gasps punctuated her walk to double Latin. Along with "No ways" and "You thinks?"

She wasn't the first to hear anything any more. She got scraps of perfect posse updates chucked to her like stale chunks of bread – usually by the Year Sevens she spent an increasing amount of time with hiding in the library.

Jassmine was going out with Uni Boy for Valentine's Day. Had something happened? Was that it?

Bree still hadn't "dropped the charges" against Hugo, so that couldn't be it. Unless he'd done something else terrible, which would make no sense. He'd been like half the Hugo recently – fewer jokes, less banter, less debauched behaviour.

Maybe he'd got with Jessica or something?

The thing was – maybe she was imagining it out of sheer desperation to know she still existed – but people were looking her way now and again.

Maybe she was imagining it, but the whispers appeared to follow her. People kept going quiet as she passed them.

She shook her head to herself.

No, definitely just imagining it. She was nothing.

The buzz seeped into her Latin class. Hushed voices spoke behind textbooks, notes were scribbled and passed around. It was like being in the middle of a gossip beehive. Eventually Bree gave up on learning and tried to overhear snippets of conversation.

"What a bitch – seriously?"

"If it really is her."

"Not just her, all of them. Do they really do that?"

"No way. It can't be."

"I don't think it's her. We would know if it was here."

"With a teacher?"

That last one made her skin get all itchy.

The moment the bell went, Bree had to confront the fact that she wasn't being paranoid.

Absolutely every single person in the hallway turned to look at her.

The whispers got louder, the stares more blatant. She honestly couldn't think what she'd done though...everyone was over the Hugo tape.

A surge in noise made her look in its direction. Heading straight for her were her ex-friends. Jassmine's face was the ugliest she'd ever seen it.

Not wanting to be part of whatever this was, Bree crossed her arms over herself and slipped into a stream of people making their way to the canteen. She looked down and kept walking.

She was sure they'd passed, when she felt a tug on her blazer. A strong one.

She staggered back into the middle of the aisle, dazed, just as Jassmine slapped her hard across her face.

It felt like her eye was going to pop out of its socket.

Bree clutched her face defensively – just as a wave of "Woooooooah" echoed from mouths around her.

"What the hell was that for...?"

Gemma answered with another slap.

Fire spread down the other side of her face. Everything stung. Bree's brain went into meltdown. What was going on? Was this real? What had she done NOW?

"I can't believe you've done this!" Jassmine screamed. And Bree knew that, pretty soon, she'd be told what she'd done wrong.

"Done what? You're the one who just slapped me."

"You bitch. You horrible sad loser BITCH."

She went for her again but Bree, always quick to learn, ducked and Jassmine missed her.

"Hit me again and I'll tell a teacher."

"Ohhhh, you just love your teachers, don't you, Bree?"

Shit.

"You just love telling EVERYBODY everything, don't you?! I can't believe, this whole time, you've been plotting, and lying...the things I told you...everyone knows...everyone's seen."

Jassmine burst into tears and the others formed a protective barrier around her.

Everyone in the school was there, and every one of them was watching.

"I still don't know what I did," Bree said, although she was beginning to harbour a guess.

Jass, suddenly outraged again, broke through the barrier of girls. "IT'S YOU! You're the 'Manifesto of being interesting' girl on the internet, you sad little freak. You've lied and cheated and you've told everybody everything."

Shock divebombed into her heart; she could hardly breathe.

"What?"

"Everyone in the school knows it's you. I didn't think it was possible to hate you more than I already hated you. You slept with Hugo – my boyfriend – for what? To write about it, you loser? I trusted you, I let you into my life and you've stabbed me in the back."

There wasn't enough time for Bree to collect her thoughts. How did Jass know about the Manifesto? It was anonymous. And she didn't think anyone read it. It was just for her really. Oh God – what had she shared? Everything? Yes, everything.

"I...it wasn't me...I don't know what you're talking about..."

Gemma stepped forward. "Stop lying. We all know you're lying." Her face was unreadable, her lips a thin downward line.

They all stepped forward in turn and Bree started to feel a little threatened.

"We know you got it on with that teacher," Jessica said, stepping forward again.

"We know you hurt yourself," Gemma said.

"We know he left you. I can't imagine why – it's not like you're a massive freak or something."

None of it seemed real. Bree kept blinking to try and double-check the authenticity of the situation. Hearing them mention Logan hurt. A lot.

More steps. Were they going to beat her up? She took a step backward but bumped into the swelling crowd.

"You're going to regret doing this," Jass said, her voice full of menace. "You're going to regret this for the rest of your life."

They were so close now. Their expressions terrifying. She couldn't get out of the crowd. Bree had no other option but to close her eyes. She scrunched her face up, waiting for the worst.

I'm not here. This isn't real. Everything's fine.

"WAIT." Someone interrupted her thoughts.

A girl she hardly knew walked in front of her, forming a barrier between her and them. "If Bree is the blogger, and Queen's Hall is the school, does that mean it's you guys who write all that stuff about people on Dirty Gossip?"

"Shut up," Gemma said.

"And does that mean you give everyone nicknames? What were they? Personality Hair? The Pleaselikemes?"

"And that means Jassmine lied about getting her drink spiked at the party," someone else in the crowd said.

"And you deliberately take photos of yourselves all dressed up to make us think you're amazing when you're all actually just desperate and insecure?"

"Don't you have a bald patch, Jassmine?"

"Gemma, apparently you look proper rank under your make-up."

The posse didn't know what to do with themselves. More and more insults, hand-picked from Bree's blog, were hurled at them like the verbal equivalent of a public stoning. They kept yelling at everyone to shut up, but the crowd was too strong.

"I can't believe it was you guys who spread that rumour about me."

"Do you have any idea how horrible you girls are? To, like, everyone?"

"Do you *blame* Bree for doing this?"

"Is Hugo really that bad in bed?"

The perfect posse went into meltdown, actually brought to tears by the mass interrogation. Jassmine's face had rivers of mascara all down it. Jessica's was so red it looked like she might explode. Even Gemma was sobbing.

Bree could only watch and listen in wonder, as her written words were repeated back by so many people. Her entire body was shaking.

"Do you girls have any idea how sad you are?"

"I cried myself to sleep after you told everyone what happened at Pizza Express. Do you even care that you did that?"

A mob. It had become a mob, of Bree's creation. It was all she'd ever wanted. For Jassmine and the others to cry, to be brought down, for them to feel as miserable and lost as she'd felt since they'd singled her out as a child and kicked her self-esteem into the dust.

Bree didn't want it any more. Finally, she stopped watching what was going on. She stepped between the mob and the perfects, and yelled:

"STOOOOOOOOOOOOOOOOOOOOP!"

And they did.

"Stop it," Bree yelled, before she got self-conscious, before she lost her nerve. She turned to Jassmine and her snotty tear-wrecked face. "Jassmine, I'm sorry, I really am. But I don't understand why you're angry at me."

Jassmine's mouth dropped. "Are you kidding me?" she asked. "Are you KIDDING ME?"

"Isn't this what you want, Jassmine? You spend your entire life making yourself and everyone else miserable, for what? For the whole school to care about you? To think you're important and interesting? If so, isn't this your DREAM? An entire blog, dedicated to you, Gemma, Jessica and Emily? Wouldn't you pay someone for that if you could?"

One by one, Gemma, Jessica and Emily's mouths dropped open in a line. Like a dance routine.

Jassmine spoke for them. "I hate you!" she screamed, her voice echoing around the tall ceilings, bouncing off the rich tapestries.

"Well, I don't hate you," Bree replied. "Again, why are you angry, Jass? So I've ruined your brand? So people know just how desperate you are to be popular? How much you let Hugo crap on you? Revealed your and Gemma's horrible bullying? Aren't you fed up of being a brand, Jass?"

She turned to the huge crowd, her voice stuttering, feeling the urgent need to get her words out. To speak them for once, instead of just writing them.

"Aren't we all fed up of being a brand? Of having to portray this perfect version of ourselves? Of being obsessed with making sure everyone else thinks we're doing and thinking the right thing? Why are we so scared of admitting to each other: 'I'm messed up' or 'I'm lonely' or 'That really hurt my feelings'? Jass…" She turned back to her. "Why are you mad? You're actually quite nice, aren't you? You're actually quite funny. Why don't you want people to know this? Why are you mad at me for showing people that you're real? Rather than a 2D cardboard cut-out?"

Jassmine's lip wobbled. "I…I…"

The bell went, signalling the end of break, but no one moved.

And Bree… Speaking on behalf of every single girl who'd ever had an awful time at school. Every girl who didn't get invited to dances when people like Jassmine did. Every girl who had, at least once, cried in a school toilet cubicle about her sad excuse for a life. For every girl who couldn't wear tight jeans and look good in them, who didn't know how to speak to boys, who overheard nasty rumours or names about themselves spread through the corridors like wildfire… Bree said: "Don't you see? How stupid all this is? How pointless it is worrying all the time what people think of us?"

The bell rang again and Ms Masoon entered the crowd, clapping her hands, breaking the trance.

"What are you all doing here? Get to class. Come on, everybody. NOW!"

The perfects and Bree stared at each other as people pushed past. Gemma was crying the hardest still; all her make-up had run off. She looked quite nice actually.

Then she heard, "Bree, BREE."

Holdo ran straight to her. Dodging and weaving through the dispersing mob until he was right in front of her. And he collected her into the biggest bear hug known to man.

"Bree," he said.

In an instant, Jassmine was forgotten. The last ten minutes were forgotten. All there was was unadulterated joy that her old friend was hugging her, just like old friends do.

She hugged him back with every molecule of her body.

"We need to talk," he said, grabbing her hand and tearing her away from the drama.

"But what about class?"

"Screw class. Bree, do you have any idea what's going on?"

"No. What's going on?" The hallways were emptying quicker by the minute, the hum of excited whispers dulled by the closing of classroom doors.

"You're an internet sensation."

"I am?"

"How can you not already know this?"

He took her round the edge of the school and they ducked out the side entrance, unseen. It was freezing cold but Bree didn't even put her coat on. Her brain was a blur.

"Where are we going?"

"To mine. I need a computer."

"Holdo, stop."

He did, and turned to look at her. It was weird – they hadn't looked at each other in so long. He'd had a new outbreak of spots, but his hair was longer and it suited him.

"What?"

"Why are you talking to me again? I thought you hated me."

"I did hate you."

"Oh."

"I really hated you."

"Oh great. Rub in some salt, why don't you? It's not like my life isn't some massive gaping wound right now."

"Your life is not a gaping wound, trust me."

"Why?"

"Bree. The Manifesto on How to be Interesting, is it really you?"

It was so surreal having her blog title said back to her.

"It…it might be."

"So you becoming a shallow idiotic twat, swanning round school like you're the best thing in the world, before getting your – no offence but – kinda just desserts, was all for the blog?"

She smiled weakly. "Well, I've *always* thought I was the best thing in the world, you know that."

Her smile was returned. Then downturned.

"Mr Fellows? Was that all true? Did he really just leave?"

Bree's eye went a bit wet. "Yes."

"That must've been awful."

"It was."

Holdo hugged her again, squeezing the air out of her lungs. It felt so good. She clamped back as hard as she could. Her friend was hugging her because a guy had broken her heart and screwed her over. That was what friends did. Finally she had one again.

Then everything that'd just happened rushed back.

"Hang on..." She broke the hug. "How does everyone know it's me? What's going on?"

"This", Holdo said, "is why we need my computer."

chapter fifty-nine

His house was empty as he led her up to his room. It had been so long since she'd been there and yet it looked – and smelled – exactly the same. Boy-blue wallpaper, art-house movie posters, the stale whiff of boy hormones and God-knows-what-else.

Holdo powered up his huge computer. "Have you not been checking internet stats for your blog?"

She pulled up a beanbag and plopped onto it, a little scared of what was about to happen.

"No. I didn't think anyone was reading it."

"Then why do it?"

She shrugged. "Dunno. For me, I guess?"

"But why go to all that trouble? Why ruin who you are? Just for you?"

Bree wasn't sure if she really had ruined who she was, but now was not the time to argue.

"Here it is." Holdo pulled up the blog.

Bree gasped. She'd never seen it from a user point of view before. Only the back end when she was uploading posts and posting the occasional photo with the faces blurred out.

It looked…quite good actually. Her hosting platform must've done fancy stuff on her behalf.

"Wow, it's actually real."

Holdo gave her a weird look. "Hang on, I'm just downloading some web-analytic software."

"Hmmm, yeah."

Bree grabbed the mouse and scrolled through the blog. Wow – she'd written so much. Her eyes scanned a few posts. Her writing wasn't actually half bad. And there were loads of comments underneath each one.

Comments? She didn't even realize she'd got commenting enabled on the thing. She saw she'd ticked the "Enable All" box, so they must've gone straight through to the front end of the blog; the bit she never looked at. How could she have been so dim?

She clicked on the post about Logan's leaving letter – there was all sorts underneath it. Written by perfect strangers.

What. A. Tosser. Honey, don't worry. He's not worth it. You're the coolest (virtual) gal I know. Your blog has MADE my year.

Three words. Get him arrested.

Are you okay, Miss Manifesto? My heart is all smashed
up after reading that, and it didn't even happen to me.

Tell someone! Seriously. This guy is a predatory jerk.
This is so much more common than people think.

Comment after comment after comment. All of them
wishing her well. All of them on her side.

No one had ever been on Bree's side.

"Who are these people?" she asked, clicking on another
post and finding just as many comments.

"Your fans, Bree."

"Fans? Bloggers get fans?"

"You still don't get it, do you? Brilliant, it's downloaded,
I'll pull up some stats."

He took the mouse, which pissed her off a bit. She
wanted to keep reading all the nice bits. Then he did his fast
typing and clicking, and she couldn't keep up until loads of
small graphs littered the page.

Holdo let out a whistle. "Holy hell, Bree, this blog is
getting over two million unique user hits a month!"

"Huh?"

"That means people. Over two million people are reading
The Manifesto on How to be Interesting."

Everything went hazy, like the words weren't real.

She had only one question. "Why?"

Holdo looked almost sorry for her. "Bree, you've done
something everyone wants to do but nobody else has the

guts for. Do you have any idea how many people have a rough time at school and feel utterly alone, but no one's reaching out to them? Or how many people wish they could change things but they don't have the tenacity at the time? Except you. You've done it. You've reached them. And you've written about it so honestly, it's like they've done it too."

"Really?"

"Really."

"But I don't think that's what I meant to do."

"What did you mean to do?"

"I just…wanted to become more interesting. I just wanted to become a better writer."

"Well, you've definitely done that."

"But it's been horrible. You hate me. Everyone hates me."

"Because I didn't know this was why you were being such a doofus. Why didn't you tell me, Bree?"

She wasn't sure. "How has everyone at school figured it out? I've changed all the names. I've pixelated all the photos."

"It must've grown so big that someone at Queen's read it and put everything together. I mean, teenagehood is pretty generic, but I don't think in every school some random girl rises to the top of the social ladder, has sex with the most popular guy in school, who films it, and then makes a teacher leave the school."

He was talking about her life like it was a synopsis. A blurb on a book cover. Which could be fine if things were fictional, but this was her life. Her misery. Her loss. And yet he was too worked up for her to shut him up.

"Look at these charts," he said, clicking on random bits. "It's been gaining popularity week on week. Must've been a word-of-mouther. How have you not realized this? Haven't you got emails from people?"

"Emails?"

"Yeah. From readers?"

Bree hadn't got one email from anyone. She would know, she checked all the time just in case some friends appeared out of nowhere and saved her from her inane loneliness. She thought back to that first night, when she'd started the blog.

"I got a different email address for it. One to match the blogging platform."

"And you've not checked it?"

"It's not my usual address. And I never thought I'd get emails…"

"Do you know the password?"

"Maybe."

She'd been drunk when she'd set it up, but drunk Bree obviously used the same password as normal Bree. She logged in without any effort, and was greeted with:

You have 45,597 new messages.

"Woooooah," Holdo said.

She opened one at random. It was from a severely-depressed fifteen year old. A self-harmer. Apparently Bree's post had really helped her feel not alone. And could they be pen pals?

She clicked on another.

Email after email after email. The room melted away. Holdo, though he was reading alongside her, hazed into nothingness.

It didn't seem real.

Bree let out a weird howling sound and finally, finally, six years of repressed tears exploded out of her heart and drained from her eyes. She held Holdo close to her and sobbed. He stroked her hair and clicked through the emails, reading them to her, as his shoulder got wetter and wetter and wetter.

And then – because February the fifteenth wasn't just a big day for Queen's Hall – Bree found the sort of email that changes one's life.

Buried on page nine.

From Brookland publishing house.

chapter sixty

Holdo began wheezing.

"Oh my God, Bree, Brookland! Brookland? You have to ring them, you have to ring them now!"

She could hardly read the email through her tears.

"They want to meet you. Look, there's a number at the bottom. They sent this almost a month ago. Do you think they want to turn it into a book? Ring them, Bree. Where's your phone? Oh my God, I'm so happy for you."

His voice faded to white noise as she got out her phone, her hands shaking, her tears splshing onto the screen.

She dialled and waited for it to ring.

Holdo grinned at her inanely as she waited for her call to be answered. He looked so lovely when he smiled.

"Hello?" a gruff voice echoed on the other line. And Bree erupted into a fresh wave of hysteria.

"Hello? Hello?"

Through sobs, she managed to get out… "Dad, it's me. Can you come home?"

chapter sixty-one

Holdo walked her to her front door, letting her stop and cry along the way. Not asking questions. He was so good at knowing when she didn't want questions.

The shock on her mum's face when she opened the door to them. "What's going on?"

"Mum!" Bree threw herself at her and fresh hysteria rose again. "Mum, I love you. I'm so sorry. I love you so much. Please, please know how much I love you and how sorry I am."

"Honey. Jesus, what's wrong, is she in trouble?"

Holdo left quietly as Bree wept all down her mother's jumper, staining it with salt. Her mum's grip got tighter and tighter.

"Mum, I love you. I'm so, so sorry."

"Shh, honey, there's nothing to be sorry about."

She gently steered Bree to the living room and got her to

the sofa. Bree started choking, she was crying so hard. Her mum thumped her back, stroked her hair, and sang to her.

Her dad arrived soon, flinging his briefcase to the floor and – without talking – joined them on the sofa. Hugging Bree tight, hugging her mum tight, rocking them, making "shhh" sounds.

Time passed. Bree eventually stopped crying so hard.

Sensing her change, they both crouched on the carpet and looked at her.

"Bree, are you okay?"

Bree shook her head so hard her brain rattled.

"No, no, I'm really not okay. I want help… I need help."

And then Bree began to talk.

Slowly, she told them everything.

epilogue

This is my last blog post.

I want to tell you what I've learned so you can get closure or whatever.

I can't have done all this and not learned something profound, can I? That won't do at all.

So you've read it now, my tale. We've done it together.

Oh, how far we've come, eh?

I guess you want to know what happened.

Well, it took a while to mend me, much as I realized I needed to be mended. Many hours were spent with Dr Thomas, crying loads into tissues, putting me back together again.

And, as a part of this mending, I have to include my apologies...

Holdo. Wonderful sweet Holdo, I cannot say sorry enough.

My beautiful parents, you will never be shut out again.

I suppose, Jass, you need one...

The most difficult apology though – at the risk of sounding all Oprah about it – is to say sorry to myself.

So, sorry to me, for being so filled with hate, so unwilling to give anyone a chance, for making myself so miserable and lonely.

You've got all the rules now, to become interesting. And, along the way, to get entirely screwed up and hate who you are.

So, in the interests of closure, to all of you who've been reading and following this and being so incredible, here's my final rule.

Rule number six – how to be really interesting: Stop caring

I don't recommend following my own manifesto. Ditch the rules. Stop trying so bloody hard. It won't make you happy and it certainly won't make you interesting.

The one good thing to take from my journey is this.

Life doesn't happen to you. You can't just sit on a park bench and expect amazing things to whizz by on a conveyor belt. Life is what you put into it. Mine didn't get more interesting because I got pretty or made friends with popular kids. That had nothing to do with it.

It got interesting because, for the first time, I actually invested in it.

And yeah, I've come out with a great haircut. But it's so much more than that. You can take those things away and I won't care. Because I've learned to invest and I've learned to let people in. That's priceless. That's what's important.

I wanted redemption – that was what I was worried I wouldn't get. And, as is always the way with redemption, I found it through love.

Love, as always, is what it comes down to. You have to love. It's the only way.

Love for life. Love for others. And, most importantly, love for yourself.

Here's the thing. I don't care any more if I'm interesting or not.

I'm fed up of my generation's obsession with leaving our mark on the world, with our who's-best-at-life competitions.

For years all I wanted was to matter. To prove my existence. To make it all worthwhile by having outside forces validate me. To tell me I'm important.

Being interesting isn't important. But being happy is. As well as being a person you're proud of.

I may disappear into obscurity now but at least I know who I am, like who I am and I'm happy. Can you say the same? If not, why not?

Because when people lie on their deathbeds, they're never saying, "I wish I'd left a mark on the world." It's "Where are the people I love? Can I see them one last time?"

Choose life. Choose love.

And always remember to live.

about holly bourne

Holly Bourne is a dazzling new voice in UK YA. Her first novel, *Soulmates*, was published in 2013 to critical acclaim, and Holly is a keen advocate of the growing UK YA literary scene.

Holly began her career working as a local news reporter on the *Surrey Mirror*, garnering a nomination for Print Journalist of the Year in 2010. She now works as a journalist for TheSite.org, an advice and information website for 16-25 year olds.

Holly is twenty-eight and lives in Surrey.

Q&A with Holly

What was your first piece of writing?

There are two notable "works". *The Adventures of Cool Pig* which I co-wrote aged five with my dad. It basically involved a sunglasses-wearing pig whose laidback attitude got him into trouble wherever he went.

I then went solo aged seven and wrote *A Bump In The Clouds*, about a squirrel in heaven who fell down to earth (literally) during an enthusiastic game of musical bumps.

As you can probably tell, all I've ever wanted to do is write books.

Which books had the most impact, or offered unforgettable advice to you as you were growing up?

It's an obvious choice but, without a doubt, *To Kill A*

Mockingbird. I first read it when I was fifteen, and love it so much I actually collect copies now. If everyone did what Atticus said, the world would be a much better place.

What research did you do while writing The Manifesto on How to be Interesting?

A lot of the research was done through osmosis at my day job – working as an advice journalist for young people on TheSite.org. TheSite's a place young people can go to get support with anything that's going on in their lives. I write lots about mental health there so I already had a lot of training and knowledge around the issue of self-harm which I used in the book.

Outside of work, I spent a long time researching the lasting impacts of being bullied at school. I read a lot about brain development in your teenage years and learned our brains form stronger memories then, so that's why we're all so haunted by our schooldays! It's chemistry! For Mr Fellows's character, I delved into the murky waters of student/teacher relationships and studied the psychology behind them. I also watched every film about high school/secondary school that's ever been made, from *The Breakfast Club* to *Mean Girls*. I had to do Bree's manifesto research for her.

But, mostly, I just asked a lot of people – *what was school like for you? Who was popular? Who was bullied? What mean things were said? What names were used?*

Then I collected them all up and put them in my book. It's scary how universal the cruelty is.

In both Soulmates *and* The Manifesto on How to be Interesting *you tackle important topics and challenge commonly held perceptions. Why do you think it is important that fiction does this?*

Fiction is a very safe place to tackle important topics – it's just words, nobody "real" is getting hurt. And yet it's a very powerful place too – a good story can change someone's life.

For me, the first thing I want to do is to get readers to turn the page. Once that's achieved, you can try and ninja-in some good. We use fictional stories to make sense of our non-fictional lives and that's why I try so hard to give readers more than just a story. To give them a few pieces of moral meat to chew over for a while.

Has your work with TheSite impacted your writing – or vice versa?

Quite simply, this book wouldn't exist if it wasn't for my job at TheSite. Every day I learn more about young people – what matters to them, what's hurting them, what's helping them. More than anything it's taught me that words can help. Just letting young people know simple things like *"You're not alone"* or *"That weird thing you think only happens to you? Yeah, it's really common – YOU'RE OKAY"* can make such a huge difference. I wanted my books to have the same impact.

Have you ever blogged?

I have! In an uncharacteristic burst of spontaneity, I quit my job as a news reporter when I was twenty-four so I could drive from one side of America to the other. I kept a travel blog the entire way. It mainly involved me complaining about the lack of vegetarian food in Texas...

As the internet, social media, and other forms of technology and communication continue to grow and develop, how important do you think books are in tackling issues, challenging ideas and changing perceptions?

I still think books sink that bit deeper than all the other new technological fandangoes. Reading a book is a real investment. It involves putting life to one side for a bit, giving yourself the headspace to really engage with a story that will take a while to tell you why it's there. I believe the frame of mind in which someone reads a book makes them more susceptible to letting ideas melt in.

Whereas if you're reading an opinion blog, whilst also

checking what other people make of it on Twitter, with eight other tabs open on your screen, and a sandwich half hanging out your mouth...well...sometimes it's easier to forget the amazing point you just read.

Were there any scenes in the book you found hard to write?

The bedroom scene with Hugo really got to me. It still does. I just wanted to reach into my computer screen and pull Bree out of there!

Do you have a manifesto?

Ha! Definitely nothing succinct and profound enough to fit on a bumper sticker. I have general "themes", I guess, that I try and live my life round, though they're pretty basic: Work hard, fight for what you believe in, don't be a douche, and always look out for and prioritise the people you love.

You quote from Alan Bennett's The History Boys: *"The best moments in reading are when you come across something – a thought, a feeling, a way of looking at things – which you had thought special and particular to you." Have any books in particular stood out in making you feel like this? Is this what you set out to achieve with your writing?*

Touching other people is the ultimate quest of a writer. Though I'm a real ye-olde-booke fan, what I do love about e-readers is that you can see where readers have highlighted a certain phrase. You get to see other people's *History Boys* moments. And of course I hope I get a few highlights along the way!

As for books that make me feel like this, as I said before, the whole of *To Kill A Mockingbird*. But, most recently, the "Cool Girl" rant in *Gone Girl* made me do an actual triumphant fist-punch in public.

Holly, what can we expect from you next?

I've just finished a book that I hope will be the first of a series about a group of girls starting their own feminism grassroots group. The first book tackles anxiety and OCD, a topic very close to my heart. I feel it's about time people really understood these issues, rather than thinking it's all to do with keeping your desk tidy. I can't wait for people to read it!

Find out more about Holly:
@holly_bourneYA
www.facebook.com/Holly.BourneYA
www.hollybourne.co.uk

acknowledgements

This book started with a squabble.

Thank you, Owen – you rotter! – for starting the squabble (*though I'm sure you'll say I started it*), as, without it, this book wouldn't exist. Seriously, thank you, for your incredible support through one heck of a year. I really couldn't have done it without you. I officially forgive you for being popular in secondary school...

Thanks, as always, to my wonderful family. To Dad, for sifting through my messy first drafts and helping me make them sing. To Mum, for bullying every single acquaintance/bookseller/librarian into getting a copy of *Soulmates*. Thanks to my sisters. To Eryn, for reading my first draft though pregnant and full of morning sickness. And to Willow, whose wise comments about remembering popular people's full names were shamelessly stolen for this story. I am so lucky and so grateful to have you all.

A huge thank you to Lisa – who champions this book so much I need you on my payroll. Your enthusiasm and support means the world. And to Ruth, who saved me from going mad in London. And, hey – Emily S, I've put your name in this book so you've got to read this one too! Your unexpected and incredible enthusiasm about *Soulmates* was just what I needed, when I needed it.

As always, a massive thank you to my agent Maddy who is STILL the loveliest person I've ever met. You continue to change my life and I continue to struggle with how I can ever adequately repay you.

The hugest thank you to EVERYONE at Usborne – I swear you need to pass some kind of amazingness test to be allowed to work there. Your collective creativity, positivity and hard work makes my writing come alive in ways I never thought possible. Thanks especially to Rebecca, my editorial guru, for making this the book you hold today. Your delicate and insightful editing MADE this story and I'm massively grateful to have your brain on board. Thanks also for letting me keep all the rude words in...well, most of them.

Finding and understanding Bree wasn't easy. And Bree wouldn't exist if it wasn't for the transformative years I've spent working at the amazing TheSite.org. I honestly believe that if she had found TheSite, she would've sought help waaaay before the plot of this book begins. I am so proud to work there and hope I've done "the issues" justice, particularly self-harm which is still so misunderstood. Thanks especially, as ever, to Emma and Nic.

Finally, I just want to shamelessly exploit this opportunity to tell any potential Brees out there that you're NOT ALONE. Don't hold it all in if you're hurting. Tell someone, get help, get support – you ruddy deserve it, and you're ruddy worth it...

...and, in my personal opinion, everyone who is half-decent in this world cried at least once in a toilet cubicle in school. It's a badge of honour really.

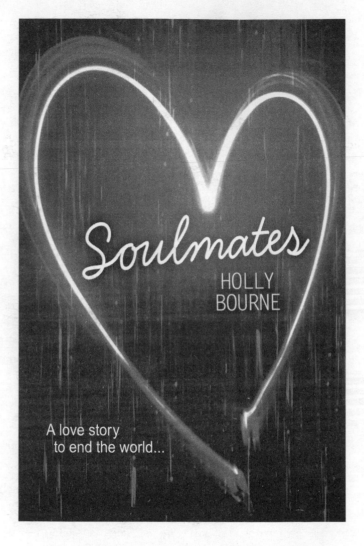

Soulmates

HOLLY
BOURNE

A love story
to end the world...

"Warning: this book will demolish your heart
as it has demolished mine."

CJ Skuse, author of *Rockoholic*

Soulmates do exist.
But not as you think.

Every so often, two people are
born who are the perfect match
for one another. Soulmates.

But what if meeting your soulmate is
earth-shattering — literally?

An epic, electrifying and
extraordinary debut about

falling in love.

ISBN: 9781409557500
EPUB: 9781409557517 / KINDLE: 9781409557524

Check out more electrifying and thought-provoking
YA reads at:

WWW.USBORNE.COM/YOUNGADULT